Confined Spaces

Paul H. Raymer

Salty Air Publishing
Falmouth, Massachusetts

Copyright © 2024 by Paul H Raymer

All rights reserved.

No part of this book may be reproduced in any form or by any electronic or mechanical means, including information storage and retrieval systems, without written permission from the author, except for the use of brief quotations in a book review.

Publisher's Note; This is a work of fiction. Names, characters, places, and incidents are a product of the author's imagination. Locales and public names are sometimes used for atmospheric purposes. Any resemblance to actual people, living or dead, or to businesses, companies, events, institutions, or locales is completely coincidental.

Confined Spaces/Paul H. Raymer - 1st edition 198

ISBN (Print Edition): 979-8-9904850-0-6

ISBN (eBook edition): 979-8-9904850-1-3

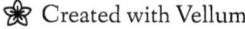 Created with Vellum

For Samantha, Alex, Lucas, Ansel, and Lily
May the world treat you with tenderness throughout your lives.

If you wish to be a success in the world, promise everything. Deliver nothing.

— Napoleon

I think I'll go to sleep and dream about piles of gold getting bigger and bigger.

— Humphrey Bogart - The Treasure of the Sierra Madre 1948

OSHA Confined Spaces

"Confined spaces - such as manholes, crawl spaces, and tanks - are not designed for continuous occupancy and are difficult to exit in the event of an emergency. People working in confined spaces face life-threatening hazards including toxic substances, electrocutions, explosions, and asphyxiation."

Chapter One

In July 1988, Jon Megquire was able to secure a twelve-month bank loan for one hundred thousand dollars. All it took was a second mortgage on his house and a guarantee from Arthur Schmidt.

Two months later, Arthur Schmidt was dead, and the bank was left holding Jon and Lisa's house and Jon was sitting on a rock in the woods in Tilley, Massachusetts, wondering if he would be reduced to living in the woods with his family if the bank required him to give all the money back.

Right now, of course, it was September and the Cape Cod weather was warm and pleasant. Birds chirped in the trees. The late summer breeze rustled the leaves, and looking up through the branches, Jon could see blue sky and an occasional fluffy white cloud.

He recognized that thoughts of living in the woods were overly dramatic, but he also knew that it was such a small step, a small twist of fortune, one wrong decision that could start the cascade from comfort to destitution.

He was trying to think—trying to be logical, trying to think like a banker. Trying to come up with options. Trying to recognize an alternative friendly guarantor, a hidden familiar in his life.

It was just money. It was just business. Nothing personal.

That was such a stupid expression—*it's just business*. Of course, it was personal! It was his company. It was his house. It was his life.

They were making the loan payments, but every month was a stretch. And even if the bank didn't call the loan and make them pay it off right away, the clock was running. Just ten months left.

Wintering in the woods would be a different story.

These woods comprised over three hundred acres that had been wisely set aside by the town of Tilley to defend against the summer resident invasion. But even at that distance, he could hear the encroaching civilization of leaf blowers and lawn mowers.

Jon hadn't known Arthur Schmidt well. Arthur was the father of his friend and teammate at Boundbrook, Dabney Schmidt. It was one of those life and death twists of fate that connected Jon to Dabney and Arthur Schmidt to the support of Jon's dream.

Woods, much like these, surrounded the Boundbrook School where he had met and played baseball with Dabney. Thoughts of Dabney and the woods surrounding Boundbrook turned Jon's thoughts to the narrow passage in the cave known as the Coyote's Gullet. It was saving Dabney's life in the Gullet that had led to Arthur's affection for Jon.

Boundbrook was an exclusive boarding school - the school of future presidents and supreme court justices. The school was its own world—a not-so-distant cousin of a medieval town, run by the headmaster who served as lord. Although there were no walls or guard towers, for the three hundred or so boys who lived there, there was little connection to the outside world. Access to television and even radio was severely limited. A movie was shown on Saturday nights in the auditorium. Short church services were held every morning with a longer liturgy on Sundays. Freshmen could not go home for months. Bedtimes, study halls, meals, and classes were regulated by Pavlovian bells. Upper class-men were given limited freedoms. Depending on his personality, the student body president was a champion or a toady. Jon was convinced that Dabney Schmidt would be a champion for the students when he became president—an inevitability. His only competition was Norman Denjer, an intellectual, a member of the Woods Squad who had no athletic interests at all and spent a lot of time with the Model Railroading Club making up fantasy lands.

There was a tradition at Boundbrook where the headmaster would randomly declare a feriatum—a spontaneous holiday from classes. The school used the Latin word for it to give it a classics flair. The day's classes would be pushed forward a day, and the next day's classes would disappear. Students would scheme and plan, anticipating when these surprise holidays would happen, playing "feriatum roulette" the night before, not doing the assignments. It was spring, and the weather was perfect. A feriatum was inevitable.

Jon was a freshman and Dabney was a Junior and the only reason they were talking was because they were both on the baseball team and Dabney had invited Jon to go spelunking if a feriatum was declared. Dabney, the team captain, was the catcher.

Jon remembered the headmaster had had it right—it had indeed been a beautiful day—beautiful beyond the blue sky, fluffy clouds, and the brilliant new greens of the leaves. It was the feeling of leaving the dark gray confinement of the winter behind. It was the shock of warmth stepping outside without a coat. A perfume of the ground and the plants summoning the pollinators to jump-start life all over again. For the students, there was an end-of-the-school-year feeling of summer vacation floating on the horizon. There was a bottled joy uncorked in their steps.

They had left the school grounds, walking at the edge of the roads until they found the trail entrance and turned in through the woods. Singing and laughing, telling stories and exchanging jokes, they walked deeper and deeper into the woods. Jon remembered the feeling of the history that Dabney had described of Indians and settlers following the deer trails before the roads existed. The air was perfumed by the pine needle blanket that cushioned their footsteps, making Jon think of Hawkeye in *The Last of the Mohicans*.

And then they had stopped. Jon remembered wondering where the cave was. He had always thought caves were massive holes in cliff sides or mountains. Where they were standing had just seemed like another clearing on the trail. The boys put their backpacks and gear down. They crinkled up their brown bag lunches and stuffed them in their packs.

"Where's the cave?" Jon had asked, as he looked around.

Dabney laughed. "Cool, isn't it? You can't even see it, can you?"

Jon moved around the clearing. There were no signs, no warnings, no trail markers. Nothing.

"Here?"

The boys pulled out their spelunking helmets and lights.

Grinning, Jon said, "You're kidding? Where?"

"Here." Dabney guided him around a big rock and showed him a hole in the ground. "It goes down. A long way down. That's why it was such a great meeting place. If you didn't know it was here, you'd miss it."

Confined Spaces

Jon looked down at the hole behind the rock. "Does the school know this is here?"

Dabney laughed. "Not officially."

"Are we going to fit?" Jon was tall and gangly, with broad shoulders and enormous feet.

The other boys had gathered around. "Sure. One at a time at the entrance. Here."

"Lunch in the dark," one of them said.

"Yeah, lunch in the dark."

Jon remembered that one of the boys had handed him a helmet with an attached headlamp. In retrospect, he didn't remember which teammate it was. "See if this fits," he said.

Jon had a colossal head, and curly red hair that bunched up inside hats. The adjustable straps inside the caving helmet allowed him to open it up to fit well.

"Ready?" Dabney asked, and one boy had gotten down on his knees and crawled into the hole.

"Anything I should know before I crawl in there?" Jon remembered asking.

"Enjoy the adventure," Dabney had said and disappeared into the ground.

Jon inhaled deeply, smelling the spring air. He took another look around at the sunshine and blue sky and crawled into the hole.

He clearly remembered the darkness and the damp. The abrupt change of temperature was shocking. Stones stuck into his knees and hands as he crawled. He could barely make out the soles of Dabney's shoes up ahead of him. He imagined himself digging his way out of a prison camp like Steve McQueen in *The Great Escape*. He did not know how long this passage was or how it would end. There had to be more magic to this cave than this dark tunnel.

Then Dabney's feet disappeared and suddenly the passage

opened up, and he was able to pull himself to his feet and stand in the dim lights of the headlamps with the other boys.

"Wow," Jon remembered saying as he looked around the cavernous space. They were standing up near the ceiling at the top of a slope that led down deeper into the ground, opening up back into the hill that Jon hadn't noticed when they were outside. He couldn't see far into the darkness of the space.

When Dabney had convinced Jon to go with them on this spelunking adventure, he had described the cave. "There is this one passage known as the Coyote's Gullet that's pretty hairy," he said, "but you'll fit okay. It's only about seven inches high. You have to go through it with your hands out in front of you, you know? Sort of push yourself through with your toes. But once you're through, it's easy going. And it's beautiful. I mean, it's not lit up like one of those touristy caves. It's the real thing. Touristy caves have those gift shops and electric lights and hand rails. It's not like that. This is the real thing."

So, when they emerged from the entrance tunnel, Jon asked, "Was that it? Was that the Coyote's Gullet you were telling me about?"

Dabney had laughed. Jon could still recall Dabney's laugh all these years later. "That was just the entrance to Shawme. The Gullet's down there." He pointed down the slope, into the darkness.

The boys started down the rocky slope, the lights of their headlamps dancing off the walls of the cave. The dimness of the light made every step unknown. The laughter of his teammates ahead of him echoed back. Jon remembered wondering about the animals that lived in these caves. Rats? Snakes? Bears? Bats?

As they got deeper, the cavity widened until they reached the bottom of the bowl, and they stopped stepping and sliding down the slope. They stood motionless for a moment, listening to the drips of the water seeping between the rocks and the sighing of moving air. The lights from the headlamps flickered across each other's faces and the surrounding walls. Jon wondered how people found their way through these caves in the dark in ancient times. And he wondered why they would choose to go there - sort of like the first people who ate raw oysters. Whoever thought that was a good idea?

"Let's have lunch," someone said, and with general agreement, they found places to sit, dropped their packs, and pulled out their brown bag lunches.

"Spelunking is a stupid sounding word," the shortstop said. He was a wiry guy and his thin rimmed glasses kept sliding down his nose. "Probably Greek. We should ask Hunter. But then again, we'd get a whole lot more than we wanted and he'd probably put it on a test."

The boys laughed in agreement. Master Hunter was an ancient British history teacher who had been teaching at Boundbrook since it was founded a hundred years ago who worshipped the derivation of words.

"How often have you guys been here?" Jon asked.

Dabney said, "A couple of times. You see a lot of feriata when you've been at Boundbrook as long as we have."

"Not enough feriata," the shortstop said.

"Didn't you say that the Indians had ceremonies in here?"

"That's the rumor," Dabney said. He looked up from his sandwich and surveyed the cave. "Kind of spooky. But if we're respectful, we shouldn't cross up any old curses against the white men."

And the Coyote's Gullet was yet to come.

"You ready?" Dabney asked. "The Gullet's up there." He pointed up at a pile of rocks. "We'll leave the packs here, but we'll need the rope."

The shortstop pulled out a coil of rope from his pack, and

Dabney led the way up the pile of rocks until they came to a hole in the cave wall. Dabney said, "That's the Gullet."

"That?" Jon asked. "Really? You fit in there?"

"It's tight, but I did last time."

The shortstop wrapped the rope around his waist, got down on his hands and knees, and with his arms stretched out in front of himself, pushed himself into the opening with his toes. His feet disappeared. Dabney paid the rope out, feeding it into the Gullet. It seemed to go on forever, and Jon realized he was holding his breath and only exhaled when the rope stopped moving and Dabney's tug resulted in a couple of answering jerks and a muffled shout.

"He's through," Dabney said. "Next?"

The second baseman repeated the shortstop's entry, stretching his arms out in front of himself as though he was diving into a lake, and then he wriggled his way into the hole and disappeared.

"What's on the other side?" Jon asked.

"Well, it's not Wonderland and we're not Alice," Dabney laughed.

"No, I mean, is it worth risking your life for?"

Dabney looked at him. "You don't have to go," he whispered. "You can wait for us."

"No," Jon said. "I just mean when you saw this hole, how did you know ... or what made you think it would be a good idea to go in there?"

"That's what exploring is all about. Finding places that other people haven't gone. Doing things that other people haven't done. Taking risks. It's like free climbing. If you don't reach, you'll never know where the edge is."

"Even if you don't know what's on the other side? I mean, maybe it's ... just a hole? I mean, at least with climbing you can see."

Dabney still had the rope in his hands, feeling for the jerk when the second baseman reached the other side, and when the tug came, he turned to Jon and said, "Your choice."

Sitting in the woods now sixteen years later, Jon remembered clearly thinking that diving into that hole in the ground with no clarity of what lay on the other side seemed counterintuitive to his self-preservation instincts. He wasn't, *oh, what-the-hell-just-do-it* drunk. Alarm bells were going off all over his mind, and there was no obvious million-dollar-golden-ticket for doing this. His Jiminy Cricket conscience voice was screaming at him. He was only fourteen. He had his whole life ahead of him.

But then there was Dabney's respect. His teammates had done this. Dabney had done this. Dabney trusted him to bring him along and offer him this opportunity. So, he got down on his hands and knees, lowered his head and reached his arms out to the hole.

"Keep your light on and follow the rope," Dabney said.

Using his toes and scrabbling with his fingers, he had pushed and pulled himself into the hole. He struggled to keep his helmet on top of his head and the light from its head lamp pointed out ahead of him. The walls seemed impossibly close. He clutched the rope and inched himself forward. A wave of fear rose from his belly, and he stopped moving, put his head down on his forearms, and closed his eyes. There was no way to turn around. He had to keep moving forward. He took a deep breath and wriggled onward.

The passage was mostly soft brown dirt. Then he came to a section that was rock. A crack in the granite outcropping, a pointed surface that he had to push and pull himself over. His belt got hooked on one of the rocky points, and he had to back up.

A tsunami of panic started rising again. He remembered

thinking, "I can't do this. I can't." But then he did. He moved farther. Back to the dirt walled tunnel, and he wondered how much longer this could go on. It hadn't taken that long for the other boys to get through. He gripped on the rope and pulled himself a few more inches forward and saw light up ahead. He would have run to it, but you can't run when you're flat on your belly, crawling like a laconic lizard. So, he continued inching forward until his arms and his head emerged and his teammates were pulling him through.

His relief at being able to stand again was palpable. "That was tight!" he said. "Now I know what it felt like to dig out of prison, you know?"

The lights from their headlamps waltzed across the surfaces of the cave as they moved, keeping the shadows dancing. The silence was oppressive, and Jon sensed the weight of the tons of earth above him, and he looked up.

The chamber was large, but, as Dabney had said, it wasn't Wonderland. There were no colorful toadstools, smiling cats, white rabbits, or mad hatters. Nature had done the decorating. Colorful stalactites hung down, dripping. He turned his head to look across the vaulted space and saw what appeared to be a frozen waterfall or curtain-like sheaves or draperies. The light from his headlamp illuminated limited sections where he pointed his head. The darkness and the shadows lurked around every rock.

"How far back does it go?" he asked.

"Let's get Dabney in here and we'll show you."

The four of them stood by the Coyote's Gullet and watched the rope as it occasionally jerked as Dabney pulled on it.

It suddenly struck Jon that in order to escape, in order to see daylight again, he had to wiggle back through the Gullet. And if it collapsed or Dabney got stuck in there, there was no way to get help. They would just disappear. They didn't have water or food. This would be their tomb and completely dark as the batteries in their headlamps ran out of power.

Jon remembered wiping his hands on his pants and brushing dirt from his face and sucking in a gulp of air as though to test the oxygen.

And they waited. And listened. Jon held his breath.

The grunts coming from the Gullet seemed to get louder. And then they stopped.

The boys listened.

Then they faintly heard Dabney say, "Uh, guys? I think I'm stuck."

The shortstop leaned down to the opening of the hole and shouted, "Dabney!"

Oh shit, Jon thought. Oh, shit. Oh, shit. Oh, shit. He's stuck. We're stuck.

"I don't know what I've done," they heard Dabney say. "I've hooked myself on something."

"You, okay?" the shortstop had shouted into the hole.

"Just stuck!" the disembodied voice came back to them.

The shortstop stood up and looked at Jon and the second baseman. "He must have put on some extra weight since last time." And he laughed.

"It's not funny," the second baseman shouted. "It's not funny. Dabney's blocking the exit. Our exit! If he doesn't get out of there, we're all going to die in here. And ...and they'll never find us. We can't get out."

That had been Jon's fear too. He remembered the feeling of blind, uncontrollable fear creeping up from his gut. He could still feel it all these years later—the utter helplessness, the total lack of control, buried alive. He had looked up at the top of the cave as though he could see the sun and the blue sky through the rock, but there was only darkness.

"We're buried alive!" the second baseman said. "I don't want to die. This was a really stupid idea. We've got to get out of here!"

"Oh, cut the shit," the shortstop said.

"What do we do?" Jon asked.

"It's simple," the shortstop said. "We just have to get him out of there. Even if we have to cut him apart!" Then, after a moment's pause, he laughed.

He leaned down to the hole and shouted, "Can you move? Can you grab the rope? Where are you?"

"I'm in the Gullet, asshole. Where did you think I was?" the shout came back.

The shortstop turned to the second baseman and said, "He hasn't lost his sense of humor. That's good."

"Jesus. He hasn't been in there that long."

"Are you on the rocks?" the shortstop shouted into the hole.

"He's just got to get himself unstuck," the second baseman said. "We can't do much to help him. And we've all got to go back through to get out of here."

"Duh," the shortstop said. "No shit, Sherlock."

With them staring at the opening, their headlamps flickered inside and made the Gullet appear to be alive.

"Grab the rope and we'll pull you out," the shortstop shouted. "Ready?"

"Wait a second," the second baseman said. "What if this just wedges him in more tightly? Is this a good idea?"

"Got a better idea?"

The second baseman leaned down and shouted into the hole, "How stuck are you?"

"Gullet's gotten smaller," Dabney's shout came back.

Jon remembered he had buried his own panic and suddenly grinned.

"What?" the second baseman asked. "What's funny? What

the hell is funny? This situation is not funny at all. We might not ever get out of here and Dabney could die in the hole. What's funny?"

"Sorry," Jon had said. "I was just thinking about Winnie the Pooh when he ate all of Rabbit's honey and got stuck in the entrance to Rabbit's house."

"Oh, yeah," the shortstop said. "And they were going to hire the Gopher to dig him out." He laughed.

Jon's smile faded when he remembered Pooh was stuck in the opening for several days and nights until he lost enough weight to get pulled out.

"We're going to have to find out why he's stuck," Jon said

"How are we going to do that?" the second baseman asked.

With the image of Winnie the Pooh and Gopher firmly planted in his head, Jon said, "I'll go back in. Maybe I can see. Face to face. Maybe he can't get enough leverage with his elbows, you know?"

"We can hang onto your ankles and pull the both of you out."

Jon straightened his helmet and his lamp, got down on his knees in front of the hole, and dove back in. He felt the other boys' hands on his ankles, and he elbowed his way further into the Gullet. Abruptly, his headlamp illuminated Dabney's face. His body filled the opening. They lay still for a moment.

Dabney's face was covered with dirt, streaked with rivulets of sweat. His helmet tilted rakishly. "Now what?" he asked.

"Can you move at all?"

"A bit," Dabney said, and wiggled. His shoulders were immobile against the sides of the hole, but his head wobbled back and forth. Jon couldn't see down his back to see if his pants had gotten hooked on the rocks.

"How'd you do this before?" he asked.

"The Coyote must be closing his throat," Dabney snorted.

"We're just going to have to pull you out of here."

"Here," Dabney said, "take my wrists."

Jon and Dabney interlocked their hands and wrists. The catcher's skin was gritty and wet with sweat, and his grip was powerful. The combined lights of their headlamps made the confined space of the Gullet unnaturally bright. The air was close and tomb-like as they stared at each other face-to-face, swallowing their fears. Jon remembered a flicker of helplessness in the older boy's eyes and he tightened his grip on Dabney's wrists and yelled, "Pull!" and he felt the grip of his two teammates on his ankles tighten and strain. Jon flexed out his elbows to push backward against the walls.

And Dabney budged. And then he budged some more.

"Can you move now?" Jon asked.

"Some," Dabney replied.

Lying on his stomach, the low ceiling of the passage restricted Jon's ability to arch his back and wiggle his ass backward or put any force on his knees. He struggled to maintain his grip on Dabney's hands while Dabney tried to move his arms back and forth to push against the walls of the cave. But they were moving. They were slowly moving like a tight cork pulling out of a bottle.

Finally, Jon felt his feet drop out of the exit as the shortstop and second baseman pulled him out, and Dabney emerged behind him as though the rocks were giving birth.

Dabney slapped his teammates on their backs and brushed some of the dirt off his clothes. "Well, that was embarrassing," he said with a grin. He took off his helmet and wiped his hands down his face. "What'd I tell you, Jon? Wonderland, right? Thanks for pulling me out."

Jon bent over with his hands on his knees and sucked in some deep breaths. "Yah. Wonderland," he said with a snort.

The second baseman turned his head to the side, bent over,

and puked. When he straightened up, he wiped his mouth on his sleeve and said, "That was close. We could have died in here."

"Nah," Dabney said. "You're too mean to die so young. They say, 'Only the good die young.'" And he slapped the second baseman on the back.

Jon would remember those prescient words.

The boys had stood in a circle, looking at each other.

"We're here. Let's look around," Dabney said. He turned toward the depths of the cavern, sweeping his headlamp over the walls and rock formations and the white gypsum flowers. "Look at those. Cool."

"Jesus, Dabney," the second baseman said. "We almost died. You almost died. And we have to go back through the Gullet to get out of here!"

Dabney looked at the second baseman. "But we didn't die, did we? We got through it with just a few scrapes and scratches. This," he waved his hand around the cavern, "This is why we came. What point would there be in leaving now?"

Dabney started moving into the darkness of the cave, stepping around stalagmites and over rocks, his headlamp sliding off one formation after another. Jon struggled with an almost irresistible urge to get out of the dark and back into the spring air above ground.

"Come on, Dabney," the second baseman had said. "Let's get out of here."

"That's probably a good idea," the shortstop said. "We need to get you back through the Gullet."

Dabney stopped moving into the cave and turned around. "Jeez," he said. "You're treating me like an old man. It's kind of a waste to leave, isn't it? We might not get another chance to get in here."

"That's okay with me," the second baseman said. "I'll go

first." And not waiting, he bent down and dove back into the hole.

"What's up with him?" Dabney asked.

"You scared the shit out of us," the shortstop said.

"Sorry about that," Dabney said. "His puke isn't going to make the Indian spirits all that happy."

The second baseman had pulled the rope in with him, and they waited to see the end of it jerk.

"Maybe I widened the hole scraping through," Dabney said.

When the rope jerked, Dabney said, "You go, Megquire. You pulled me out. I hope you don't have to do that again, but you'll be there."

Jon got down on his hands and knees, looked back at his teammates, and pushed himself back into the hole. At least this time, he knew what to expect at the other end. He knew how long the passage was. He could anticipate getting out from under the ground. He could carry the vision of sunshine and the clear spring air with him as he pushed through the darkness and the dirt. It still seemed to take a long time to get through.

But this time Dabney didn't get stuck. The shortstop squirmed his way out of the Gullet and they all stood together for a few moments, brushing off the dirt and joking about Coyote attitudes. They picked up the packs and the brown paper lunch bags they had left behind and moved back up the entrance slope to the exit. The crawl through that short tunnel seemed almost effortless compared to the Gullet, and they emerged into the sunshine, where they stood together, breathing in the spring air and congratulating each other on the adventure.

That was why it was so inconceivable a month later when they were told that Dabney had killed himself in the school woods.

Chapter Two

And now Dabney's father was dead too. Not from suicide. Apparently, a heart problem. And Jon was in the woods again—different woods and different circumstances—wondering if he should tell the bank.

Jon had found this thinking rock not long after he and Lisa had bought the house in Tilley and Jon had teamed up with Ace Wentzell. Jon had a vision for a state-of-the-art design/build company that would specialize in energy-efficient and healthy homes. Then came Sam ... Jon and Lisa's son. He was the joy of their lives. But to be clinical about it, Sam was expensive. Maybe he should have been ... planned. Maybe they could have waited and paid for some of the other stuff first and built up some savings and, oh, and not started a business that didn't deliver predictable paychecks.

All around him, nature did the things that nature did so well. The birds chirped and whistled and twittered. The leaves swished and whispered in the breeze. The sunlight filtered down to the bed of pine needles, warming them and perfuming the air, naturally, unlike the pine air freshener that Ace Wentzell hung from the mirror in his truck.

All that just happened.

He didn't really believe that things would get so bad that he would have to leave the house to live on the street or in these woods. But he wondered what it would be like. He wondered how people did it. He wondered how they showered. He wondered where they found food. It wouldn't be pleasant to trap rabbits and cook them over an open fire. There was a sort of romantic Hemingway notion of living off the land, but that wasn't an option he wanted to consider to solve their problems.

Lisa got a predictable paycheck as a Massachusetts State Trooper. He and Ace had built a solid reputation, but how many houses could a family build? The Cape was running out of room. Until Arthur Schmidt died, Jon had been feeling comfortable with the bank. Now he wasn't sure.

That was the reason he was sitting on his thinking rock in the middle of these woods. Would he be able to find another guarantor? He wanted to be on the daylight side of the Shawme Cave and out of the trap of the Coyote's Gullet.

They say that when you ask someone to invest in your company, you're offering them an opportunity to travel with you on your adventure and to profit from your success. But to Jon, it felt more like asking for a handout. And if he hadn't invested everything he had personally, how could he ask someone else to take the risk?

When they started the company, Jon had gone to the bank. The smiling banker had said, "No." Banks weren't interested in investing in small enterprises like Wentzell and Megquire. There wasn't enough history and there wasn't enough equity in the business on its own. "Can you get someone to guarantee the loan?" the banker had asked helpfully.

Jon's father had suggested that he approach Arthur

Schmidt to become a member of his board of directors. "His name would look much better on your paperwork than your old man's name."

And Arthur Schmidt made it easy. He invited Jon to come to the house on Pocatuck outside of Plymouth. Jon had no idea what Pocatuck was. It turned out to be a massive estate that had been in the Schmidt family forever. Arthur was justifiably proud of Pocatuck. He guided Jon along paths through the woods, past old stone walls, and sudden clusters of flowers that perfumed the air. They stopped at an enormous elm tree that reached out and up to the sky. "This tree is hundreds of years old. It was here when George Washington was president. It witnessed the indigenous people hunting the deer along these trails.

"I want to tell you something, Jon. When I die, I want these woods and fields and trees to be returned to the Wampanoag tribe. But I am afraid that they will develop it, cut down the trees like this one, and build a loud and glittery casino."

He stepped up to the tree and laid his hand on the trunk as though he could feel the history and the essence of its being. "They can't be allowed to do that. That's why I want you to help Minky, if anything happens to me. Get her to talk with that friend of Dabney's—Norman Denjer. He seems to have a thorough understanding of real estate and the law. Will you do that for me?"

Jon remembered protesting that such things were so far in the future that they weren't worth talking about, but of course, he would do what he could.

After studying Jon's business plan, Arthur Schmidt said he would be glad to guarantee the bank's loan. "Dabney told me you were the one who pulled him out of that cave when you were at Boundbrook together."

Jon agreed that had been a very scary moment, murmured

condolences about Dabney's death all those years before, and expressed his sincere wish that he had been able to do more.

"Those are difficult teenage years," Arthur had said. "We just didn't see his despair."

Jon thought again about Dabney as he sat on his rock. He had to be sure about the company's potential for success, but the fact was that death was about the only totally sure fact of life. But he had to feel the successful future in his gut.

He watched some ants working on their pile of sand. They didn't have mortgages or car payments or electricity payments or taxes. They just lived. When the indigenous people lived here, they had just lived too. And then the colonists moved in, built these stone walls that ran through the woods, cleared off the trees, raised animals, planted stuff. And now the summer people were moving in along with the urban commuters that drove to Boston and Providence every day, and they let the trees grow back over the old fields and the stone walls fell down. The world kept turning, and the clock kept running.

His thoughts turned to Lisa. He'd known her for almost ten years now. She'd swept him off his feet when he came to the Cape in 1979 to play in the Cape Cod Baseball League. He loved her natural smile and the drift of her auburn hair, her high cheekbones, and the sharpness of her mind. She grew up in Tilley. Her father was the chief of police. And to be fair, Lisa was what had brought him back to the Cape after a stint of working in Florida. And actually, when he boiled it all down, this money mountain problem was all her fault. She had encouraged him to work with Ace Wentzell. She had agreed to marry him. She had agreed to buy the house. She had brought Sam into the world. So, in fairness, whatever he did now to solve their economic problems would be okay.

She might not see the long-term value in the short term risk the way he did. She was practical. She was an immediate impact thinker. Take care of these problems now and the future will take care of itself. At least that seemed to be how she thought.

Business was gambling. The firm of Wentzell and Megquire was taking a chance on the future. But unlike throwing money on a roulette wheel that would blow it or reward it in the chance of a moment, it was investing in their efforts and their skills and their imagination. Take a little from the now... well, maybe more than a little... to be secure in the future.

When Jon had originally "washed-ashore" on the Cape in the summer of 1978 to play in the Cape Cod Baseball League, he had lived with Ace and Babs Wentzell, and Ace had initiated him to the wonders of construction. Ace was an experienced and talented contractor who resisted change, but was willing to listen to Jon's explanation of a changing world.

He would just have to find a new guarantor. And then tell the bank about Arthur Schmidt. How hard could it be?

WHEN HE GOT BACK to the house, he said, "If I don't find someone else to guarantee the loan, the bank is going to want us to pay it all off."

"You don't know that," Lisa said. "You don't know that they'll do that."

"We just don't have a lot of options." He paused, not sure if he should tell her his thoughts. "I was just out in the woods wondering what it would be like to live there."

Lisa looked at him. Her features softened. She pushed her hair back off her forehead. She reached out and put her hands on each side of his face and angled his head down toward her and he dropped into the depths of her warm brown eyes.

"That will not happen," she said.

And at that moment, he knew she was right. The bond between them was so strong that he had no doubt they would figure it out. He just didn't know how.

"That's not going to happen," she said again. "This is just a twist in our story to keep life interesting. I've never enjoyed camping." And she smiled and kissed him.

They held that embrace and then returned to their evening chores.

She turned back to the sink.

"Why don't you call one of those preppy friends you hung out with? You said they all have money. Can't you get one of them to help you out?"

Jon thought again of those Boundbrook years, to his teammates on the baseball team, the near-death experience in the Shawme Cave, the dining hall, the squeaky floors in the rotunda by the mailboxes, the stuffy classrooms, the plaster busts of famous philosophers, and tried to pick out a single face he could consider a close friend.

"It's going to work," he said, stepping back. "I know it's going to work. We're going to build this fantastic business. This is the future, Leez. I mean, when we run out of oil around 2000, everyone is going to need to be using solar heat to stay warm. They're going to want to save energy. They're going to want comfortable, healthy homes. And that's what I'm trying to give them. It can't lose. I'll think of someone."

Lisa turned to him.

Jon's face reflected the innocent urgency of his thoughts. The house creaked. The refrigerator compressor clicked on. He could hear bluejays scolding each other outside.

He stepped up and hugged her again. "I have to do this. You know I have to do this."

Lisa pushed him back and studied his face. "I know," she said.

He held his breath until she finally gave him one of her smiles. "We're in this together," she said.

There was a solution. He just had to find it.

* * *

SEVERAL WEEKS LATER, on a drizzly early fall morning, they were juggling schedules. Lisa had to go to work. Jon needed to get to a job site. And two-year-old Sam wanted everything.

Lisa asked, "Can't you just stay home today?"

"I can't today, Leez."

"Neither can I. I've taken too many days off."

Jon looked around, noting all the things in the kitchen that needed work. The oven needed to be replaced, and so did the refrigerator. He had been reading about cast concrete countertops. All the pictures in the building magazines made their little house look shabby and tired.

And when he went off to work on the houses that he worked on with his mentor and partner, Ace Wentzell, it was even worse. The houses that Ace loved to work on were the houses of Cape Cod royalty, with grand water views, sweeping, manicured lawns, and kitchens that could feed the attendees at a rock concert. On Martha's Vineyard, they were trying to restrict the construction of houses that were greater than forty thousand square feet! At just over one thousand square feet, Jon and Lisa's house would be a small closet in one of those. Jon wondered who needed a forty thousand square foot summer house?

Even though it was small, Jon was proud of their house. It needed work. They'd known that when they bought it. The real estate agent had smiled and said it had potential! Sweat equity, they called it. Fixer upper, they called it. How hard could it be? And working for a professional contractor meant they had access to plumbers, sheet rockers, electricians, painters, masons, floor installers, and all the other trades that are necessary to build a house... if they could afford them and the needed materials. Over the years that Ace had been building on Cape Cod, he had assembled a reliable and professional team. They accepted Jon, and although they were professionals, they often volunteered to help with his projects.

Their house had only one bedroom, and if they were ever going to have more children, Sam was going to need to have a room of his own to give his parents some privacy. Where was that money going to come from? Just one child was expensive enough. Like day care. If both Jon and Lisa were working, they couldn't leave Sam alone. And they couldn't always rely on Lisa's mother, Dot. Having her in town was a real asset, but she had her own life. They could get Ace's wife, Babs Wentzell, to help. But asking your business partner's wife to take care of your kid rubbed Jon the wrong way.

It was a daily conflict.

"All right," Jon said. "I'll figure out a way. There's stuff I have to do here, anyway."

"Always is. Just don't forget about Sam and don't let Stogie get into the neighbor's yard again. Don't get so involved in something that you lose track of time."

Jon made his 'I'm-shocked-you-would-think-that' look.

"You do that sometimes."

Jon considered his son, Sam, to be a genius. He was taller and more intellectually advanced than any of his two-year-old peers. And that didn't surprise Jon as one of his brilliant parents. That Sam had peers was surprising to Jon. During his previous visits to Tilley, he had never noticed the number of small children. They seemed to have just popped up since Sam was born. He had thought small children were just visitors, short tourists who arrived with their parents and made a lot of noise. He couldn't ignore them now. They were in play groups at the church and story time, and Mother Goose at the library. Jon participated in events that he never would have believed possible before he became a parent.

Lisa seemed to be a natural at these parenting things. At Sam's pre-school, she sang along with the nursery songs, showed up in her State Trooper uniform when required, and was a great mom in every way. It appeared she had been given the handbook on parenting. Somehow, Jon's copy was missing.

Jon's focus was on the construction business. He was intrigued by the thought that homes might produce as much energy as they used. Simple energy-efficient design could make a world of difference. But chemicals in materials made people sick, especially little kids like Sam, who lived and breathed close to the floor.

After Lisa had gone off to work, Jon looked at Sam and said, "Right, buddy. What do you want to do now?"

Sam looked at him like a confused robin.

"You all good? No diaper change required? Listen, I've got to work on the kitchen lights. You've got your things and I've got mine. Right?"

The living room had, in fact, become Sam's playroom. Toys were everywhere: a highway rug on the floor, things to step on, things to climb on, a world of childhood entertainment. What could go wrong? Jon got out his tools.

The light in the kitchen was a single fluorescent ring light on the ceiling that they both hated. It gave everything a kind of pale, washed out patina that took the joy out of vegetables. The room was sunny enough in the daylight, but at night it felt like a 1950s gangster movie on the lower east side of Manhattan.

The ceiling fixture should have been easy enough to

replace. Lisa's voice echoed in his head, warning him to turn off the power before he took down the old fixture. The fuse box was in the basement. It was one of those screw-in-the-fuse boxes where you could insert a penny if you didn't have the right fuse—if you wanted the circuit to work immediately and were willing to risk your life. He had to decide which circuit and fuse were connected to the ceiling light in the kitchen. If he shut off all the power to the house, it would shut off the refrigerator. It would have been a lot easier if the fuses had been marked. As it was, the process required turning on the kitchen light, running down to the fuse box, taking out a fuse, running back up to the kitchen to see if the light had gone out, running back down to the fuse box, reinstalling that fuse, taking out another one, and so on. It was a tedious process.

Of course, with the power off, the light in the kitchen was dim. Jon set up his drop light.

Finally, with Sam happily playing in the living room, the fuse box runs completed and the power off, Jon moved the kitchen table with its red checkered tablecloth, climbed the ladder, and removed the fixture and surveyed the wires. They were old and there was no electrical work box in the ceiling to mount the new fixture. Two fuzzy wrapped wires just ran through a bracket and stuck out of the ceiling.

Jon stood on the ladder, holding a flashlight, staring at the wires. To do the job right, he should run a new Romex wire and install a steel, electrical box. That would mean that he would have to go to the hardware store to buy the box and the wire and cut away the ceiling. He climbed down off the ladder, took the cover plate off the switch on the wall, and thought about how he would somehow snake a new wire up through the wall and across the ceiling.

Returning to the basement, he aimed his flashlight up over the unexcavated crawl space under the kitchen. The myriad of cobwebs, undisturbed for thirty years, twisted throughout the space. Jon had yet to venture into the crawl space both because he hadn't needed to and because tight spaces brought back bad memories. There was light from the backyard shining through a narrow foundation window. Opening that window from the outside might give him access and limit the amount of crawl space crawling he would have to do to get to the wire.

Back in the living room, Jon said, "Hey, buddy, let's go outside. It's beautiful out there."

Sam said, "No." It was his initial answer to everything.

Stogie, the family bulldog mix mutt, stood by the door wagging his stubby tail enthusiastically. He had the look of Winston Churchill ready to take on the Boche.

"Where's that big dump truck of yours? You know, the yellow plastic one? You could build a road. You could help me. How's the diaper?"

"Why?" Sam said.

Jon checked it anyway, found Sam's sun hat and the bottle of sunscreen, which Sam never liked, and they hopped down the back steps into the backyard. Sam took off. The yard was fenced in, and Jon was not concerned that Sam would run out into the street despite his natural curiosity about everything. With his hands on his hips and a smile on his face, Jon watched Sam race around the yard, stopping periodically to pick up a stick or pine cone or leaf and then race off again. Jon shook his head at the wonder of it all. Then he turned back to the house.

He walked around to the side and found the opening in the foundation wall. It was generous to call it a window. It was just a piece of glass in a frame mounted in the opening in the foundation wall, held in place by paint and age. With a bit of coaxing, cutting, prying, and scraping, it didn't take long for Jon to remove it. He set it on the grass and peered through more cobwebs and into the gloom. He poked a long stick he found in the yard through the window and swirled it around to remove cobwebs, much like winding cotton candy at a fair. He craned his head so he could look up at the floor joists and recognized that even with the bright daylight in the yard; he was going to need his flashlight to find the wires, so he returned to the house to retrieve it.

He considered maybe the wires didn't really need changing. He could leave the old wiring in place and figure out a way to jury rig the new fixture onto the kitchen ceiling. What he was doing was mainly just an exploratory exercise.

When he came back out into the yard, Sam was gone.

"Sam!" he called. "Hey, buddy. Where'd you get to?" It was not that big a yard. The gate to the side street was closed and latched. He looked under the bushes where Sam sometimes liked to play forts. "Sam! This isn't funny." And it wasn't funny. It wasn't a scene from a movie where the camera would move off to a bird's-eye view of the Megquire's backyard in Tilley. There wasn't some big evil man in a trench coat and black leather gloves with his hand over Sam's mouth. It was an empty backyard with green grass and abandoned Tonka trucks.

Suddenly, it occurred to Jon that Sam had gone into the crawl space. Why? Because he was two, and he was curious, and it was different.

Jon ran over to the open foundation window. "Sam," he shouted. "Are you in there?" He tried to control his voice, swallowing the fear.

The little voice that came back to him pulled the tension out of his shoulders. "Dowk. Little Bear's cave."

Jon reached into the opening with the flashlight, looking for the source of the voice. "Okay," he said, bile rising in his throat. "Okay. That's great. Come out now. You shouldn't be in here. This isn't a place to play. It's yucky."

But Sam was exploring.

Confined Spaces

It was barely a crawlspace. It was just the right height for a curious toddler. With two feet of height from the dirt to the bottom of the floor joists, it was a stomach drag for an adult. There wasn't room to turn over. The ground inside the space had not been touched since the land had been cleared and the foundation was built. There were construction remnants — boards with nails, scrap pieces of insulation, rocks, a beer can, and the skeleton of a dead animal that had climbed in and died. It was an undignified job site that was never meant to be seen again.

The window opening was just enough for Jon to pull his shoulders into the space, and after a moment's hesitation, he pulled himself in up to his waist.

"Come on, Sammy. Come back now. It's yucky."

The light from Jon's flashlight was an enticement for Sam to explore further, and he moved deeper into the space.

Memories of the Coyote's Gullet and Dabney Schmidt flooded his mind as he peered into the darkness and considered how to get his son out of there. Responsibility overwhelmed his thoughts. There was no one in the house. Sam was unpredictable, autonomous, and helpless. The space was congested and oppressive. He tried to reason with Sam. "Come on, Sam. You're going to get all dirty in here. It's not a place to play. You're going to get stuck."

Sam was small enough to turn and sit and stare back at his father through the gloom and the cobwebs. "Why?" he said. "What's this?"

He wasn't referring to anything in particular. "It's just the space under the kitchen. You know, the kitchen is up there." Jon leaned on his elbow and pointed up. "Let's go back there. And have a snack?"

"Why?" Sam asked.

"Oh, come on, Sam. Please?" Jon could feel desperation creeping into his voice. That was the last thing he wanted to do.

Sam said, "I can't."

Jon took a deep breath, closed his eyes, and lowered his head onto his forearm. He told himself that it was all in his head. It was just like lying on the grass in the backyard and letting the sun warm his back. There was nothing threatening about it. The menace was all in his mind. He looked up at his son.

Abruptly Sam screamed, an indecipherable jumble of toddler twisted sounds that tangled Jon's guts. He forced himself to focus and try to break the problem down into solvable pieces. He had to get Sam out. He couldn't carry him out because he couldn't stand or even kneel. He couldn't forcibly drag him out without hurting him. He needed to be persuasive, reassuring, kind, fatherly. He pulled himself through the opening and into the crawlspace, wiping cobwebs from his face.

Sam screamed in fricative, meaningless bursts.

Jon angled his body so that he could tilt his head to see Sam. He took a deep breath and let his muscles relax and tried not to think about turning around and crawling back out. Sam was only about six feet away. "There," Jon said and smiled.

"It's dowk!" Sam yelled.

"We're okay. We're okay. I have my flashlight. We can slide back out now. Okay?"

Jon was amazed at the array of expressions that rapidly appeared and disappeared on his son's face. As he had many times before, he wondered what was going on in that little mind. In the dim, indirect light from the flashlight and six feet away the wrinkles on Sam's forehead, the pink on his cheeks, the wideness of his eyes, the frizz of his hair transmitted messages that were indecipherable. Trust? Fear? Hunger? Did toddlers have deep, questioning feelings?

Jon wanted to wipe the sweat from his eyes, but hesitated because his hands were covered in dust.

It was clear to Jon that Sam would have to get himself out. At the same time, it was clear to Jon that he would have to use his voice as a persuasive, parental bond to pull Sam to him. Logic wouldn't work and neither would anger. Yelling "You come out of there right now!" would not be productive. Nor would fear generated by Jon turning around and sliding back out through the window and leaving Sam in the dark to fend for himself. All of these alternative approaches would leave deeper scars that could haunt Sam in his later years. There would be time for Jon to doubt his parenting skills later, when this was over.

Jon put his head back down on his forearm again and took another deep breath, raised his head, and smiled at his son. "All right, Sammy. Let's do this. Let's get out of here and go have a snack. Maybe you can help me?"

Sam stopped wailing. "Why?" he said and started crawling back toward his father.

Jon said, "Be careful." Jon watched Sam crawl over the rocks and dirt. "That's it."

Jon eased his own body around as Sam approached.

When Sam got back to the open window, Jon said, "Carefully," and then, "Wait for me out there. I can't move as fast as you."

Sam laughed as he stood on the grass in the backyard's sunshine.

Jon pushed his head through the opening and sucked in the infinite fresh air. As he pulled himself out of the opening, he felt as though he was being born. He turned over onto his back in the grass and stared up at the blue sky. His son came over to him and looked down. "Nack!" he said.

Paul H. Raymer

* * *

Jon sat in the kitchen, by the light of his drop light, nursing a mug of coffee and watching Sam play. Maybe Sam wouldn't be scarred for life by what had just happened. Would he even remember it? Would it enhance the monsters under his bed when it got "dowk"?

The experience was traumatic for Jon. It was more than a notch in his memory. It was a gouge on the walking stick of parenthood. It was that moment when you turn away for just a moment and turning back your child is lost. It's just a moment. A breath-sucking split second. The reason parents never want their children out of sight.

But there was still the light fixture to be dealt with.

Putting the old ceiling fixture back was the most reasonable way to resolve the situation—putting it all back the way it had been. Someday he was likely to have to deal with crawling in crawl spaces. But not today. Not with Sam unattended. It was clear to Jon that there wasn't much one could do around an inquisitive two-year-old that took your eyes away from the toddler for a moment. He couldn't put him on a run in the backyard or cage him. He wondered how people did it.

He lingered at the kitchen table in the weird light from the drop light and watched Sam playing with his traffic jam of toy cars and wondered why simple tasks in old houses always turned out to be more complicated than they appeared to be initially. Unraveling the tangled web of the layers of undocumented decisions made in the building and repairing the building by various craftsmen threatened every step on the path to success. The simplest route was to just tear it all out and start over. Delete all the history—all the miscellaneous decisions. That caused him to wonder what would the world be like thirty years in the future for Sam? That would be in the next century—2018.

Finally, he heaved himself up and found some bigger screws, climbed the ladder, put the old wires back on the fixture, remounted it, and hoped for the best. He stood looking up at it and shrugged. Then he turned to Sam. The fuse still had to be replaced.

"You all right?" he asked.

"I'm going to go down and put the fuse back now. You okay for the moment?" Jon tried to think of all the trouble that a toddler could get into while he was alone. Jon was sure that there were a dozen unforeseen, impossible to imagine hazards that Sam could discover even with limited mobility. He would just be a minute. Maybe two. He closed the kitchen door, the front hall door, the closet door, the door to the porch. He hoped Sam hadn't figured out how the door knobs worked yet.

His hand was on the basement door when he heard the front door open and Lisa return.

"Hi," Jon said, when Lisa walked into the kitchen and threw her keys down on the table. "How was your day?"

Jon always found it amazing how Lisa's Massachusetts State Trooper uniform transformed the character of his wife. Perhaps that was what it was intended to do. It was like a magic cloak that transmogrified his short, sweet, beautiful wife into a part of a legal machine who had the authority to punish him for his transgressions. The uniform stirred up the guilt in his soul. When she was in uniform, they couldn't just be good-old Lisa and Jon.

"What's going on here? How's Sam?"

"Fine! He's fine."

Sam was ignoring his mother until he looked up and said, "Daddy took me under the house."

It was indeed a full sentence with subject and verb and the

concept of 'under', all of which was an amazing step forward in Sam's communications skills. Many of his s's were missing in his general speech, and he often needed interpretation. He got irritated when his parents heard different words from what he said. He also recognized that his mother understood him better than his father. So, 'Daddy took me under the house' could have meant something entirely different, such as "Daddy found a mouse" or "Daddy slept on the couch".

Jon laughed. "Let me explain."

"What? Did he say you took him under the house? Why would you do that?"

Jon gave his wife a kiss and asked if he could get her anything.

"Why would you take him under the house?" she asked again.

"Well, that's not exactly what happened. Do you want to change? Then you can tell me about your day and I can tell you about ours."

"But he's all right?"

"Oh, of course," Jon grinned. "He's fine. We're all fine. Everything's fine."

"What's happening to the light?"

"I'll tell you all about it."

Lisa smiled. Although it wasn't one of the light-up-your-life smiles that Jon loved, it would have to do.

When she returned, the uniform had gone away, and they were Lisa and Jon again. Jon explained what had happened with the ceiling fixture and the incident in the crawl space.

"You know you can't leave him alone like that!" she said.

"I had to. I couldn't carry him around. And it was just for a minute." Jon explained why he needed to go back into the house and leave Sam in the backyard. He threw his hands up. "I guess I panicked, Leez. I did. I panicked. He was just gone!"

Confined Spaces

Her eyebrows went up, and she put her hand over her mouth.

"There was that moment, you know? That horrible moment when he was gone. I mean, I tried to imagine all the things that could have happened to him in those few brief seconds. It was literally moments. Seconds. It was like a magic trick. He was there and then he was gone. I mean, he's mobile, but how far could he go? Rational thought disappears."

"What were you thinking?" she asked. "No, don't answer that. You weren't thinking."

"That's not fair. How am I supposed to get this job done if I have to watch him all the time? Why would he go through that window and into the crawl space? It's dark and full of cobwebs and who knows what. You know how I feel about tight spaces. But he was perfectly fine in there. The space is so small, I can't even turn over, but he was just sitting there. The cobwebs and the dirt and the dark didn't bother him at all. I think he would have been perfectly happy playing there. Is that normal?"

Lisa had picked Sam up while Jon was explaining all this.

Sam said, "So we no change ... to the house today?"

"No."

"Can you put the fuse back and get the light on in here so we can get supper?"

"Sure ... as long as I put the wires back right."

Lisa smiled at him. The steps squeaked as he headed back to the basement. He addressed the fuse box, crossed his fingers, and screwed the fuse back in place and stared at it, willing it not to pop.

Back up the creaky stairs in the kitchen, he flipped the switch, and the old fluorescent bulb shuddered to life. No harm. No foul. No ... progress.

"Do we need to hire an electrician?"

"No," he said. "No, I can do it. But we might want to

change out the fuse box for one of the new-fangled, modern breaker boxes. And that's beyond me."

"Do we need to do that now?"

Jon pulled a beer out of the fridge and settled at the table. "Priorities," he said.

"What?"

"What we do and when we do it is controlled by our limited budget."

Lisa had developed a strong 'don't-tell-me-something-I-already-know' look. She put her hands on her hips and looked down her nose from the top of her eyes over the top of her glasses.

Jon said, "So, how was your day?"

* * *

"Domestic violence again," she said. "At Summer Meadows. That development that Ace worked on over in Mashpee. What makes couples think that the best answer to their troubles is to beat on each other? I hate those calls. Makes me feel like an armed therapist."

"I hate it when you have to deal with domestics."

"When people are screaming obscenities and threatening to kill each other, it can easily spin out of control."

Sam ran up and jumped into a chair head first. "Big truck! Dad sed under how. Why?"

"It is dirty under the house," Jon said. "Because that's outside of where we live."

"Why?" Sam asked.

"You wouldn't want to live down there, would you?"

"Why?"

"We live up here where it's much nicer."

Jon and Lisa moved around the kitchen in harmony. Jon

pulled down the drop light and coiled it up and put it away. He returned his tools to the toolbox and closed the cover with a click. He put the box back in the tiny closet built in under the stairs and sat back down at the kitchen table again while Lisa pulled pasta out of a cabinet and a large pot and cover out of another.

"Any mail?" she asked.

"I forgot to check." He got up and walked to the front door and pulled open the mailbox that was attached to the outside of the house. Advertising flyers, credit card offers, the telephone bill, what looked like an unfriendly letter from a credit company, and a fancy envelope with a gaggle of surnames on the return address which could only mean lawyers.

Jon remembered when getting something in the mail was a pleasure. It validated your existence that someone was getting in touch with you. There might be a connection to new opportunities, an update from an old friend, or a note from a long-lost uncle who was willing you his castle in Scotland.

Dunning letters were an unfamiliar experience for him. But the letters were better than the collection phone calls that made answering the phone a dreaded event. Letters from lawyers, however, never meant anything good. One in the mailbox was the shot across the bow—the warning. One at the post office was certified or registered and things were getting serious.

"Anything good," Lisa called.

"Nope," Jon replied, walking back to the kitchen, stepping over a line of toy cars that Sam had parked at the threshold.

He dropped the pointless papers on the table and held the legal manifestation out in front of him. It was addressed to Wentzell and Megquire Construction, from Barnaby, Waggleworth, and Fram "This doesn't look good."

Lisa kept working on preparing supper. "What doesn't look good?"

"Oh, just something from some law firm." Jon peeled it open, unfolded the heavyweight foolscap, and scanned the words. "Shit," he mumbled, as he digested the content.

"Jon!" Lisa said, indicating Sam on the floor with a nod of her head.

"Sorry."

"What is it?"

"The occupants of one of those houses in Summer Meadows. Where you were just talking about. You remember where Ace built that house? Those never were Ace's type of houses, anyway. The occupants are apparently going to sue us."

Lisa put down her spoon. "Why?"

"They say it smells in the house."

"What would cause that?"

"I don't know. New houses always smell because of all the new materials, you know. Like that 'new car smell' that comes from all the plastics. But those houses are three years old! Who knows what these people brought into the house? How do we know if it came from the construction or their stuff? I never liked that project from the beginning. There was something about it that didn't sit right."

He took a major gulp out of his bottle of beer. "It just sucks. People never want to take responsibility. They always need to find someone else to blame. I hate thinking about money all the time."

Lisa turned and looked at him as he slouched over the table. "I thought you said that bank loan was all we needed."

"It was. It is. But they may want a new guarantor now that Arthur Schmidt is dead."

"But we should be all right. Right?"

"We are. I mean, we are all right."

"What then?"

Jon scratched the label on his beer bottle. "I don't know."

"What do you mean, you don't know?" Lisa crossed her arms over her chest. "My mother used to throw stuff when she was worried about something. She banged around, slamming things down in the kitchen. It was like she was trying to kill it ... whatever was bothering her. Stomp out the problem. Like smooshing an ant or something. Her face got all twisted up, like things were pulling it from the inside. I knew enough to stay out of her way."

"Did she ever hit your father?"

"Hit him?" Lisa laughed. "Hit him? Christ, no. Have you seen my father?"

Lisa's father was an imposing figure as the Tilley's chief of police. He was tall and bulky, with thinning hair, florid cheeks, a small black mustache, big ears, a constantly quizzical expression, and almost gray eyes that could make a criminal squirm.

"No. She certainly never hit him. He stood back and let her vent it out."

"Did she ever hit you?"

"Never," she said without hesitation. "It was just frustration. Usually money. Trying to make life fit together when you don't have the tools to do it."

"What did she throw?"

"Almost anything. Glasses. Paperweights. Pots."

"Damn," Jon said. "Does she still do that?" He was thinking about the safety of Sam when Dot came over to babysit. She seemed like such a quiet, passive sort of person.

"Stress makes you do strange things," Lisa said. "They never talked about their money issues in front of me."

Lisa sat down at the table and held Jon's hands. "So, what's the problem?"

"Well, there's this!" Jon flourished the legal letter in the air.

"Have they actually sued? Find out what Ace thinks. Maybe he'll have a quick answer."

"I doubt it," Jon said, glumly. "And then there are all the day-to-day expenses."

"Maybe you shouldn't go to that Providence conference next month. That's going to be expensive."

"You gotta go to these conferences," he said. "You gotta keep learning - making connections and learning the science and promoting the business."

"I'm just saying it's expensive and maybe we can't afford it right now. This house needs a lot of work."

"I'm already committed. Paid the fee. I've gotta go," Jon said. "Gotta go. I've got to keep learning. Just like you had to get your degree to do something you wanted to do. We'll make it work." He grinned.

Wentzell and Megquire would be successful. But there was the frustration of the lack of just being able to ... to do something, whatever it was. When it was right there. Within reach. Like a donkey with the carrot hanging over its nose. If he ran just a little faster, he could catch the carrot.

Attending the International Clean Air 1988 Building Science Conference was an investment! Technically, it was more like asking for a blessing.

In the thick of the silent kitchen, Jon waited. He wondered if she still thought he'd made a mistake all those years ago when he had been approached by the scout from the Los Angeles Angels, where he could be earning at least half a million dollars a year now. That was the 'road not taken'.

"Sorry about the light," he said.

"At least you didn't electrocute yourself!" She smiled.

And that made all the difference. That smile. Life might get tough, but as long as he had that smile, he knew she had his back. That was all the blessing he needed. The rest of it would work itself out.

"Maybe you could talk to your father at the picnic? At least tell him what's going on."

"I'm not asking him for more money. It was hard enough asking him to help with this house."

"I don't know why," Lisa said. "I'm sure he would support you. You've convinced me that solar energy is the future. And you've read all those books about the end of the 'fossil fuel-based economy'. Why wouldn't he want to guarantee his son's pioneering?"

Jon had read a book that outlined the process for getting investment money from venture capital firms, and the first step was to create a business plan. Most of it was fiction because it was mainly a description of all the things that Jon *wished* the company to do, most of which hadn't happened yet. It was a five-year dream world that was backed up with dream facts about what Jon dreamed was going to happen.

The financials, one of the most important sections, forecasted sales and costs for the next five years. How many houses was he going to sell in 1993? How many air quality projects? It was imaginative financial fortune telling.

Luckily, Ace had been building and selling houses for a long time, so there was all that historical information. And there were stories in the newspapers about energy shortages that he used for illustrations.

Jon might have been going about this totally wrong because a construction business was not a whiz-bang, high-tech wizardry of the future enterprise that some money-bagging venture capitalist might want to invest in. It was truly bricks-and-mortar, windows and doors, heating and cooling systems, wiring and plumbing. Where was the flash and sizzle of that? It wasn't exactly a Microsoft or Apple computer model.

Jon had advanced ideas on how to use the heat from the sun and the warmth from the earth to make homes more energy efficient and comfortable, but Ace wasn't convinced to try innovative construction approaches. He'd been building houses the same way for over twenty-five years and "none of them have fallen down yet!"

He needed fellow Boundbrook alumnus Norman Denjer's magic real estate touch. Denjer had emerged as a world-recognized real estate mogul. Jon regularly heard about him on the news. Apparently, people tripped over themselves in the rush to give him money. Real estate wasn't high tech, but it worked.

"Dad's seen my plan," Jon said. "I don't think he believes it. And now there's this," he waved the lawyer's note.

"You'll have to convince him. You believe it, don't you?" Lisa asked.

"Sure. Of course. I mean, I've got to make this work. Right? I mean, I don't know how you can predict what's going to happen five years from now, but that's what you're supposed to do. And I guess you've got to believe it if you're going to ask people to invest in it. I still don't understand how you can sell shares in something that doesn't exist."

"You'll figure out something."

Chapter Three

A few weeks later, the family gathered to renew connections, share old memories, and mark the passage of time.

"Who's idea was this?" Jon's father, Andrew, asked. "This is a brilliant spot, and whoever thought this up is a genius."

"You did, Dad," Jon replied, lugging a cooler out of the car.

"I guess you get smarter in your old age! We should do this every year."

The idea of mingling with relatives at a picnic was not at the top of Jon's pile of fun ideas. It would be worse for the participants who were honorary family members like Ace and Babs Wentzell. Cousins had piles of historical memories that they could fall back on in casual conversation. Both of Andrew's brothers and their wives would be there with some of their children.

Since this was September and with the presidential election coming up in November, there were bound to be the rumblings of politics no matter how hard people tried to avoid the subject. It was like any other topic one struggled not to think about. Inevitably, it was what you thought about. And this gathering was happening in Massachusetts, which was Governor Michael Dukakis's home state.

Andrew had reserved a pavilion in Plymouth Woods State Park. The pavilion sheltered enough picnic tables for an army of family members. The park was a natural wonderland, including baseball fields and a lake with paddleboats, a pool with a water splash area, a petting zoo with farm animals, and a small train with open-air cars that chugged around the perimeter.

Although it was the end of the summer, the park was still busy with full parking lots, crying toddlers, and a line at the lady's room. There were people throwing Frisbees on the field, the train was still chugging around, and the paddle boats were bumping into each other on the small lake. And the Megquire family was gathering.

Jon and Lisa's mini-van was filled with toddler paraphernalia as they drove up from Tilley, leaving little room for Stogie to curl up on the back seat next to Sam's car seat. Jon was amazed at the amount of stuff that was necessary to lug around for kids. All that stuff had to be unloaded and hauled into the pavilion.

There were plenty of hugs and laughter and struggles to keep everyone's name straight.

"How's the little one?"

"Getting any sleep yet?"

"Did Janney ever move in with that guy she was dating?"

"I've lost track. I think everyone lost track."

"We should update the bible—you know where all those family details are."

"They grow up so fast, don't they?"

"Good thing they get older and we don't!"

Laughter, laughter, laughter. Fist bump. Fist bump.

Confined Spaces

And so the families spread out their goodies and set up their lawn chairs out in the sun. They put charcoal in the grilles and got them ready for the burgers and the hot dogs and the kielbasa.

Cornelia, Jon's sister, was glad to see him, and Stogie was glad to see her.

"How's Quark?" Jon asked. Quark was Cornelia's border collie.

"Getting old. Someone should invent health insurance for pets. How's married life?"

"Getting old." Jon laughed. "No, seriously. It's great. So's being a father. It's just finding time for everything. Time and money."

They spread out the tablecloth and stacked the plates.

"Maybe you need to get a real job," Cornelia advised.

"How's Texas? Space Agency got anything going on I should know about?"

"Well, STS-26 is going up at the end of the month. It's good to get flying again. We're still getting over Challenger."

"Well, let me know if they're going back to the moon. I hear the view is pretty good from up there."

Sam came running up and then stopped abruptly in front of Cornelia and looked up at her. "I'm Hoolu," he said.

Cornelia smiled. "Hey, nephew. What's happening?"

"I'm Hoolu," Sam repeated.

"It's a character from one of his books," Jon explained.

"Oh. Hi, Oolu. Good to meet you."

"No, Hoolu."

"Hoolu?"

"No, Hoolu. I'm thirsty."

A pickup softball game drew the adults out to a sunbaked baseball diamond. Jon had come close to playing professional baseball, and his uncles reminded him that this was an amateur game and not competitive or serious. But the Megquire family was competitive about everything, from the games they played to the food they ate.

Jon wondered what it would be like when Sam was old enough to join them.

The game ended with a collision on the base path between Jon and his uncle Langston, with both of them refusing to yield, ending up with Langston on his back and Jon still holding the ball.

They all gathered around Langston and helped him to his feet, relieved that they wouldn't have to head off to the hospital.

"I'm really sorry," Jon said again.

"Don't worry about it," Langston said. "It was my fault. I know you're a professional killer!" And he laughed and then coughed. "This is where you feel your age catching up to you."

When they reached the picnic pavilion, Langston was dropped into a nylon webbed folding camp chair and handed a beer.

Lisa wanted to know what Jon had done this time.

Ace confirmed he was glad he had declined to take part in the game. "You Megquires are way too competitive for me." He laughed.

Steaks were thrown on the grilles, beers were popped open, and the conversations lapsed into family memories and reminiscences of times and people who had passed. Less physical games were set up for the youngest among them, like wrapping adults up in rolls of toilet paper or tossing water balloons.

Jon settled into a beach chair beside Ace.

Ace was a gruff Santa Claus of a man without the beard. Big shoulders, big belly with his suspenders stretched to the limit, clean shaven, intense eyes, sharp as a razor knife, with an encyclopedic knowledge of construction and the skills to match. He was sixty-eight now, old enough to retire if there was such a thing as retiring for an independent contractor. There was no pension plan and wasn't much in Social Security since, working for himself, Ace had paid little into the system. Besides which, Ace didn't much like the idea of socialism.

Babs had managed their finances for years and had squirreled away a small fund for rainy days. As far as Jon knew, their expenses were low and as long as Ace didn't do something stupid like contract some long-term disabling disease that laid him up in the hospital for months, they should be okay.

Jon turned to Ace and asked, "So, what about this lawsuit?"

Ace coughed. "What?"

"This thing with the stinky house in Summer Meadows. You saw the letter from the lawyers."

"Lawyers. Jesus!" Ace muttered.

Jon had helped Ace through his legal issues when a client used his house to murder his mother-in-law and blamed it on Ace. Ace's opinion of the law had not improved.

Jon asked, "What do you think is happening there? Could it have been anything we're responsible for?"

"No! Absolutely not. After three years? Are they serious?"

"They say they can't live in the house."

"What the hell do they want us to do about it?" Ace demanded. "What's it supposed to smell like?"

"They didn't say. Just that it stinks."

"Where? Where does it stink in the house? The whole house?"

"They didn't say. You read the letter."

Ace gulped his beer. "You always get whackos like that in construction. They probably are raising pigs in the basement or something. Never liked those houses anyway."

"Well, we're going to have to do something. We can't afford a lawsuit."

Companionably, they sat back, sipped their beers, and watched the controlled chaos around them.

"What do you know about Norman Denjer?" Ace asked abruptly.

"Not much," Jon replied. "Why?"

"He's been all over the news. Apparently, he donated a bunch of money for a youth center. Special Olympics."

"That's great," Jon said.

Jon watched Sam and wondered again about his son's future and was silently overwhelmed with love and fear and responsibility.

Ace disturbed his reverie by saying, "Denjer's apparently building all over the place."

"You know he went to Boundbrook? My boarding school."

"Did you know him?"

"We weren't in the same class."

"Did you know him, though?"

"Not really. But he certainly was a presence even then."

"I heard he wants to build some sort of resort," Ace said. "He has a big name and a big money reputation."

"What are you talking about, Ace?"

"I'm just saying, if he wanted us to get involved in some development project on the Cape, we should consider it."

They sipped their drinks and watched Jon's family members food compete: who had steaks instead of burgers and hot dogs, who had the biggest cake or the most brownies, whose whoopie pies were the best.

"What have you heard?" Jon asked.

"Not much," Ace said. "But Mr. Denjer has made it abundantly clear that he wants to own a world-recognized golf resort with his name on it. He's bragged about it."

"What would we have to do with it?"

Ace rubbed his hands on the arms of his chair. "You might

just want to get your name in. You know, as an old school chum."

Jon laughed. "Would you want to build for him?"

"I could," Ace said. "For a price."

"No, you couldn't. Don't kid me. He'd drive you crazy."

"I'm already crazy." Ace chuckled and took a sip of his beer. "The problem is the land. The Wampanoag want land for a casino and they've got twelve thousand years ahead of Mr. Denjer's golf club."

Jon's uncles were debating meat cooking issues. Uncle Langston's wife, Francine, was spreading out a red checkered tablecloth and setting down a gigantic bowl of potato salad.

"Don't much like casinos," Jon said. "You see those old people staring at those machines, putting in the quarters, pushing the button over and over again. All the 'ching, ching, ching' of the electronic bells. 'Maybe this time. Maybe this time.' I don't see the fun in it."

Ace laughed.

"Maybe Denjer will put a casino into his golf club."

"Think they'll pay any attention to the energy issues or the air quality?"

"Yeah," Ace agreed. "It's the granite and the marble and matching the grain on the birch paneling. And then they want it to seem old. Venerable. And then they add the gold fixtures. And they keep changing their minds. A project like that takes forever, even after the lawyers, politics, and Indians."

Jon and Ace paused to contemplate the surrounding activity.

Ace said, "Land ownership is a strange thing. It's mainly a social relationship, isn't it? You can't really own this land we're sitting on. We can just agree to let you use it. Land ownership can never be absolute, like the ownership of a book or a watch."

"Sounds like a very Native American attitude, Ace!"

"We'll see. Have to let the courts decide. Don't know if we want to get involved with a project with that much press attention. How well do you know Mr. Denjer?" Ace asked again.

Jon watched Lisa chatting with Francine and Babs. He loved her laugh. It made him smile. They kept glancing over at him and Ace, and he wondered what they were gossiping about. He reached up and pushed his hair back.

"Don't have to worry about it. As I say, I don't know Denjer. Really, just what the press tells everybody, and I pay little attention to that. But it's hard to be alive and not see the Denjer name."

"You've got a nice family," Ace said. "You're lucky."

"Sometimes I wonder about them," Jon replied. "You don't get to pick your family."

"Thanks for inviting me and Babs."

"You're family, Ace. Frankly, I don't know why you would want to spend a day with my noisy, obnoxious family, but life is full of surprises."

At that point, Sam ran up to Jon, who was about the same height, ensconced as he was in his short beach chair.

"You're short," Sam observed. "Oh, yeah. I pay anymore on the inside."

"Okay," Jon replied. "But this is where we are now."

"I said that in your dream that they can't call anybody," Sam said. At least that's what the words sounded like to Jon. Sam had an extensive vocabulary for a two-year-old. And he loved to use it. Sam's logic, revealed by how he put the words together, was baffling. And until Sam came along, Jon hadn't realized how important consonants were to form understandable speech.

Ace leaned over and asked Jon, "What's he saying?"

"He says a lot of things that I don't understand, but he gets angry if I don't get the word he's using exactly right. Lisa is better at this."

"I went to pay more," Sam said.

"Why don't you play with Bart? You two should get along great." Jon thought of Bart as an infant, comparable to Sam in age, but in fact, Bart was eight and, from Sam's perspective, Bart was a big person and not a playmate.

"I don't ike Bart. No. No. I went to pay a different game on the table in there."

Sam's opinion of Bart was fluid, changing from moment to moment, from hero to annoyance. Jon marveled again at the wonderland that defined the thoughts in Sam's mind.

Jon looked at Ace and then heaved himself out of the chair. "Let's go see what's happening, Sam. More later, Ace." Then he paused and added, "We should probably talk about the bank. Now that Arthur Schmidt has died."

* * *

Jon followed Sam over to where Jon's stepmother, Mirasol, was sitting. Jon still hadn't gotten used to the thought that he had a stepmother.

Mirasol was almost ten years younger than Jon's father, and she was smokey and mysterious in a tropical way. She had long, glossy black hair, sparkling brown eyes, and brilliant white teeth that lit up her face when she smiled. She was uncomfortably young and attractive to be his stepmother. He was glad his father was happy, but he wondered how, in his mid-fifties, Andrew had the energy for a young wife and a new child. Jon had enough trouble keeping up with Sam.

Mirasol's effusive nature allowed her to blend naturally into the mélange of family memories and relationships that defined this group of people. Having none of the references to their childhood memories didn't seem to make a difference to her. She was an exotic spice sprinkled onto the standard family stew. She laughed at their jokes, flashing that brilliant smile, and laying her hand affectionately on Uncle Langston's arm. And Mirasol brought her spicy Caribbean cooking to the cookout as well. The smells of onions, garlic, paprika, olive oil, and peppers mingled with the aroma of frying hamburgers and hot dogs.

Jon wondered how his aunts, Francine and Edith, felt about her.

Sam said, "Nack!"

"We're going to have lunch soon," Jon replied.

"Nack!"

Jon said, "Hey, Leez. Sam says he wants a snack."

Lisa replied, "Why don't you get him up at the table and we'll get his lunch going?"

Jon picked Sam up and slid his legs into the gap between the picnic table and its bench. Sam had grown a lot, but his chin only came up to the table surface.

"Think we're going to need something for him to sit on," Jon said. Furniture wasn't built for small people, probably with the thought that they wouldn't stay small long enough to make it worthwhile. A cooler on the bench would be too tall and there weren't any phone books or dictionaries around. Jon assembled a pile of towels, picked Sam up, and resettled him on the pile, hoping that the pile would stay together long enough to get Sam through lunch.

"They grow up so fast," Babs said, coming up behind Jon as he wrestled Sam into his seat.

"I guess," Jon replied.

"Every day they change. You need to treasure these moments."

"And the dirty diapers. And the tantrums." Jon laughed.

Babs had become another aunt for Jon. She was far more than his business partner's wife. He'd known her for almost ten years, ever since his first summer on Cape Cod, playing baseball and trying to figure out where his life was going. And now she was helping with his son. It was one of those connections life makes that seems momentary and incidental initially, and then time weaves the paths together without intention or effort going on for years or decades.

"Pfsst! Those things will pass soon enough. And you'll forget how to change a diaper." She smiled. "Until the next one comes along."

Jon turned quickly and stared at her. "Not ready for that yet," he said with a nervous laugh. "One's enough for now. Especially a handful like Sam."

Babs said, "He's a joy."

Enthroned on his pile of towels, Sam happily dug into pieces of peaches and peanut butter-covered slices of bread laid in front of him, leaving the crust behind in a pile.

"You're an air quality expert now, aren't you?" Babs asked.

"I wouldn't say I'm an expert."

"Do you know much about this toxic mold? I read about it online."

"You're reading articles online?"

"Oh. Just a bit. You know when I took that accounting class we bought that computer, and it's addictive, isn't it?"

Jon laughed. "Bet Ace doesn't spend much time on it."

"No. No. I think he thinks it's cursed. He gets so mad at it when he can't get it to print something. I'm afraid he's going to throw it in the trash!"

Ace did not like change. He had been in construction since Alley Oop came out of his cave and he knew from experience what worked and what didn't. He wasn't against technology, but how computers worked - or didn't work - was unfathomable to him. It was difficult for him to accept that computers, like religion, were beyond his understanding, and he just had to accept them.

Babs, on the other hand, had accepted her traditional role of wife and mother, but had the wit and curiosity to seek new ideas so Jon was not surprised that she happily accepted what computers could do just as she accepted her car without knowing how all the stuff under the hood worked.

"It's so much fun when that voice pops up with, 'You've got mail!' It's always a surprise. Most of it is just junk, but it's still a surprise.

"But I was reading about toxic mold down in Texas. A woman got very sick just touching the stuff. I think they said it was stacky something."

Jon thought that there was a line that divided professionals in a field from the general public. It was the job of professionals to know all the technical terms like doctors knowing all the minutia of body parts. The public, however, was not expected to know that stuff. Computers blurred that line and now the most surprising people, like Babs, were familiar with the term stachybotrys chartarum mold. Did that make Babs an expert? In fact, because he knew the term, did that make Jon an expert?

"Sounds like stachybotrys chartarum," Jon said.

"That was it. See, I knew you were an expert. Don't they also call it 'toxic black mold'? Do we have that around here?"

"It's universal," Jon said. "Actually, the spores are too heavy to float around in the air, so it gets into the compounds they use to make Sheetrock in the manufacturing process. So, it's sitting around - dormant - until the Sheetrock gets wet."

"Oh," Babs replied. "That's interesting."

Babs was a very smart woman, but there was no need for her to have or even want to have a deep understanding of various biological genera of molds. Jon had learned that most times it wasn't necessary to know what classification of mold a substance was any more than investigating what type of shit was sitting on the middle of the carpet. The issue was to remove it and deal with the cause. A curious mind could get sucked into the vortex of scientific investigation and lose sight of the original purpose.

"Oh," Babs repeated. "No, I was just wondering if it was common around here or is it a southern problem because my sister has black mold in her house and she was wondering how dangerous it might be."

Jon said, "As long as she doesn't get up close and personal with it, she should be all right. Where does she live?"

"In Summer Meadows, you know, the development where Ace worked."

Jon stopped adjusting Sam's towel seat and looked at Babs. "Summer Meadows? Really?"

"Yes. Summer Meadows. She's lived there since they built the houses. Why?"

"Did Ace mention that we might have a problem with the house he built there?"

"Something about a smell?" Babs asked. "He's always getting questions like that."

"How bad is you sister's mold?"

Babs laughed as she wiped some yogurt from Sam's chin. "Who knows? You know that's the problem with the internet, isn't it? Could mean something. Could mean nothing. She just got nervous, you know? It gets scary!"

Jon had been learning all that he could about microbiology, but much of what he had learned was from the internet as well. He had ventured up to Cambridge and visited the MIT bookstore, which offered a wonderland of information on many scientific subjects. Most of it was so detailed and required a much higher level of math skills than he had ever pursued in his college career. And he put books back on the shelves as fast as he pulled them down and flipped through the pages. He had to keep remembering that what he had learned meant that he knew more than many people, but he was way below the level of expert, and he had to be very careful not to offer categorical solutions. It was like a police officer on a TV show promising, "We'll find out who killed your son, ma'am" when, in reality, you can't promise things like that!

And then it occurred to Jon that Lisa had just been to Summer Meadows. "Hey, Leez," he called. "Weren't you just over at Summer Meadows for a domestic disturbance?"

Lisa looked up from the cooler where she had been pulling out salad ingredients. She reached up and pushed back her hair.

"Uh, yeah," she said. "Why?"

"No reason," Jon replied. "Babs was just telling me that her sister lives there."

Lisa smiled and ripped open a bag of shredded lettuce and dumped it in the big bowl. "Have you talked to your father yet?"

Jon did not want to talk with his father about money. He dreaded discussing money at all. It was like acid. It was a magic that changed any conversation. Two people having a happy, interesting conversation would magically change roles when the question of money was sprinkled into the air. The source and the sink. The giver and the givee. The bank and the debtor. Even ... Even if it was a gift. It immediately established an obligation. Family was the worst. Owing money to a family member showed failure.

Rich people weren't supposed to discuss money. That was one of the unwritten rules. "If you have to ask what it costs, you can't afford it." But of course, that was just another one of those lies. The manifestations of wealth underlined everything.

But ... Jon could not deny that money drove business.

* * *

"So, Dad," Jon said as he drifted over to where his father was standing next to the grill, flipping burgers. "How's life?"

"Great. Tiring, but great. Never thought I'd be a new father at this point in my life. Thought I was through with diapers when you went off to college."

They both laughed. "But Bart's great," Jon said. "He's not in diapers at this point. I mean, he's eight, right?"

"I think that's right," Andrew said. "I lose track. Sometimes I think you're still in diapers!"

Jon laughed. "I'm not! And I certainly didn't think I'd have a little brother at this point in my life. And Mirasol. She's great too. You want help with that?" Jon looked around for a plate to catch the burgers his father was maneuvering.

Uncle Langston ambled over to the father and son's conversation to supervise the progress of the meat on the grill. Jon asked if he had recovered from the softball game, and Langston grunted. "When do you decide you're too old for something? People start referring to you as 'sir' or adding the 'Mister' to your name? You were an athlete, Jon. When do you stop telling yourself to stop whimping out when you exercise? When you're young, you want to push through the pain, right?"

Jon was holding the empty plate, watching Langston's face.

"When you get old," his uncle continued, "if you push through the pain, you end up in the hospital with a hernia!"

"Oh, for Christ's sake, Langston. Stop whining," Andrew added. "We have the greatest healthcare system in the world. You've got insurance."

Langston Megquire looked at his brother. "We don't, you

know. We don't have the greatest healthcare system in the world. Are you going to put cheese on all those burgers?"

Jon knew from experience that family disagreements could continue endlessly and unproductively, and had deep roots in previous disagreements. And they pursued such disagreements simply because they enjoyed disagreeing. But Langston's presence didn't make talking to his father about money any easier.

"Maybe you should sit down," Jon suggested. "Have another Manhattan and rest. You don't want to aggravate your muscles."

"That's probably a good idea," Langston replied.

"I'll bring your burgers over to you, old man," Andrew called after his brother. He lowered his voice and confessed to Jon, "He can be such a whiner. He needs to lose some weight and get some exercise and stop complaining. You know, Jon, there are some things in life that you can't do anything about. But most things can be confronted and dealt with head on."

"I know, dad. Speaking of which, I wanted to talk with you about the business."

"Oh? How's that going?"

"No, seriously. It's going great. I love working with Ace."

Andrew shoveled the burgers onto the plate that Jon was holding. "So, what's the problem, then?"

"Cash flow, mainly. I want to build up the technical side. And I'm worried about the bank."

"Maybe you need a consultant who could look at your numbers and evaluate the market and give you a direction to move in. I know nothing about construction."

Jon did not believe that a consultant was what Wentzell and Megquire needed. It was pleasant to think that some hot shot business wizard could step in and turn their little company into a multi-million-dollar enterprise, someone who could take on all the responsibility and make it 'all better'. Nice thought,

Jon thought. But as tempting as that was, that only happened in business fairy tales.

"What about Denjer?" Andrew asked.

"Who?"

"Norman Denjer. He's a star. Worth millions."

"Ace was just talking about him, too."

"He's all over the news. He's making a lot of money for many people. Returns get back to the investors like clockwork. He's a genius. He must know something about construction. Wasn't he at Boundbrook when you were there? Those are lifetime connections, Jon. You should take advantage of them. Isn't that how you got Arthur Schmidt to guarantee your loan? That was a terrible thing about his son. Terrible."

"Did you know that Arthur Schmidt died? Recently?"

"What? No. What happened?"

"Something to do with his heart. Apparently, it was sudden."

"That's a shame," Andrew said. "What are you going to do? About your loan?"

"I don't ... I'm not ... I don't think we need a consultant. What we need is someone to guarantee the loan. What I want to do is learn more about pollutants. Maybe take a course in public health. I didn't really know Denjer."

"He's got a big name and reputation. But there's your answer. He's a star in the press. I bet he could help you out. Make some connections."

"Do you have another plate for the buns?" Jon asked.

Andrew said, "We invested with him."

Jon looked at his father. "We? Who?"

"My company. Patera Healthcare. His real estate development plans have been very successful."

"Who?" Jon asked.

"Grab that plate on the table."

Jon set the plate with the burgers on the table and picked up an empty one and held it up to his father.

"Who?" Jon asked again. "Was that you? Did you decide to invest, or was it Patera Corporate?"

"That's part of my job, Jon. Denjer makes remarkably consistent returns. They only take investors by invitation. You should take advantage of that connection."

Jon should have had a plan before he ventured into this conversation with his father. Did people really plan conversations in advance? Did they really maneuver the words to achieve a goal? Or did that just happen in the movies at the hands of a clever writer?

"Actually, Dad, we need to do some work on the house."

"Oh?"

"Don't get me wrong, it's a great house, but we knew it needed work when we bought it. New wiring. Gonna need a new roof. A few of the windows need to be replaced. Bunch of stuff."

"You run a construction company!"

Jon said, "I do, but it still costs money. Lisa's getting frustrated living on a construction project. And we don't want Sam to eat lead paint dust."

Andrew turned and looked at him. "You have lead paint?"

"Sure. I mean, it's an old house. They only stopped selling paint with lead in it in 1978 - just ten years ago. Probably all the paint in the house is lead based."

"Did you know that when you bought it?"

"I don't know. I don't think we thought about it. I mean, it's our first house. We liked it and the price was right. I don't think we thought about the paint."

The burgers were cooked. The salad was on the table. There were ebbs and flows of laughter from the relatives. Francine, Langston's wife, was singing a song about spiders to

Sam, who was grinning and trying to sing along. Lisa joined in with the hand motions - over, under, over, under. Twist and turn. Twist and turn.

Jon thought back to the Boundbrook English history teacher, Master Hunter, who said this was a political song describing the peasant struggle to escape from poverty and just when they reached the top, the nobles would wash them back down again so that they would remain in place. Sort of like Sisyphus pushing that rock up the mountain only to have it roll back down again. Nursery rhymes were much more fun when you could just take them as simple stories.

Andrew looked down at the platter of burgers he was holding and then up at his son's face. "Well, look," he said with a sigh. "Talk to Denjer. I bet he would guarantee your loan and could help you make a plan. I think you need some comprehensive business advice. You didn't study business in college, did you? Things are tight right now. But talk to Denjer and then we'll go from there. Okay?"

That advice was like swallowing vegetables that Jon didn't want to eat. It stuck in his throat and then dropped into his guts. But as he ruminated on the wisdom of his father's thoughts, it gradually became more positive. If he could actually get Norman Denjer to guarantee their loan, that would be a plus on the company's resume and enhance the chance to get funding to build the business. Denjer's name would carry a lot more weight with investors than his father's. By the time the picnic ended and they were driving back to Tilley, Jon was excited about the prospect of a well-funded enterprise and sang along with Lisa and Sam about the zealous spider.

Chapter Four

Having people over for dinner meant cleaning—even if it was just one person, even if it was an old friend, even if it wasn't the queen of England. There was sweeping and vacuuming and dusting, but the biggest challenges were the piles of things that had magically accumulated on every flat surface of the house. It was a fact of life, Jon thought, that setting a single item on any surface automatically attracted other items to join it, from a single piece of paper to a pencil—anything that had yet to be provided with a permanent home, things that were in transit from the mailbox to the trash. So, when an event like a visitor entered, much of that detritus migrated into drawers or boxes to be dealt with later.

"Who?" Jon asked, when Lisa had announced that an old friend was coming over for dinner.

"Nita," she said. "Nita Avant. She was in my class. High school."

"Oh. You've never mentioned her before."

"You probably didn't notice, but she was one of the

groupies who hung around those Longliner games. You were too busy being a stud."

Jon had played for the Longliners in the Cape Cod Baseball League, representing Tilley. The Cape Cod Baseball League brought Jon to the Cape in 1977 and introduced him to Tilley and brought him together with Lisa in what seemed like a million years ago.

"I only noticed you," he said with a grin.

She slapped him on the back of his head and said, "Bull. You couldn't take your eyes off Nita. She's a beauty. It's terrible, but we teased her about being our Indian princess. She's also a very talented musician. She's at Berklee now in Boston."

"So, what's the occasion?"

Lisa pushed a pile of newspapers together and shoved them into a paper bag. "What? Do we need an occasion to have someone over for dinner?"

"No. Of course not. We just don't do this very often."

"You've been talking about your classmates ..."

"Who?"

"Dabney Schmidt and that Norman character."

"Norman Denjer?"

"Yah, him. It's not just preppies who have classmates. A small-town high school class can explode like dandelion pappus after graduation, all over the country."

Jon looked at his wife. "Like what?"

"Dandelion pappus. You know, those fuzzy things that go floating off everywhere."

"Geez, Lisa. You are more than just a pretty face." He jumped backward before she could give him another love tap.

"Nita called me and wanted to catch up. So, I invited her to dinner. To show off Sammy and the house. That's all. No occasion."

Jon realized that although he had known Lisa for almost ten

years, he knew little about her as a teenager. He hadn't been there. And she didn't talk about it. His own memories were clearly populated by the years at Boundbrook, by the smell of the dormitories, the bells between classes, the babble in the hallways, glee club events, baseball, the stern faces of the masters, and the camaraderie of his fellow students. There were no girls except the rare dance weekends, and when he went home on vacation.

But Lisa hadn't left home for high school. She'd been surrounded by familiar places and people throughout those formative years. Her father was the police chief, for Christ's sake. THE authority figure. Like living with the Pope. Was that why Lisa didn't talk about those years? Or didn't she talk about them because he didn't ask her about them?

* * *

Lisa had embedded a Pocahontas image of Nita into Jon's mind with her Indian princess label.

"Hi," he said when he opened the door for her. "Nita?"

"I remember you," she replied with a smile, and held out her hand. "Whatever happened to that professional baseball career?" She had a formidable handshake, and she was short and fit and tanned, with long straight brown-black hair, and high cheekbones. Jon found her eyes seemed to dance to inner music. He pushed the door all the way open and stood back to let her in. He tried to remember her among the groupies that had hung around their games, but Lisa had dominated his thoughts then … and now.

Lisa came up behind him and held out her arms. "Nita!" she gushed, as they wrapped around each other in a bear hug. "Wow. You haven't changed a bit."

Sam hung back at the corner of the kitchen door.

Confined Spaces

Jon held out his hand for Nita's jacket that she had been wearing against the late October chill, and then they all moved through into the living room, with Lisa and Nita going through a rapid-fire catch-up.

Jon was lost, smiling as he listened. He opened the wine and poured glasses for the three of them. It appeared the local connections between Lisa and Nita had never been broken.

The house tour was quick. "You remember this place?" Lisa asked. "We probably drove by here a thousand times over the years and never noticed it."

Nita asked, "Who'd you buy it from?"

"The Hollands. They'd lived here for years. Remember them? As they grew, the Hollands marked their children's heights on the basement door."

"Don't remember them."

"Kids were older. Before us. I think Mr. Holland taught Latin."

Nita snorted.

Sam was fascinated by Nita, hanging back but gradually warming up to their visitor. He rushed into his room ahead of the tour and danced around, pulling various toys off shelves, shoving fuzzy bears and soft rabbits up into Nita's face. "Iggy! And Bob! My whole life. It's good."

Lisa smiled at her enthusiastic son.

Nita asked, "How old is he?"

"Two."

"Wow! He has a lot to say."

"Been talking since he was born," Jon said.

Lisa asked, "Any men in your life?"

Nita laughed. "Sort of."

"Serious?"

"Don't know yet," Nita said with a smile.

When they were back in the living room, Lisa recounted her experiences at UMass.

"You always had that authoritarian streak in you," Nita said. "It must be tough competing with your father."

Lisa laughed. "What about you?"

"Albuquerque," she said. "I headed out to Albuquerque. They didn't teach us much native American history here. There was an opening for an intern, so I got on a bus and headed out there. Figured I could learn and teach at the same time."

"And did you?"

"You know, this is a nice little New England town, but bigots are never easy to get along with. I'll never know if people are born with bigotry in their hearts or if they learn it along the way. And you probably never saw it."

Lisa looked at Jon. "Kids can be cruel."

"Whatever happened to Billy Pistol? Didn't he join the marines? He was always complaining that the Vietnam war ended too soon."

Lisa got up and stood looking at a bookshelf for a moment. She pulled out their Tilley High School yearbook: *The Lighthouse 1978*. She flipped through the pages and handed it to Nita.

"Yeah," Nita said. "There he is. Didn't he have some fancy car?"

"He had a bright red Oldsmobile Starfire convertible. The girls all thought he was cool."

Nita looked at Jon and asked, "Didn't you have some sort of sporty thing too?"

Jon smiled. "Maybelline. She was an MG Midget."

Nita laughed. "You called your car Maybelline? What is it with men and cars?"

"That's why I liked him," Lisa said. "It wasn't the baseball. It was his car. I was always attracted to British sports cars."

Jon looked at her in surprise.

"I remember you two tooling around in it. What happened to it?"

"I sold it to get a minivan to carry all of Sam's stuff around!"

Nita laughed and looked at Sam building a housing complex on the living room floor with his Duplo® blocks.

Lisa looked at her friend and asked, "What made you go to New Mexico? I don't remember you ever talking about the Southwest."

Nita looked down at her wrist and pushed her silver bracelets around and around. "Something to do."

The house was quiet. Then the heat kicked on in the basement and the pipes ticked as they warmed.

"Something to do," Nita said again. "You know, you get out of school and they make those grand graduation speeches about the world being at your feet and putting away childish things and what?" She looked up. "It's like up until then there's a script and then it's over. But it's not over. It's like they said, 'We know. But we're not going to tell you! You have to figure it out for yourself.' Like ... get a job at MacDonald's or get married.

"When I went to the Wampanoag Pawâw in Mashpee, there was a flyer about summer intern positions in New Mexico near Albuquerque, so I thought, 'What the hell?,' got on a bus and headed out there." She shrugged.

"Wow," Lisa said. "What did you do? Where'd you live?"

"With a family at first, but eventually I got my own place. They're nice people. Most of them."

Jon watched Nita's face. She was the same age as Lisa and ten years had passed since they'd left high school. He remembered some poet talking about how people aren't adults until their 'expression was set'. The skin of Nita's face was smooth and calm with no signs of aging. He tried to see what she was seeing as she described the arid landscape and small boxy houses. She described a rocky, treeless land circumscribed with mountains, lunch counters with confederate flags called 'Park Ur Butt' and clothing stores called 'Nothing But Boots'. She said there was one movie theater on First Street called Lux and the whole town came out to gather around the brilliant green grass for football on Friday nights in the Fall and baseball in the Spring. Her students played in the marching band. She taught them music theory and how to play the flute and they taught her ancient indigenous traditions, harmonies, respect for the land, and a language where there was no word for 'goodbye'.

"The contrast between Cape Cod and rural New Mexico is shocking. When I arrived," she said, "I knew nothing. The program just dropped me there. I sat in the family's kitchen I was staying with and no one talked to me. I didn't know where anything was or how anything worked or what I was supposed to do. It kind of struck me like a slap on the head with a pregnant porcupine that I'd made a huge mistake."

Jon looked at Lisa. She had barely ventured over the bridges to get off the Cape. She hadn't had the opportunity to see the Appalachian Mountains, much less the Rockies. New Mexico was as foreign as a fairy tale. Her travel experience was what she had seen on TV. Once they got this house under control, they would have to do some traveling. Places were different when you could touch them and smell them. It made the world more understandable.

"But after a while, they adopted me," Nita said. "They were proud of their town and their history. They had this massive county fair in the summer—like the Barnstable County Fair—with whirly-swirly rides and cotton candy and pigs and cows and horses. And my band played and marched. It was awesome. Until one of the girls disappeared."

Lisa said, "What? What happened?"

Nita pushed her bracelets around on her wrist. "She didn't come back when we were getting ready to get on the bus to come back home. We thought that maybe she'd gone off with some boy. I mean, she was young. And she was pretty. And the fair was a big adventure. All the flashing lights and music blaring from the loudspeakers and the crowds laughing and yelling. She was Apache."

"What do you mean, she disappeared? You left without her?"

"The bus had to. It had to get back with the other kids. I was the youngest chaperone."

"Did you tell the police?"

"Oh, yeah," Nita said. "We told them. We told this fat cop in a khaki shirt with sweat stains under his armpits who barely took the corn dog out of his mouth to listen to us. 'Just a kid,' he said. 'She'll turn up. Probably necking under the stands with some farm boy' and went back to chow down on his corn dog."

"Did you leave?"

Nita looked up at the ceiling as though she were watching the scene. "I couldn't," she said. "I had to look for her. I was responsible for her safety. It was like one of those moments when you look away and your child is gone."

"I know that feeling," Jon said, looking down at Sam on the floor at their feet.

"I know," Nita said. "She was just gone. There were crowds of people. She could have been anywhere. I ran around to all the places we had been at - all the rides and the animals' pens and the portable toilets and food stands. I'd always known her to be responsible. She could have been off with a boy, that was certainly a possibility, but girls disappeared out there."

"They what?" Lisa said. "They disappear?"

"And the authorities don't seem to care. It doesn't even make the papers."

"When was this?"

"Five years ago now."

"Did you find her? Did she come back?"

"She didn't. I didn't." Nita looked at Jon and Lisa. "I know you're a state cop, Lisa, and you probably would have kept looking for her. Chasing down any clue. Any lead. But they didn't. It fucked up her parents and her family."

"Understandable."

"But she just disappeared from everyone else's thoughts so quickly. Like 'poof. She's gone. Who?'"

"That was it, for me. After five years there, it just didn't feel right anymore. I wanted to get lost in my music. The music of the desert and the mountains was gone, and I applied to Berklee and they gave me a scholarship. That was one place where my indigenous ancestry made a positive impact." She laughed.

Jon took Sam up to bed, read him a story, and sang *Scarlet Ribbons* to him, tucked him in, turned out the light, and slipped out of the room.

They gathered around the kitchen table. The aromas of garlic and seared fresh scallops filled the air. The house felt warm and cozy on the chilly October night. It was Cape Cod in the off-season when it flowed back to the year-round residents.

"This is what I missed in New Mexico," Nita said. "I couldn't imagine ordering seafood in the middle of the desert. These are wonderful."

The wine warmed their bodies and pacified their minds as Nita and Lisa reconstructed memories.

"So, what are you doing now?" Lisa asked. "I mean, besides Berklee and your flute?"

"Don't laugh," Nita said with a smile.

"Never."

"I'm working as a domestic for this rich dude who lives in Winchester."

"Really?"

"You said you wouldn't laugh!"

"I'm not laughing. I'm not laughing. But that's weird."

"He's in the news. I guess he's kind of famous."

"What's his name?" Jon asked.

"Norman Denjer. Norman P. Denjer. He's some kind of real estate wizard."

Jon looked at Lisa. "The Norman Denjer?"

"That's the one," Nita said. "You know him?"

"I went to school with him."

"No shit?"

"We weren't in the same class. But we went to the same boarding school. We might do business together."

Nita took a sip of her wine. "Pretty aggressive guy - but that's not too unusual in his world."

"What do you do for him?" Lisa asked as she cleared away the dishes.

"Domestic stuff. Vacuum. Dust. Take out the garbage. His wife's pretty nice, actually. Skinny. What Tom Wolfe would call a 'social x-ray'."

Jon opened another bottle of wine and poured it into their glasses. "What do you mean 'aggressive'?"

Nita swirled her wine around in her glass and took a sip. "I don't know how to describe it, but you know, hanging around some of the elders helps you to see things if you look hard enough. He has this kind of brown haze or aura around him. And he seems secretive about things. He asks me if I enjoy working there and where I'm from and when I tell him I'm an American, he insists that my family must be from someplace else."

"That's terrible," Lisa said.

"And there doesn't seem to be logic in what he says sometimes. I think your son, Sam, is more logical than Mr. Denjer."

Jon rolled up his sleeves and started the water running in the sink for the dishes.

Lisa laughed. "Sam has his own logic."

"So does Denjer," Nita replied.

Lisa asked, "Do you think he's dangerous?"

"Powerful, illogical men generally are. He has this weird magnetism too that seems to attract people to him."

"Maybe you should leave," Jon suggested.

"Can't," Nita said. "I need the money to pay the rent."

Chapter Five

The lawyers from Barnaby, Waggleworth, and Fram wanted to know what action Wentzell and Megquire was going to take to resolve their client's smelly house problem. Jon asked Ace what he thought was causing it. "We're going to have to go and look," Jon said.

"Smell," Ace replied. "We're going to have to go and smell."

"That too."

"Do you have a sniffer tool? Something that can sniff odors and identify them?"

"I don't think there is such a thing," Jon said. "The human nose is an exceptional tool. Of course, a dog's nose is even better. The problem is getting the dog to detail what it's smelling."

Ace said, "I never liked that Summer Meadows project from the beginning. It didn't feel right. The ground smelled. Didn't think it was a good idea for Babs' sister Brenda to buy one of those houses, but I couldn't talk her out of it."

Jon looked around his kitchen while he lifted his coffee mug. The kitchen was nothing fancy, but it was comfortably sunny. He set the mug down on the table and sniffed. Home. It was a wonderful mix of smells - dog, food, toddler, fabric softener, with a sprinkling of steam heat from the warming radiators. Home. It would be miserable to have some major pollutant dominate that aspect of his life.

"I guess I can understand why those people are upset," he said.

"But why us?"

"Who else are they going to blame? It's a house. They bought a new house. They expected it to come with a roof and windows and a heating system. They eagerly anticipated moving in. They didn't expect it to come with a stink, and, according to the lawyers, it won't go away. So, they're angry and frustrated and uncomfortable. And they hear all those stories about crappy builders who cut corners and buy cheap materials and cheat their customers. And now that lawyers can advertise their services, they find a law firm who promises to cure their problem and get a bunch of money."

Ace stood up and took his mug over to the sink. "We're not some mega-million dollar construction company," he said. "You can't get blood out of a stone. Do we need to get our own lawyer? You know how I feel about those beasts."

"Probably, but let's not start that clock running until we get a look at the problem."

* * *

SUMMER MEADOWS WAS a development with curving roads and cul-de-sacs and a homeowner's association to keep everything frozen in time. Jon knew that most of these developments were constructed by one builder who cranked out the buildings from standardized plans with a handful of options for customization, saving money by being able to coordinate the materials and the tradespeople who could move from box to box.

Summer Meadows had apparently had economic issues with the builders and had to splice the project together as mortgage rates ebbed and surged along with the fortunes of the participants.

Wentzell and Megquire had been drawn in when construction slowed to a crawl with eighteen percent mortgage rates in the first part of the decade and even the custom home market dried up. Summer Meadows was one of Wentzell and Megquire's first projects. And Jon didn't want a stinky house to be their last. Even the hint of a lawsuit could be devastating in the tight-knit local Cape Cod market, especially among the regal vacation home customers who passed their builders' names between them like an entry pass into the New York Yacht Club.

The Ramsbottoms were apparently not occupying their house because, as their lawyer had stated, the smell was so bad that they had been driven out. Luckily, it was a summer house. They actually lived in New Jersey.

Ace parked his truck in the driveway beside an idling royal blue Audi.

"Remember this one?" Jon asked.

"Oh, yeah," Ace replied. "Glad to get out of here."

"Anything in particular?"

"Nope. Just too ticky-tacky. No time for refinements. No money either."

Jon and Ace stood beside the Audi. The driver had one of those new cellular phones that only doctors and lawyers could afford. The driver finished up a call and heaved himself out, wiping his mouth and tucking in his shirt.

He stuck out a pudgy hand and announced, "Bitaf. Bitaf

Schnable. Barnaby, Waggleworth, and Fram." He peeled a business card out of a card case.

"Hi, Mr. Schnable. Thanks for meeting us," Jon replied, reading the name off the card. "I'm Jon Megquire and this is Ace Wentzell. He built the house."

"I know," Schnable said. "It stinks."

"I hope that's not a reflection of the quality of construction," Jon replied with a laugh.

"Oh, no. House is built like a tank. It just smells."

Ace grunted.

"We're giving you guys a chance to fix whatever it is that went wrong. Our clients, the Ramsbottoms, are not interested in getting involved in some protracted legal action. They're good people, but they live in New Jersey. Know what I mean?"

"It's been three years, Mr. Schnable. The materials will have out-gassed by now," Ace said.

"Whatever that means. The place stinks. It's unlivable. It's the worst in the den. They removed all the furniture in there and shut the door."

"How often are they there?"

"They tried ... and I say tried ... to use the house this summer. But it's unlivable. It stinks."

"We got that. But do they just keep the place closed up? What have they brought into the house?"

Schnable glared at Jon. "Don't try to turn this around on the Ramsbottoms. They're good people. They haven't been cooking meth or something in there. They just want to enjoy the Cape Cod air and go to the beach. Of course, they close it up when they're not there. What do you think? Otherwise, there would be squatters in there. That happens, you know? These vacation homes."

"Did it?"

"Did what?"

"Did squatters get in there?"

"No! It's been locked up tight. Hell, I don't think even squatters would want to be in there now."

Jon turned and looked at the house. "Okay. We'll take a look, but you have to know that it's unlikely that any materials used in the construction process would produce overwhelming odors after three years. If it was the materials, they would have been worst just after construction. Not three years later. Something changed since we finished the construction and turned over the keys."

Schnable snorted. "We're giving you a chance to make it right, but I'll tell you, the Ramsbottoms are losing their patience. They're nice people, but there's a limit. Expensive. It could be expensive for you."

They walked up to the front door and Schnable fumbled with a bunch of keys and unlocked it.

"Don't open it," Jon said. "We want to check the outside first."

"I'm not going in there," Schnable said. "I'll be in my car."

Jon and Ace walked around the outside of the house. Jon took pictures of every aspect of the walls, windows, doors, trim, overhangs, and landscaping. The materials were weather-aged, but there were no obvious signs of rot. Flashing details were in place. Weep holes in the masonry weren't blocked. Gutter run-offs were in place. Landscaping - which happened after construction - was closer to the house than Jon or Ace would like. But that was typical.

They opened the front door and stepped into the foyer and were immediately struck by the smells of a closed-up house in a humid environment. And something else. It was beyond 'musty' or 'stuffy'. The stink was concentrated from the lack of ventilation. It didn't smell deadly, but deadly gases like carbon monoxide don't smell at all.

"Sniff!" Jon commanded. They stood still, sniffing the air like bloodhounds. The house was silent. Tightly built houses stifle noise and trap air.

The house had a living room, one bedroom, a bathroom, the kitchen, and a TV room or den on the first floor. A stairway behind a door in the kitchen led down to the basement. And by the front entry, stairs ran up to the second floor.

"Three bedrooms and a bathroom up there," Ace said as they stood by the stairs.

Jon opened the basement door and walked down the unfinished stairs. The odors there were different, a hint of Cape Cod dampness with a sprinkling of heating oil and combustion odors from the water heater. The barometric damper in the chimney swung back and forth, tapping with the moving air. They scanned the surface of the basement walls and floors for signs of leaks or cracks when the foundation settled, but it all looked as Ace had left it. There were summer sports toys—paddle boards and some water skis, but no pile of stinking towels or moldy bathing suits near the washer and dryer.

"Heat's been on," Jon said. They could smell the dust particles that had settled on the baseboard convectors over the summer and burned off when the boiler first fired up.

"Do you smell cigarette smoke?" Jon asked. "I don't mean actual smoke, but you can tell that odor that clings to your clothes when you're near a smoker."

Ace nodded. "Maybe a bit, but there's something else. Mold. And not damp mold, but serious mold. It's not materials. It's something else."

They moved through the kitchen, which showed little signs of use despite the high-end range and massive refrigerator. Jon opened the refrigerator door, half expecting to find body parts, or at least a rotting horse's head. But it was empty.

The mold smell was stronger in the living room. They

looked for stains on the ceiling or walls that would show water leaks, but found nothing. Jon got down on his hands and knees and felt the surface of the wall-to-wall carpeting for dampness. It wasn't wet.

The door to the den was closed, and when they opened it, the smell was overpowering. Ace staggered back. "What the hell?" he muttered behind the palm of his hand, which he was holding over his mouth and nose. "What the hell is that?"

The room was empty. Jon half-expected to see a decomposing body in the gloom of the closed-up room, but nothing appeared to be dying, dead, or decomposing. Jon stepped out of the room.

"That's not building material stink," he insisted. "That's not formaldehyde or acrolein. What do you think it is and where is it coming from?"

"There's one of those plug-in air fresheners in there."

Jon snorted. "Those things are bad, but they're supposed to smell like lemons or pine needles. We have to find the source of the smell."

Jon stepped outside the back door and breathed deeply to clear his nose, took a deep breath of the chilled October air, and went straight back to the den before breathing in. He moved around the room, sniffing and trying not to gag. The stink was strongest near the outside wall. Jon got down on his hands and knees and sniffed an electrical outlet. He removed the cover with his pocket tool and tiny black corkscrew shaped pellets tumbled to the floor.

Back in the living room, he said, "Critters."

"That'll do it," Ace replied.

Back outside, Jon tapped on Schnable's driver's window. "Critters," Jon said when Schnable powered down the window.

Schnable peered up at Jon. "Critters?"

"Definitely not building materials or attention to detail. When did they first notice this smell?"

Schnable hauled himself up out of the car. "What do you mean?"

"When did they notice the smell?"

"This summer. When they came up in August."

"Well," Jon said. "Something's been living in the den wall. Probably shrews. They defecate and urinate in the same spot. It accumulates and grows mold. We'll open up the bottom of the wall and show you. But it's definitely not something we did in construction. They'll have to get an exterminator in here and clean out those wall cavities. But it's not us."

"What?"

"Come on in the house and we'll show you when we open up the wall. You have to see it and you have to smell it or you won't be able to convince your clients that it wasn't us."

Schnable stepped back. "I'm not going in there. I believe you."

He was not a big man, and he was slouching. Jon looked down at the top of his balding head and said, "I'm afraid I must insist, Mr. Schnable. We're not opening up that wall without you being there, and if we don't open up that wall, we won't know the extent of the damage."

Back in the house, Ace had removed the baseboard from the wall and set up a work light. He told Schnable that he was going to cut out a section of the sheetrock, and Schnable nodded, squinting his eyes and holding his hand over his nose and mouth.

When Ace pulled away the piece of wallboard, it exposed a pile of tiny balls of excrement almost a foot up the cavity in front of the fiberglass insulation.

"I see it. I see it!" Schnable blurted, and ran out of the room.

"I can't leave it like this," Ace said so while Jon opened windows, Ace opened up more of the wall so that the damage was fully exposed and removed damaged insulation and feces. Jon took pictures and bagged a small sample for physical evidence.

Schnable was leaning on the roof of his car.

"Okay?" Jon asked.

"That was awful. How'd they get in there?"

"Don't know. You'll have to get an exterminator to find the holes and make sure the critters aren't living there anymore. Probably just shrews. Let it air out a bit. I opened some windows."

"No! No! When you're finished, close them. I'll lock up and make some calls."

"So we're good then? You tell your clients it's not us?"

Schnable looked up at Jon and then jumped into his car. "Can't promise anything. We'll see," and he hurtled down the driveway and disappeared down the street.

Back in Ace's truck headed back to Tilley, Jon said, "I don't think that was what Shakespeare had in mind when he talked about taming the shrew!" and they both laughed. "But they haven't signed off on it yet."

Chapter Six

A couple of weeks later, Jon attended the 1988 International Clean Air Building Science Conference at the Patriot Grand Hotel in Providence, Rhode Island. The hotel featured an enormous, soar to-the-sky glass enclosed atrium with walkways and levels crisscrossing the space and dominated by a towering waterfall that made the air continuously damp and smell faintly of chlorine.

When Jon entered the lobby, hotel guests and conference attendees were milling about and flowing out through tunnels to meeting rooms named after patriotic New England places like Lexington, Concord, Bunker Hill, and Plymouth.

Jon checked in and went up to his room on the ninth floor. He dropped his bag and walked over to the window overlooking the city, and stared down at the traffic.

He recognized Lisa was not thrilled with his attendance at the conference—in terms of neither money nor time. She would have to find people to stay with Sam while she went to work. It would only be for a few days, he reasoned, and they had family support. But he wondered if she thought about the stories of men attending conventions and getting drunk and partying and wearing trashcans or lampshades on their heads and connecting with hookers. It was typical fodder on TV shows - men misbehaving at conventions.

Jon doubted that sort of thing would happen at an air quality convention. This was an assembly of international scientific geeks who wouldn't know the first thing about raucous partying. He didn't expect to find beautiful women in low-cut dresses wearing stiletto heels! Jon had mentally stereotyped the few females he expected to attend to be the classic studious type with thick glasses and chunky shoes. And the men would wear jackets and bow ties and vests with pens nestled into their pocket protectors.

Jon had doubts about his own attendance at the conference. He hated feeling like a rookie. He was sure that most of these people were scientists with multiple degrees and international reputations—advising governments and the United Nations. They would use scientific words and terms that were unfamiliar to him, but flowed out of their minds as easily as the water in the waterfall in the lobby. He was an outsider—a civilian. He was a T-ball player walking into Fenway Park. He wouldn't know anyone and no one would know him. They would ask him what he did, and he would have to tell them he was a contractor on Cape Cod, and they would step back and say, "Oh. That's interesting" and walk away.

But he knew stuff. He had been reading and thinking. He was familiar with the names of some of the speakers. He had been reading microbiology textbooks and learning about prokaryotic diversity and unicellular eukaryotic parasites, but he had trouble pronouncing the terms because he had never heard anyone say them out loud. He found it fascinating that these microscopic creatures could live in his body without him knowing. They were so tiny. Could they actually affect the grossly sized environment of a house? And there were fungi and mold and all sorts of spiders that could show air flows and ants that could serve as a guide to sources of moisture. It was an overwhelming, mind blowing, microscopic world, and he could never remember all the details and names.

He turned away from the window and returned to the lobby. He knew enough about buildings to wonder how the moisture from an active waterfall would affect the hotel structure and the occupants. And how could you fill the lobby with indoor air quality experts who would analyze all their surroundings? Or maybe the issues were so big that these scientists just didn't notice them. But they couldn't miss the faint smells of bodies, perfumes, cigarette smoke, or chlorine.

He wandered down the hallway and found the conference registration tables where he received his name badge with a lanyard to hang around his neck, along with a packet of information about the events of the conference. The schedule of sessions was accompanied by a handful of promotional literature for companies selling the latest diagnostic equipment, equipment that would allow you to see the microbes. And that was cool.

Attendees holding their packets and their cups of coffee gathered in subgroups and laughed or looked terribly serious. Organizers and volunteers scurried between the groups to set up classrooms with slides and overhead projectors and screens.

The opening plenary session was set up in one of the hotel ballrooms. Jon sat in a seat in the middle of the room and began reading through the informational materials in his packet, trying to figure out what sessions he should attend. The session titles were technical and serious, and he didn't know how they matched the work he was doing. Then the person sitting beside him said, "Lot of people here. I'm kind of surprised that this many people are interested in the air quality in buildings!"

Jon looked around the room that was filling with mumbling, shuffling attendees as if to confirm that what the man said was correct.

"Where are you from?" the man asked.

"Cape Cod," Jon replied.

"Oh, not far then. Where on Cape Cod?"

"Tilley."

"My family used to vacation on Cape Cod. Brewster, I think it was. Maybe I'll get there this time. I'm from Michigan. The name's Walter," and he stuck out his hand.

And so, their exchange moved on to small towns outside of Detroit and how the air quality in buildings was bad everywhere and Walter's occupation as an architect. The room continued to fill and the instigators of the conference took the stage and the lights went down and a title slide lit up the screen.

The keynote speaker was a professor from McGill University in Montreal who spoke with a French Canadian accent, making the words sound smooth and melodic but no easier to understand.

The slides darkened and blossomed on the screen. Jon tried to absorb the printed and the spoken words forecasting a grim future if humankind didn't clean up its act of making and disposing of stuff. Laws and regulations and sub-paragraphs of legal documents describing the toxic content of absolutely everything, it seemed, predicted future misery. And the problems were universal from the seats they were sitting on to the building that surrounded them.

Walter leaned over the empty seat between them and whispered hoarsely to Jon, "That waterfall in the lobby is terrible! I'm sure there's mold everywhere."

Jon shook his head, wondering what it all meant. If the problems were that universal, why wasn't someone doing something about them? Why weren't there more stories in the news about people getting sick?

Then the speaker discussed the work that the World Health Organization had done studying sick building syndrome. It was Jon's first encounter with the WHO and SBS, and it opened up what he had considered a local or provincial problem to a global one. The speaker was referencing the outbreak of Legionnaires Disease at a Philadelphia convention and that made the audience squirm, laugh nervously, and hold their hands over their mouths as though that might filter the air they were sucking in.

Maybe going to this conference and getting together in this building was a terrible idea. It was a modern building, presumably built to all the codes and standards. Although Jon had noticed some dark spots on the wallpaper in his bathroom, but he attributed that to the overwhelmed maintenance staff.

It made him wonder. All these people. All these rooms. All these mechanical systems. All these structural elements. How could they possibly pay attention to all of them? Every day? Just from his limited construction experience, he knew buildings degraded. Nature wanted them back. Buildings and whole towns and settlements cascaded back into rubble and trees and bushes, and then got buried in the jungle and disappeared the way the Mayan temples had.

Out in the hallway when the opening session ended, attendees were checking their schedules, seeking coffee and bathrooms, and confabbing about what they had just heard. Out of the sea of anonymous faces, one familiar to Jon appeared. He couldn't miss her high cheekbones, piercing eyes, and the small gap between her front teeth. And 'GAIL' on her name badge confirmed she was indeed the Gail Barker whom Jon had met at a memorable building science conference on the Cape five years before. There were some streaks of gray in her blond hair.

He was even less sure about what to call her than he had been when she was teaching at that conference. Ms. Barker? Professor Barker? So he said, "Hi."

It took a handful of moments for her to react, to check out his name badge, and then his face, and then say, "Jon?"

Jon grinned. "It's me. Jon Megquire. From Cape Cod."

Her face lit up. "Burying any more bodies?" she asked.

Jon laughed. "Guess I should have figured that you'd be here. Are you teaching any of these classes?"

"I've got one tomorrow on the inner-city tenants' rights work I have been doing in Fall River. Finally finished that Doctorate."

"Wow!" He wondered how inner-city tenants' rights fit into an indoor air quality conference. "This is all new to me," he said.

"I thought you were a builder?"

"I am." He followed her to the next session on The Role of Buildings on Health and Public Policies. When that talk ended, he sat with her at the buffet lunch, and told her about working with Ace and trying to get their business rolling and marrying Lisa and having Sam. And he told her he hadn't heard anything more about the participants at the Tilley conference.

"Yeah, the place is still there," he said when she asked him what had happened to that facility. "I haven't heard of any more conferences there, though. I think they had a bluegrass festival a couple of years ago, and they are still growing stuff. But I don't know what they do with it."

She told him she was practicing law but couldn't give up her connection to buildings, so she'd finished her doctorate in public health and was working with families in Fall River.

As they were walking with the after-lunch crowd across one of the bridges in the lobby to the afternoon sessions, she said, "I don't know about you, but these fancy bridges make me nervous. They don't seem well supported and with all the moisture from that waterfall ...."

"I know what you mean. And with all these people. And hanging one bridge over the other .... But I guess we have to trust the engineers and the building inspectors."

"I still don't like it. I don't need these dramatic spaces. They just make me nervous."

During the afternoon, Jon's head filled with a world of information that bewildered him. Elements spun from the macro world to the microworld and back again. He was amazed at the array of natural phenomenon that surrounded him every day that he never noticed and never saw. Chemicals in the air. Chemicals in the food, clothing, pajamas, pillows, toothbrushes, and shower heads. Information piled up in his mind with no orderly place to store it in his thoughts. All afternoon the slide projectors clicked around and the speakers peeled the Mylar slides off their protective backing, and leaned over the illuminated surfaces of the overhead projectors, their faces blasted by the intense light giving them an otherworldly look that matched the content of their words.

When the presentations ended for the day, Jon staggered out to the reception in the exhibit hall, thinking about what he was going to do with all this information. These people were intense, and after what he had heard during the sessions, Jon understood why. This stuff could make you sick or even kill you.

There were vendors selling diagnostic tools and combustion analyzers and software. Much of the stuff was for commercial or scientific laboratory purposes. Not that all these chemicals were not in homes, but there was little information on how they affected occupants. This was all interesting stuff and cool tools, but Jon needed to connect the technology to the

Confined Spaces

work he was doing with Ace—to justify why he was spending money to attend the conference.

And so he wandered along the aisles, scanning the titles of the companies, trying to figure out what they were offering before getting sucked into the pitch of the salesman or, worse yet, ignored. There was a disconnect between the scientific and the practical in this audience. Finding the means to make those connections was what Jon was looking for. The lights, buttons, and switches on a fifteen-thousand-dollar spectrum analyzer were cool, but not something that he could carry around in houses.

Some companies offered devices whose purposes were unfathomable to Jon as he tried to connect concepts to reality. The equipment offered technically brilliant solutions to laboratory and scientific problems in organic chemistry. Jon needed real world answers to tell him why houses worked the way they did or if the people in them were getting sick. Some booths pulled people in with swag—pens, candy, squishy stress reliever creatures, or caps.

It was simpler for companies to make high-tech equipment for a few laboratories than it was to address the vast world of homes and consumers and potential liabilities—like finding shrew feces in wall cavities.

He drifted with the crowd moving from vendor to vendor, sipping drinks, piling food on little plates, chatting about the effects of toxic chemicals and whether stachybotrys mold was too heavy to be airborne.

He caught up with Gail and asked her how her sessions had gone, and she asked him if he was learning anything. "This is cool stuff," he said, "but I have found nothing for homes."

They moved with the crowd out onto the bridge across the lobby.

Partway across, Gail grabbed the railing, which was vibrating. "What the hell?," she said.

Jon felt a vibration through his shoes. "There are a lot of people out here."

Then he felt the floor pop as though it had slipped a notch on a belt, dropping a few inches. And then the platform dropped away beneath them.

* * *

Suddenly, the world around Jon changed. He had stepped into an invisible hole and for a moment his stomach surged up into his throat, and he reached out to grab anything around him as he fell with bodies and concrete and wires and glass and seemed to keep falling and crashing into things around him. The noise of the twisting and snapping materials and people screaming was deafening.

Abruptly, he stopped moving.

Time skipped and lost its meaning.

And then whatever he was on moved just a little more and for a second that seemed to last forever, he wondered if he was going to start falling again all the way down to hell. His consciousness cleared, and he realized the bedlam that surrounded him and wondered if he might be making those unearthly sounds. His instinct was to scramble, to get out from under the rubble and bodies and get outside and breathe fresh air again.

It was dark.

Despite the blast of disorientation, he recognized that the bridges in the lobby had collapsed on each other. All those people and the vibration of their footsteps had been too much for the structures. He was entangled in a pile of people and building materials and he was lucky to be alive, and that thought drove his stomach back up into his throat.

Images of Lisa and Sam and the crawlspace under his house and the Shawme cave at Boundbrook climbed up into his consciousness.

"Don't move," he thought. "Don't move. Stay still and maybe this will all resolve itself."

He scanned a rapid mental inventory of what parts of his body he could feel and move and what hurt. He was on his side. His conscious connection to his body parts was detached. He forced himself to think of his feet, his knees, and his hands.

What had happened to Gail?

He moved his head. Someone underneath him moaned, and he shifted his body to take his weight off whomever it was. How many people were under here? For a moment, panic surged up through his body. He didn't want to die in a pile of bodies and building rubble in a hotel in Providence, Rhode Island. The panic was dampened when the corollary thought of where he did want to die almost made him giggle.

Time was fractured. It was shockingly dark. The noises were overwhelming. He smelled wet concrete and sweat and traces of cooked meat.

He tried to pull his feet up. Just above his head, there was a concrete slab. He was lying on a body that moaned as he shifted his weight.

"Gail?" he said. "Are you all right?"

The body didn't answer.

Gail had been just beside him when this happened. He needed more light. He should have his penlight flashlight. He couldn't see anything. He wondered if he had gone blind.

He struggled to not panic, to not let the overwhelming instinct of being trapped in a tight space with no way out force his mind to explode. He closed his eyes and centered his thoughts.

Of course, his mind wouldn't explode. He was in a hotel lobby in Providence, Rhode Island, not five hundred feet down in a coal mine or stuck in the Coyote's Gullet. People knew they were there. Emergency services would come, and they would lift these concrete slabs, and they would get all these people out of here. They might not complete the conference tomorrow. So, he would probably go home and this would all be just a story to tell his grandchildren—about the time he was in that hotel collapse in Providence, Rhode Island.

He had to move. He could move—head, shoulders, arms, hands, hips, thighs, knees, and feet. All there. Noises sorted themselves out. The broken mass of building materials had stopped creaking, screeching, and popping. Human voices distinguished themselves—screaming and yelling.

Time passed.

"Gail?" he yelled.

He got himself up on his knees. His left arm hurt like hell. He felt beneath him, hoping to find the concrete floor of the walkway, but recognized it was a body. He needed to get off. He reached out in front of him.

"Gail?" he called. Was it her body that he was kneeling on? If he could see ... It could have been any of the dozens of people on the bridges. He couldn't tell if the person was even alive. "Are you all right?" he shouted again. He hated that question. Of course, the person wasn't all right. They were trapped in a collapsed building, most likely with broken bones. It was a general question. Not specific.

He closed his eyes, but he had to get his weight off the body beneath him. He tried to control his breathing. He felt around himself to distinguish how the person was lying, and if he could shift his weight off to the side. He needed to define what were shoulders, back, head, and legs.

The body groaned.

"Shit. Can I help?"

"Get off me!"

A sudden slight glimmer of bright light filtered through the rubble, and Jon could recognize the color of Gail's clothes.

"Gail?"

"I can't feel my legs. Is it really dark?"

"I'm here," Jon said. "It's Jon Megquire. It is dark, but they might have gotten some lights on."

"Where are we? What happened?"

"The walkways collapsed."

Jon's sensory synapses fired off in a near overwhelming tumult of sound and smell and feel. He reached again for calmness and control—to be logical and analytical. But, except for that faint shimmer of light, it was blindingly dark, and when he moved his thinking out of his head and into his surroundings, the cacophony was overpowering. So many unidentifiable sounds - what they were and where they were coming from. Screams of pain. Creaks and screeches as building materials shifted and groaned under unaccustomed weight. Jon felt each vibration, anticipating another crush of the tons of material over his head. He sensed the building's pain. And his own.

When he moved his left arm to feel around, the pain was excruciating, and he grunted. "Shit!"

"I can't move," Gail said.

"Are you hurt? Where's your head?"

"It's still attached to my neck," Gail replied with a snort.

"I just can't see ... which way you are ... you know ... lying?"

"Can you move?" she asked.

"A bit," Jon said. "I'm good. My arm hurts. I just can't see anything. The lights must have gone out. And it's night. I think."

"What time is it?"

"I can't see my watch." It could have been hours since they had stepped onto the bridge.

"What the hell happened? These bridges made me nervous the first time I stepped on them. I can't feel my legs. I may be kneeling on them."

"We're alive. I'm sure they'll get us out of here."

"It hurts," she said, and they lapsed into silence, listening to the noises that surrounded them. Jon thought of an old naval TV show that portrayed a group of sailors trapped in a room on a sinking aircraft carrier. They were trying to be normal. Talking about life and their families. Playing cards as the sinking ship made dying noises all around them. They heard a crew attempting to cut through the deck above them to let them out as the water in the room continued to rise. The rescue noises stopped, and the ship pitched to one side and then the TV screen went to black. That show haunted Jon. The unavoidable inevitability of the rising water and the possibility of escape snatched away at the last moment, robbed him of his sleep.

There was no rising water in the hotel lobby. And there were people out there beyond the rubble. And maybe, if he could see, there was a way out of this space between the slabs. He moved forward a few inches and reached out with his right hand, trying to catalog the surfaces and substances around him. He was clear on which way was up and which way was down - above him and below him. They had been walking across the lobby, so if he could move forward ... or backward, would that take him off what was left of the bridge? Had the bridge dropped all the way down to the floor of the lobby or was it still suspended part way? Would moving upset the balance? And where were all the other people who had been walking with them?

"Why can't I move?" Gail asked.

"Can you move your arms or your legs?"

Gail screamed.

Jon reached out and put his hand on her back. "It's okay. It's okay. Don't move. It will be okay. They'll get us out."

Just then, they were doused in a piercing spray of water.

"Shit!" Jon yelled. "What the hell? Where is the water coming from?"

"Oh, god. Oh, god. Oh, god!" Gail mumbled. "Am I bleeding? I can't tell if I'm bleeding or if it's water. Oh, god. Oh, god."

Water. The last element. Jon forced himself to eliminate the sinking ship from his mind. They were in a hotel lobby in Providence, for Christ's sake. When he was in college, he had taken a class in Buddhism, and he tried to remember the breathing exercises they had taught him to calm himself. Long, slow breath. No sinking ship. Lisa, Sam, and Stogie were waiting for him to come home. One moment, one thought at a time. One. Moment. The next. Moment. The next. Moment.

"I'm sure it's water," he said. "Either the sprinkler system broke or they're spraying this because of a fire risk."

"Fire! Are we going to burn up in here? If we're going to die, let it be quick. I don't want to burn. If they were going to crush me, they should have finished the job."

Jon winced as he pulled his jacket off to cover their heads to shield them from the spray of water. "No, no, no. It has to be the sprinklers. If they were spraying it with a hose, it wouldn't be constant. And what would burn? I mean, this is all concrete and glass. Right? Nothing to burn. We just have to be patient. They will not leave us here."

"Patience is thin when you are in excruciating pain," Gail mumbled.

Jon wondered if she was going to black out. Again, he wished he could see. He felt her underneath him. He wished he could help her move, but she seemed wedged and frozen in place, and any movement caused her intense pain. Unlike the men on that sinking ship who could at least sit at a table and play cards while they waited to die, Gail and Jon were twisted into a small cavity between slabs of concrete, tenuously held apart like slices of bread ready to drop like a bologna sandwich. Moving at all might be the worst thing he could do.

Beneath him, he felt Gail breathing. Water from the sprinklers thrummed on his jacket, and when it finally stopped, he heard the shouts of rescue workers, the whine of saws, and the screech of shifting materials.

"Hey!" he yelled. "Hey! In here! We're in here! Help! We're in here!" He grabbed a chunk of concrete and cautiously tapped on the slab. "Tap." "Tap." "Tap." Like the sailors on the steel bulkhead of the sinking ship. "Tap." "Tap." "Tap."

Then he waited. No noticeable change in the surrounding noises. He willed the slab of concrete above his head to just lift away like the cover of a box, but with every vibration he feared it would go the other way, dropping on them and crushing them. So, he tried to stay still.

Forever. Time crawled past. It was taking forever.

The air was thick with dust and had that sharp odor of something burning or something that had burned. Each time the pile of rubble around them vibrated, his hopes and his fears rose simultaneously. For the moment, they were safe in the pocket they huddled in. Getting out was likely to be painful.

Gail was silent. He put his hand on her back to make sure that she was still breathing.

"Listen," he said. "It sounds like there are a lot of people out there working on this pile."

Frustration blended with blindness and helplessness. He had lost any connection to time. It was simply forever. Logically, he understood it was going to take a lot of time to carefully disentangle the materials from the people, but logic didn't ease anxiety. Dozens of people had been on the bridges and in the lobby beneath them. He understood building materials. He appreciated the tools that they were using. But his understanding did not make it easier to be patient and not move.

"Hey!" he yelled again. "In here! We're in here!"

Sudden silence.

Why had they stopped? Had they given up? "Tap." "Tap." "Tap." They couldn't have given up.

Then the shouts and the noises began again, and suddenly there was a shaft of light.

"Hey! In here," Jon yelled.

A disembodied voice came through the hole. "How many of you are there?"

"Two of us. Two of us. Me and Gail Barker. And she's hurt pretty badly."

"All right," the voice replied. "Can you move?"

"I can," Jon said, "but I don't think Gail can. But I can't see. I think she's pinned."

"All right. Just stay put. We'll get to you. We're stabilizing the pile."

Stay put! Jon thought. Where the hell am I going to go?

Gail was silent. Jon wondered if he should have tried to keep her from passing out. They always did that in the movies, yelling at the character to keep them awake because if they fell asleep, they would die. It was always, "Go on without me. Leave me behind. I'll only slow you down." How much of that was real? How much of our actions in life are controlled by something we've seen on TV or in the movies? We trust people to get those details right, but how many writers had actually been in those situations? These situations?

Jon's mind was wandering. He couldn't recall hearing about anyone ever being in a situation like this before. Hotels were not supposed to fall apart. Engineers were supposed to design these things mathematically so they would stay up. We trust engineers to keep buildings standing and airplanes flying and cars from exploding.

The surrounding debris began vibrating. The air became thicker with dust. Water ran down on them and Jon ducked his head. Oh, god. Was that slab finally going to fall and crush them like the bologna he had envisioned? He didn't even like bologna.

And then light flooded in and the slab floated up into the air, and he could see the details in the lobby like the recessed lights in the balconies that continued to shine as though nothing had happened. They were resting on a pile of rubble about two stories above the floor. He could see that Gail's legs were pinned under a heavy piece of glass from the walkway railing. She wasn't moving.

* * *

"CAN YOU WALK?" the rescue worker asked.

Jon was stiff from the contortions he had experienced in the rubble cavity. It was good to be able to breathe. He tried to look at his watch, but bending and twisting his wrist cause him to emit a grunt of pain.

"I don't know. How long? How long was I under there? I seem to be intact," he explained.

"Let's get you out of here."

"I'm not leaving without her," he pointed to Gail. "What about Gail? She's not moving. We've got to help her."

"We'll take care of her too," the rescue worker said.

He leaned over and pushed the hair away from Gail's face. "Gail. We're safe now. We're safe. We made it. We're going to get you out of here."

Gail groaned. Jon ran his hand across his forehead and back across his hair, feeling the grit and wiping back the sweat. He surveyed Gail's position. She had gone down on her knees with her arms out in front of her, as though she was worshipping some phantom god. A heavy section of glass railing was lying on her back, pinning her, as though she had been folded up like a pocket knife. Her legs might be broken and she might have suffered internal damage, but the pile of rubble they were standing on wasn't stable and might shift again at any moment. Getting her out and getting her medical attention was the priority.

Jon put his hand on her back and felt her breathing. He turned to the rescue worker standing behind him. "What's your name?" he asked the rescue worker.

"Vincent," the man replied.

"All right, Vincent. Come on," Jon said. "Let's get this thing off her back and get her out of here."

They positioned themselves to get a grip on the railing. "Come on. Lift!" Jon shouted. He felt the bone in his wrist pop, but managed to maintain his grip as they pivoted the glass up and pushed it back. Jon got down on his knees and brought his face down close to Gail's. Her eyes were closed.

"Stay with us, Gail. Stay with us," he said. "Can you get a stretcher up here for her?"

"On the way," Vincent said. "We'll take it from here. Let's get you out of here too."

Jon stepped back, out of the way, while Vincent and

another responder manipulated a stretcher to position it beside Gail.

"What did you say her name was?" Vincent asked.

"Gail," Jon said. "Dr. Gail Barker. She's a lawyer. Treat her well."

He watched as they gently maneuvered Gail onto the stretcher and then hoisted it up and out of the space.

As Jon became more aware of his surroundings, the lobby of the hotel was a distorted caricature of what it had been. It reminded him of the images of building bombings he had seen on the news—something unreal. He was standing on a pile of rubble two stories high, level with the surrounding balconies. Rescue crews had forced a crane through the glass windows, and the concrete slab that had rested precariously over his head was now suspended in the air above them. First responders struggled to move debris and guide victims away. The space echoed with shouts and the whine of power tools. Unaffected hotel guests stood on the surrounding balconies, leaning on the railings, watching the drama as though they were witnessing a show.

Jon felt himself asking, "What happened?" even though he knew they wouldn't have an answer.

"How many people?"

"Did anyone die?"

It was too busy and too early for any answers.

When he reached the floor of the lobby, he was guided into one of the hotel ballrooms, where triage was being performed on what must have been hundreds of people. Somehow, the hours under the rubble with Gail seemed very private, as though they were the only people going through this. But on the contrary: it was an experience shared by a crowd. It was like Jon imagined a field hospital in a war zone with people bleeding and moaning and being attended to by medical personnel.

But it wasn't a war. It was just a damn fancy, modern hotel in Providence, Rhode Island, where they were holding an indoor air quality conference. It wasn't microbes. It was construction and engineering details. They should have been safe and not fighting for their lives. He swallowed his anger with the engineers and the developers, and was grateful that it had not been the last day of his life, squashed in the rubble. Physics were real.

In the lobby, jacks and winches screamed as the heavy blocks of concrete were moved. The crane they had pushed through the glass front of the building was like the head of a dinosaur, reaching in to lift massive pieces up and out of the way. Rescue workers and construction crews yelled instructions at each other. Chain saws whined and sparks flew off their blades as they chewed through pieces of metal. Bodies of the dead were carried out on stretchers with their faces covered. Dangling wires sparked as they touched exposed pieces of rebar.

Jon looked up at the untouched parts of the building and the hotel guests on the balconies, like spectators gawking at a train wreck. He remembered reading about citizens who rode out in their carriages to watch civil war battles, as though life and death struggles were a sports event.

He had to call Lisa and let her know he was okay. There were masses of TV cameras and bright lights when they brought him through the lobby. He didn't want her to just see all this on the news and be sitting in the living room gaping at the TV in shock, wondering what had happened to him.

He wanted to hear her voice. Time had twisted. The reality of the hours he had spent trapped did not follow the normal, predictable sequential flow of his life. A lifetime had passed.

Without waiting for medical attention, he headed off to find a phone. Lisa answered on the fourth ring in a sleepy voice. "Hi," she said.

"Sorry to wake you," Jon replied. "Just wanted to check in."

"It's late, Jon. What's up? I expected you to call earlier. I waited up. What happened? Did you lose track of time partying with those pretty biotech women?"

Jon laughed. Hearing her voice sent a flood of relief surging through his body.

"Not exactly. How's Sam? I'm sorry I didn't get a chance to say goodnight to him."

"He's okay. Didn't want to go to bed. Kept asking for more stories. We've got to get his room finished."

"I'll get on that when I get back."

"How's the conference?" she asked.

Jon paused. "Good. The conference is good. I'm learning a lot."

"That's good."

"The hotel ... not so much."

"What do you mean?"

And then the trauma of the hours under the rubble hit him and his knees trembled and he nearly dropped the phone. "Oh, Christ, Lisa. The fucking hotel collapsed!"

There was a moment of silence on the phone that contrasted with the uproar that surrounded him at the hotel.

"What?" Lisa yelled into the phone. "What do you mean 'the hotel collapsed'?"

"The walkways. The walkways across the lobby. People are dead. People have been killed. People were crushed. A lot of people have been injured. There are pieces of the building all over the lobby."

"Oh, my God, Jon! Are you okay? Are you okay?"

Jon sucked in a huge gulp of air. "Yeah. Yeah. I might have

Confined Spaces

broken my wrist, but I'm okay. They just got me out." He could hear Lisa breathing on the other end of the line.

"Leez? I'm okay, but I've got to go help."

"Were you on it?" she asked.

"Uh, yeah. I was heading back ...."

"When was this?"

"I guess it must have been about six thirty. Something like that."

Silence again on the phone line.

"I was walking back with Gail Barker. Remember her? I met her at that conference in Tilley. We were trapped in the rubble. They just got me out a few minutes ago."

Lisa gasped. "Holy shit, Jon! Are you really all right?"

"I'm okay. Really. Just hearing your voice. You can have a lot of negative thoughts when you're trapped like that. But I've got to go find out what's happened with Gail. They wanted me out of the way, so they sent me to get checked out."

"Did they?"

"Not yet. I wanted to talk to you first. Let you know I was okay before you heard something about it on the news."

"Holy shit, Jon," she said again. "No, go get checked out. I'll get someone to take care of Sam and be over as fast as I can get there."

"No. No. No, don't do that. I'm okay. Really! They don't need more people and more cars to get in the way. This is an amazing operation. I don't think this hotel is going to recover. No. Go back to bed. Sorry I woke you. I'll call you when I know more."

"I want to be there."

"I know. I know," Jon said. "I appreciate that."

"I want to be there with you to make sure you don't do something heroically foolish. Be sure you get yourself checked out."

*　*　*

Hotel staff stood behind the front desk as though waiting to check in new guests. Recessed lights glared down on the shiny surfaces covered with a coating of dust. The potted plants in the corners added a touch of nature. The grand waterfall continued to drip.

Jon couldn't get over the guests who were leaning over the balconies. The contrast between what was still normal and what was disaster was startling.

His wrist was throbbing, so he returned to the triage room. A doctor took one look at him and told him to sit down. "Let's get you checked out," the doctor said.

"I'm okay, doc. Really. It's just my wrist," he said.

"You don't look okay," the doctor replied. "Have you seen yourself? You look like you just crawled out from under a building collapse. Oh, wait. I bet you did!"

Jon let the doctor poke and prod him, look in his eyes, and check out his arms and legs. "This hurt?" he asked as he put pressure on Jon's left wrist and Jon winced. "That might be broken. We'll get you an x-ray when we can."

"Maybe you can just tape it up," Jon replied. "I need to find out what happened to my friend. See what I can do to help. I'm a contractor."

"You'll probably need a splint and a cast," the doctor said. "We'll get it taped up and get you a sling for now. Then you should fill out this paperwork so we can get you into the system."

After getting Jon's wrist restrained, he handed him a clipboard and a pen.

It angered Jon that his hand was shaking as he filled out the form—even in a disaster, there was paperwork. There would be lawyers all over this one.

He handed the clipboard to a man sitting behind a table that had been pulled out of one of the conference session rooms and was still draped with the conference logo, then he set off to find what had happened to Gail. He emerged just in time to see Gail being carried through the lobby doors to a waiting ambulance.

Chapter Seven

Life would never be the same 'normal' again. Two months later, Jon was still haunted by the crushing, confined space under the rubble.

The end of a calendar year was always a crazy and confusing time, twisted up with Thanksgiving and Christmas, holidays and shopping, religion and politics. Jon wondered what George Bush would be like as a president. There was talk of another recession and that might affect mortgages and home construction.

Good news came in a surprising coda from Barnaby, Waggleworth, and Fram, who postulated that Wentzell and Megquire had not been the cause of the stink in the Ramsbottom's house in Summer Meadows, bringing that legal action to an end.

It was Sam's third Christmas, and there was joy in his face as the awareness of all the packages and the lights and music filled his mind. The baseball equipment that Jon got for him in anticipation of a brilliant career in the big leagues was ahead of Sam's years. He could put two hands in the baseball glove!

Sam was Lisa's parents' only grandchild, so the kid was buried in the riches of Croesus. The presents piled so high and came so fast that Sam was compelled to dash from one to the next, barely looking at the pictures on the boxes. Jon's father-in-law, Mark Prence, suggested that Jon was going to have to build another room on the house just to hold all of Sam's stuff.

And when the holidays ended, and the festivities had settled into the trash bins of the past, they all erupted into the new year of 1989, wondering what the coming days and months would bring. Jon showed no signs of physical injury after the hotel collapse, but he continued to have nightmares about what had happened and wondering if Gail had survived.

"Hey, listen," he said, "I've got to call Gail Barker. Find out if she's okay."

She said, "Good idea, and by the way, the bank called."

Jon was sitting on the floor cross-legged, assembling a shelf for Sam's toys. He put down his screwdriver on top of the assembly instructions. "When?"

"Yesterday. I forgot to tell you."

"What did they want?"

"I don't know. They want you to call them."

Jon picked up the instruction sheet again.

"You can't ignore them, Jon," Lisa said. "Ignoring them just makes it worse. They want to know you're there. They want to know you care."

"I'll call them. I'll call them. They just want their pound of flesh. It shouldn't be a problem. We've been making the payments. Never missed any."

The anemic gray light of this January day was not conducive to putting a smile on Jon's face. The Cape had been abandoned by the tourists and the snow birds - residents who escaped to Florida for the winter—were returning. They were elderly and the thought of funerals brought Jon around to wondering about his own mortality. He had a sudden, shuddering flashback to his hours under the rubble in the hotel. He thought again about the people injured in the hotel collapse who had to have limbs amputated after being pinned.

News reports said that thirty-eight people had died in the collapse. Thirty-eight people! Under the rubble, he had felt so alone—except for Gail.

Jon wondered at the contrast between what surrounded him now - despite the grayness of the day, the winter leafless trees, the dormant lawns and hedges. He was in his own house with his family. He could look out of the windows and see the sky as opposed to being confined between slabs of fallen concrete, waiting to be crushed like a slice of bologna. He had nightmares about being trapped—not able to escape, nightmares about being in dark confined spaces with no way out—spaces where he couldn't breathe or move - dark spaces. Waiting spaces—spaces where he was waiting for something horrible to happen. Spaces where he was surrounded by bleeding body parts and torn off limbs.

He pulled out the conference attendee list, got Gail's phone number, picked up the phone, and dialed. He listened to it ring, wondering about the spaces on the other end of the line. But Gail never answered.

On nights when Lisa woke him from his nightmares and pulled him up from the dark depths of his haunted sleep, the relief was palpable. He could taste the freedom of being able just to get out of bed and walk around, lean over the sink and splash water on his face. He wondered if prisoners in solitary confinement lost their minds when they were locked in those cold and dark spaces. Could you get used to such a space? Could you make that your world? They say you can get used to anything. How did people who went blind get beyond feeling trapped? The future gets lost in a confined space. Both place and time are restrained.

He wiggled his fingers, tapped his nose, and slapped his hand on the carpeted floor. His thoughts drifted back to the Shawme cave at Boundbrook, to that inner chamber with Dabney stuck in the Gullet. There were moments when they all could have died.

But then Dabney did die. That was senseless. With Dabney dead, Norman Denjer became president of the senior class and leader of the school. Now the world recognized Norman as a hero.

Jon called the bank.

* * *

"Just a check on how things are going," the friendly loan officer said with a smile in his voice when Jon called.

Jon's call had been routed from person to person through a maze of telephone connections. Jon wondered if he should feel comforted that Wentzell and Megquire's business wasn't big enough to merit a dedicated banker. There was always the hope that maybe they would lose the paperwork in the bureaucracy.

"How IS it going?" the banker asked.

"Great," Jon said. "It's going great. Might ask you for some more money soon!" he laughed.

"Buildings seem to be falling down," the banker said. "Did you hear about that hotel in Providence? What a mess. You hear about that?"

Jon hesitated before answering. "I was there," he said.

"What? Really?"

"Yeah. I was there."

"That must have been horrible. Are you okay?"

Jon briefly described the Patriot Grand Hotel experience.

"If you're going to get yourself into dangerous situations like that," the banker said, "we might have to ask you to get key man insurance. If something happened to you, what would happen to your business?" The banker chuckled.

Insurance. Another of Jon's favorite subjects. He was convinced that insurance companies started in horse-drawn wagons driven by snake oil salesmen promising safety and security to the rubes across the plains, making bets that their customers would never die or have an accident. And yet, insurance companies owned the biggest buildings in major cities across the world. It was definitely magic—another disconnected piece of reality.

"Seriously, Mr. Megquire, your company is doing great meeting the payments, but we're getting a little nervous about the state of the construction world. Mortgage rates are coming down, but it would be good if you could pay down a chunk of the loan. Your debt-to-cash-flow ratio is tighter than we would like. Know what I mean? If you could bring it down by ten thousand dollars, that would bring it more in line with that financial statement you sent us."

"Ten thousand?" Jon asked. He held the phone out from the side of his head. "Really? Ten thousand?"

"That's what the bank would like to see. Good faith."

One of the things with banks was walking the razor's edge between positive and negative - success and risk. It was simple to borrow money if you didn't need it.

Jon didn't want to know if this was a suggestion or a demand. He didn't want to know *when* the bank wanted the money. So, he didn't ask those questions because he didn't want those answers. He just said, "Okay," and hoped the banker would have a nice day.

Norman Denjer looked like his best answer.

Confined Spaces

* * *

Norman Denjer's fame made Jon hesitant to call him. Jon appreciated famous people are still people. They have childhoods and families and classmates, and as Bob Dylan said, "Even the President of the United States sometimes must have to stand naked." A little fame rubs off the closer you get to intimacy—same town, same school, same class, drinking buddies, dated the same girl.

Denjer was a man in the news, and some day, he was the news. Like Dow Chemical or Microsoft, Norman apparently aspired to be a brand.

Norman always did his best to stand out and gather the crowd to himself. At Boundbrook, all members of the senior classes were regarded with awe by the underclassmen. When freshmen or plebs entered the school, the upperclassmen took advantage of their ignorance of the school systems and routines selling passes to breakfast—which was in fact part of the meal package their parents paid for—selling them passes for the elevator in the main building, which didn't exist, and taking advantage of their naivety in every way possible. A freshman, who was probably living away from home for the first time, was open to all the older boy influences. Looking for comfort. Looking for guidance.

Of course, seniors rarely talked to underclassmen. There was no point. Except where they could be made into the butt of a joke. The world of the school belonged to the seniors and freshmen were interlopers, interrupting a finely developed machine.

Norman Denjer had appeared to be above all that. He was senior class president, leader of the student body. Since seniors were the world of the school, it was Norman's world, and after he graduated and stepped beyond the walls of

Boundbrook, he had done his best to make that world his own as well.

Jon's experience at the school had been mediocre. He got through it. He had watched Denjer from afar, but never got close to his orbit of followers. And that was almost fifteen years ago, so he was surprised when Denjer took his call and agreed to meet with him and talk about old times and talk about Jon's business issues.

He didn't know what to expect from Denjer. He might fantasize about Denjer whipping out his checkbook and writing Jon a check for ten grand for old times' sake, but Jon recognized the fairy godmother quality of that thought.

And as for the business consultant angle, he had little hope that Denjer would guide his business anywhere. Denjer was most likely unaware of the science behind buildings. Jon's vision was that with Ace's construction skills and his own familiarity with technology, Wentzell and Megquire could be a world class construction firm. And Denjer was a developer, and he had money, so Jon thought, "What the hell?" and he had picked up the phone, and now he was sitting in a glass office tower in downtown Boston in the lobby outside Denjer's office.

An office like this manifested power—like a big house or a fancy car. Surrounding yourself with these views and all these people and the fancy carpets and the artwork and chandeliers was all very cool but functionally meaningless. Except to impress other people. And maybe that was the whole point, Jon thought. You impressed other people with money and power and they helped you to get more money and more power. But you didn't actually do anything ... except get more money and more power. It was an exercise of pushing paper around.

Jon knew, if you followed that string from the paper to the boots on the ground, the shovels in the earth, the hands on tiny electronic components, you arrived at the people who actually created things.

He watched the office staff float across the thick pile carpeting and waited to be summoned. He thought of sitting outside the headmaster's office at Boundbrook. Headmasters didn't make this kind of money, and their power was limited to the world of the school, although that extended out through the veins and arteries to suck in the economic blood of people like Denjer.

The good thing about having gone through the boarding school rat's maze was that he wasn't intimidated by all these trappings of fame and fortune. Jon could imagine his own source of power. He felt comfortable in what he was wearing—it was appropriate for the environment. But he could not imagine having penthouse offices like these. He just didn't want to. He could have had them, he thought, but he chose not to.

Ace would never have been able to do this.

A handsome young woman in a tight-fitting dress suddenly appeared before him, offered him a stiff smile, and asked him to follow her.

"Oh," Jon said. "Sure." And he scrambled to his feet and trailed in her purposeful steps and the swish swish of the fabric of her skirt across the lobby, down the hall, around a corner, and into Denjer's massive office.

The young woman turned and walked out, closing the glass door behind her.

Denjer was on the phone facing the panorama of the city spread out beneath him.

Despite Jon's sang-froid attitude about grand office environments, Denjer's office took his breath away. It was high above the street—very high. Like the observation tower at an airport. It touched the clouds, looking over the Boston Common and down the Charles River. And it was all glass. There didn't appear there were any outside walls. As though you could walk right out into the air space above the city.

Jon stood where the young woman had left him, clutching his business plan.

Denjer continued his heated phone discussion, raising his free hand into the air to gesticulate his thoughts to the unseen body on the other end of the connection.

The single side of the discussion that Jon could hear was a nonsensical babble of balderdash. He debated if he should just sit in one of the large, over-stuffed leather armchairs facing the desk, sit on the floor, or if he should turn around and follow the young woman out the door and back to the lobby.

Denjer continued his heated conversation.

Jon watched. This was a game, and Jon knew it. He stepped away from the door and drifted to a trophy shelf where there were pictures of Denjer with other powerful people. At least Jon assumed they were powerful. He didn't recognize most of them. Jon hadn't seen Denjer since Boundbrook, except for pictures in the papers. Denjer had put on weight since they'd left school. But then, in school, Jon remembered Denjer as being short and scrawny. He'd grown a mustache—a black layer of fuzz across his upper lip, and he lacked a defined chin. His face flowed into his neck with no apparent jaw line. His head reminded Jon of a pumpkin and his eyes seemed to have drawn closer together, and melted to slotted squints. He was over two hundred pounds and balding. His slick silver suit did not flatter the fat on his body. He wore a blue striped shirt, unbuttoned at the neck.

Denjer turned away from the windows but continued his rant on the cordless phone. He finally dropped the phone into its cradle on the desk and looked at Jon.

"So, Jack, how the hell are you?" Denjer almost shouted, grinning. "It's been years. Almost too many to remember!"

"It's Jon," Jon said. "Almost fifteen years now. But the school won't let us go, will it?"

"Oh, yes. The old Boundbrook. All for one and one for all. Old school ties. Never enjoyed wearing ties. Even now. Never liked the way they made you do things by the book. Know what I mean? Time to get up. Time to lie down. Time to go to chapel. Time to eat meals. Too many rules. More rules than anyone has ever seen. I don't know who has time to create all those rules and write them down."

Jon smiled.

"But when I was there," Denjer continued, "you might not remember. Do you remember? When I was there ... What class were you? When I was there ... When I was president ... Do you remember that? I don't think I remember you. But there were so many students there. So many and I tried to remember all their names. That's how you win, Jack. That's what my father told me. I've made a lot of money since then." He turned and waved at the city behind the glass as though it all belonged to him.

"Real estate," Denjer said. "Remember that. Real estate."

"Norman," Jon said, "it's great to see you."

"It is," Denjer said.

"It's great to see you and see how well you've done since school."

"It is, isn't it? It hasn't been easy. Success is never easy. It has to be nursed and stroked and coaxed like a flower.

"Sit. Sit. Sit," Denjer indicated the leather chairs while he dropped into the swiveled throne behind the desk.

"We've got a couple of Boundbrookers here. Phil Bosun and Reid Trask. You remember, Reid? Class ahead of you, behind you? I don't know. Maybe you don't remember him. Just because they went to Boundbrook doesn't make them memorable, does it? He's my right-hand man now. I take care of my own."

Jon's chair had been selected to be lower than Denjer's.

"What's on your mind, Jack ... Jon? What have you been up to? How can I help you?"

Jon described the work that he had been doing with Ace and handed Denjer the business plan.

Denjer asked, "What's that?"

"Wentzell and Megquire business plan."

"Jesus! What the hell are you building? An aircraft carrier?"

Denjer thumped his fist down on the plan. "Never seen anything like this," he said. "Never! This is like War and Peace. Do you expect me to read all this? Did you type all this? When I wrote my thesis at Harrow, I never had to read anything this long. Great school. Very hard to get into. Boundbrook helped, and being president ... That was important. Where did you end up going?"

"North Carolina. UNC. Class of 1980."

"Excellent school too. That's an excellent school. Not like Harrow, but still good. Best thing about Harrow, if I can be honest with you, was Eleanor, my wife. Her family practically owns that place."

"I didn't know your wife was British. And you lived in England. How did you like it?"

He couldn't see the expression on Denjer's face, but there was a pause.

"She's from Indiana," Denjer said. "Valparaiso. Got to get your education in an American school. People get confused about that. I guess there is another Harrow in England and people get confused about that. I can understand that confusion. But they're different places.

"So, what does this encyclopedia say? I'm not going to read it. Here, you can have it back. I'd just use it to prop the door open." And he laughed.

Jon reached over and pulled his business plan back and explained his vision for Wentzell and Megquire.

"How much cash have you got?" Denjer asked.

"What?"

"How much cash have you got? Right now."

Jon reached back for his wallet.

Denjer laughed. "I don't mean cash in your pocket. Although that's good too. You can buy me lunch. You have to know how much cash you have every day. Each day. Start of the day. End of the day."

"I'm not sure."

"Is it a dollar? A hundred dollars? Ten thousand dollars? Do you have a hundred thousand dollars in the bank?"

"No. I'm sure we don't have that much."

"Who's 'we'? How many people do you have working for you?"

"We have crews working on houses."

"Yah, but who's 'we'? Who's Wentzell? Where did he go to school?"

"Asaph Wentzell. He has an engineering degree from Rutgers."

"That's good. Rutgers is an excellent school. Engineering is good. What year?"

Jon said, "Nineteen forty-one, I think."

"Holy shit! How old is the guy? He must be ancient. Nineteen forty-one! Did he fight in the Civil War? Where did you find the guy? Holy shit!"

Jon explained he had worked for Ace as a summer job when he came to the Cape back in 1979 to play in the Cape Cod Baseball League, and he had enjoyed working in construction and when setting up a baseball franchise in Florida for his father hadn't worked out, he had come back to the Cape and joined forces with Ace to set up Wentzell and Megquire.

"You should have called me," Denjer said.

"What? When?" Jon asked.

"When you were in Florida. Robbie is a friend of mine. Joe Robbie. The guy who built the stadium for the Miami Dolphins. A baseball franchise in Fort Lauderdale would have been great. I could have gone there. Been a part of that. You should have called me then. I need a sports team. I don't know about this technical construction business. People don't want to live in technology. They want bigger, cheaper houses. So that's what you've got to give them. What you want to do is give them what they want, not what you think they need. Give 'em candy and not some disgusting medicine. People don't want stuff that's good for them. I might be able to help you with that. Let's get some lunch."

Jon almost imperceptibly shook his head as he rode the wave of Denjer's thought processes.

He stood and turned toward the office door.

"Not that way," Denjer said. "We'll use my elevator."

Jon looked around. Denjer grinned and walked to a wall that concealed a door, depressed the hidden handle, pushed the door open, and stepped inside. "Like the oval office," Denjer said. "My way out."

The lights in the small hallway flickered on from their motion. They walked past a bathroom and reached an elevator door. "I love this," Denjer said, "but it can give me the creeps when the lights go out. Gets dark fast. Surprised the hell out of me. Even though I know it's at the top of this building, it's confining because you can't see out. Walls closing in. That gives me the creeps. But it's my elevator. Only for me. It's always waiting right there where I left it."

Jon smiled.

"And I have my safe room. Just like the kings had their castle keeps and the priests had their hidey-holes. A place to hide in case the bad guys get in. Can't be too safe."

Jon looked around.

"It's very hidden. Very hush-hush. Just a bit bigger than a broom closet. You can't see it. I'm not going to show it to you, because then it wouldn't be a secret anymore, would it?"

"I guess not," Jon said, and they stepped into the diminutive elevator.

The restaurant Denjer selected was out of Jon's price range. A McDonald's or a Friendly's would have been more his choice. He could have afforded to buy Denjer a burger but not wine, snails, and steak au poivre! And there was Denjer's comment about his cash position and that dominated Jon's thoughts throughout the meal, and he felt his back pocket to make sure that his wallet was still there.

The maître d' greeted Denjer by name and patrons looked up and smiled as Jon and Denjer were guided to a favored table. He informed the maître d' that Jon was a classmate, and they were having a mini-reunion. The man smiled politely and handed them enormous menus. Denjer ordered a bottle of red wine.

As soon as they were seated and were opening their menus, a man slithered up to the table clutching his napkin, and said, "Excuse me, Mr. Denjer. Is it okay if I talk to you? Sorry to bother you. I saw you come in, and I've been reading about you in the papers. I'm working on a project that you might be interested in. Digital telephone networks are going to be big. Big! I'd love to talk with you about it."

Denjer lowered his menu and glared at the man. "Call my office," he said, and flicked a trace of a smile at him.

"Okay," the man said. "I will. Thank you. Sorry to bother you. And your friend."

When the man left, Denjer said, "I always wonder how movie stars put up with things like that. People always want their attention. Really. I can't go anywhere. I should hire a security detail. It might make life easier. Safer too. Know what I mean?"

Personal security was not something that had ever crossed Jon's mind.

While they ate, Jon described his vision for Wentzell and Megquire, and the more he talked about it, the more enthusiastic he got. He didn't consider how much of what he was saying Denjer heard. The noises of the restaurant swirled around them. The laughter and the voices of the other diners blended with the tintinnabulation of the lyric Italian country music ringing through tinny speakers. The aromas of the food - the onions, the pasta, the warm bread - tantalized their nostrils. And the rich palate of flavors in the red wine fuzzed the sharpness of Jon's thoughts.

He was having lunch with a powerful, internationally admired business authority. Getting this man to share in his vision of the future of housing could change the world for many people—including for Jon, Lisa, and Sam. Little firework pops of excitement shot up in the galaxy of Jon's thoughts. They could get the equipment, set up the offices, meet payroll, get a new roof on their house. But before he could run off into the world of shiny new test equipment, he needed to get Denjer to guarantee his existing loan and come up with ten thousand dollars to satisfy the bankers.

"Look," Denjer said as they were snarfing down dessert, "this is exciting. No, seriously. This is really exciting. I haven't come across a project this exciting in years. Probably never. You can't lose with construction. Real estate never goes away. Know what I mean? Thank you for bringing this to me. All those years at Boundbrook paying off. Right?"

Jon grinned.

"We can make this happen," Denjer continued. "I have friends. I'm already in real estate. And I've done construction." Denjer laughed while he wiped his mouth with his napkin. "My consulting fees are reasonable. I mean, you get me. Right? People like that loser who came by the table earlier ... I can charge a guy like that through the nose - a hundred thousand just to look at his project, and it would thrill him to breathe the same air that I'm breathing. Know what I mean? He would just be happy to just say that he'd consulted with me. He would put that on his resume and slap it on his sales brochure. Whatever the hell he's selling. Don't know. Don't care. But he'll probably do it just because he interrupted our lunch."

Denjer dropped his napkin on the table, looked up, and waved his hand at the waiter.

"But we're classmates, know what I mean? You do things for classmates that you wouldn't do for strangers. Am I right? Christ, I give enough money back to that school every year. People call me all the time. Every day. There is probably a stack of while-you-were-out slips sitting on my desk right now.

"But this is different, Jon. You've really got something here. We can scare the pants off people with this stuff you're telling me. Fear is a wonderful sales tool. You know that? Insurance people do it all the time and so do drug companies. People will do almost anything to avoid being afraid. And after they buy the insurance and they're feeling all warm and fuzzy about life, they figure they've beat the devil!"

The waiter placed the bill on the table between them.

"We might need to make some minor changes. Some details that I'm sure you'll agree with. Small things. Tweaks. Adjustments. Nothing major. What you've got is good. We want to make it better, right? Want it to be the best that it can be. Want it to exceed ... And I mean that in the best sense of the word ... EXCEED not just succeed. And that might take a few minor changes. But we can talk about that."

And the bill sat there between them. Jon summed up the hors d'oeuvres, the entrees, the deserts, the coffees from the prices that he remembered from the menu. He hadn't even seen the prices of the bottle of wine because Denjer had just ordered it, but this bill was going to exceed a month of groceries. He wondered if there was enough room on his credit card. It would be a killer if his card was declined. Picking up the check meant that you were in control. This was your lunch meeting. When this day started, Jon hadn't even intended to get lunch.

Denjer pushed back his chair and put his hands on the edge of the table.

Jon reached back and pulled out his wallet.

"Well," Denjer said. "Thanks for lunch. Reinforcements in the middle of the day. Know what I mean? Call me next week, and we'll set something up."

Jon reached out for the check, turned it over, and swallowed hard.

* * *

DENJER PROVIDED a glimmer of light for the future - both distant and immediate. Money was money and business was business. Maybe Denjer's changes to the company wouldn't be all that bad. What Jon had to focus on was what was best for Sam and Lisa. Working with Denjer might be something he had to do for them, for their welfare. For their future.

A week later, when he called Denjer's office to follow up, he had to leave a message because Denjer wasn't available.

Days passed. Jon got out on Ace's job site and helped with some of the grunt work. His carpentry skills were gradually improving, but he wasn't capable yet to meet Ace's standards as a finish carpenter. He could handle hauling shingles or stuffing insulation into the wall cavities or mounting the chutes in the soffits. Physical labor distracted him from worry. He had sent samples he had collected from the ground around the shrew house out to a laboratory to be analyzed, and the cornucopia of chemicals the results revealed was shocking. It wasn't just the shrews at Summer Meadows.

"That place is polluted," Jon told Lisa. "It's no wonder that you are getting juveniles with problems. If they've been growing up there with all the lead and mercury, it's like a suburban community of zombies."

"Have you told Ace yet? Babs must be worried about her sister living there."

"Not yet. I mean, what the hell can they do about it?"

"Do you think it's bad enough that Brenda should move?"

Jon looked down at Sam playing with his trucks on the living room floor and was glad that they weren't subjecting him to a toxic environment. Their old house might have some lead paint issues. Jon hadn't noticed Sam chewing on the windowsills. But they couldn't watch him all the time. He was curious—always wanting to know 'why', touching and tasting things that struck his fancy. That was the problem with old houses and dust and paint flakes: they were hard to avoid.

"Did you ever get ahold of Gail Barker? Didn't you say she was a lawyer?"

Jon said, "Great idea. She didn't answer when I called. Maybe there is a legal solution for Brenda. It would be good to find out how Gail's doing. But I need to get more information about Summer Meadows, too. Who built it and when? Don't know if she'd know anything about that."

Lisa said, "What about that guy you met at the Institute? At the conference when we dealt with that guy, the woman buried in the foam. You remember him? The computer guy. Maybe he could find out something for you."

"Oh, yeah. Lash. Lash Ashton."

"Have you been in touch with him?"

"On and off. He's not the greatest letter writer."

"You should call him."

"I mean, it costs a quarter now just to mail a letter," Jon said, throwing up his hands. "Can't keep track of it. Remember when it was five cents? Maybe we just don't write that much anymore."

"Call him. Have you got his number?"

"Somewhere," he said.

* * *

JON REMEMBERED Lash Ashton as a big, enthusiastic bear wearing wire-rim glasses, button-down shirts, paisley ties, khaki pants, and high-top Keds sneakers. His blond crew cut encouraged a quick rub like a profound pile rug and his arched eyebrows and big ears gave him an exotic lineage.

But it had been almost five years. Maybe all that had changed. Jon wondered if Lash was still promoting desktop computing. Jon rummaged through the paper clips, free pens, postage stamps, and papers in his desk drawers and found the small notebook he had used to take notes at the conference at the Institute in Tilley in 1984, where he had met Lash.

He should have stayed in touch. He should have written or called in the intervening years. Time just slips away. Days, months, years just quietly drift into the past, and suddenly it is five years later. It felt like barely yesterday as Jon thought about it, recalling moments, words, thoughts exchanged. Was he still driving that AMC Pacer or was it a Gremlin?

Jon dialed the number he found at the top of one page in the notebook, uncertain if the number would still work. It was like putting new batteries in an old toy and wondering if it would still move its arms and legs or flash its lights.

At least the number connected. There was no disconnect notice. It rang.

Jon was sitting at his desk. He spun around in his chair, holding the phone to his ear, stretching the cord. He stared out of the window at the gray January sky.

It rang again.

This might not be the best time to call.

It rang again.

Ten rings were the limit. Ten rings gave enough time to get to the phone - if they chose to.

Nine rings and no answer. Well, it was a good thought. He could have used Ashton's computer skills - assuming that he was still working with computers.

Jon was pulling the handset away from his ear when there was a click and a man said, "Hello?"

"Oh, hi. Lash? Is this Lash Ashton?"

"Who's this?"

Jon identified himself.

"Hey! Jon! I wondered what happened to you. Shoot anyone recently?"

Jon laughed. "Jesus, no! Been working with Ace up here in Tilley."

And the conversation flowed on from there. Updating.

Jon mentioned he was trying to expand his business into air quality and energy efficient construction. He told Lash about attending the conference in Providence and about the walkway collapse.

"Whoa," Lash said, "that sounds like a horror movie. Man, you always get yourself into the most extraordinary situations. Makes my life sound tame."

"You don't still drive that AMC Pacer?" Jon asked.

"Gremlin," Ashton replied. "It was a Gremlin. That was a magnificent car. Ran forever. What about you? Didn't you give up the MG?"

They moved on from cars to families—wives, children, work. Jon admired people who were chatters on the phone. His sister, Cornelia, eight years his senior ... she used to lie in the hallway of their parents' house and twist the phone cord around her hand while she talked and talked to her friends. Jon thought her ear must have grown callouses. But maybe that was why Jon didn't talk long on the phone: he didn't get the chance.

Apparently, Lash had never lost his love for computers. He laughed when he described his office at home with all the computers and monitors and hard drives and wires that turned the room into an electronic jungle. His wife, Windsor - "yeah, like the castle" - was afraid to open the door. She said that things went in there to die and were never seen again, including all the plates and soft drink cans that disappeared. She often threatened to hire a cleaning staff to come in and detox the room.

He was working remotely for Apple computers and teaching at the New Jersey Institute of Technology. "What have you got for a computer?" Lash asked.

Jon admitted he was stuck with his Mac 512k. He wrote a few letters and did his taxes once a year and played with the VisiCalc spreadsheets, but not much beyond that.

"Maybe you could check something out for me," Jon said.

Lash said, "Sure. What'cha got?"

Jon explained about the toxic stuff that he had turned up at Summer Meadows. "I'd like to know more about that development. Is there anything there that would cause it to be particularly toxic? An old factory? It is close to the air force base - Otis."

"No problem, Jon. I'll see what I can turn up."

When he was off the phone, Jon related his conversation to Lisa. "I'm glad you two reconnected," she said.

"I have to get back together with Denjer," he said. "Maybe set something up for next week."

"Be careful with that man," she said. "There's something about him that bothers me."

"Sure, that isn't just the cop in you who mistrusts everyone?"

"That's not fair. It's part of the job."

Chapter Eight

In Norman Denjer's mind, he knew that all the toxic mumbo-jumbo namby pamby bullshit just got in the way. For Christ's sake, when he was a kid, they ran behind weed sprayers because it was fun. All this safety stuff just reduced the freedom of choice, adding more rules for everyone because of people who just didn't want to suck it up. It was a play land for lawyers.

He had so many lawyers working for him, he sometimes wondered if anyone lived a life that wasn't dominated by lawsuits, paperwork, discovery, depositions, and legal findings. When he was king of the world, he would gladly replace lawsuits with guns and decapitation. Those who didn't do the right thing would simply be removed without wasting time and thought about whether someone was going to be offended.

The toxic shit actually worked to Norman's benefit because it helped him to find cheap land. Of course, then he had to do the little dance with an environmental consulting firm. La-di-dah-di-dah. Pip-pip. Wave his hat in the air and whisper that everything was on the up-and-up. The land was fine. The air was fine. Now let's build some houses for these fine people who needed lovely new homes to live in. Wasn't that what they were always saying? "We need more affordable housing!" "People need a place to live!" So that is what he was giving them.

"Bosun!" he yelled. "Get your ass in here and bring that happy-ass paperwork with you."

Phil Bosun reminded Norman of a fire-hydrant. Besides the fact that his face seemed to be perpetually red, he had a shiny, shaved head that seemed to flow down in a tubular fashion to his oversized feet. He had been on the football team at Boundbrook, six years ahead of Denjer, and wrestled at Yale. Norman was sure that he had family connections that he couldn't put on his resume, family connections that let him get things done that couldn't be done otherwise. But what Norman loved about him was that he was loyal as hell. He matched the spirit of the Yale bulldog.

Bosun came into Norman's office carrying a thick file, which he placed in front of Norman on his desk and stepped back.

"So?" Norman asked.

"The site has to be checked," Bosun said.

"Who says?"

"The bank. They need the site work before they'll close."

Norman slammed his hand down on the desk. He had one of those hula-girl dashboard dolls on his desk and he'd unconsciously learned how to hit his desk in just the right spot with just the right force to make her dance and swing her skirt. And so he did it a second time.

"Bullshit!" he shouted. "I've done more than enough work with that bank that they should take my word for it. Where the hell do bankers come from anyway, Phil? It's not their goddamned money."

"No, sir," Phil said.

"Damn right. It's my money. They're just keeping it for me until I need it. I should open a bank. Maybe I'll do that. I haven't done that yet. I'll get the lawyers to look into how you start a bank. Ever started a bank, Phil? How hard could it be? Even a banker can do it! It can't be that hard."

"Yes, sir," Phil said.

"God, I hate dealing with lawyers. 'Lawyers to the right of them. Lawyers to the left of them. Into Valley of Death ...' whatever, whatever. Call that environmental company and get that squared away. Summer's coming. People need homes, Phil. Good people. Fantastic people. They need homes. The best people. We want the best people in there. We want to give them magnificent homes. A good place to live. A place to spend Thanksgiving and Christmas with their families. We need to build a future for them."

Phil said, "Yes, sir."

Norman stood up and glared at Bosun. Bosun didn't blink. "You'll make that problem go away. Right?"

Bosun was a good man. A man who did what he was told. Not one of these men who makes up excuses or constantly apologizes for not accomplishing what was asked of them. Why couldn't all people just do it? Stop whining about the unfairness of life. Get over it. Norman knew he could trust Bosun.

That flicked his thoughts back to his meeting with that other Boundbrooker ... Jon Megquire. Norman hadn't quite put that one together. Starting a bank would be a much better bet than some sort of environmental construction company, but something about the concept intrigued him. He could probably work it to his advantage for his public image. Boundbrookers everywhere. Hell, two of them worked for him and some of them were investors in his real estate projects.

Who could blame them when every real estate deal he did turned to gold? Paid the investors back tenfold. It was like one of those perpetual motion machines that they said couldn't exist. Norman had invented a perpetual motion money machine that everyone wanted to get in on. He had to beat them back with a stick as they were forcing money on him. He had to keep finding new properties - new projects to develop. That's why he needed people like Phil Bosun to straighten out the occasional problem - the occasional grain of sand like these environmental reviews that only clogged up the works.

Megquire might help with that. He was a kid. Years behind Norman. Each class was like another world. He seemed like one of those clean living environmental types that hugged trees and recycled aluminum cans.

"What?" Norman asked when he realized Phil was still standing there.

"It's the lawyers, sir," Bosun said.

"What about lawyers? I hate lawyers. Who are we suing today?"

"They want to meet with you, sir."

"You know, Phil, I hate meetings. Everyone sitting around. Picking their noses, trying to speak up to prove how smart they are when they have no more to say than spitting dust. Do you know how much more productive the world would be if people weren't always sitting around in meetings? Say what you have to say and move on. That's what I say."

Phil said, "Yes, sir."

"Look, lawyers. My grandfather was a brilliant professor and scientist and lawyer and engineer. Dr. John Denjer. You probably haven't heard of him. MIT - good genes, very good genes, very smart, Harvard Law School, okay, very smart. That's why I always start off: Went to Harrow, was an exceptional student, went there, went there, did this and that, built a fortune - you know I have to give my credentials all the time because we are disadvantaged, a minority really. But you look at these lawyers, the thing that really bothers me - it would have been so easy, so very easy really. But that's not as important as these lives here. My grandfather explained toxics - and guns, toxics and guns - and a lot of other stuff to me many, many years ago. Toxics can kill and so can guns and that was thirty-five years ago. I was still in high school. And he was right - who would have thought - all those years ago, but when you look at what lawyers are doing now - my grandfather would be rolling around in his grave like a one armed paper hanger at a water cooler convention.

"So how many fellas have we got in there—and it is fellas because you know they haven't figured out that the women are smarter right now than the men? They are letting the women into law schools now, you know? Beautiful women. They assume that just because you're beautiful, you're not very smart. You can't know that unless you're beautiful. They're a minority too, aren't they? Beautiful women are a minority and should be treated that way. You can't understand that. You have to be it to know it. So how many fellas have we got?"

Bosun was standing with his hands clasped together at his waist. "Four, sir. Will you be joining them?"

"I'll be there. I'll be there. Get them some coffee or Danish or something to stuff in their mouths. Jesus. Four of them. Why does it take four monkeys to bring down a clump of bananas? You'd think that one of them would be enough. They're just trying to run up their billable hours. They charge for their hours when they're picking their noses or pissing. And I have to pay for it! I'll be there."

He sat back at his desk while Bosun left the room to settle the lawyers in the conference room. It had all come down to this. But of course, that was always the case. Every moment was connected to every preceding moment. Every thought to every preceding thought.

Norman looked around the room and down at the city at his feet and wondered if his father would approve of what he had accomplished - the traffic on the streets many stories below. He was convinced that he could fly out over the city. As a kid, he was sure that if he ran fast enough and flapped his arms hard enough, he could just take off and fly over everyone's heads.

He heard the huff and bother of the people in the office outside his door. A room full of lawyers waiting for him. They would all look up when he walked into the room, puffing out their chests and shuffling their papers. They couldn't exist without him. He paid their mortgages and their children's tuitions. His thoughts, his ideas, his challenges paid for their lives. And they adored him and were terrified of him. He could drive them to their knees and chop off their heads.

Maybe he should sue Jon Megquire. No reason. Just for the entertainment. But Megquire didn't have any money. He had nothing, so there wouldn't be anything that Norman could take away.

But maybe Megquire could be useful. He worked with land, didn't he? Maybe, just maybe, he knew where THE piece of land was. The holy grail. The optimum location for the Club! Maybe he could be good for something after all.

Denjer slammed his palm down on his desktop to watch the hula girl dance, stood up, and slipped through the hidden door to his private bathroom to take a piss before he stomped off to see the lawyers.

Chapter Nine

Although there had been a slug of cold weather, the temperature dropping to ten degrees, Nita Avant hoped that winter was losing its grip. There were hints of warmth in the air. She noticed the green stems of the snow drops poking their heads up between the old leaves that hadn't been blown away by the winter winds as she walked from the bus to the Denjers' house. The cold weather made her fingers ache as she practiced her music. The heat in her apartment was unpredictable, and the landlord was unresponsive. The pipes banged in an unsyncopated rhythm and the steam hissed and whistled throughout the wintry nights. But she was grateful that it worked at all. The windows rattled when the storms came, despite the fact that the houses were tucked in together. The wind could sashay around the buildings, knocking on the walls, and pushing snow into drifts across the street. When it snowed during the night, she could hear the plows scraping the asphalt and beeping when they had to back up. It was the Boston winter symphony of the city.

But spring would come again. The remaining patches of

dirty snow were melting. Slick, icy spots on the sidewalk remained. There were days when she missed the New Mexico heat and there were many days when she missed teaching and had to force herself to go to work cleaning someone else's house. There was distinct dissonance in the Denjer home—a lack of balance and harmony. It wasn't a happy home.

Eleanor Denjer was a troubled woman, and Nita couldn't blame her. Mr. Denjer could not be easy to live with. He saw a different world than everyone else. What was obvious to him looked very different to other people. Maybe that made him a genius because geniuses were supposed to see the world differently, but Nita would never crown him with that nobility. Nita had heard people speak of Norman Denjer with awe, as though it was magic merely to get close to him. She had seen articles that said that celebrities lined up to be a part of his companies.

But the man treated his wife as an object, as his possession.

It must be challenging to face every morning reproducing the constant beauty of a Mona Lisa, a Maserati, or a Steuben wine glass. Every day she must have contested the challenge of comparison with those around her—her friends, her social club members, and even those who worked for her like Nita.

Nita did not consider herself beautiful, but people had told her she had an exotic charm with her ruddy skin, brown-black hair, high forehead, prominent cheekbones, and dimples. Her appearance contrasted with Eleanor's, and maybe that very contrast terrified Eleanor that she would lose her husband to the younger woman. Nita tried hard to appear as dowdy as she could. It was Nita's goal to remain invisible and just keep her job.

The icy surface crunched as she stepped up on the granite block sill and put her key in the lock of the Denjer's back door. She had been there hundreds of times. They had given her the key. The key turned. The knob turned, and she stepped up into the kitchen and listened.

Before she had left her apartment that morning, she had debated the Denjer discord with her roommates and whether she should return to work. There had been no yelling or raised voices. But at least one side of the love was missing in the marriage.

"Who cares?" one of her roommates said. "That's their problem. You're not a marriage counselor."

"Should I go back to work?"

Her roommate shrugged. "Why not? I would. What have you got to lose? It's a job, Nita. It's just a job."

"I don't feel welcome."

Her roommate laughed. "They'd be lost without you."

So Nita had begun the day just the way she had begun a hundred days before—taking the bus, walking to the house, unlocking the door, and stepping into the silent kitchen. When she heard nothing, she began her routine, taking off her coat, pulling her apron out of her bag, and stepping into the kitchen to make coffee. She stopped when she noticed she was holding her breath. "This is stupid," she said to herself. "This is stupid. This is stupid. This is just a job." Yet there was that feather of discord in her stomach as she moved around the kitchen.

She relaxed as she flowed into her routine. Moving pots and emptying the dishwasher, putting plates and glasses away in their proper places. She emptied the trash, stepping back out into the winter cold to shove the smelly remnants of the previous night's supper into the large cans by the back step. The kitchen in order, she started breakfast. She was laying strips of bacon in a frying pan when she heard the swish swish of slippers scuffing the floor behind her.

She turned and saw Eleanor reaching for the coffee carafe.

"I don't think it's finished brewing yet," Nita said.

Eleanor was bending slightly, peering into the carafe lodged in the coffeemaker. She grunted. Much of Eleanor's public beauty was carefully painted on. And every night Nita imagined she had to strip it off, putting the costume away for another day, and putting it back on the next morning. There in the kitchen, without makeup, jewelry, or the splendor of her clothing, she was stripped of her public identity, like the tiny body of a knight without armor. Her hair stood out in all directions. Her eyes were baggy and bloodshot. She hugged her silk robe around her like a cerement and her crimson painted toe nails stuck out of the open ends of her pink, fluffy slippers.

Nita waited.

Finally, Eleanor turned her eyes from the carafe to Nita. "Bring the coffee to me in the living room," she said. "Just toast this morning and Mr. Denjer has gone to work already, so he won't be needing breakfast." And she left the kitchen.

Nothing else. Nita's stomach settled as her fear of confrontation subsided, and she turned the heat off under the pan of bacon.

She moved through the house following her routine—dusting, vacuuming, emptying trash—doing her job. She slipped into the comfort of her own thoughts, hearing the music in her head, the rhythm of her world. And when she got into Mr. Denjer's study, she felt a tiny vibration in her body—an animal shiver.

Apparently, he had left it abruptly. All was not in order. The desk was covered with file folders and crumpled up papers.

Nita stepped methodically around the room, surveying. The room was usually neat enough for Nita to do a quick dust and vacuum, but not today. It was so out of character not to put everything back in its place. Even crazy people have predictable traits.

It occurred to her that perhaps she should just leave everything as it was, exit, and close the door quietly behind her. She picked up one of the crumpled pieces of paper from the desk and unfolded it so that she could read it. Names, numbers, and people.

Nita had an affinity for numbers. Numbers could be clear and concise. Clearer than words that could have multiple meanings. Numbers and patterns of numbers could tell a precise story. It seemed to Nita that all this information was not what Mr. Denjer was looking for. Assuming that it was Mr. Denjer. Who else could it have been?

The Denjers paid her to clean, so that is what she would do. She wouldn't move the folders or crumpled papers on the desk. She grabbed the wastepaper basket and moved around the room. She paused occasionally, standing still, holding the basket in her right hand, and listening to the house. Maybe she was overthinking it. She was just a dumb foreigner in his eyes, doing what she was told to do. "Yes, effendi. No, effendi. I offend, effendi," she murmured in her mind.

She placed the basket by the door and vacuumed the floor, and when that was complete, she returned to the kitchen, emptied the trash into a bag, and went on with her chores about the house.

She put coffee and toast on a tray and brought it to Mrs. Denjer, who was sitting in the subdued light of the living room, staring at the empty quiescent fireplace. Nita set the tray down on the coffee table. As she was pulling away, Eleanor stopped her by reaching out and putting her hand on Nita's forearm. Eleanor looked up.

A moment passed.

Nita asked, "Yes, Mrs. Denjer?"

Eleanor released her grip and Nita stepped back.

"Did you clean his study?" Eleanor said.

Chapter Ten

The beauty of this office, Norman thought, was that he was above all the sloth below. Boston, even from the lofty altitude of Norman Denjer's high-rise office, was a dirty city. Cities were dirty. That was their nature. It was part of the mud and the blood and the sweat of manly battle. It had to be dirty. None of that sylvan scene with butterflies and Bambis prancing around. Unless, of course, you were going to shoot them and eat them. He remembered liking the part when Bambi's mother was shot in that stupid Disney movie.

Disney, of course, was a classic manipulator of youthful minds and adult pocket-books, ringing the money out for the ducks and butterflies and princesses prancing with their golden hair flowing out behind and making little girls believe they could actually achieve something like that and screaming at their parents, "Buy it for me! Buy it for me!" What a money-making machine that man was!

Those people down there on the street were just little ants scampering back and forth. Norman could understand how it would be enchanting to be a sniper to just randomly pick one of them off, like when he would shove a firecracker into an ant hole and watch all the ants hopelessly scurry for cover. It was a beautiful thing. It made him think about lawyers. Put out a pot of money and anything that pissed you off and watch the lawyers scramble for the crumbs, like those ants. "My coffee's too hot!" Sue 'em. "My princess doll's hair falls out!" Sue 'em. "My 12-year-old nephew broke my wrist when I hugged him at his birthday party!" Sue 'em. It was like a kid in a candy store. You really didn't have to work anymore. Lawsuits flew around like snow on Christmas day. It was a wonderful world.

If you did anything - anything at all meaningful - you could expect to get sued. All because of Walt Disney. Kids are brought up with a "gimme-gimme" attitude. He has it. I want it. Norman suffered with that every single day. He had things and people wanted them. It didn't matter if there was any truth to it. The lawyers would twist things around and ring a few million out of the dirty laundry.

Norman turned away from his windows and summoned Reid Trask to his office, not noticing that he was already there, standing quietly by the door.

"I hate the way you do that," Norman shouted.

"Yes, sir."

"You skulk around like a thief in the night. Do you wear 'brothel creepers'? My mother used to call shoes like that 'brothel creepers' because you couldn't hear them coming or going. Remember Toft ... Mr. Toft ... at Boundbrook? He used to wear one shoe walking down the dormitory hallway at night, so we'd think he was twice as far away as he was. 'Click' Silence 'Click' Silence. What a creepy old bastard. Remember him? Latin teacher. I hated that man. I hated Latin. Stupid waste of time to learn a language that no one uses anymore. Dead language. He's probably dead by now. Thank god. It's not right to speak ill of the dead, and I don't do that. Do I, Trask?"

"No, sir."

"What?"

"Excuse me, sir?"

"What do you want? Don't just stand there scraping your shoes on the floor. Where are you from, Trask?"

"Here, sir."

"Jesus. You mean you were born in this office? I don't believe it. You're lying to me, Trask. I don't like it when people lie to me. What do you mean 'here'?"

"Massachusetts. Lincoln, Massachusetts. I thought you knew that, Mr. Denjer."

Norman spun around and glared at him. The man was a toady. A simpering, smiling toady with a gelatin spine and brothel creeper shoes and a shiny suit. Some days people could get to Norman's soul. Some days he did not consider himself a 'people person'—whatever the hell that meant. What was that stupid song about "people who need people are the luckiest people in the world"? Who writes that shit?

"Of course you're from Massachusetts, but don't tell me what I know and what I don't know. It's what I don't know that you should tell me so that I know it. Is that clear? So tell me something that I don't know."

"The lawyers ...."

"Oh, fuck the lawyers. They're always whining about something. I suppose they want more money. Tell me something positive. Lawyers are always negative. I think they all live in those trenches from the first world war and never got out."

"They say that there are going to be significant damages from the hotel event," Reid Trask said.

"Oh, they did, did they? How is any of that my fault? It was the engineers. Let the engineers and lawyers get into the ring, take off the gloves, and fight it out. That would be a beautiful thing, wouldn't it? Seeing them actually doing something. I boxed at Harrow. Did you know that, Trask? And I was very, very good at it. Better than anyone."

"Yes, sir."

Norman dropped into his desk chair and began aligning the hula dancer with his pen tray. He looked up at Trask, who was still standing in the same position.

"So? What? What about the lawyers? Take care of it, Trask. That's what I pay you for, isn't it? To take care of things. Do I have to do everything myself? If I did everything myself, it would get done right, but why would I need to pay all these people to do this stuff? That's what I pay lawyers for. To take care of these things. Maybe I should sue the engineers. Should I sue the engineers, Trask? Maybe I should sue you."

Trask's eyebrows flicked up. "No, sir."

"'No, sir' what? No, I should sue the engineers? No, I shouldn't sue you? Who should I sue? Look. One thing is obvious. This problem needs to go away. I have more important things to do with my time. So, Trask, if you want to keep your job, make this problem go away. Is that clear?"

"Yes, sir," Trask said.

Norman turned toward the windows and glared out at the city. Getting good help is always a problem, he thought. How could you know who was on your side? Even when you're the captain, you couldn't tell when someone was about to stab you in the back. Norman was sure that Trask wanted to see him fail —well, everyone did. "I'm the king of the castle, and you're a dirty rascal. Ashes, ashes, all fall down."

But he was the king of the castle. He had to keep remembering that—keeping that in mind. And being king had privileges. Henry VIII had it right: when the woman wasn't performing, he had her head chopped off and moved on to the next one.

Norman had a vision, and he intended to make it a reality.

It wasn't clear how yet, but his vision was of rolling hills and manicured acres of woods and lawns with a palatial club house where he would entertain movie stars and royalty who would all clamor over each other to hand him money to join. It would be his kingdom where his power would be unfettered, built upon his years of toiling to accumulate the wealth and connections to make his vision a reality. He had always known the connection between the words realty and reality, which was why he had dedicated his life to real estate.

The Indians kept saying that the land was theirs, and they wanted it back. Well, too bad. Norman was not a religious man, but he appreciated the expression that if god hadn't wanted him to have a piece of land, why did He offer it to him—show it to him, give it to him? Norman knew that the blood of both royalty and god flowed through his veins—particularly for the ownership of land. History told us that history changing leaders and history changing explorers knew that owning the land was akin to divinity. Genghis Khan, Julius Caesar, Odysseus, Christopher Columbus, and Adolf Hitler all knew that. Even JFK knew that, reaching out beyond the earth to the moon.

"I should get a son," Denjer thought, staring out his windows at the city below. "I should get a son and then I could say, 'Someday, son, this will all be yours'." He huffed.

Chapter Eleven

Jon believed in his schoolmate's heroic public persona. The man had done a lot and made a great deal of money. Jon knew that from the frequent news stories, even though Jon had never paid attention to them, except to comment that, "That guy went to Boundbrook. I was there when he was president of the senior class." There were mentions about charitable things he had done in the school promotional magazine that listed all the people who had donated money to coerce other alumni, who, it was assumed, were equally successful to follow suit. But not all alumni got out of the school and went off to make their millions. There were those, like Jon, who wrestled with debt and who wondered if their lack of economic success painted them as failures no matter what field of endeavor they pursued.

Jon's years at Boundbrook had passed in a blur. He'd done well enough academically to get into the University of North Carolina. His capability in sports had helped the school to achieve some athletic recognition. But he had never tied into a *Boundbrook Forever* state of mind.

Confined Spaces

He had been a sophomore when Denjer was a senior and senior class president, with all the bells and whistles that the position entailed to the younger class-men. There was no question of economics among the students: in order to afford to be at the school, they all came from wealthy families except the ones on scholarships. There were students with branded last names who owned car companies or baseball teams or chemical companies, who obviously stood out. But the students rarely cared. Money was their parents' concern. Not theirs'.

When Jon had finally gotten through to Denjer to resume the discussion about the business, Denjer told him to come to his house in Winchester and gave him the address.

As he drove up to the Georgian mansion on a quiet street, Jon realized Ace would love the place with its turrets, leaded windows, and wrap-around porches. Jon expected a butler in white-tie and tails to open the front door when he rang the bell, but Denjer opened it himself and then stepped back into the house, leaving Jon to close the door behind him. It was exactly the sort of house that Ace loved to work on—the wood of the floors glowed where they were visible around the oriental rugs. The entry stairway whispered subtle craftsmanship in the curving wood of the steps and the carved balusters. The crystal chandelier sparkled in the morning light.

Working with Ace had taught Jon to appreciate the skill required to put all the pieces of a house together, and he wouldn't have expected anything less in what he expected to be Denjer's opulent life.

Denjer grunted when Jon said, "Nice house."

Denjer led him down a hallway past massive portraits and classic bronze statues with naked women and wild animals to a large office, sliding the door closed behind them. He pointed to a large chair in front of a cold fireplace, and Jon sat down.

Denjer stood behind him, forcing Jon to twist in his seat to follow him.

"I haven't got a lot of time," Denjer said. "I've thought about your plan. It will not work."

"Oh? In what way?"

"It will not work. It's as simple as that. There are too many 'imagine this' and 'imagine that's'. You don't build a business with imagination. Not a real estate business. Take a house like this: I didn't build it. I bought it. Someone else built it. Built it fifty years ago. More. Maybe lots more. I don't know, and frankly, I don't care. Don't know who those portraits are out there. Bought them too. My wife liked the house. So I bought it. Women are the decision makers when it comes to houses. Did you know that?"

Denjer paused in front of the windows for a moment.

Jon said, "Umm."

Denjer turned and paced rapidly back to where Jon was sitting.

"Who chose your house? I bet it was your wife. You married? I bet your wife chose your house. When I was a kid, I was building blocks with my brother Danny. He's younger than me. Lives in Toledo or somewhere out there. I don't have a clue what he does. He's a dink. He doesn't talk to me. We were playing with blocks, and I needed more to finish my building. I was always good at blocks. Maybe that's why I'm so good at real estate. My mother knew that. She would come floating into our playroom wearing a filmy sort of gown and there we would be on the floor playing with our blocks. Danny and his blocks and I had my blocks. And she would say, 'Oh, isn't that lovely, Norman. Is that the Taj Mahal? You are such a clever boy.'"

Denjer dropped into the twin chair facing Jon and glared at him, his hawk-like eyebrows arched up to the top of his face.

"I was clever." Denjer laughed. "I am clever. I'm still clever, and Danny was a dink. I needed more blocks to finish, so I told Danny to give me some of his, and that I would give them back to him later. But when I was done building my building, I glued it together and Danny never got those blocks back."

Denjer paused. "The only problem with Danny ... No, not the only problem. He has lots of problems ... One of Danny's problems was that he liked to crawl under his bed. Then he would pop out and scare the shit out of me. HE was the monster under the bed. He tried to convince me that if spies ever got into our house, we would have to hide under the bed. He'd try to get me to crawl under there with him. He'd say that we had to practice. That it was the only way we would be safe. That it was bound to happen. I didn't even want to look under his bed."

Denjer leaned back in his chair, still staring at Jon.

Jon looked down at his hands. He had no idea what any of that had to do with financing Wentzell and Megquire.

"Do you want coffee or something?" Denjer asked. "Don't know if we have any. But I'm sure I could find some if you really wanted it. Always makes me want to pee. It's embarrassing to have to get up during those meetings. I had to do that in the middle of a meeting with Lee Iacocca. I had to stop in the middle of his description of what he was doing with Chrysler. He wanted to know my opinion of acquiring American Motors, you know, those dinks who build those weird cars. But they did own Jeep, so I told him he should do it. 'Just do it,' I told him. And he did. But I had to interrupt that meeting by having to pee. So I don't drink coffee at meetings like that. But I'll get you some if you want it."

Jon didn't have a segue that would fit into Denjer's monologue and divert the conversation back to the business plan for Wentzell and Megquire.

"Look," Denjer said, leaning forward in his chair. "Look,

you're a nice guy. I remember you from school now. You were a nice guy there, too. Didn't you play baseball? Course that was the end of my senior year. Where did you go after Boundbrook? Someplace down south, wasn't it?"

"UNC," Jon said.

"What did you study?"

"Electronics and broadcast journalism." Jon shrugged.

Denjer laughed. "Really? Journalism? What the hell does that have to do with anything? I don't much like journalists, personally. You know you gotta get the exposure. That's at least half the battle. People want to work with people who are bigger than they are. But when I was on Letterman, they asked me if I wanted to sing. I told them they were crazy. If I sang, they would have lost half their audience. I mean, I'm good at a lot of things, but singing isn't one of them.

"You should have studied business if you wanted to run a business. That's what I did at Harrow. I've got to tell you it made me what I am today."

"I wanted to play baseball," Jon said.

"So why didn't you? Aren't you very good at it?"

"No, I was very good at it," Jon replied. "The Angels nearly drafted me."

"Nearly? Nearly drafted? No such thing as being close except in hand grenades and horseshoes."

"No. I turned them down. I could have gone pro."

Denjer stood up and Jon wondered if that was all they were going to talk about - if their meeting was over.

"Want coffee? Coke? Water?" Denjer asked and started walking out of the room.

"So, what about Wentzell and Megquire?" Jon called after him.

Denjer stopped. "What?"

"I thought we were going to talk about my business. Wentzell and Megquire?"

"We could. We could do that. You know I charge a lot for consulting. I'm not sure you can afford me. I mean we're friends - classmates. That's true. But I can't give it away. If I did that, I wouldn't have a business. I mean, why would Bechtel pay me to consult on their next weapon design if they heard I was working for free? Right? That's something even you could understand." He turned back and continued walking out of the room. "Follow me!" he commanded.

Jon stood and followed Denjer through the formal dining room with dark blue walls and twinkling crystal wall sconces and waist high urns in the dark corners with scenes of cherubs and heavenly clouds painted on them. Denjer pushed through a swinging kitchen door into a glistening white kitchen with stainless steel counters and an enormous commercial range.

Denjer reached down and opened the door on a counter high butler's fridge and pulled out a can of Coke. "Help yourself," he said, turning away.

Denjer stopped, leaned on the counter, and sighed. "I don't know, Jon. I don't know. I can help you, but Jesus, it's tough. Sort of like breaking trust. Breaking a confidence. Know what I mean? It's like revealing the winner of Miss America before the judges have finished. I don't know."

Jon's hope was that he was still following Alice's white rabbit, and that Denjer had a perfect solution—Willy Wonka's golden ticket or the New York State Lotto number—a solution that would magically solve everything. A solution that he was keeping in his pocket or would pull out of a drawer in this massive kitchen.

"Tell you what," Denjer began, and took a sip of his Coke.

Jon held his breath.

"Tell you what. Maybe there is something I can do." Denjer smiled. "But there are a couple of things you're going to need to do for me. You do have an interesting business idea. It is interesting. Can you make money with interesting? Maybe it's something we could develop. Something we could build on. Something bigger than anyone has ever seen before. We could turn this around. I'm the best there is at real estate. I've got projects everywhere. It's in my blood. My father was in real estate. Did you know that?"

Jon nodded numbly.

"You're into that toxic crap, aren't you? That's part of what you do, right? Figuring out what's bad in the air, in the room, in the ground. All that shit."

"Well, it's not exactly 'toxic crap'," Jon said.

"Whatever. Personally, I think it's bullshit." Denjer laughed, enjoying his own humor. "Get it? Bullshit. I mean, we've been living with this stuff for hundreds of years, right? It's never hurt us before. And now suddenly it's killing us. It's like all those cavities we didn't get because of that fancy scientific toothpaste. You know it's all marketing. You know that, right? It's like what that Barnumand Bailey said about, 'You can fool some of the people all the time, but you can't fool all the people all the time.' But you sure as hell can fool enough of them to buy into any bullshit when you do it right. Am I right or am I right?"

Jon hated this part of the business - the part where you had to listen to people like this and then invite them to share in your dream, be part of your team—to trust them and believe in them. They had the fuel to let you keep going. Imagine driving into a gas station and explaining to the attendant the reason you needed gas, where you were going and why you were going there. Getting them to share in the vision of your destination from visiting grandma on her deathbed to buying a box of donuts to going to a stuffy office and sitting behind a desk for another eight hours of your life. Wentzell and Megquire needed the fuel to keep going, but was it worth listening to this?

Denjer was picking at the stub of the pop top on his can. Dink. Dink. Dink. "I think you said something about building science. That's good. That makes it sound like there is something official about it. Scientific. Scienterrific, I like to say. Scienterrific. People like science. You can do anything you want as long as you base it on something scientific. If it's scientific, people will believe it. We can get some scientific guy to say he did tests. We can build on that. But you've got a problem."

Jon waited. He wondered where everyone else was in this massive house. Shouldn't there have been cooks in the kitchen using all this glistening shiny steel? Where was Denjer's wife?

"What about now?" Denjer asked.

"What?"

"What about now? How are you keeping the doors open? What's your debt level? How are you financed?"

"We have a bank loan. Nothing else."

"Hmm, huh? Sure. How much?"

Jon looked at Denjer's eyes. "A hundred thousand dollars."

"Psst," Denjer snorted. "A hundred thousand! What was that for? Office expense? Where you get that loan? The Salvation Army? Did they give it to you because of your good looks and your hearty handshake?"

"Arthur Schmidt guaranteed it."

"Who?"

"Arthur Schmidt. Dabney's father."

Denjer put his can down on the counter. "Dabney Schmidt. Man, I haven't heard that name in years. Boundbrook just continues to haunt us. How did you get connected with him? I'd forgotten Dabney."

Jon shuffled his feet. "I contacted Arthur Schmidt to be on

the board of my company and he invited me to visit them on Pocatuck."

"On whoosy-whats-now?"

"Pocatuck. That's the Schmidt estate. It's huge. I guess it's been in the family for a long time. Unfortunately, Arthur died."

Denjer crushed his can and glared at Jon. "How big? How big is 'huge'?"

Jon was startled by Denjer's sudden ferocious attitude change. "Uh, I think they said it was around twenty-seven hundred acres. Something like that."

"Where?" Denjer demanded. "Where is it?"

"Pocatuck?"

Denjer slammed his hand down on the counter. "Of course! Pocatuck!"

"It's outside of Plymouth. West of Plymouth."

"When?"

Jon was confused. "I suppose it's always been just west of Plymouth."

"No! When did Arthur Schmidt die?"

"Last July."

"Shit! Why didn't I know about this? What's happened to the land?"

"Arthur wanted it turned over to the Wampanoag. But Minky Schmidt—Mrs. Schmidt—still lives there, so she hasn't done it yet."

Denjer slammed his palm down on the counter again. "Perfect!" he said. "Perfect! We can make that work. We can deal with problems. 'Problems' is my middle name. Norman Perkins Problems Denjer. It's not too late. It's not too late." Denjer laughed again. It was a hollow, gleeful giggle.

"Your partner's old," Norman said, looking directly at Jon.

"Ace?"

"Wentzell. Is his first name Ace?"

"Asaph. Asaph Wentzell. He goes by Ace."

"He's old. A modern, scientific, state-of-the-art company can't be connected to an old man set in his old ways. Doing things the way he's always done them. Old builders do that. They don't want to learn anything new. They want to keep doing things the way they've always done them. 'If it ain't broke, don't fix it.' If I'm going to work with you, he's got to go."

Jon needed money. The company needed money. Jon recognized that there would need to be compromises to get the financing the company needed to thrive. But Ace was the reason the company existed. But maybe Denjer had a point: he was old, and he didn't like change. Maybe he'd like to retire. Maybe it would be good for him. He'd already had a heart attack.

"I'll back you," Denjer said. "We can build the company into a powerhouse. Scientifically built houses would be at the cutting edge. Nobody's ever thought about that before. You're in first, and the first one in gets all the biggest fish. Maybe we can take it public in a couple of years. People like science. What do you think?"

"Ace is a big part of the company," Jon said.

"But he's old. Is he one of those old-world craftsmen, the kind you see in brochures for fine furniture, picking away at the wood with some sort of hand tool? Bullshit like that? Maybe we can get him to do the fancy shit on the club-house." Denjer scraped his Coke can across the counter and picked at the stub of the pop-top.

Then he turned away. "If you don't want to do it, I can see that. I respect loyalty. Loyalty is important. And maybe you're not ready for this."

"I wouldn't be here if Ace hadn't agreed to work with me."

"How's that house of yours going? Cute little place. Delightful spot."

It surprised Jon that Denjer knew anything about his house. "Have you seen it?" Jon asked.

"I enjoy driving. I drive around a lot looking at stuff. Always liked the Cape. Got some properties there. Tilley's a way out, but it's more exclusive out there. Sort of like the Hamptons on Long Island. People go a long way for privacy." Dink, dink, dink.

"We like it."

"But it needs work. I bet there are a lot of things that you would like to do to it, and that would increase its value. Give you more of an asset. Tell you what: I'll buy it. Give you all the cash you need to finish it up the way you want it. You can just live there mortgage free. Make the wife happy. That would be our joint investment in the company. I'll just buy the house for a couple of hundred thousand more than you bought it for and you can use the extra to build the company. It's a risk for me and a solid future for you. I'm going to be betting on an old Boundbrook School chum and the future of technological home construction. Doing the world some good. People are getting all twisted up about running out of oil and global warming and all that shit. That's fear. Selling on fear is a winner. That's what makes insurance companies so successful."

Jon felt the pall lifting from the company. Denjer was willing to invest. No mortgage. Enough money to do the work they wanted and money to grow the company into a technological power-house with Denjer's backing. Ace could retire. They would have the power of Denjer's name, connections, money, and business acumen to build a best-in-the-world, technologically based home construction business. Problems solved.

At that moment, the swinging kitchen door was pushed open, and a woman walked in, pushing her blond hair back out of her face, shuffling her feet in her fuzzy slippers. She struck Jon as spectacularly beautiful, despite looking as though she had just rolled out of bed. She was taller than Denjer. She had the sharp features of the marble statue of a goddess softened by whimsical eyebrows that defined her deep blue eyes.

"Hi," she said. "You still here?"

"My wife," Denjer said. "Eleanor. She does nothing."

"Pleased to meet you," Jon said, addressing Eleanor.

Eleanor smiled at him. "You're sweet," she said. "Why are you still here?"

"I live here," Denjer replied. "Where's Nita? You didn't fire her again, did you? We don't eat if we don't have someone to cook. You can't cook. It might spoil your nails. You're such a dink, Eleanor."

Denjer glared at his wife, his eyebrows pulling even closer together, his little mustache trembling in caged fury. Jon wondered if he was going to hit her.

Denjer slammed his fist down on the countertop again, making the kitchen echo. "We need to eat, Eleanor. Do you have any idea how hard it is to find people who want to work? One of these days, Nita will not come back. What did she do this time? Did she butter your toast wrong? Put your socks in the wrong drawer?"

"I didn't," Eleanor said. "I didn't fire her. She's here."

"Where? Jesus! You are perhaps the worst people manager I have experienced in my entire life. Do you know anything about people? You need to get out and do something. Do something. Do you understand? I don't care if it's volunteering in the library or working as a greeter at Walmart. You need to be out of this house."

At that moment, Nita stepped into the kitchen doorway. "Did you need something, sir?" she asked quietly.

For a moment, it shocked Jon to see Nita here in this context as Norman Denjer's staff. "Nita!" he blurted out.

Denjer looked at him. "You two know each other?"

Jon said, "Sorry. Yes. Nita went to school with my wife."

Denjer was silent, his eyes swiveling between the occupants of the kitchen.

"Well, well, well. Isn't that a coincidence? Isn't that a coincidence?"

Nita dropped her eyes to the floor, but not before Jon noticed a look pass between her and Eleanor.

Denjer smiled. "Well, well, well," he said again. "Nita, maybe you could rustle up something for lunch? That would be great. Mrs. Denjer can give you some ideas. Couldn't you, Eleanor?"

Jon was not eager to sit down to lunch with Denjer and his wife and have Nita serve them, but his discussion with Denjer was in suspension and incomplete. The solution to his problems was dangling just out of reach.

"Excuse me," Jon said. "Maybe I should come back at another time."

"Lunch, Eleanor. Come on Megquire." Denjer pushed through the swinging door without another word to his wife.

"Nice to meet you, Mrs. Denjer," Jon said to her as he followed Norman.

"So, what do you think?" Denjer asked when they had reached the living room.

For an instant, Jon was not sure what Denjer was referring to and was tempted to offer his concepts of domestic relationships, but he skipped that thought, realizing that Denjer was back to business. "Sounds interesting," he said. "You've given me a lot to think about."

"Don't hesitate. Don't diddle. This is the best you're going to get. Think about it. You're smart. Think about it. I'm the best, and if I'm behind it, it's going to work. So think about it, and I'll get the paperwork together. But don't take too long. I'm just doing this to help you out. Take it or leave it. It doesn't matter to me. Don't take too long."

Jon turned to leave the house as Denjer added, "And just one more thing: I need you to help me get Pocatuck."

"What?"

"This deal only flies if I get Pocatuck. Arthur's dead. Ms. Schmidt needs to find something smaller. For a kinder, gentler future. And I need Pocatuck for my club. And you can get her to do it. You have the connection. You have her trust. You do that and I'll do this. Tit for tat."

Jon wondered how Denjer had put that whole scenario together from a simple mention of the property. Denjer hadn't seen Pocatuck. He hadn't met Minky Schmidt. He knew nothing about their family, their future, or their fortunes.

"Sure," he said. "Pocatuck." How hard could it be?

Jon left the house smiling. He had an answer. It may not have been the best answer, but it was an answer. It was something to hang onto.

He didn't know how Lisa would feel about selling the house to Denjer, and the thought of severing ties with Ace made him queasy. Ace was family. But the business was business.

* * *

ON THE ONE HAND, Jon thought to himself as he drove back to Tilley, Wentzell and Megquire wasn't exactly a solid enterprise. They had made little progress since they started. Ace was building a house or two, and Jon was scrambling to convince architects and engineers that air quality in houses was an issue, and they should pay him to make things better. And that wasn't paying the bills. And that wasn't building momentum for bringing in investors. And it wasn't paying the bills. And the house wasn't getting finished. And they were relying on Lisa's income. And Sam wasn't getting all the attention that he should be getting.

On the other hand, there was Norman Denjer's proposal. All right, Jon thought, all right. The guy was not the nicest man, but you didn't have to be nice to be a business success. In fact, nice guys finish last. Business required a shark-like attitude, and Denjer had that in spades.

Tracy Chapman's *Fast Car* was playing on the radio. This was a soft song, a somewhat melancholy song that pushed Jon's thoughts to the edge of benign joy but pulled him back before he slipped over into mawkishness. He turned up the volume on the radio and rhythms of the music soothed his soul. It was so much better than listening to "The Wheels on the Bus" or "You're Special" - Sam's favorites.

Denjer had given him a vision of the future—debts paid, money in the bank, house finished and shiny.

All right, so maybe asking Ace to step down wasn't a nice thing to do. But he should understand. It was business. And he was old, and when Jon thought about it, he was dragging down the future. He just wanted to keep building those whales of houses. Obviously beautiful. Solid. Works of art, each one taking a year or more to complete. They would never go very far, building one house a year.

And Ace didn't want to try new things—new materials, new technologies, new tools. He didn't know a thing about blower doors or infrared cameras. He didn't want to go to conferences and learn more. He didn't even want Babs to use a computer to do their books. But he was old. Learning new stuff got harder when you got old. You couldn't be as flexible in body or in thought.

Jon would do him a favor by getting him to step down. Babs would be pleased too. He'd already had one heart attack.

Denjer was right. He could see things like that, things that other people might miss. You just had to trust him.

The long drive between Winchester and Tilley gave Jon plenty of time to think. Bobby McFerrin's *Don't Worry Be Happy* came on the radio. Seemed like good advice to Jon. "Just do it!" as Nike said. "Just do it." If he was going to sit around worrying, he wouldn't be doing anything. He had to take that first step that Antoine de Saint-Exupery described in *Wind, Sand, and Stars*, as his friend was crawling away from his wrecked plane in the Andes. To stop was to die, and if he died in the snow in the Andes, his body would never be found and his family wouldn't get his insurance. So, for each step, he thought about the future of his family. "What saves a man is to take a step. Then another step. It is always the same step, but you have to take it," Saint-Exupery wrote, or at least that sounded like what he had written.

Jon was taking this step for his family. It wasn't physically the same as crawling through the snow at the top of the Andes mountains, but it was like crawling out from under the rubble at the Patriot Grand Hotel in Providence. It was for his family.

That thought made him think about Gail Barker. She would understand what he was trying to do with the company. She would appreciate the importance of good indoor air quality. Maybe he could hire her or make her a partner. That exciting thought made him press a little harder on the accelerator. He would have to call her when he got home. See how she was doing?

There is nothing particularly interesting about Route 3 between Boston and Cape Cod. It is just mile after mile of relatively straight highway, filled with traffic. Cars ahead. Cars behind. Cars in the breakdown lane. Cars on the on-ramps and the off ramps. Nothing to read except license plates and bumper stickers like "Dukakis/Bentsen" or "Visit Edaville Railroad". Semi's and delivery trucks and all the other elements of daily commerce hissed and thundered along. And they would do it all over again tomorrow.

Jon imagined trucks with the Wentzell and Megquire logo painted on the side. He needed to come up with a slogan. "Healthy living for all". No, that sounded like a spa or a commune. "A breath of fresh air every day". "Breathe where you live". "Houses for health". Lisa was good at that sort of thing. They needed something like that Nike line: "Just do it". That had nothing to do with sneakers. It was a lifestyle statement. Something like "Breathe Easy". That sounded too good. Someone else must have thought of it. Lisa would come up with something.

But Lisa might not like the idea of turning the house over to Denjer. Of course, she hadn't met him. Denjer was a different person, live and in-person than he was in the papers. Maybe he could set up a meeting before they closed the deal. He could get her to give him advice. He just needed to get her to think that working with Denjer was her idea. She would see that working with Denjer would be like adding a supercharger to the company. It would put them into the big-leagues.

Maybe the fact that Nita worked for him was a good thing. Nita was Lisa's friend. Maybe Nita knew some things about Denjer that would give them an edge.

Have to think about that. Maybe he shouldn't tell Lisa right away. He could wait until he had a clearer picture of what was going on. Maybe it wouldn't happen, so why initiate a problem that might never exist? The problem was that he was excited.

Jon smiled to himself. Yeah, he was pretty excited, and he knew he might just blurt something out. And Lisa would ask him what happened and why he was smiling, and then he would have to explain. He could give her the highlights without giving her the economic details. He didn't have those, anyway. So that would make it easier.

* * *

When Jon walked in the door, he was filled with the excitement of a solid future, and he was greeted by Sam, who ran up to him holding a truck.

Sam said, "I went to pay a different pace today. Okay? This truck? Anty Babs gave me this truck. Cool?"

Jon hung up his coat on the hook in the front hall. "That is cool, Sam. That was very nice of Anty Babs. Is she here?"

"Oh, yeah. It was broken, but you can't look inside the Honda anymore because it's hard."

"Is she still here, Sam?"

Stogie trotted in with his stubby tail wagging.

Sam stopped moving and looked up at Jon, and it suddenly occurred to Jon that something wasn't right.

"What is it, Sam?" Jon asked. "Is everything okay?"

"Mommy's mad."

"Oh, no. What happened?"

Sam didn't reply, but ran back into the other room.

Jon followed, with Stogie trailing along behind, toenails clicking on the hardwood floor. Lisa was in the kitchen and she seemed to be struggling with a loaf of bread that wasn't cooperating.

"Hi," Jon said and gave her a quick peck on the cheek. "What's going on? Sam said you were mad."

"I'm not mad," Lisa said. "I'm not mad. I'm frustrated. Do you know that feeling?"

"Anything I can do?"

Lisa didn't reply, but continued to struggle with the bread. There was a big pot of water boiling on the stove.

"It smells great in here. What'cha got cooking? Has Stogie been out recently?"

Lisa slammed the loaf of bread down on the counter and spun around to face him.

Jon stepped back.

"The dog got into the shoes again. Sam wet his pants. The electricity is going on and off in here. Babs couldn't stay, so I had to rush home, which my sergeant wasn't happy about at all. And, Jesus, Jon, the bank called again. You've got to talk to them."

"What did they want?"

"They wanted to talk to you!"

"Okay. I'll call them. Did they leave you a name?"

"By the phone," Lisa said, and turned back to the kitchen.

It wasn't the garlic bread that Lisa was fighting with.

"We work hard," she said. "We aren't buying luxuries." She waved her hand around the kitchen.

"I know," Jon said.

"I hate those phone calls."

"I know," Jon said. "I did talk to Norman Denjer this afternoon, and he might have a solution for us."

"Great," she said. "When?"

"We have to work out the details still." Jon recognized it wasn't the best time to explain.

Jon walked back to the little room they used as an office, picking up the paper that Lisa had left on the table in the front hall as he went. He dropped into the chair behind the desk, and picked up the phone, dialed the number, and entered the world of banking phone frog, leaping from connection to connection. When he gave his name to the banker Lisa had written on the slip of paper, the man said, "Oh, yes. Mr. Megquire. We've been trying to get in touch with you. Glad to know we have the right number for you." He laughed.

"Sorry," Jon said. "Been working. We've been busy."

"That's great to hear. Great to hear."

Jon waited in the silence. "You've been getting our payments, right?"

"Oh, yes. Just checking in. It would be helpful if you would send us an up-to-date balance sheet since we don't have a long history with Wentzell and Megquire. In fact, I can see from your paperwork here that Wentzell and Megquire doesn't have a long history itself." He laughed. "Anything we should know about? Any changes in your status?"

"Nope. It's all good."

"Heard something about a lawsuit," the banker said. "Is that something we should know about?"

Jon sucked in a deep breath. "Oh, no. That's nothing. We built a house for some people and these little animals - shrews. I think they're called Asia House Shrews. They moved into one of the walls and made a mess. Piles and piles of shit. It smelled awful, but it wasn't us. Happened long after we were finished and out of there. The lawyers agreed it wasn't our fault. They're going to wrap that all up."

"Wow," the banker said. "Sounds awful. Glad to hear it's all taken care of."

"And," Jon started to say, "and I've been talking to an old classmate about investing in the company. You might know the name. Norman Denjer."

"Oh, my," the banker said, "that would be something. That sounds like a positive development."

"It's not settled yet. We're still working out the details."

"Good to hear. Good to hear. Well, listen, stay in touch and send us a balance sheet - recent and year to date. Helps us to help you, right?"

Jon hung up the phone and went back to the kitchen. "We'll get through this," he said, giving Lisa a hug.

And then the phone rang. The two of them looked at each other. They let it ring again.

"I'll get it," he said.

* * *

He lifted the receiver and said, "Hello?" Did the bank forget something?

He didn't recognize the woman's voice who responded. "Jon? Jon Megquire?"

A variety of snarky responses ran through Jon's mind like, "I did what you asked. They're all dead and there's blood everywhere." Or "Never heard of him. Wrong number." Instead he asked, "Who's this?"

"Gail. Gail Barker."

Expecting a nasty bill collector on the other end of the call, Jon was momentarily lost. A flood of guilt for neglected contact poured into his thoughts. "Gail? How are you? I tried calling you."

Jon put his hand over the mouthpiece and turned to Lisa. "It's Gail Barker," he said sotto voce.

"I found the card you gave me at the conference," she said. "It somehow survived the destruction."

"I'm so glad you called. I feel terrible that I didn't check in with you." Jon described how the EMTs had whisked him away and other elements of the collapse aftermath. "But how are you doing?"

"It did a number on my legs. Put me in a wheelchair," she said.

"That's terrible! I am so sorry! Are you going to be all right?" Stupid question, Jon thought. Stupid question. She's in a wheelchair, you idiot.

The catching-up conversation went on. Gail told him it had changed the way she worked, and he told her about his family and his work with Ace and that he was trying to build up the business by specializing in toxic conditions in homes after all the things they had talked about at the conference before disaster struck.

"That's actually what I was calling you about," Gail said. "I wondered if you had joined the lawsuit against the development company?"

Jon said he hadn't heard about it.

"As you can imagine," Gail said, "the insurance claims have been astronomical. The whole thing just screams NEGLIGENCE. I'm surprised you haven't heard from one of the lawyers that gathered like gadflies around all the victims."

"Nope," he said. "But we don't always answer the phone. I avoid lawyers like the plague."

"Did you give your name to the EMTs when they took care of you?"

"Probably. I can't remember. Things were so crazy."

"Damn," Gail said. "It was enough to give anyone PTSD. Like being in a war zone. You should check. Money can never heal all the mental wounds, and maybe you don't need it." She gave him the name of the insurance company and the lawyer.

"Ever hear of a guy called Norman Denjer?" Jon asked. "I'm trying to get him to invest in the business. Take it to the next level."

One of those stunning silences on the phone when it seemed like the connection had been broken.

Then Gail said, "Denjer?"

"Yeah. Norman Denjer. I went to high school with him - boarding school. He's done a lot of real estate developing and he might invest in my company."

Gail said, "Denjer?"

The hesitation in her voice made the hairs on the back of Jon's neck rise. "Do you know him?"

"It's his development company, Jon. He developed the Patriot Grand. He's the one we're suing."

Chapter Twelve

Looking good today, Norman thought to himself. Sometimes his wisdom and his skill surprised even him. It was rare ... it truly was rare when he felt this good. Most of the time, someone screwed up something ... usually something brutally simple, something for which he had provided clear and precise directions. But people had the attention span of a tick. Turn left. Turn right. And they were lost. They couldn't handle the third instruction. Pssst. It was gone. There was no room in their brains for anything more than that. People were inherently stupid. And that was a scientific fact. He had tried to hire the so-called best and the brightest, but the ones with a higher level of intelligence were not always the best looking ones.

He couldn't do that. No. No. That was a no, no. There were all these stupid rules now. You couldn't do anything that you wanted to because there were rules against it. But Norman was convinced that unless you looked attractive, you didn't have your bottles in the bank. You couldn't get the socks on the roosters. Cleverness, in Norman's mind, was matched by being graced by god to have an attractive face and a glorious body.

He gazed out his office windows at the city below. One of the beauties of this penthouse office was that he could see the Back Bay—where they had filled it in years ago—on one side and a seaport on the other. On the seaport side, cranes were piercing the sky as building after building reached for the stars. That was where all the barons of Boston industry had always had their offices—where they watched their ships come in laden with the treasures of the world where their wives walked on the 'widow's walks' waiting for their husbands to sail back home with silks and spices for the winter balls.

And now ... and now there was Pocatuck. It took Jon Megquire to bring him back to Pocatuck. "Bring me back to old Virginny," Norman hummed in this mind. Norman twitched as he imagined those twenty-seven hundred acres. And they belonged to his old friend, Boundbrook classmate, and competitor for class president, Dabney Schmidt. But Dabney was dead. And so was his father.

Dabney, Dabney, Dabney. What a shame.

Norman wondered why people couldn't just enjoy beauty, and wit, and intelligence. Why did they have to be envious? Norman knew people were envious of him. They wanted to do the things that he did, have the power that he had, generate the adoration that he generated. Great people ... really great people ... were always the targets of envy and lust. There certainly was pain in leadership. But someone had to lead. Someone had to assume the responsibility of the presidency of the senior class. Some people had said it should be Dabney Schmidt.

Dabney was captain of the baseball team. He had an inflated ego, of course, but no true greatness. It was baseball that transformed him into a hero. It wasn't real.

And there was Schmidt's family, of course. Everyone knew

the Schmidt name. It was all over their beer brand. Everyone had seen those ads on TV with the Schmidt brothers. They weren't real either. Pete and Barry Schmidt never existed. They were figments of the imagination of a Madison Avenue advertising executive.

The Denjer name was not on a can of beer or a snack food bag. Norman's father, Barry Denjer, had simply been a real estate genius, and like all genuine geniuses, he didn't need to brag about his wealth or his success. People just knew when you were a genius. Like father. Like son.

Schmidt probably even thought that he was the best candidate for president. Norman had had to help him recognize he was not capable of leading people. What he understood was mano-a-mano combat, so Norman had decided that that was what they were going to do.

Dabney irritated Norman. He had a head like a cube and blond hair, freakish blue eyes, and he was the proverbial six feet tall. Taller than Norman. And he wore those unbuttoned pink polo shirts and leather boat shoes without socks.

Confronting the problem head on, Norman remembered telling Dabney that they had to get the president thing straightened out. He remembered being particularly nice about it. He had suggested that they find a quiet place in the school woods and sit down and talk about it - man to man.

Schmidt had laughed and said it was a waste of time. He was scared. Norman knew he was scared. He could smell it. But Norman knew if Dabney's manhood was threatened, he would stand up on his hind legs, beat his chest and roar threateningly. Norman had counted on that.

Boundbrook had a lot of rules. Alcohol was forbidden. And guns. Norman had both, and he brought them with him to the cabin in the school woods. Students weren't supposed to be out there during the week, but it was spring, classes were almost over for the year, and Dabney and Norman were school celebrities. Their college applications were done. Norman couldn't remember where Dabney had said he was applying to. Yale, perhaps. Something like that. He remembered Schmidt giving him some bullshit about envisioning what you want to happen, and that makes it happen because you know that it's going to be true.

Sitting at the crude picnic table in front of this remote cabin, Norman had opened the bottle of bourbon and offered it to Dabney. Dabney had proffered some kind of watery excuse like, "We shouldn't be doing this," but Norman knew the athletes were always drinking, proving their camaraderie. Norman told him it sharpened the senses. They were classmates, weren't they? Boundbrook forever!

But then Schmidt got antsy. He wanted to get on with it. And when he laughed, it was like dragging fingernails across a blackboard. Even today, Norman could still hear that laugh. He heard it every time he heard a bluejay. More like a screech than a laugh.

Norman had laid his grandfather's pistol on the table between them. His grandfather had given it to him on his sixteenth birthday. He'd really liked that gun, and he regretted he had had to leave it behind. It was his greatest regret about that afternoon. He could still remember the feel of the metal, the weight of it in his hand. He'd kept it polished and stored in a wonderfully soft felt bag, like the ones to store silver teapots in. He didn't consider it threatening at all. It was just a beautifully engineered and machined metal object. A tool. Thinking back, he remembered the way the sun had glinted off the barrel while it sat there on the table and wondered what had ever happened to it.

Norman remembered Schmidt looking at him and asking if he was going to shoot him.

Even at seventeen, Norman knew macho men were all cowards at heart. When it came right down to putting the pedal to the metal, they were cowards. They could yell their heads off in synthetic rage, but there was no substance behind the noise. Occasionally, men like that enjoy flirting with the taste of danger or death. Norman knew it was stupid, but somehow it got their adrenalin pumping, arousing them sexually, like hanging from a cliff without a lifeline or climbing Mount Everest or playing Russian roulette.

Norman had asked Schmidt if he'd seen "Deer Hunter". The roulette scene played vividly in Norman's mind. Nothing separating life from death except a finger on the trigger. Like the edge of the cliff with a thousand feet of free fall and deadly rocks below.

Schmidt had insisted that things like that didn't happen in real life and he'd started to stand.

But Norman was a leader. He was a leader then, and he was a leader now. He remembered ordering the macho boy to sit down. Norman chuckled as he thought about it.

And Dabney did. He sat down again.

It would have been better if they had done this in the school gymnasium, surrounded by the student body. Instead, Norman was facing this fat faced, self-indulgent ass who expected everything to go his way in the middle of the woods. Witness-less.

So Norman pointed out Dabney's shortcomings, that no one wanted him to be president of the school, and they had to work this out between them, and Norman put the gun up to his temple and pulled the trigger. Even though he knew the gun was empty, there was a momentary shock and a twist to his scrotum when he heard that click. He could still hear it.

He had challenged Schmidt to do it, but Schmidt said it was meaningless because the gun was empty. So, Norman had pulled a single bullet out of his pocket and held it up between his thumb and first finger and waved it around, picked up the gun, inserted the bullet, spun the cylinder, closed it, and laid it back on the table between them.

Schmidt had again insisted that it was a crazy and stupid thing to be doing, so Norman had given him the opportunity to concede. He clearly remembered saying, "Concede the election and we're done here. Or one more time, and I'll concede. I will bow to your bravery. Free and clear. All yours." He promised that if Schmidt conceded, he wouldn't tell anyone that Schmidt had chickened out. "Scout's honor," even though Norman had never been a boy scout.

Norman sniggered a little as he remembered putting the gun in his lap, noting the position of the cylinder, putting it up to his temple again, and pulling the trigger.

He loved that gun. He knew everything there was to know about it, including how to see where the bullet was in the cylinder. He'd played with it for years. He knew that when he pulled the trigger, the cylinder rotated. He knew where the bullet was.

In hindsight, he could have gotten it wrong. He could have made a mistake. It was probably a crazy risk that he shouldn't have taken. But those were the days and boys will be boys.

It seemed so clear now, but at the time there was a certain fuzziness emboldened by the bourbon, a fuzziness that colored Norman's memories of the scene with bluebirds and a fantasy sylvan setting. He had reminded Dabney that the odds were in his favor - it was just one in six, something like an eighty percent chance the chamber would be empty and he would be president of the school. Just like that.

Dabney had yelled at him that he was crazy, but Norman could tell that he was going to do it. He'd whispered, "Concede. Concede, Dabney. Does it really mean that much to you?"

Norman had put the gun back down in his lap and checked the position of the cylinder, like checking his watch while trying not to be rude. He'd gently replaced the gun on the table and rotated the handle to make it easy for Dabney.

Oh, that was a special moment. Reminiscing, Norman looked out at the city. Such a special moment. He couldn't remember another time when he had felt that way. Euphoria. Dabney was going to do it. Despite all his swear words and protestations, Dabney had accepted the challenge. And now, all these years later, standing at the windows of his penthouse office in downtown Boston, a tear trickled down from Norman's eye. His only regret was that he couldn't repeat that moment of elation over and over again. He could see Dabney lift the gun, aim it at his temple, and pull the trigger.

The sound had been deafening. Dabney's head was gruesome to look at. There was so much blood on that pink shirt. Norman had wanted to pick up his gun and wipe off the dirt, but quickly recognized the wisdom of leaving it behind - sacrificing it to history like John Wilkes Booth's derringer.

It was clearly suicide, they all said in the aftermath, although they couldn't understand why Dabney had done it. Norman remembered the descriptions of Dabney were all sugar and spice and everything nice as they always are, even with murderers and drug dealers. No witnesses ever appeared. It was such a tragedy. Such a tragedy.

Norman had stepped up and described running into Dabney walking through the woods, but nothing more. No signs of a troubled soul. Such an unexpected tragedy.

And now their paths crossed again—Norman, the Schmidt family, and Pocatuck. It was truly a small world.

Why wasn't it his already? If he'd known about Pocatuck, he would have just bought it. If he'd known about it. If he'd known about Arthur dying .... He should have known about it.

Someone should have told him. You can't do anything about something if you don't know about it. If he'd known about it ....

They were practically family. He could have inherited Pocatuck. He should have inherited Pocatuck. Arthur would have given it to him. He had been Dabney's friend and classmate. Tight. Thick as thieves. Buddies. Pals.

But, no. No. They were pals with Jon Megquire.

A twist of a smile flickered into the corner of Norman's lips.

They had told Jon Megquire about Pocatuck. Twinky Schmidt had told Jon about the land. His land. Norman's land.

No. It wasn't Twinky. That would have been a stupid name. It was Dinky. No, Minky. Norman could see that. He could see that Minky Schmidt could adopt big, cuddly, curly haired Jon. Maybe think of him as a son. Think of him as a replacement for Dabney. He could see that. They'd guaranteed his loan, for Christ's sake!

So all Norman had to do .... All he had to do was get Jon to give him Pocatuck. And that should be like taking candy from a baby.

* * *

He yelled, "Trask! Trask! Get Trask in here. Now! Jesus Christ. Cynthia! Get Reid Trask in here now."

Cynthia ran in, her blond hair flouncing, her face twisted into a look of concern—like a goat who'd been kicked in the balls.

"Get Trask!" Norman yelled again. "Where the hell is he? Twenty-seven hundred acres of land is in the wind? Why the hell didn't I know about this? Why the hell didn't Trask tell me about this? This is the place for my club. World renown golf course. Development. Trask! That's what I've been looking for. What I've been waiting for all my life. Crown jewel. My crown jewel. It has to be mine. Golf is the way to make money. Retirement houses and a golf course." Denjer wiped his mouth with the back of his hand.

Reid Trask ran into the office. "I was just ...." he began.

"I don't give a rat's ass what you were doing. Why didn't you tell me about this ... about Pocatuck?" Denjer yelled. "Twenty-seven hundred acres, Trask. Twenty-seven hundred acres in Plymouth, Massachusetts. What are you blind? What do I pay you for?"

"Is it on the market?" Trask asked. "How did you hear about it? It wasn't in any of the trade sheets."

Norman looked at the two people standing in his office. Moe and Curly. Goofus and Titly. What else was he missing? Why did some frog-face like Megquire have to wander into his house to tell him about the score of his lifetime? Norman was the best. Always. He had been the best from the day he started. He knew more about the real estate market in Massachusetts than anyone in the world. This. This was like forgetting to zip your fly up after you pissed. He turned to the windows.

"I know more about the real estate market than anyone in the world," he said. "You see those cranes out there?"

The two clowns turned toward where he was pointing.

"You see those cranes out there? That's me. I made all that happen. Me! It's because of me that this city is growing. It's because of me that this state is growing. It's me. And I hire people—people like you clowns—to get me the information that I need to fight these battles, to win these wars. Great generals make great history because ...." And he turned away from the windows. "Great generals make great history because they fight great battles, because their troops understand they're making history. Do you understand?"

Titly looked like she wanted to scurry out the door. Trask smiled for some stupid reason. What the hell was he smiling about? This wasn't funny. There was absolutely nothing funny about this situation.

"How much do I pay you?" Norman asked. Never mind, Norman thought. Whatever he was paid, he wasn't worth it. Norman had rescued him out of pity. The kid came from an excellent family. Should have been smart. Should have had good connections. He wasn't really a kid anymore, but Norman thought of him as a kid, thought of him as a wet-behind-the-ears freshman at Boundbrook. Some people never grow up, do they?

"Why do I do that?" Norman thought out loud. "I've got to learn to be less caring. I've got to stop coddling idiots." That used to drive his father crazy when his mother did the "poor baby" thing. His father would say, "The boy won't grow up to be worth a hill of beans if you go on treating him that way."

Hill of beans, Norman thought, turning back to downtown Boston. Now look. Boston beans. Top of the hill. Top. Of. The. Hill. Norman snorted.

Then he said, "Let me make this clear. I. Want. That. Land. Understand?"

Silence in the room.

Trask and Titly fidgeted and shuffled.

Sirens on the streets below echoed up against the crystal glass surfaces of the buildings. Any sense of the coming spring was lost to life inside the glass office boxes.

"So?"

Trask said, "I know that land was listed in state documents, but it isn't listed for sale."

"Why didn't you tell me about it?" Norman dropped into his regal leather desk chair. His mother had picked out the furniture for his office. She would have bought the "Resolute" desk from the White House if she could have, but like Pocatuck, it was there, but it wasn't available. So she bought this massive thing with all sorts of fancy twists and turns of burnished wood. The inlaid black leather top was covered with the desk accessories that Norman's mother thought were appropriate: a pair of gold desk pens speared into their holders in the launch position, a mountain goat golf trophy she had found in a yard sale, a three candle-stick lamp with a brass base, a glass tray with a few paperclips and a mechanical pencil, and another tray with three mechanical stamps in it that Norman loved to slam down on documents. REJECTED. PROPRIETARY. FAIL. He would have loved to have had ones that read SECRET or TOP SECRET, but he couldn't be bothered to go through the paperwork and interviews. His mother would have hated his hula dancer.

"What would I have told you, Norman?" Trask asked. "There are thousands of pieces of property—tens of thousands that are not for sale."

"Don't you read the obituaries? Don't you?" Norman asked.

Trask looked like a sick doe.

"Maybe you don't understand this, but when people die, property transfers. You should know this. New owners don't know what to do with what they've inherited. They sell. They donate. What the hell have you been doing out there? You know—or at least you should know—that we have been looking for land for my club. There are things we know and things that we don't know and there are things you need to know that you don't know but should know. I know you know them, but you're not thinking because you don't know how to think. Thinking doesn't come naturally to everyone, and it is clearly obvious that it doesn't come naturally to you. I should have known that when I hired you."

"I'll look into it," Trask said.

"NO!" Norman yelled and slammed his hand down on his desk again. "No. It's too late. The man's dead already. It's too late. The door is opened. The pants are dropped. The world is watching. The horses have left the barn. The fire's already started. It's too late.

"Megquire's going to get it for me. You remember Megquire from Boundbrook? No. No. No. You don't have to do anything, Trask. You don't have to do a fucking thing. You're fired."

Chapter Thirteen

Jon was out walking Stogie and thinking about the future and wondering where life would lead and how the pieces would fit together.

Joining forces with Denjer wasn't perfect. Jon knew that. But it was an answer. Some sort of cosmic fairy with bags of money would not appear and make it all better. Denjer was far from being the good fairy. What he was demanding was akin to God asking Abraham to kill his son to prove his fealty. The promised land on the other side was tempting, and it seemed there was no acceptable alternative. Or maybe there were other choices, and Jon didn't see them or know about them. He only knew that he wanted no more of those phone calls. He hated thinking of his phone, his mailbox, or even his house as his enemy. He hated going to sleep on Sunday evening, dreading what might wait for him on Monday morning. So maybe Denjer wasn't the ideal solution to his problems, but it was a valid, tangible solution. Jon knew taking chances was the only way to redirect destructive energy. Taking chances was how millionaires made their millions. In the meantime, he would keep building houses with Ace and looking for environmental consulting projects.

There was no way that he would comply with Denjer's demand to force Ace out of the company. Ace was the integrity of the company—not an option on the table.

Stogie laid down his own toxic dump in the neighbor's yard. Jon was tempted to just push it into the bushes, hoping that no one would see. It was biodegradable after-all. Maybe dog shit could be recycled for its embodied energy. That didn't seem to be an immediate viable alternative to picking up Stogie's waste and properly disposing of it, however.

While he was contemplating the excrement problem, a car eased down the street, coming toward him, gradually slowing until it stopped right beside him. He didn't recognize the car or what he could see of the male driver.

"I was going to pick it up," Jon thought and turned to look with a smile.

For a moment, the driver didn't roll down the passenger window, and Jon wondered if the driver was just lost or was incapacitated. It wasn't uncommon for tourists to ask the way to the Kennedy compound or the bridge to Martha's Vineyard. That was annoying when he was mowing the lawn and a driver would waggle a finger at him, summoning him to the side of the car, which meant shutting off the mower and then trying to understand what the driver was asking. Jon did his best to think of himself as a visitor to some vacation spot, with no idea where he was or how he could get to wherever he wanted to go. Courtesy was required on both sides.

Jon bent over and scraped Stogie's poop into the paper bag he had brought with him for this purpose. It was always so weird walking down the street with a lunch bag filled with dog dung.

He turned when he heard the whirr of the electric car window. He stood up, holding his paper bag, and stepped back.

The driver leaned over the empty passenger seat.

He reminded Jon of a bouncer that would be a permanent fixture at the door of a nightclub—chunky, balding, with fat white fingers that he laid on the edge of the open car window.

"Hey," the man said.

Jon said, "Hi," and looked down to check out what Stogie thought of the situation.

"You're Jon Megquire," the man stated.

"I guess I am." Jon bent over to peer more closely into the car. "Do I know you?" The man did not look the least bit familiar.

"You do site investigations. Are you licensed?"

"Who are you?"

The man leaned back in the driver's seat and looked up at his rear-view mirror. Jon couldn't tell if he was checking his makeup or looking for other cars on the street.

The situation made the hair on Jon's neck frizzle.

Jon asked, "Can I help you? Who are you?"

"Look," the man finally replied in a voice that rumbled from down in the bowels of the earth, "Look. Situations are complicated. A lot of people are involved. You might want to choose a different direction. You have a nice family. Cute wife. Cute kid. Don't mess around where it won't be good for anyone. There can be misunderstandings and unintended consequences."

"Who are you?" Jon asked again as the car window slid back up. The man gave Jon a ghastly grin and slowly drove away, leaving Jon standing on the sidewalk holding Stogie's leash and a paper bag full of crap.

* * *

"Well, that was interesting," Jon said to Stogie, who responded by wagging his tail. "What the hell was that all about?" The whole thing was creepy, especially the man's references to Lisa and Sam. Who was he? Where had he come from? What did he want?

He memorized the car's license number and flipped it over and over in his head to make it register before he could write it down, but it probably wouldn't be much use. It was a Massachusetts plate. He'd have to ask Lisa if she could "Run a plate" for him. Maybe the man had gotten him confused with someone else, although that was hard to accept since he knew Jon's name.

Back at the house, he threw Stogie's poop bag into the trash and found Lisa in the kitchen feeding Sam. Jon dropped into a chair at the kitchen table.

"Hey," he said.

Lisa was in her uniform, ready to go to work.

"If I gave you a license plate number, could you track down who it belonged to?"

"What license plate?"

"Nothing. Just curious. They do that kind of thing on TV cop shows. Just wondering ... if, say I saw something, if you could find out who the car belonged to and tell me."

Jon got up and pulled a coffee mug out of the cabinet and filled it, and sat back at the table.

"What's going on, Jon?" Lisa asked.

"Nothing. Really. I just saw a strange car driving weirdly."

Lisa put Sam's breakfast plate in the sink. "What's weirdly mean? Swerving like the driver was drunk? Bouncing off the curbs? Hitting other cars?"

Jon laughed. "No, no, no. Just, you know, kind of cruising slowly down the street looking for something. Could you look it up and tell me?"

"I could look it up," Lisa said, "but telling you what I found is something different. We're not supposed to do stuff like that."

"Oh," Jon said, cradling the coffee cup between his hands. "I'm just wondering if there is anything particularly dangerous in environmental consulting work. I mean, it doesn't seem like a threatening job, you know?"

"What's going on, Jon?"

Jon described his strange encounter with the man in the car.

"Did you get the license plate?" Lisa asked.

Jon wrote it down on the edge of a scrap envelope.

"The guy was probably just lost. Looking for the ferry or the Kennedys."

"But he seemed to know who I was. By name."

"What are you getting into?" Lisa asked. "Don't do anything stupid."

"I'm not," Jon said. "I'm not. Just doing my job. I suppose when you find toxic stuff on someone's land, they might not be happy about it. It costs money to clean it up. And you know it's like finding bones on a construction site. You know that. There was that job site last year where they found those bones and you had to shut the site down while the archeologists tried to figure out who was buried there and when. Like maybe it had been a murder or maybe just an old grave. They had to stop the construction, right?"

Sam ran off into the living room to create another traffic jam with all his trucks and cars.

"Delays don't make contractors happy."

"So, do you think this guy was threatening you?" Lisa asked.

"I have no idea. I don't know that anything I'm doing is anything that anyone would want me to stop. I had nothing to do with that hotel collapse. I'm not part of that investigation. I don't think Ace is building anything threatening, although he has wealthy clients who can get frustrated. There is Brenda's - Bab's sister's - house in Summer Meadows."

"Yeah, seems like there may be something nasty there."

"Maybe. Lash is helping me with that. But that's already built. Been there for years. What I'm doing wouldn't hold up construction."

"Maybe the guy just had an unpleasant morning and doesn't like the way you look." Lisa laughed and put her arm around him.

"That's probably it. He was just driving around yelling at ugly people."

"He got that wrong," Lisa said. "Nothing ugly about you. The man ain't got no taste."

* * *

"Hey, Lash. What's up?" Jon asked when he got Ashton on the phone. It was a week after Jon's encounter with the guy in the car—a typical late winter Cape Cod afternoon. Gray sky with a hint of rain. Jon was glad that his work with Ace was indoors. Propane fired, salamander heaters put out a lot of heat, but they also produced a cloying smell, and the roar of the rushing air was deafening. Jon had come home with a headache, but he was curious about what Lash might have discovered about Summer Meadows.

"Interesting stuff," Lash replied. "Digging into this stuff is always interesting."

"Is interesting good? That word can mean a lot of different things - particularly regarding the value of what you discovered."

"No, it's interesting. I mean, not everything is digitized, so you can never be sure that the information is complete, but it turns out that there was a company that made thumb tacks right near where that development was built."

"Thumb tacks? Doesn't sound all that threatening to me," Jon said.

"And other stuff," Lash said. "The company was there for a long time. Since the turn of the century. They also manufactured nails and wire products."

"Fascinating."

"Yeah, but the really interesting stuff is that they discharged wastes containing cyanide and heavy metals into an unlined acid-neutralizing lagoon close to the building and next to a saltwater tidal marsh."

Jon was sitting in the hallway of his house where they kept the phone on a little table with a lamp that looked like a replica of a cannon from Old Ironsides. Jon twiddled with the twisted phone cord.

"How did you find all this out?" he asked.

"Wait. There's more," Lash replied. "They also dumped process wastes containing acids and metals such as copper and nickel and solvents that they discharged into drains in the floor of the main building. Apparently, some of these chemicals permeated the floors and timbers of the building and migrated to adjacent soils and groundwater."

"Whoa. Nasty interesting stuff."

"Yeah. And there were other contaminated areas of the site, including a filled wetland, a former dump, and other chemical spills."

Jon looked up at the ceiling in the hallway and noticed a water stain. He wondered if it was new or one that he just hadn't noticed before.

Lash paused before he said, "It was classified by the government as a toxic site."

"So why did they let someone build on it?"

After another pause Lash said, "And then that designation seems to have disappeared."

"How?"

Jon couldn't see Lash shrug on the other end of the phone connection. "Don't know, man. That's your job."

"Oh, thanks," Jon said. "No wonder people are getting sick there."

"It is surprising. Surprising that they could build that development there."

"Who was the developer?"

"Haven't gotten that information yet," Lash said. "As I say, not everything is digitized."

"Do you know when they built it?" Jon asked.

"Six years ago. 1983. It's the usual bureaucratic pile-on behind the project," Lash said. "You know, lots of 'this' and 'that'. It's a challenge to unravel the people behind the corporate names. But you've stumbled upon a clusterfuck of the first order. There's nasty stuff in that ground. I wonder how the guys that built it are doing. I bet they didn't wear any protective gear when they were digging up that dirt to put in those foundations."

"You're probably right there," Jon replied. He had a sudden thought. "Shit. Ace built one of those houses."

"Your partner?"

"Yeah. And his sister-in-law lives there."

There was a pause and then Lash asked, "So what are you going to do about it?"

"Don't know. See if you can find who was behind this." Jon's immediate thoughts were that Babs' sister should just quietly sell her house and move. He didn't know of any process where he could seal the foundation to prevent any more toxics flowing into her house. It would take a major earth moving project to clean up the site.

"Thanks for the help," Jon said. "Let me know if you find out anything else."

* * *

Nita wondered how chefs could come home and cook a meal. After you had been dealing with food and pots and pans all day, how could you come home and keep doing it? Did people who shuffled papers all day enjoy shuffling papers at home? Maybe that was why she had aspirations of being a professional musician and not a professional house cleaner, because cleaning her own apartment was very far down on her list of activities that she wanted to do when she got home.

Music was different. She shared a small but high end stereo system with her roommate that filled the apartment with sound and was accurate enough for her to play along with some of the greatest flute music. She could stand with her music stand with the score of the piece and play along as though she were in Carnegie Hall. Or she could transport herself to another world, swept away in the confines of the couch. Occasionally, her cellist roommate would join her and together they would venture into musical wonderlands.

Sometimes, it was work when she was struggling through a new piece. Not work really. She never felt it was work. Hard. Challenging. Something .... but not exactly work. Not like cleaning-a-house-work. When she could find the tone or shape the sound, or effortlessly move her fingers. Maybe that was it. Effort. She loved attempting to get the sound she wanted, but sometimes the love was lost in the process until she could get to that moment of just letting go. But that was one thing about music—she didn't have to find the right words. She didn't have to describe it. She just had to do it.

So the apartment wasn't clean. There were pots in the

kitchen. Food wrappers and empty plastic shopping bags littered the counters. There were clothes on the floor and her bed wasn't made. Books stood in piles or splayed out open face down as though giving up from exhaustion. Bills and messages were strewn across the desk. Pictures were angled ungainly on the walls. Throw pillows and blankets were scattered unfolded across the couch.

Nita's roommate wasn't home this evening, so Nita had the apartment to herself. She had eaten a packaged and reheated macaroni and cheese dinner and was working through the intermezzo of her latest piece. It was going around and around in her head, but wouldn't come out straight. It should be so simple. It needed to be simple to connect smoothly to the complex elements that came before it and followed it. It was the calm before the storm when all the noise stops for a moment and nature holds its breath, that moment when the tsunami sucks all the water back to itself and unsuspecting and unaware islanders dance in the unnatural beauty laid out before them. It is the moment of the promise of peace, sprinkled with the pending darkness of primal terror that manifests itself on the small hairs on the neck and arms.

That was what she wanted. That was what she was looking for in these few simple bars of music. Sometimes the simplest elements are the most challenging, to find just the right amount of color, tone, and rhythm, to blend and not interrupt the flow of the piece.

She listened to the city outside the windows. She heard the sirens. She listened to the refrigerator cycle on. She heard the little shudder of the compressor. She listened to the hiss of the steam from the radiators. She heard the pinging of the metal expanding. She thought about Eleanor Denjer's discomfort. She listened to the beat in the bass notes of her neighbor's stereo. She heard their voices through the wall. She wondered about the Denjers' discord. She listened to the footsteps in the ceiling above her head. She heard the creak of the floor.

Focus! The voice in her head shouted.

Whadayahgetit?

Whadayahgetit?

Whadayahgetit?

Where are you going? What are you thinking? Find the peace. Find the serenity. Remember the babbling brook? Remember the whispering desert wind?

But just as the tune of the mournful sound of a loon on a Vermont lake was taking shape in her mind, Eleanor Denjer called.

* * *

"You're very pretty," Eleanor began.

"Mrs. Denjer?" Nita replied, taken aback by this interruption in her evening.

"You're very pretty," Eleanor repeated. "I thought you were the one. He's not there, is he?"

Nita pulled the cordless phone away from her ear and looked at it as if she could see Eleanor Denjer on the other end. "Who are you talking about, Mrs. Denjer?"

"I was sure you were having an affair with him. Those dimples."

"Who are you talking about? I'm not having an 'affair' with anyone. And, Mrs. Denjer, my private life is none of your business!"

"It is if it involves my husband."

"Your husband? That's crazy."

Eleanor Denjer didn't reply.

The silence twisted Nita up. She wanted to scream into the phone that she found Norman Denjer, a despicable piece of human trash that she wouldn't touch in a crowded subway or a sinking ship.

"I know," Eleanor said finally. "But there's someone. There's someone or something. It's happened before. You can't blame me for thinking it was you. You're very pretty."

Nita strode out to the kitchen, holding the phone between her chin and her shoulder. She filled a glass with water at the sink.

"I need your help," Eleanor said.

Eleanor Denjer began confiding in Nita like a high-school friend. Several times in her monolog, Eleanor insisted she didn't know who else to turn to and apologized for disturbing Nita's evening. She suspected her husband was having another affair, but she hadn't been able to find any evidence. Naturally, she thought it might be Nita because of her exotic beauty and proximity.

"I contemplated letting you go," Eleanor said. "Removing the temptation, but if it wasn't you, he would have just found another way."

"Thank you for the compliments," Nita said.

"But how can you tell?" Eleanor asked. "When you love a man, how can you tell? You try to find the good parts about him. When you're a fool ... like witnessing a murder. You can't know the murderer unless you're there—unless you see them do it. Unless you see the smoking gun. And even then. You can't be in the bedroom with the lovers. God, what a thought!"

"You don't have to worry about that. I promise you. Not on my account, anyway."

"He plays games, you know? Did it since we were first married. He uses dice. He showed me. Convinced me to invest my family money. He has elaborate rules, and he throws the dice and makes his bets."

Nita didn't want to hear about Mr. Denjer's private life.

She leaned back against the counter and listened to Eleanor Denjer ramble on. Nita moved about the kitchen, abstractedly tidying things, when she suddenly realized that Mrs. Denjer had asked her a question.

"Excuse me?" she asked.

"I want to give you something, something I found on his computer."

"Oh. I don't know, Mrs. Denjer. I'm not sure if I'm the right person."

"It's important that he doesn't know."

Nita looked up at the ceiling before she asked, "Doesn't know what?"

"I'll see you Thursday."

Chapter Fourteen

Norman could sense his dreams coming true. Ferrari had an ad that read, "What can be conceived can be created." The Denjer Grand Ocean Bath and Golf Club was more than just an idea now. With Pocatuck, it would be created. Denjer smiled at his reflection in the glass windows of his office.

Boston was an industrial forest of buildings. The sun glinted off the glass of a million windows. He could see people in their offices - at their desks, in conference rooms, staring out through glass as he was. When he had wandered through the woods at Boundbrook, he knew every rock and every root in the paths. He could hear the birds, an occasional car on the roads far away, and the breeze rustling the tree branches in the overstory, scratching at the sky. Isolated in this glass box perched on the top of this tower, the sounds of the city were faint echoes—car horns, emergency sirens, truck backing up alarms—were hints of the life on the streets below. But he knew every inch there, too. The rocks and the roots were the people who got in the way that he was forced to step over or walk around.

Power was a burden that he shouldered, willingly doing his part, making his mark on history. The admiration of the masses wanting to hand him money and guide their lives and their futures warmed his heart and filled him with an innate joy that he could do so much for so many. Would his father be proud of his success? Thoughts of his father made him wince—made him drop back into his past as an insignificant kid.

But now, he stood like the captain on the poop deck of his flagship. And that recalled Marlon Brando in *Mutiny on the Bounty*. Would Captain Bly's father have been proud of him? Poop deck. Norman snorted. Such a stupid term. English was full of stupid words. When he was king of the world ... and that wouldn't be far off now ... he would clean up the English language. Everyone would have to speak his version of the common language. How could a country function if people didn't all speak the same language in the same way? How could they possibly understand each other? It was little wonder that there was so much conflict in the world. Differences, by definition, equaled conflict. Harmony was the only answer ... everyone speaking the same language. Everyone believing in the same god. Not that he was religious.

He could fix that, too. If he were the god, it would remove all the confusion as to what to believe and who to believe in. Religions were stupid and confusing. It was simple, Norman thought. Believe in me. It was that simple. Believe in me. I am the one. I'll take care of you. I'll protect you and save you from yourself.

There were so many things to fix. So many. It was too bad that he couldn't do it all himself. That would be so much simpler. It was when you had to depend on other people that things came apart.

He turned away from the glass and shouted, "Cynthia!" He dropped into his desk chair and looked expectantly at the door to his office, resting his elbows on the arms of the chair, steepling his hands together with his fingers touching tip to tip while funneling his lips.

For a moment, Cynthia shocked him with humanity as she stood in his doorway. Amongst all the glass and marble and metal, she was human warmth and Norman smiled as she fidgeted, shifting her weight back and forth, twisting her hips.

"How are you this morning, Cynthia?" he asked.

"Fine, sir. Thank you." Her tentative smiled flickered and faded like a faulty connection.

Norman leaned forward onto his desk. "And how's your family?"

"Fine, sir. Ricky has an ear infection again."

"That's a shame," Norman said. "It's not contagious, is it? Wouldn't want ear infections going around the office." He laughed a deep from the belly laugh and heaved himself up. Although Cynthia was across the room, she took a step backward.

"No, no," Norman said. "Come in. Sit down. We never talk. Let's talk." And he smiled again.

"Where, sir?"

Norman pointed to the big leather armchairs in front of his desk.

"Should I bring a notebook or anything?" she asked.

Still smiling, Norman said, "No, no, no. I'm sure you will remember whatever we talk about. You're a smart young woman. How old are you now? Can I ask that? I know you're not supposed to ask a woman her age. It's not polite. My own mother was twenty-five for years. Never looked a day over forty. I can't tell how old women are any more. Make-up, dresses, foo-foo frocks. Can't tell. Just can't tell."

Cynthia slid into the office and lowered herself gingerly

into the chair, crossing her legs and pulling her skirt tightly around her.

Norman perched his ass on the edge of the desk, resting his hands on either side of himself.

"So, what did you want to talk about?" he asked, staring into her crystal blue eyes.

"Sir?" she asked.

She was quite pretty; he thought. Nicknaming her 'Titly' was a bit abusive. But it fit her. What did her parents think of her working for a celebrity?

"Did I hire you?" he asked. There were so many people. Where did they all come from? Had she been offered to him as part of the selection from personnel?

"Are you going to fire me, sir? Did I do something wrong?"

"No, no, no," Norman laughed again, leaning toward her and putting his hand on her shoulder to reassure her. "No, no, no. You're doing just fine. Just fine. How long have you been with us? Do you like it here?"

"Yes, sir," she said.

"Are you married, Cynthia?"

"Yes, sir. Four years now."

"That's wonderful. I hope he's good to you?" Denjer said with a smile and a slight tilt of his head.

"He is, sir. He's a fireman."

Denjer leaned back in surprise. "A fireman! I always wanted to be a fireman. When I was in elementary school, they took us to visit a fire station. They had a dog. A Dalmatian. Just like in the children's books, with the Dalmatian riding on the fire truck with the ears and tongue flapping. It looked so exciting. I wanted to be one too. Is it exciting, Cynthia?"

"It's dangerous."

"And that makes you worry? Of course it does. Of course

you worry. All wives worry about their husbands, don't they? Children?"

"Just Ricky, sir."

"You want more children, I imagine. That's an enormous responsibility, though, isn't it?"

Cynthia mumbled agreement, recrossed her legs and adjusted her skirt.

"It's different from raising a dog. It is different. I guess you can't tie a kid up in the backyard to relieve himself, can you?" Norman laughed again. "Can't put the kid on a leash and walk him to the park. Although people do that, don't they? Put kids on leashes. I've seen that. I've seen them do that. They're not choke collars like you might use to discipline a dog. They're almost like a harness. Is that cruel, Cynthia? Do you think that's cruel?"

"Yes, sir. I mean, no, sir. I don't think that I'd ...."

"No, of course you wouldn't. You're too nice." Norman smiled again. "You're too nice."

Norman looked into her pretty eyes, seeking the sincerity in her words. "Wait," he said, pulling away from his desk and striding around to the master's position. He opened the right hand top drawer of the desk and pulled out a narrow royal blue leather box.

"I've got something for you. Just a token of my appreciation for all your good work." He stepped around the desk and stood beside her as he handed her the box.

Cynthia looked up at him and then opened the box.

Norman watched her face as she displayed the small diamond tennis bracelet. Her mouth formed a delicate O and her carefully plucked eyebrows lifted.

"Oh, sir. Thank you. It's beautiful!"

"It's a tennis bracelet," Norman said, waving away the appreciation and stepping back around to the master's side of the desk. "Do you play tennis, Cynthia? I've never understood why anyone would want to wear a bracelet playing tennis. But there it is. That's what they call it. I just want you to know that I appreciate all you do. Kind of spontaneous thing."

"Thank you," she said with a smile.

Still standing, Norman leaned forward on his desk. After a protracted pause, he smiled and quietly said, "I've got something special I want to show you, Cynthia." He held out his hand. "Come with me."

Cynthia stood up. The touch of her hand was electric. The skin of her fingers was smooth and soft as she touched him like a feather.

Norman nodded and led her over to his private door. He stopped and turned and looked at her. "Did you know this was here? It's a secret. It's my secret. Did you know I have my own bathroom and elevator? Can't even see the door, can you? Hidden. It's like the oval office. You know, like the White House? In Washington? Where the president lives?"

"No, sir," she said with a smile.

"Did you ever go in here when I'm not around?"

Cynthia stopped and put her hand over her mouth. "Oh, no, sir. I wouldn't. I mean, I couldn't. I didn't even know this was here!"

Norman grinned. "That's good. That's good. Here, let me show you how this works." He pushed on a section of the wall behind his desk. "Come on," he said encouragingly. "Come on. I won't bite."

They stepped through the doorway, and the lights on the ceiling blinked to life.

"There's the elevator, just there." Norman pointed down to the end of the hall. "And there's my bathroom. We won't go in there, of course, but I'm sure you can imagine." He laughed.

Cynthia was clutching the blue box with the tennis bracelet to her ample chest. And smiling.

"What else do you see?" Norman asked. "What else?"

Cynthia looked around the narrow hall.

"You can't see anything else, can you? Look carefully now. Pretend you're a detective. Look carefully."

Norman stood back, watching Cynthia look up and down and back and forth. She looked confused when she didn't see anything.

"Perfect!" Norman almost shouted. "It's hidden. A hidden door within a hidden hallway. Perfect. Watch this."

Norman squatted down and ran his hand along the baseboard and pushed at a seam where two pieces joined and a section of the wall swung away. Norman stood back up and said, "See? It's my safe room. It's a place where I can be safe from invaders, wars, hurricanes, aliens. Anything! Go ahead. Step inside."

"Oh, I don't know, sir. I don't much like small spaces."

But Cynthia stepped forward into the confinement of Norman's safe room and looked around. "It's cozy," she said.

Norman remained in the hall. "If you close the door, you can lock it from the inside. I won't be able to open it from out here. You'll have to unlock it. You'll be safe in there. Safe from all the mean and evil people in the world. Just like a baby in a womb."

Cynthia looked out at him through the doorway. "Do you ever just come in here to get away from everything? I mean, it is kind of quiet, and you've got everything. Can you tell what's going on outside?"

"I can see what's going on in my office on that little closed circuit TV."

"That's cool," Cynthia said. "Are you coming in?"

Norman had never shown his secret safe room to anyone

before, and he realized how small the space actually was. Initially, he had thought it would be a great idea to take Cynthia in there. He knew it would impress her to give her insight into his secret world, to let her see behind the power, to provide her with a vision of a world she would never know, to give her stories that she could tell her friends and family. It abruptly dawned on him that his secret safe room wasn't a secret anymore.

"Come out of there," he demanded.

Cynthia looked startled.

"Come out of there," he said, more loudly.

Cynthia scuttled out of the safe room and brushed past him into the hall. Norman pulled the door closed, and it clicked into place.

"You can't tell anyone about this," he said, staring fiercely into her eyes. "No one. You can't tell anyone. Ever. Understand?"

"No, sir. Of course not, sir. I won't tell a soul."

"I mean it. Not a soul. Ever. No matter what."

Cynthia scrambled out of the hall and back into Norman's office.

"You can go now," he said.

* * *

Yes, yes, yes. Cynthia was a good thing. He'd done a good thing. She loved him and he loved Pocatuck. His spirits soared.

"I just met the land called Pocatuck," Norman sang to the glass in his office. "And suddenly that name will never sound the same to me!" His singing voice was deplorable, Maria was screeching in pain, and Leonard Bernstein would run screaming into a wall. But Norman was grinning fiendishly.

Suddenly, his dream would come true. All these years of

searching for the perfect place for The Club. He could see the rolling hills and the ancient trees, the blue skies with the fluffy white clouds. Twenty-seven hundred acres close to Boston. It would bring that old Brahmin sanctuary, the Brookline Country Club, to its proverbial knees. That place was old, but it had only two hundred and thirty-six acres! They had their noses so far up in the air that they could smell their own asses without bending over.

They had the gall to turn down his membership application! The Denjer family didn't go back to the Mayflower. His mother wasn't a member of the Daughters of the American Revolution. No doubt she could have been. She just didn't see the point.

So now ... now he would be able to stand on the porch of the grand club house, spread out his arms, and greet the greats of golf to his club. The Denjer Grand Ocean Bath and Golf Club! The DGOBGC! Admittedly it might have been slightly more perfect if it had actually been on the ocean, but he had picked out the name long before he had met Pocatuck.

And the funny thing was that the Brookline club claimed to have native American connections. Pocatuck had much, much deeper roots. He was sure of it. He would have to look that up. You could just tell from the name.

Still smiling, he turned and dropped into the desk chair and rubbed his hands across the smooth surface.

Why, he wondered. Why wasn't it his already? It wasn't his yet. It wasn't his. So he'd buy it. He'd just buy it.

Norman was contemplating candidates to carve his life-sized statue for the lobby of the clubhouse, when two yahoos tumbled into his office unannounced. Their faces were familiar. Norman never forgot a face. But their names escaped him. They were part of the great crowd of hoi-polloi who circulated in the hallways and hung around the water cooler and sucked on the corporate tit. Cynthia hadn't announced them. They didn't wear jackets and their ties were hanging loose and their sleeves were rolled up to their elbows. One of them was losing his hair and his bald spot glistened under the fluorescent ceiling lights.

The other one wore black-rimmed spectacles that made his eyes bulge out like those paintings of big-eyed children that were supposed to make you go, "AWE!"

It was a sudden and threatening interruption of Norman's day, and he pushed back in his chair.

"What do you want?" he shouted. Phil Bosun should always be in his office. How did Cynthia let these hooligans past her desk?

The two men stopped just inside the office door and looked at each other.

"What do you want?" Norman shouted again. "Who are you, and what are you doing here?"

"Sir," Glasses began. "We can't do this anymore."

Norman wiped the spittle from his lips.

"Yes, sir. We can't."

Norman pushed back closer to the glass and farther away from the uninvited pair.

"Who are you?"

Glasses began closing the door. "You probably don't want to have this conversation be public," he said, nuzzling the door until the latch clicked.

Although the world of Boston and the hint of New England and the rest of the country spread out all around him through the glass box of his office, Norman felt trapped.

"We've been doing this now for six years," Baldy said. "And we haven't said a word to anyone. I mean, it's like ... the land of make-believe. Because that's what it is. You tell us ... well, you don't tell us directly. You tell us indirectly and we do it. And you pay us, but ... we don't think you pay us enough."

"Yes," said Glasses. "We're afraid that when this all comes out that it won't be good for our families."

Norman looked at the two men. Why did they have to hire morons? Why did he have to trust morons with his life and his dreams? They weren't big. Sort of average size. Sloppy build. Out of shape. He could take them, if he had to. Phil Bosun definitely could. If he got in a bar fight with Phil at his side, he could take on an army of dingleberries like these two.

Norman was a very important man. World leaders and corporate executives like Lee Iacocca and Steve Wynn had asked him for advice. He had received many awards and accolades for his charitable work. His name was on buildings. His face was all over magazine covers. People begged him to let them give him money to invest in his projects. His net worth was greater than some countries.

People just didn't barge into his office any more than they barged in to see the Pope or the President of the United States. His time was precious. Single moments were like drops of gold. This interruption was totally unacceptable no matter who these people were. And for them to actually close the door behind them without permission ... well, that was a capital offense. When he was king of the world, beheading would be too good for them.

He pushed his chair back to his desk, lowered his eyes, paused, and then slowly raised his head and said in a whisper from the back of his throat, "What are you talking about? Who are you?"

Baldy eased himself around behind Glasses, who said, "We generate the paperwork for your real estate projects."

"So?"

"We make it up."

Confined Spaces

"Lots of paperwork is generated in this office," Norman hissed.

"But we make it up," Glasses said again.

Norman started uncoiling from his chair, straightening out his body, the volume of his voice increasing as he said, "Of course you do. That's your job. Isn't that your job? Isn't that why we pay you? Should we stop paying you to do your job? Should we? Is that what you're asking us to do? Is that what you're asking me to do? I'm a very important man. I have very important things to do every day. I don't have time for your troubles."

The two men stood several steps from the door. It was apparent that they didn't know what to do with their hands. Baldy stuffed his into his pockets while Glasses attempted to cross his arms across his chest in a more defiant stance. Baldy looked at Denjer and then said, "We think we deserve more money ... that is, if we should keep quiet about this. And not tell someone ... the press maybe ... about what we're doing. About what you've asked us to do."

"Are you threatening me?" Norman roared. "What have I asked you to do? I ... haven't ... asked you ... to ... do ... anything. I ... don't ... even ... know ... who ... you are."

The two men took a step back until their backs were almost pressed up against the office door.

Norman dropped his voice again. "Explain yourselves. Are you cheating? Are you lying? Are you stealing from the company? Do you even work here?"

"When you give us a property name ...."

"I give you a name? I give you a name? What kind of name? Fiddle o'fladdle? What are your names? Hoolu and lulu? "

Glasses had dropped his hands to his sides. He shuffled his feet. He looked at Baldy and rephrased his statement. "When we are given a property name, we generate all the commensurate real estate documents to make it look real. But it's not real. They're not real. All they are are pieces of paper."

Norman glared at them and reached for his phone. "This is scandalous. It's scandalous. It's criminal. You are criminals. I never asked you to do this. I have to call the police and have you arrested. I have to report this. Did I ever ask you to do this? You're saying ... you're saying that you misled me into taking money from people for properties that don't exist? That never existed?"

Norman waved the phone receiver at them.

"You told us to," Baldy said.

"I told you to? I told you to?" Norman dropped the phone handset back into its cradle and slammed his hand down on his desk until his hula dancer wiggled her grass skirt.

"Yes," said Glasses, "and we can't keep doing it. We can't keep lying. We're going to end up in jail!" He hesitated. "You're going to end up in jail."

Suddenly, Glasses and Baldy became Tweedle-dee and Tweedle-dum dressed like jokers in a Disney version of Alice in Wonderland. Norman's office became a forest with green ferns and red and white polka dotted toadstools the size of tables in a Paris street cafe. Animated baby animals scampered about and smiled at him, and the Cheshire Cat puffed on his hookah. Jail did not exist for the king of the land. That was a dingy confined space for paupers and thieves that didn't apply to kings of industry who conferred with royalty and Lee Iacocca. Norman struggled to find his voice. "Off with their heads," he wanted to say ... and do. Wasn't it the Queen of Hearts who wanted to chop everyone's head off for any random whim?

Finally, he said, "I don't know what you're talking about, but I don't want you talking about it anymore. Here or anywhere. Do you understand? Do you understand? I don't know what you're talking about, but if you want more money to stop talking about it, you'll have more money. Now get out of my office!"

The two men hesitated. Baldy was reaching for the door when Norman stopped them.

"Wait! I want you to look into a property called Pocatuck."

"Sir?"

"Pocatuck. It's a real place. It's real. Indian name. I'm going to buy it. I'm going to own it. You're going to seek and find my outstanding interest in the property. You're going to find the fact that my grandfather won it in a poker game."

"Sir?"

"Aren't you? It's there. You just have to find it. That's what they call it, isn't it? Outstanding Interest? It impacts the Color of Title or some such gook. You can do that, can't you? You're the men," he smiled. He spread his arms wide. "You're the guys. You're the ones I can count on. Aren't you?"

Baldy and Glasses looked at each other.

"Pocatuck," Norman wrapped his tongue around the word. "And stop sweating on my Persian carpet!"

Chapter Fifteen

Jon always thought that Lisa looked beautiful, although through some sort of twisted logic, he refrained from telling her that. But sometimes it just struck him like a slap in the face and the words burst out uncontrollably. "Jesus. You look great!" Sometimes it was a bit much.

"Is that a surprise?" Lisa asked.

So, he backpedaled, "No, I mean you always look great. But sometimes you look greater." He grinned.

Lisa tilted her head and gave him her appraising look. And then she smiled.

"I mean, it's different when you're not in uniform."

"I don't look great in my uniform?"

"No, you do. I mean, of course you do, but ..."

"I'm not supposed to look attractive in uniform."

"Oh, but you do. You know that, but ..."

"Shut up, Jon. Let's go before you get in any deeper."

Nita Avant had invited them to her gig in Cambridge, and it was a rare treat to take the evening off. Jon didn't know what sort of flute music Nita played or how good she was, but it didn't matter. He was getting to spend the evening with Lisa.

You have to do stuff like this once in-a-while, Jon thought. And Lisa looked great. Sam and Stogie were with Lisa's parents for the night.

The mini-van took a bit of the sparkle off the romance of a night on the town, but the sound system was surprisingly good. Added to Jon's collection of cassettes that he had brought over from his MG Midget were Raffi and Bill Harley singing songs that Sam loved, telling the tale of Zanzibar and "Don't bring it home, oh no". But tonight was an adult event, and they didn't have to listen to "The wheels and on the bus go 'round and 'round, 'round and 'round, 'round and 'round". They could transition from Jon and Lisa - mom and dad, back to Jon and Lisa - lovers.

So as Jon drove, they talked about Sam and Stogie and the house and Lisa's family.

The miles slid by. They crossed the Sagamore Bridge over the Cape Cod Canal. They swung around the rotary where summer traffic clogged coming and going on summer weekends, and launched up Route 3 toward Plymouth and Boston.

"Are we going to make it?" Lisa asked.

"What?"

"I don't mean just financially. I mean you and I."

Jon turned and looked at her. "What do you mean?"

"It's not just the money, Jon. You're not here. Your head is in the clouds. You hop from scheme to scheme, snatching at the first shiny solution that pops up. And all the time ...all the time you're not looking at what you're already holding in your hands."

"Do you want me to quit? Want me to get an office job with a regular paycheck?"

Lisa turned her head to look out at the passing scenery.

"One thing leads to the other," he said. "I want to stop those phone calls. I can't break through the responsibility to get to the pleasant dreams of us ...of Sam ...of our future. I just can't see any future in stocking shelves in the supermarket or working as a janitor."

They listened to the babbling voices on the radio and stared at the road ahead of them.

"You had a dream. Becoming a police officer. And you did it. The fact is that I don't have that dream. The only dream I'm sure of is you. You and Sammy."

Lisa reached over and put her hand over his. "Have you called that lawyer for the insurance company that Gail Barker told you about?"

"Not yet," Jon said.

"Maybe you should. Maybe we shouldn't wait for them to call us."

Jon's thoughts slipped back to the hours under the rubble and all the screaming and war-zone turmoil. "Maybe I should. No, I will. I'll call them."

Then he said, "Business success is more of an hallucination than a dream."

"You think too much, Jon," Lisa said with a laugh. "You need to keep your mind on your driving."

"It's just interesting," Jon said as they were passing the exits to Plymouth and signs showing the route to the Mayflower and Plymouth Plantation. They dropped into their own thoughts.

"The pilgrims had dreams. It's kind of interesting to think about the pilgrims and the Indians. How much of the stuff they taught us in school was real? I mean, they say that 'history belongs to the winners'. We haven't been here that long. The Indians were here long before. The Indians say, 'you can't own the land'. Ace told me that.

"I know that money isn't everything, but it helps. They say

it takes money to make money. Most of the kids at Boundbrook came from money."

"Like you?"

Jon laughed. "I never thought about it."

"Really? You never thought about coming from a rich family?"

"We weren't rich," Jon protested. "We were comfortable. Money wasn't an issue."

"Holy shit, Jon," Lisa said. "Money wasn't an issue? Do you know what that means? Your parents gave you a sports car for your twenty-first birthday. You don't have any college debt. You were one of those spoiled little rich kids who went to Florida for spring break. I don't think there's a more yuppiefied town in the universe than Millbrook, New York, where you grew up and hung out at the country club. Give me a break, Jon."

"I guess," Jon said. "But I never thought of us as rich. We were just the same as everyone around us. And there were certainly people who were richer than we were. The people with the multiple houses and the yachts. Money just wasn't a big thing. At least not for me. I mean, I guess it's the comparison. 'Rich' or 'poor' are a comparative terms."

"What would you call us now?"

That struck Jon that Lisa had a point.

"Would we be rich or poor?"

"Well, that's a real mood crusher!" he said. "Do you think we're poor?"

Lisa twittered and put her hand on his arm. "That's not what I'm saying. It's just interesting the way people get comfortable where they are and tune out what they don't want to see or hear. Black or white. Rich or poor. Old or young. We disregard the rest. It's survival. Weak or powerful. They're all adjectives."

The road rolled by and the trees slid past. Vague white highlights of houses were visible between the naked trees.

"Great," Jon said.

"It's not your fault."

"Fault? It's not my fault that I had a comfortable childhood? I'm paying for that now!"

"That's not what I'm saying. It's just happenstance. It's just the environment that you grew up in. My environment was different. I grew up where the rich tourists came to vacation and build fancy houses on the ocean. I lived there. You visited there. You see the difference?"

"Not really."

"And some things can be blamed on other people. You said so yourself. All that work you are doing with toxics and healthy homes. People make these places toxic. And then people live there. That's not the fault of the people who live there. That's the fault of the people who build there. Like Summer Meadows."

"I have nothing definitive about that yet," Jon said.

"I know, but that might explain the level of juvenile delinquency coming out of there. I worry about Ace's headaches."

Jon glanced at her. "What?"

"Ace's headaches. He started getting them after building that house in Summer Meadows."

"Lash and I talked about that. We wondered about the people who worked on those houses. Shit. I hope those things aren't connected."

They drove past the Plymouth County Jail and its associated farm. The fields were straight and regimented and dormant in the cold.

"Jails and graveyards," Jon said. "Confined spaces."

"I didn't mean to crush the mood," Lisa said. "Let's listen to something else. Talking heads scare me."

"Sure. Find a tape that's not 'Skinamarinky-dinky-dink'!"

They passed the three massive radio towers of WPLM with their blinking lights to warn off aircraft.

"We should throw out some of these," Lisa said, as she held the bag of tapes on her lap and clicked through them.

Jon said, "I have a hard time with that. I mean, we paid for those things."

"Yah, but you've had some of these tapes for at least ten years. I mean, here," she held up one cassette. "Mantovani? Really? How old are you?"

Jon laughed. "It's soothing. My mother liked to listen to that stuff. She called it schmaltz."

"Growing up is one thing, Jon. Growing old is another."

"Find some jazz," Jon suggested. "We can get in the mood."

"Nita didn't tell me what the concert ... session ... jam was all about."

"I associate jazz with saxophones or pianos. But there's Mingus ... Charlie Mingus with the base and Groove Holmes on jazz organ. Jazz flute is unique. Find that Yusef Lateef tape. Or the Herbie Mann one."

"Having a night out is great and I'm excited that Nita has done so well," Lisa said. "I think she's suffering trauma from that girl who disappeared in New Mexico."

"Spontaneous!" Jon said. "Tonight, I mean. Not Nita's student's disappearance."

Lisa laughed. "Spontaneous is the last word that I would associate with you."

"No, seriously. This is just one of those spontaneous things."

"You don't do spontaneous things."

Jon turned to look at her with his best 'you-cut-me-to-the-quick' face, but he couldn't hold it for long. Instead, he put his hand on her thigh. Mini-vans with their individual seats are not romantic vehicles - at least in the front seats. And although the move was spontaneous, the timing was not great.

"Um?" Lisa said as Jon moved his hand up her leg, pushing up her skirt. "What'cha got in mind?"

"Just being spontaneous," he replied with a grin.

"Later," she said. "Boston traffic is not suited to spontaneous displays of affection!"

They were passing through the Braintree Split in the highway and the Boston skyline was appearing on the horizon. City traffic built up as they wove over and under the bridges and streets that crossed the highway. Finally, they crawled past the massive gas tanks painted with the rainbow swash by Corita Kent. Jon didn't have time to pick out the face of Ho Chi Minh along the edge of the blue splash.

They curved around under and over ramps into the city and onto Storrow Drive along the river and then turned right up on Harvard Street, crossed the river and crept up into Cambridge. Gangs of students bounced up and down the sidewalks—serious or laughing, reading or eating, carrying books and papers and bags and backpacks. Other places in the country had student communities gathered around colleges and universities, but there was something different in the music of the Harvard University community in Cambridge. To Jon, most colleges and universities were part of the city or town where they were located—even like Boston University on the other side of the river was part of Boston. Harvard was the beating heart of Cambridge, and Cambridge itself was its own commonwealth.

He turned to look at Lisa, who was crunched over against her door, staring out the window.

"It's another world," he said.

"Hm hm," she agreed.

"There's something about this place."

"Hm hm."

"Don't know what it is. I can see how someone can get sucked into it and never leave like some sort of enchanted kingdom with wizards and warlocks. Did you ever want to go here?"

They stopped at a light and watched the pedestrians saunter across. She turned and looked at him. "How?" she asked. "Why?"

"Didn't you ever want to study Greek or philosophy?"

"No," she said. "I don't think there are many state troopers who are Harvard grads .... Not that they couldn't be. It's just that these people are different. The stuff they learn here doesn't seem practical. They wouldn't learn to bake a cake. They wouldn't matriculate to devil a moist Windsor sponge. Blah, blah, blah."

Jon laughed. "What the hell is that?"

"I'm not just a pretty face, you know."

"I know that."

"Are you implying that I'm not pretty?"

Jon could feel the slope tilting under the logic of where this line of conversation was going. "Now we just have to find a place to park. Have you been to Grendel's Den before?"

"It sounds like a place that fits into your witches and warlocks world. When did you go there?"

"I came with my sister when she was thinking about graduate work at MIT. She was just checking it out and someone told her about it."

"Checking out what? Restaurants?"

"No. Schools. MIT's got a great reputation."

Lisa snorted. "You think?"

Jon gave up on finding street parking and pulled into a garage, winding around up the ramps, and finally sliding into a slot. Jon didn't immediately get out of the car and Lisa asked, "What's wrong?"

He peered through the open sides of the building, wide slits of daylight, and thought about all the concrete and vehicles above them held up by structural pillars. It gave him the creeps.

"Maybe this wasn't such a good idea," he said.

Lisa laid her hand on his arm. "It's going to be okay. It's just a building. You've been in a lot of them."

"It's just ... I don't know ... Sometimes I just feel the building, you know? I FEEL the building. I remember all those drawings in physics class with the stress arrows and the force vectors, and I can feel all those things pushing against each other - pushing down. And sometimes I can feel like a molecule in the middle of all those forces. You probably think I'm crazy."

"That's why I love you. Let's get out of here and have supper."

He took a deep breath and got out of the car.

They scuffed down the concrete stairwell to the street and joined the flow of pedestrians, stopping for a moment to get their bearings before setting off toward Harvard Square.

* * *

THE RESTAURANT WAS at the bottom of a building just off the Square. It was a small basement space, and they were lucky to get a table.

Lisa was relaxed and natural. They talked about Sam and the house and Jon rambled on about the quality of the air around them and the big fans in the restaurant's kitchen putting the space under negative pressure, and Lisa smiled and tilted her head at him.

He said, "We should do this more often."

"That would be nice."

"What would you think about taking a trip somewhere next summer?"

"Where?"

"I don't know. Have you been out west? To the Rockies?"

"My parents didn't do much traveling. They enjoyed staying on the Cape. I don't know the last time my mother went over the bridge."

Jon laughed.

"We didn't go off to the south to visit Civil War battlefields or to see the cherry blossoms in Washington. They were perfectly satisfied with the world around them on the Cape."

"Wow."

Lisa looked up from her food and put down her fork. "What do you mean, 'Wow'?"

"No, nothing," Jon back stepped. "I mean that's great."

They ate in silence for a while. "But didn't you ever want to travel?" he asked. "There's a lot of world out there. Lot of things to see: Statue of Liberty, Eiffel Tower, Big Ben, the Rockies, the Pacific Ocean."

"I've had an ocean all my life," she replied.

"I know. That's true. But people are different in different places too. They speak different languages. Have different customs. Different food."

"We get a lot of that on the Cape. People bring a lot of that stuff with them when they visit. We have a lot of different restaurants with lots of different food."

"I know. But it's not the same. Seeing different places gives you a different perspective, a different set of viewpoints to make different decisions."

The restaurant was packed with people. One woman's screeching laughter rose above the others, like someone dying on a battlefield. Diners shouted to be heard across their tables.

Dishes clattered. It wasn't the place for a quiet, heart-felt conversation.

Jon had an urge to widen Lisa's horizons - to show her the world, to be her mentor, to give her something that her parents never had. She didn't need to accept a limited universe. He would give her more to her life. Maybe. In the future. When life was more settled. When there was time to sit on a beach at sunset with a glass of wine and the lack of money was no longer a threat. Maybe then.

"I think we're doing okay," she said.

"I'm just saying. We could plan some vacations."

"There are other priorities. I can't think about vacations."

They finished their suppers submerged in the restaurant's noise.

* * *

THEY LEFT The Den and wound their way through the streets. Cambridge was a jumble of lanes and streets and alleys that had just happened over the centuries. There was no logic to the names of streets.

"Do you know how many streets in Boston are called 'Harvard' something?" Jon asked. "A lot, and they're not connected. 'What are we going to call this street?' 'I don't know.' 'How about Harvard Street? That's a nice name. Makes it sound important.'" Jon tried using his best Bostonian accent for this fictional conversation. "Where did Nita say she was playing?"

"Malkan's on Harvard Close," Lisa said.

"Oh, that's helpful," Jon laughed. "Hope you know where we're going. What the hell is a Close?"

It was still early, so they poked into the Harvard Coop and wandered among the books, records, and magazines. Jon pulled out the home building and scientific magazines, looking for articles on air quality and energy efficient housing.

Back on the street, they walked past bars that were bustling with early Friday night revelers, celebrating a life that neither Jon nor Lisa were part of. They were an 'old' married couple in a youthful crowd. The student life was in their past. The Harvard student life was a world they would never know. Jon refused to feel old at thirty. It amazed him how choosing a path with a single person, a single place, or a lifestyle defined his world as he passed through time, lingering a while, but moving on. Lisa took his hand.

They finally discovered Harvard Close that Malkan's was on - the name of the place proclaimed on a green awning that sheltered the small flight of stairs down to the entrance at the base of an old brownstone building. They pushed through the door into the space, which began with a bar along the right side and small tables on the left, both of which were crowded. The room was smokey and noisy and warm. Jon peeled off his coat and followed Lisa past the bar to the entrance of a large room at the back guarded by a large woman perched on a stool, smoking a cigarette and collecting the cover charge. Her gray hair had apparently exploded and her makeup looked like war paint. Massive earrings dangled from each ear and the cleavage between her prominent breasts dove into the cut of her dress.

Jon smiled at her as he pulled out his wallet.

The woman asked, "Two? Ten each, then. Sit anywhere. It'll start when it starts."

Lisa glanced at Jon, turned and led the way through the tables and chairs.

The lighting was dim, with wall sconces pointed up toward the ceiling. There was a stage at the front of the room and a bass player was hugging his human-sized instrument, plucking at the strings and twisting the tuning pegs. A scattering of patrons sat on twisted metal chairs, chatting and drinking.

"I wonder if there is a waitress or something?" Jon said.

"Maybe you have to go up to the bar."

A drummer sashayed through the tables and climbed up on the stage, exchanged a few words with the bass player, and then settled himself in the middle of his equipment. He picked up his sticks and gave the drum a quick rat-a-tat-tat, concluding with a rap on the high-hat cymbal.

"You want a drink?" Jon asked, standing. "Guess it's 'help yourself'."

"Sure."

Jon walked back between the tables. He stood at the end of the crowded bar and waited for the bartender to notice him. The crowd was shoulder to shoulder in the warm and smokey room. Jon wondered about the quality of the air in the place. He had heard that the British called this 'fug'. They had an advertising slogan for a fan they called 'The Fug Fighter'. Jon didn't see that making a hit in the American market, but after all he had read about air quality, they needed something. He put the fact that they were in a basement out of his mind. There were ceiling fans lazily stirring the air, their indolent movement seemed out of sync with the hub-hub of the crowd.

Jon secured a couple of glasses of draft beer and exchanged money with the bartender. Holding the two full glasses high to keep them out of the way of elbows, he made his way back through the crowd. Small amounts jostled out of the glasses and ran down the side and onto Jon's hands. But then a large man stepped back, bumped Jon's arm and beer slopped out and dripped down onto a woman's dress.

"Hey!" she said. "Watch it! Jesus."

"Sorry. Accident."

"You bet you're an accident," the woman said. She was

short, almost disappearing into the bodies at the bar. She peered through large, black-rimmed glasses and her long gray hair was pulled back in a ponytail.

"Trying to get back to my wife," Jon said with a smile. He shouldered the rest of the way through the bodies to the entrance of the music venue.

"Cover?" the woman on the stool by the door said.

"Remember me?" Jon asked, holding up the two less-full glasses of beer. He nodded toward Lisa. "My wife's over there. We came in a while ago."

The woman on the stool dragged on her cigarette and blew smoke up at the ceiling while Jon stood there, beer dripping on his feet. "Unh huh," she said finally.

Jon took this as permission to continue. He moved back and forth between the tables, peeling his feet off the sticky floor, coming back to Lisa. At the table, he set the beers down and dropped into his chair. "Busy place," he said.

Lisa said, "Yup, it's filling up in here."

They sipped, waited, and watched.

"Did she say this was a concert?" Jon asked. "Seems like an odd place for a concert."

"She didn't say."

The room was full and their beers were emptied by the time the rest of the quintet had assembled on the stage and Nita stepped up to the front. She looked spectacular, dramatically different from her maid persona.

A spotlight hit her, and she raised her hands in the air, and the chattering and nattering hushed.

"Hi," Nita said into her microphone.

The crowd responded with an echoing "Hi."

"Thanks for coming." She peered around the room, holding her hand as a visor to block the glare of the spotlight.

Then Nita turned to the other musicians, picked up her

silver flute, which flashed as it reflected the white light of the spotlight. The bass player started a thumping, walking beat. The drummer followed, sliding his brushes on the surface of the drum. The piano and violin chimed in and Nita lifted her flute to her lips, and a snake charmer tune slid out into the room, rhythmically wandering through the notes like dancing through a field of gold. Jon felt the walls of the room disappear and the space expand, and they were no longer in a basement. The audience disappeared. The thumping of the bass swelled like running footsteps. Nita's melodic line was almost breathless, building up, taking the audience with her until it felt as though it couldn't go any farther, and then an abrupt pause. A disconnect. It was only a moment, but it felt like forever. Everything stopped. Jon held his breath.

It was just long enough for concern to start. He felt his stomach in his throat in what his father called a "Thank you, marm" on a hilly road. They'd reached the top, gasped and then started down the other side, the notes slipping and sliding around each other, twisting and turning, bouncing and bumping. Jon had never known that a flute could say so much.

And then it was over. The applause began tentatively, as though the audience didn't quite know how to respond, but then it swelled into a roar. Nita bowed, turned, and waved at her fellow musicians.

"Thank you," she said. "Thank you. That was something that I wrote called 'Riverrun'. Now something that I heard Bobbi Humphrey play called Harlem River Drive."

So the music wove around them, transporting them to other places and times.

Lisa leaned over to Jon's ear between numbers and said, "We should do things like this more often. Thanks." And she smiled and put her arm around him.

When the set ended, Nita put down her flute and stepped

down from the stage and moved between the tables, acknowledging the praise to her left and to her right, smiling, touching hands. She finally reached Jon and Lisa, and giving Lisa a hug, she said, "Thanks for coming."

"Wow! That was amazing," Lisa said, grinning. "Your music is wonderful. I didn't know flutes could do that."

"Thank you." Nita hesitated and studied Jon's face. "Are you a friend of Norman Denjer?"

"Umm ... not a friend, exactly. We went to the same school, and I'm working with him. Or trying to."

"Do you know anything about his business?"

"Just that he's a real estate genius. What we hear about him on the news. What made you start working for him?" Jon asked.

"A friend," Nita replied. "A friend in the tribe told me he was looking for someone." She paused and added, "I'm a musician."

"Well, that's obvious," Jon said with a laugh.

"I know little about accounting and numbers."

Jon waited for the connection in thoughts. He watched Nita's forehead wrinkle and her eyes dart around the room, looking for listeners. She was trying to decide.

"I'm a musician," she repeated. "Not a detective or a secret agent. My heart is with my music and my people. And trust is scarce, but ... listen, something is going on with that man. I don't know what it means, but he is not a good man. Even his wife doesn't trust him.."

Jon said, "Oh?" He felt Nita studying his face.

"He forgets I am a person—that I am visible, that I am not just a maid."

"Oh?"

"His wife, Eleanor, you met her, right?"

Jon nodded. "She seemed nice."

"They haven't got the greatest marriage. In fact, I think he treats her like shit."

"Oh."

"Anyway, she thinks he's up to something and doesn't want to get caught up in it, so she made a copy and gave it to me."

"Copy of what?" Lisa asked.

"I don't know." She reached into the pocket of her colorful flowing caftan and pulled out a computer disk, and handed it to Lisa.

"What's this?"

"Data," Nita said. "Check it out."

"It's a computer disk," Jon said to Lisa.

"I know," she replied. "But what's on it?"

"Eleanor gave it to me."

"But what did she want you to do with it?"

The audience was settling back into their seats.

"Listen, I've got to get back up there. Can we talk more after the show?"

Smiling at the acknowledgment of audience members, Nita turned and headed back to the stage.

Jon and Lisa resumed their seats.

"You want another beer?" Jon asked.

"You can't do this," Lisa said, leaning over the table and lowering her voice. "I'm not a lawyer, but this doesn't smell right. This may be evidence of a crime. Or it could be a crime itself."

"I know."

"And if you accept stolen evidence from her, you—"

"Is that true?"

"And you want to work with him, don't you? He's going to invest in the company?"

Jon twisted in his seat. Looked around the room. Watched the musicians assemble on the stage. He wondered how Nita could shift into focus on the music and away from mundane questions of daily life. How do you just drop into the river of creativity and leave reality behind?

"She's my friend and she might be in trouble."

"I can't read this disk anyway," Jon said.

Lisa looked at him. "Why not?"

"I have a Mac. Different disks. My disks are smaller."

Nita's music didn't lie. The notes from her flute were pure. They took the audience for a stroll on the beach, a walk through the woods, the streets of the city.

Jon tried to stay with the music, but his mind kept wandering and wondering. They needed to get home to Sam and Stogie. It was a long drive. There was work tomorrow. What the hell was going on with Denjer?

As they were getting up from the table after the drummer hit the last thump and the bass player plucked the last string and Nita headed off stage. Jon and Lisa followed her backstage, wending their way between the people moving in the opposite direction toward the exit.

The band members looked up as Jon and Lisa entered the small space that was cluttered with stage lights and chairs and instruments. Nita was nowhere to be seen.

"Nita?" Jon asked. "We're friends. She asked us to meet her after the show."

The drummer, who was boxing up his sticks, said, "Sorry, pal. You missed her."

"Wow," Jon said. "That was fast."

"Ya. Surprised us too. Some big guy appeared and hustled her out the door without a word."

"Did she know him?" Lisa asked.

"Don't know," the drummer replied. "He looked familiar, and she didn't complain, if that's what you mean."

"Did she say where she was going?"

Paul H. Raymer

The drummer shrugged.

Chapter Sixteen

Norman gave Cynthia the list of investors to call. The fact was that his investors loved him. They were knocking at the door and climbing over walls to give him money to put into his projects. They thought he was a genius. Everything he did made money. He had investor genes - investing ran in his blood. His father was an investor. Very smart. Norman felt that he always had to recite his credentials every time he started a conversation. People didn't understand Harrow College in Indiana. And when he told them he excelled at the Kellogg School at Northwestern University, they thought he was talking about breakfast cereals. But there was money to be made with mundane commodities like that, and that helped him build a fortune and make connections. Norman understood people were so blind and you had to convince them repeatedly that you knew what you were doing.

The fact was that he was helping them. The days when he had worked in the half-way house as a kid, he'd given away his time and it felt good. He'd just been sweeping floors and cleaning up, but it felt good. And he wanted to do more of it, but his mother didn't feel it was dignified for him to be cleaning up after drunks.

He was still cleaning up after drunks. He snorted. Bankers and investors were all drunks and drug addicts, so he would continue to help them take care of their money, nurse the piles of cash and help it grow. They didn't want to watch the sausages get made. They just wanted to eat the results.

They had to move on Pocatuck now. They had to move on this before some other vulture spotted the carcass and got there first. This was his dream. His dream. This would be the culmination of his life's work. It would bear his name and carry his legacy.

There were indeed vultures in the world of real estate—operators who had no passion, no soul, no dream except to be Scrooge McDuck with a vault full of coins to dive into. They didn't understand what it meant to build a legacy. They didn't understand the sacrifices that had to be made. They just wanted to lean over the table and pull all the piles of chips and money into their arms meanwhile looking around for the next move. They had no attention span. Norman understood a legacy required commitment. His uncle had taught him that. He was a brilliant professor - a scientist and an engineer. When you had the vision for a project, the passion flowed from it and you had to follow that passion to the end.

This was going to be the crowning touch for the tribe of investors that he had built up with his successful investments—one upon the other, each project feeding the next. And this time he could give them membership in the Denjer Grand Ocean Bath and Golf Club.

Norman didn't know why Pocatuck had dropped into his lap. It probably all went back to that day in the woods at Boundbrook. He had helped Dabney Schmidt move on to a better place, and this was his reward. He smiled when he realized how perceptive he had been that day so many years before.

* * *

CASH IS THE KEY. The rest of it is just bullshit. Norman always liked those comedy routines when they pass money around.

Abbot says to Costello, "I have to make a call. Loan me fifty cents."

Costello reaches in his pocket and pulls out a handful of change and says, "All I've got is forty cents."

Abbot says, "That's okay. Give me the forty cents and you can owe me ten cents." And it spirals on from there, going faster and faster like a shell game until both Costello and the audience are totally confused and blinded by Abbot's impeccable logic. Somehow, it always worked with Costello as the banker, always in debt.

With Norman, it was a case of real estate and wealthy investors who didn't care where the money came from as long as it kept coming in a steady stream. And Norman was good at lining up a bread line of Costellos, passing the cash from the back of the line to the front. If you ignored reality and hung on to fundamental facts, it worked every time. Money was only worth what we mutually agree it was worth.

And at the bottom of all that, there had to be trust. Norman could trust his mother, but there weren't many other people in his life that he could count on to be there when he needed them. Trust was like being sure that the day would begin, like there would always be stars in the sky, like knowing that water was always wet. People were these fuzzy masses of constantly moving molecules that could rearrange themselves in unpredictable arrays like shape shifters.

He trusted Phil Bosun. Phil didn't change his shape—his haircut, the clothes he wore, the frequency of his voice, or his answers to questions. Norman knew that when he asked Phil a question, he would get the answer he wanted and the response he expected. Norman knew nothing about Phil's life outside of the office, and he didn't want to know. He didn't want to be Phil's friend or buddy, to go to his house on fall Sunday afternoons and watch football and drink beer. He didn't want to know Bosun's origin story. He didn't want to know about Bosun's family. He didn't want to know about Bosun's love life or if he had a girlfriend. The man was built like a tank and was as reliable as a rock. That was all that mattered.

"All right?" Norman asked when Phil rolled into his office.

"Yes, sir," Phil replied.

"Where is she now?"

"Safe," Phil said.

Nita Avant was not a reliable constant. She was as unreliable as a bad TV picture. Apparently, she was a musician on top of everything else. And she was an Indian. Having people in his house was scary as hell. Things disappeared. That old expression, "Well, it didn't just get up and walk away" wasn't true when you had strangers walking through the rooms of your house. He had had a reasonable sense of trust in his wife, Eleanor. So why had she betrayed him? Why had she conspired to give that information to the Indian? Didn't she know that information could hurt her too? Conspiracy and betrayal—could there be anything worse? Although families did steal things from each other, didn't they? Getting up in front of a minister and swearing to be true to each other didn't mean you would be. There wasn't anything about stealing in the marriage vows.

Phil Bosun hadn't sworn to be true. He just was.

Nita Avant hadn't sworn anything either, but things had

gone missing and now she was a problem that had to be dealt with.

Norman sighed. "Anyone looking for her?"

"Not so far, sir."

Norman looked at Phil standing in his office doorway with his hands clasped loosely over his crotch. Norman giggled as he had a random thought of Phil in that famous picture of three patriots carrying the drum, the fife, and the flag, marching in the light of the 'rockets' red glare' and smoke in the air.

"Good," Norman said. "I'll let you know when you can throw her in the river. We just have to be sure. Have to be sure. Can't be sure of anything. Not now. Not these days."

Phil didn't reply.

Gazing out the windows with the city spread out below him, Norman thought of superman and wondered if he could fly, if he could just spread out his arms and glide over the buildings, the streets, the parks, and the people like the man of steel in the movies. He was such a strong flier he could hold up falling people and airplanes. Superman didn't have wings. Was it the cape that helped him to fly?

It was always the details that caused the problems, wasn't it? He shrugged off the vision and turned back to Phil. Removing this woman was certainly the right thing to do. Did she know anything? Probably not. She probably didn't have a clue about anything. Didn't have a clue. Why was she digging into his computer? Was there someone behind her? Maybe she worked for the FBI. And how did he know what she knew or didn't know? How did he know what she knew? How did she know his computer passwords? He and Eleanor were the only ones who knew his passwords. Maybe that was a mistake, but what's done is done, as his mother always said.

"What does she know? Does she know what's on the disk Eleanor gave her?"

"She didn't say, sir."

"We need to know what she knows. We need to know what Eleanor knows and why she would do such a stupid thing. We need to know who the bitch has talked to. I knew I shouldn't have let her into my house. I knew it, but Eleanor insisted. You just can't trust these people. Find out what she knows and then make her disappear. I don't want to deal with this right now. We've finally got the land I've been dreaming of, and that's special, Phil. Do you know what that means? All these lands of make-believe, all these property dances, all these piles of dollars finally have a home. Do you understand?"

Phil didn't reply.

Norman could see the light at the end of his tunnel. He could see that there was a place where he could finally ... finally stop running. He would have to untangle some things ... like this loose end, but he could see that there would be a resolution and a restitution and a revolution and a constitution and a constipation - a conflagration and an indigestion. Whatever.

"I don't want to hear about it anymore."

"Yes, sir," Phil replied and turned and left the office.

Chapter Seventeen

The morning after Nita's concert, Jon got a call from Denjer demanding that he meet him on Martha's Vineyard.

"What? Why?" Jon asked.

Denjer said, "Because that's where I will be and I'm excited about your project and I like the Vineyard. I have projects out here."

"You're there now?"

"I am. I like the Vineyard. It's where all the movie stars have summer places. When they call me, I have to be there. You have to look for the diamonds in South Africa, not in New Jersey. You look for honey in the beehive, not on the sidewalk. I'm your honey, Jon. I have time at one o'clock. Meet me at the Flying Horses carousel in Oak Bluffs and we'll talk. If you're ready to go, I can write you a check. But I want to show you something."

"Damn, Norman. It's a haul. I have to drive to Woods Hole and take the ferry." But Denjer had hung up before Jon could say any more.

Jon found the concept of 'a check' tantalizing, even though he didn't know how much or what it was for. Even if it was from Denjer, to have the money problem resolved and behind them would allow him to move on and focus on the challenges that he wanted to focus on. Constantly thinking and worrying about money was a waste of time. He wanted to get on with his life.

So he told Lisa that he had to meet Denjer on the Vineyard and hoped that she could get her mother or Babs to take care of Sam.

"Why?" Lisa asked. "I thought you'd decided you couldn't trust him. And why Martha's Vineyard? Couldn't you meet him in Woods Hole and not have to take the ferry all the way out there?"

"Denjer is Denjer - an unexplainable force to be reckoned with. I can't explain why he does what he does. He just said that that was where he would be and if I wanted to meet him, that's where I had to go. He said he could give me a check."

Lisa was dressed in her state police uniform and had her left hand on her hip and her right hand on her gun holster. "A check?" she said. "A check for what?"

Jon was pulling on his coat. "I don't know. We'll see. I want to ask him about Nita, too."

"I thought you'd decided not to work with him?"

"We still need development money, and maybe I have this wrong. The press on the guy is overwhelmingly positive. Who knows what's real and what's rumor? I don't have to take it from him, but no one else is offering.

"I mean, it's exciting, isn't it? I mean, it could be exciting," he said with a grin. "Maybe all these money problems can be behind us today. I'll be back. Wish me luck." He gave her a quick kiss and headed out the door before she could say any more.

Confined Spaces

As Jon drove up the Mid-Cape Highway, he tried to think of all the scenarios that this overcast March day might play out. His thoughts were fragmented. There were so many unknown pieces. He kept falling into the paraphrased ear worm, "Please come to Denjer in the springtime ..."

He'd been over most of these thoughts before - parting ways with Ace, selling the house to Denjer, giving up control of Wentzell and Megquire, working with famous personalities that were connected to Denjer. No more bill collectors, dunning letters, collection agency phone calls! He would be able to concentrate on stachybotrys and carbon monoxide and lead poisoning. He could get the tools to test and measure homes and businesses. The possibilities were limitless. He didn't like the guy and he didn't trust him, but as they say, business is business.

It was still the off season, so when he reached Woods Hole, he was able to find street parking. He walked to the Steamship Authority building and bought a ticket and waited. And watched.

Big people. Small people. Workmen and mothers. People with suitcases. People with dogs. Sweatshirts with hoods. Baseball caps from New York and Detroit. All these people who wanted to be in a different place for work, for adventure, for fun, for resolution. What lives did they bring with them that were interacting in this place on this particular day and would never see each other again?

Jon wandered outside and leaned on the railing overlooking Great Harbor and the scattering of winter mooring sticks bobbing in the white-capped chop. The wind was picking up, and it was starting to drizzle.

What did Denjer want? What did Denjer want? Why Martha's Vineyard? It annoyed Jon that he wasn't working—

that he wasn't helping Ace, that he wasn't taking care of Sam, that he would even consider working with Denjer.

When the ferry finally pulled into the dock and the cars and trucks began pouring out of the ramp and the walk-on passengers flowed down the gangways to rush off to shuttle buses, Steamship Authority staff pulled back the gates and allowed the Vineyard bound passengers to file back up and into the boat.

Jon wound his way up the boarding ramp, into the ferry, and through the hallways, past empty benches to the boat's snack bar and out to the deck at the bow, where he could watch the handful of boats navigating through the treacherous Woods Hole passage between the mainland and Nonamesset Island.

Jon wanted to know what he would say to Denjer. He wanted a clear position. The path through Denjer's thoughts, however, was far less clear than the passages for boats through these waters. There were few markers. What Denjer wanted and why he wanted it was a mystery. It wasn't a one-to-one money for service arrangement. It was something else, but Jon didn't know what.

When the ferry blew its horn and pulled away from the dock, the breeze and the incipient rain on the foredeck drove Jon inside to the overheated snack bar where he sat and thought and watched for the half-hour boat ride. "Please come to Denjer .... Hey ramblin' boy, why don't you settle down ...."

* * *

As the ferry was pulling into the Oak Bluffs dock, the passengers filed out to the passageways and stairs down to exits. The boat bumped into the fenders as it came to rest and the dock lines were passed out and secured by the Steamship Authority staff. There was a tangible feeling of impatience and anticipation in the crowd as they waited to be released.

Bumped and jostled by the crowd, Jon made his way down the gangway and up the dock to the street, and stood for a moment getting his bearings. He pulled the collar up on his jacket and adjusted his cap.

It wasn't his first visit to Oak Bluffs, but it looked different in the offseason with the diminished traffic and offseason scattering of visitors. Businesses were just opening up and the street displays of T-shirts and postcards hadn't been pulled out to the sidewalks yet.

Lisa and Jon had brought Sam out to ride the horses on the Flying Horses Carousel. They were intricately carved and garishly painted, and as the carousel spun, the riders could reach for brass rings as they flew past. Jon smiled as he remembered Sam's laughter as the horses rose and fell and the calliope music filled the building and echoed off the walls. It was a family adventure ...Lisa with mustard from her pretzel on the tip of her nose, Sam bouncing through the streets clutching the string of a balloon.

Today was a different day. It was a midweek drizzling morning in March and the carousel hadn't yet opened for the season and Jon was early, so he wandered down Circuit Avenue and found a lunch counter, sat down, and scarfed down a cup of clam chowder with oyster crackers. He didn't want to buy another expensive lunch.

Back out in the rain, he stood under the carousel's roof overhang while he waited for Denjer to arrive, thinking positive thoughts about his future and everything they would be able to do when they had the resources to do it. Visions of offices and trucks and staff and testifying in front of Congress as an expert witness danced through Jon's head as he watched the flow of people.

By half-past one, Jon had begun to think that Denjer was standing him up and that this entire visit to the Vineyard was just a waste of time. Jon looked at his watch again and started to make plans for getting home before Sam went to bed. He'd picked up a ferry schedule at the terminal in Woods Hole, and he was scanning down it when a car pulled up and he heard someone yell, "Hey!"

Jon walked over to the open window and recognized Denjer, who shouted, "Get in!"

"Jesus, you're all wet," Denjer said as Jon climbed into the car.

"It's raining," Jon said.

"Well, try not to get my car seats wet. They take forever to dry out and it makes the car smell like a wet dog, which is overtly unpleasant.

"But this is the best time of year here when all the tourists aren't wandering around having their pockets picked by these enterprising pocket pickers. People buy the most amazing shit. I remember as a kid getting my parents to buy me this ceramic black fuzz covered skunk when we went to Niagara Falls on vacation. I thought that was just the best because Niagara Falls was printed on its tail. I don't know why I cared.

"I want to show you something."

Jon gripped the *Oh Shit* handle over his door as Denjer swerved to avoid a pedestrian who stopped to give the car the finger as Denjer laid on the horn.

When he had regained his composure, Jon asked, "I'm curious, Norman. Why are we here?"

Navigating through the small streets, Denjer turned to look at Jon as though he was affronted to be questioned.

"We're here because I'm here, and I want to show you something," Denjer repeated. "If you don't care, we can call this whole thing off. I've got other things to do ... a lot of things.

A whole lot of things that I could be doing rather than giving you a guided tour of Martha's Vineyard."

Jon knew he didn't need a tour of Martha's Vineyard. What he needed was a commitment of financial support.

Denjer rambled on, spewing out the description of his greatness, dropping famous names, blasting people he couldn't stand, condemning the future of the world and all the people in it, and Jon tuned it out and hung on for dear life. He wondered that Denjer's heroic public persona could be so different from the personal living reality.

Suddenly, Denjer slowed, and then swerved into the entrance to what appeared to be a private club. A subtle and dignified sign at the entrance read 'Los Tres Pinos - private'.

"This is what I wanted to show you," Norman said, as they pulled to a stop in front of a grand, New England mansion style club house. He turned to Jon and said, "See?"

Jon considered the building through the rain spattered car window. The building was pretentious, with white columns supporting a Palladian roof and full story windows glaring out at the surrounding golf course. Jon leaned over to peer up at the roof, looking for saints perched at the peak.

"Okay," he said.

"What do you mean, *okay?*" Denjer demanded.

"It's a golf club."

"*It's a golf club,*" Denjer mimicked. "*It's a golf club.* Brilliant! It's not just any golf club. This is Los Tres Pinos. THE Los Tres Pinos. This is where presidents play. This is where movie stars play. This *golf club* is known around the world. This is where the PGA holds world class tournaments."

Jon knew he was meant to be impressed, that he was meant to express his awe and wonder and just sitting there in the rain in front of this clubhouse for an experience that he would never forget.

But he wasn't impressed. "Wow," he said.

"Get out of the car," Denjer demanded, jumping out onto the drive and storming off in the direction of the building's entrance.

Jon followed more slowly.

Inside the lobby, the doorman greeted Denjer by name. "Good afternoon, Mr. Denjer. I'm afraid the course isn't open today."

"That's okay, my man. That's okay. I'm just showing my friend the building in case he wants to join. What's the waiting list now? A few hundred names? A few thousand dollars a year just for the privilege of waiting?" Denjer laughed.

Jon nodded to the doorman and smiled. He felt underdressed in his jeans, boots, and Carhartt work jacket.

"This could be yours," Denjer said. "You could be a member here or anywhere you liked. You play golf?"

"Don't exactly have time for it."

"No? Well, you should. That's how you make connections. Move up in life. The best business connections get made on the golf course. You could make putts with royalty. You could get that pretty wife of yours into the movies. Clubs like this are the doors to the castle. Maybe I'll let you join mine."

Jon had no desire to join a club like this. The magic of following a little white ball around the manicured grass trying to whack it into a gopher hole had never grabbed his soul.

Denjer was spinning around in the lobby like Julie Andrews in the Alps, waving his arms around, and then he turned and stormed back out through the doors and into the rain. He stopped at the edge of the drive, looking out over the rolling fairways of the course and put his hands on his hips.

Jon came up beside him and tried to see what Denjer was seeing.

"Pocatuck," Denjer said. "That's what you said its name was, didn't you?"

"Yes. That's the name of the Schmidt's property."

Denjer turned and looked at Jon. There was water dripping off his eyebrows.

Denjer rushed back to the car. "We've got to hurry. Reservation on the freight boat back to Woods Hole."

Jon hung on as Denjer rushed back through the narrow roads to the Oak Bluffs ferry terminal, arriving just in time to join the line of tractor trailers, pickup trucks, and cars driving onto the boat.

Denjer was grinning. "I'm sure they would have held the boat for me. They know who I am. So there was no need to rush."

The freight boat, the Katama, had an open vehicle deck and a small area to accommodate passengers. Denjer's car was dwarfed by the semis parked close to it on either side. Denjer made no move to get out.

"More comfortable here than up there in the passenger area," Denjer said. "Unless you have to tinkle. Can't do that in my car."

"I'm okay," Jon said.

The wind had picked up and despite the size of the ferry, they could feel the pitch and yaw of the disturbed sea.

"So that's what I'm going to do with Pocatuck. I'm going to create the most impressive, world class golf resort on the planet, a place where the PGA will be honored to hold tournaments. Pete Dye is going to design the course. I've already talked to him about it. You know Pete, don't you? He's designed Harbor Town on Hilton Head and Sawgrass in Florida. Brilliant guy. Brilliant."

Jon wanted to get out of the car. He was feeling nauseous. He wanted to get home. He didn't want to talk about golf course designers, so he interrupted Denjer and asked, "Are we going to talk about Wentzell and Megquire? Are you going to invest? You said something about a check?"

Denjer looked at him. "I want you to help me buy Pocatuck."

"Okay," Jon said. "I don't know what I can do, but I'd be glad to do what I can. But it's up to Minky Schmidt. Arthur wanted it turned over to the Wampanoag. He asked me to help Minky to make that happen."

Denjer open the utility box between the front seats of the car and pulled out a revolver and put it in his lap.

Jon's eyes widened.

"I want you to help me," Denjer repeated.

"What the hell is that for? Are you going to shoot me?"

Denjer laughed. It was an uncanny, hollow sound, like the branch of a dead tree scraping against the side of a house. "No. No. Of course not. I don't like guns. I really don't. Revolvers are special, aren't they? You can actually see where the bullet is if you know how to look at it right. No. No. I'm not going to shoot you in my car. Blood would be so much harder to clean up than that rain water you brought in earlier.

"No. No. I just want you to understand how serious I am about Pocatuck. Guns are serious, Jon. I'm just underlining my point here. That's why I took you to see Los Tres Pinos. You've got to protect yourself ... and your family."

Denjer had the revolver in his right hand and he looked up from it to Jon's face. "I'll help you. I told you I'd help you build your business, and I always do what I say I'm going to do. As soon as I have an agreement to buy that land. And I want to buy it. I wouldn't have to, you know? I have what they call an *outstanding interest* in the property, you know? My team found the paperwork. Some sort of family gambling debt a long time ago. I didn't know about it. No one ever told me, but apparently it went back years. Years! So I wouldn't have to buy. I could just defend my rightful claim to it."

Jon had nowhere to go. The ferry was in the middle of Vineyard Sound. Wrestling the gun away from Denjer in the front seat of the car was a poor resolution to the situation.

"Okay, Norman. Okay," Jon said. "I get the message. I'll do what I can. Why don't you put the gun away? We'll be in Woods Hole in a few minutes. I'll talk to Minky for you. Let her know how serious you are, and I'm sure that she will listen. Okay? You don't need to have that gun. I get your message."

"Soon?" Denjer asked.

"Okay. Okay. Soon."

Denjer studied Jon's face, and the silence was oppressive.

Finally, Denjer smiled and opened the utility box again and laid the revolver down inside it. "Okay," he said. "Okay. I'm going to trust you."

He paused, and then continued, "But I know where you live."

Chapter Eighteen

Jon's head was spinning when he got home, busted through the front door, and threw off his coat.

Lisa was getting Sam cleaned up for supper. She turned as Jon stomped into the room.

"How was that?" she asked.

"You won't believe it!" Jon said, trying to keep his voice down and smile for his son.

Sam said, "I'm very nice that you tried to share with everybody. Yes, it's very nicely trying to try it yeah and you liked it when mommy read that to me or daddy read that to me yeah do you like going to the library don't you? I like going to the library. Yeah, libraries are a fun place, so exciting because there's books about everything."

"Who took you to the library?" Jon asked.

"Aunty Dot took me. She wanted a book. She knows all sorts of things."

Dot was Lisa's mother and Sam was her only grandchild, so he was bound to be full of sugar after the day.

"I'm glad," Jon said. To Lisa he said, "I need a beer ... or something stronger." And he left the room.

When Lisa joined him in the living room, she asked, "So what happened? Did you have a nice sea cruise on your day off?"

"You won't believe it. He pulled a gun on me."

"He what?"

"He had a gun in his car and he pulled it out and waved it around."

"Did he threaten you with it? What did he do?"

Jon jumped up and paced across the room.

"The whole thing was strange. I mean, why did he need me to go all the way out to the Vineyard on a shitty day like this, and drive me to a country club?"

Lisa sighed. "Was the gun loaded?"

"How would I know?" Jon asked. "How? He didn't shoot it. We were in his car on the ferry. He wasn't going to chase me around the ferry with the boat bobbing and rolling and the rain coming down, firing his gun!" Jon snorted.

"Start from the beginning," Lisa said calmly.

Jon recounted getting to the Flying Horses early, standing in the rain, and wondering if Denjer was going to show up. "I hate waiting," he said. "There's no way to know if the other person is going to show ... especially Denjer. I shouldn't have gone."

He told Lisa about Denjer's hair raising, driving through the streets of Oak Bluffs and then out to the fancy country club. "Ever hear of Los Tres Pinos? Denjer said it was famous."

"I think I remember some chatter about celebrities out there, but that is out of my jurisdiction."

"Anyway, apparently he's a member there. Then we rush back to the ferry, the Katama, and drove right on. He said they would have held it for him. Not likely!"

"Why didn't you get out of the car?"

"The Katama is a freight boat. The passenger accommodations are an afterthought."

"So what did he want? Why did he pull out his gun? We can arrest him for that."

"He wants Pocatuck. He wants to turn it into a resort."

Lisa asked, "What does that have to do with you?"

Jon sat down on the sofa next to Lisa and said, "He thinks I have some magic connection to Minky Schmidt because Arthur guaranteed the Wentzell and Megquire loan."

Lisa got up. "You have to get away from that man, Jon. Even if he gave you a million dollars, it would be so tangled up in spider webbed strings that our life would be pure hell."

"But that still leaves the problem of the bank," Jon said to Lisa. "We don't have an extra ten thousand dollars kicking around. If they call the loan, we're really screwed."

"I thought you said that Denjer was going to give you a check?"

Jon snorted. "He said he was, but it never came up. But, I think the bank is being unreasonable. I mean, if we had that kind of money available, we wouldn't need the bank! It's the proverbial Catch 22."

As Lisa worked on supper, Sam was entertaining himself in the living room, singing songs he made up as he went along, crashing cars. The house had a bit of a chill from the late March air. The steam heating system was making the pipes click and hiss. Jon thought of the old boiler in the basement burning up the oil. They had to buy oil a hundred gallons at a time, and at a dollar seventy-five a gallon that was a hundred and seventy-five dollars a pop, which happened at least once a month during the cold weather. He was eager for the winter to end.

"I've got to get that disk that Nita gave me over to Babs and see what she can extract from it. We need to know."

"I hope Nita's okay," Lisa said. "I haven't heard from her. Too bad we didn't get to talk with her after her gig. I hope she's okay."

"I do too," Jon said. "Maybe we'll know more when we find out what's on that disk."

"Call Babs. See if you can go over there tonight."

"I will. After we eat," Jon said.

* * *

IN THE WENTZELL'S KITCHEN, Ace was reading the *New York Times*. When he had stopped smoking his pipe, it appeared his face was missing a piece - the pipe had been so much a part of him. Jon had a hard time getting used to it. But Ace's doctor had told him he had to stop - and Babs enforced it. And he stopped, but he fidgeted with his fingers.

Jon described Denjer's Vineyard craziness and Nita's concert in Cambridge. He pulled out Nita's disk and handed it to Babs. "I don't know what's on it," he said.

"Oh, how exciting! A mystery!" Babs said. "I'm flattered you think I can open this."

"I have no doubt."

Jon and Ace chatted about the business. "You know the bank wants us to pay down the loan," Jon said. "The banker said that he thought it would be a *good idea* if we reduced the principal amount by ten thousand dollars."

"Pssft!" Ace huffed. "Bankers. Lawyers. Politicians. They don't have a clue about how the world works. Probably done nothing useful in their lives."

"I mean, if we had an extra ten grand hanging around, we wouldn't need the loan."

Ace sipped his reheated coffee. "So, what are you going to do?"

"I'm hoped that Norman Denjer would invest. That would take a load off, but he wants to make changes to the company, and I don't know if we want him to have that kind of control. He may know a lot about business and he certainly has a lot of connections and having him as an investor ... you know ... gives the company a kind of legitimacy. Know what I mean? I mean, the guy is a star. He's all over the media. It's like having a Rockefeller as a personal investor. But he's crazy."

"Pssft!"

"You don't think so?"

Ace folded up the newspaper and reached for his coffee and coughed. And coughed.

Jon asked, "You okay?"

Ace struggled to control the coughing. "Damn! Giving up the pipe was supposed to stop the coughing. Seems worse. Maybe I should go back to it."

"Can I get you some water?"

"Nah. Got my coffee." He took a gulp. "I've dealt with people like Denjer before. They're like a farmer's back porch light in the summer. The moths flutter around it, believing they can absorb the light, that they too can shine that brightly, repeatedly banging against the glass until they crash and burn." Ace watched Jon's face. "It's best to stay away. It might seem like a good idea, particularly when everyone else is fluttering around too. But then the farmer turns out the light and goes to bed. Where does that leave the moths?"

"That's deep, Ace."

He laughed and started coughing again.

"How does that help us with the bank? Are you saying I shouldn't ask Denjer for it?"

"I can do that."

"You'll talk to Denjer and ask him for ten thousand dollars?"

"No," Ace said. "Babs and I'll put the money in and get the bank off our backs."

Jon laughed. "Really? You holding out on me, Ace?"

"The fact is, I'm never going to retire. What the hell am I going to do? My golf game sucks, and I have no desire to go cruising - in any sense of that word. I like it here. No, we set aside some money, but I don't know what it's good for if it doesn't let you do what you want to do. You've got a great family, Jon," Ace said. "Money isn't life. Sometimes we lose track of that. The fact is ...and I've said this before ...the fact is that we work to live. We don't live to work. Money is just a token. It might sound hokey, but I'm old enough to be a bit hokey. But there are a lot of people who love you. That's what's in your bank."

Jon smiled. "Wow, Ace, you are a never-ending source of surprises."

"I'll have to check with Babs, but I think she likes you. And she loves that son of yours!"

Serendipity, Jon's mother used to say. It's just an instance of serendipity. Positive and unexpected.

Babs came into the kitchen with a handful of papers and a guilty smile on her face. "Is this what they call 'hacking'?" she asked.

"I don't think it's hacking," Jon said. "You didn't break into a computer system by stealing a password. What did you find on the disk?"

"Well," Babs said, drawing out the word, "seems like a bit of hanky-panky to me. I can't be sure without seeing his other accounting, but it seems like Mr. Denjer is making up stories by playing with his numbers. He's imaginative with his names like 'Betty Davis Isles', 'Thumper's Thicket', and 'Pinocchio Plaza'. Who names places like that? Doesn't that sound fishy to you?"

Ace got up and poured some more leftover coffee into his mug and heated it in the microwave.

"What are you going on about?" he asked his wife.

"No, you see. There are these names that are associated with the profit-and-loss statements and cash flows that are highly improbable. They just make little sense. I mean, I've looked at a bunch of balance sheets and P and L statements, and these are definitely fictional - even if they weren't associated with the peculiar names."

She spread the papers out on the kitchen table and explained what she was describing.

"Someone must have known," she said.

"Why do you say that?" Jon asked.

Babs dropped into a chair at the end of the table. "Because," she said, "someone gave you this disk. Is it from Mr. Denjer that you've been talking about?"

"Lisa's friend Nita gave it to me."

"How did she get it?"

Jon sucked in his breath. "She works for Denjer. Cleaning his house."

"Didn't you just tell us that someone dragged her away at the end of her concert?" Ace asked.

* * *

When Jon got back home, he told Lisa about Ace and Babs coming up with the ten grand to take care of the bank and they hugged and Jon did a little dance. Getting the bank off his back without having to beg Norman Denjer for the money was like getting out from under a collapsed hotel lobby - a unique and very personal experience.

Maybe economic insecurity isn't a big thing. Things could be worse, Jon rationalized. They could live in a cardboard box on the street. There could be rebel takeovers, religious insecurities, and conflicts, Gestapo banging on the door, the Inquisition about to haul them away to be tortured. It could be worse than a thousand dollar credit card bill or being late on the electric. But economic insecurity caused people to fling themselves out of the windows of high-rise buildings, attempt murder, or commit serious crimes. He wasn't there yet. He was surrounded by people he loved and people who loved him. But he still wasn't eager to answer the phone when it rang.

"Hello?" Jon said when he finally picked up the receiver.

It wasn't one of those snarky voices demanding to know if Mr. Megquire was at home. There wasn't a canned flow of threatening or cajoling phrases demanding payment on an overdue bill. But Jon didn't immediately recognize the female voice.

"Jon?"

"Yes?"

"It's me. It's Gail Barker."

A momentary pause as Jon's thoughts shifted from anxiety to pleasure. "Gail!" he said. "It's so great to hear from you. I'm so sorry I haven't checked back with you. I hope you are doing well."

"I'm okay," she said.

"Thanks for calling. I should have called you. Damn. I think I'm getting old. I forget things all the time. So how are you?"

Jon put his hand over the receiver and shouted to Lisa in the kitchen, "It's Gail! Gail Barker. False alarm."

"I'm good," Gail said, when he lifted the receiver back up to his ear. "I don't know if I'll ever get used to this wheelchair. Stairways become impossible mountains. Until you get there, you can't imagine a world without working legs."

"I can imagine," Jon said.

There was a moment of silence.

"What's the prognosis?" he asked.

"I'm in rehab, and god, that's a lot of work. The doctors say that it looks good. It's not like I'm going to have to get my legs amputated or anything."

Jon winced.

"Walking just seems so basic," she said. "Gives you a different perspective on life when you can't."

"We did that in summer camp. They wanted to sensitize us to handicaps, so they blindfolded us and made us try to walk around and do things. They covered up our ears so we couldn't hear anything. That was great. I couldn't hear people yelling at me."

Gail laughed. "Why would people yell at you?"

"I don't know. You know camp counselors are just kids with new power. They want younger kids to jump when they say 'Jump!' But when you can't hear them, you can ignore them."

"Unfortunately," Gail said, "this isn't summer camp and they won't be taking restraints off my legs. My life has changed. People look at me differently. They certainly treat me differently."

"I can imagine." Actually, Jon couldn't imagine. He could only speculate. Imagining only kissed the surface. It couldn't get immersed in the sensations, feelings, thoughts, emotions of losing the ability to walk. Jon felt anger for what had happened to Gail rising from his stomach.

There was another chunk of silence. "Listen," she said,

"That's not why I called you. I didn't call you to complain ... except about the cause. I called to warn you. Did Norman Denjer invest in your company?"

"We're still talking about it."

"Don't," she said.

"Don't what?"

"Don't let him invest in your company. In fact, don't let him do anything. He's an evil man. You don't want to associate with him. You need to see that. I told you he was the one that developed the Patriot Grand Hotel."

"I remember. I remember it all. The noise. The sound. The smells. Jesus, I'll have nightmares about that for years. Probably for the rest of my life. I know you said Denjer had something to do with that?"

Gail said, "Absolutely."

"Oh." Jon pulled the receiver away from his ear and looked down at Stogie, who was lying at his feet, casually wagging his tail, thumping against the floor.

"I've been doing research. Reading all the accounts. I have engineering friends who have been getting me updates."

"I know they say the person at the top ... you know, the buck stops here kind of thing, but was Denjer himself involved?"

"They didn't even bother to review the engineering reports. Those walkways were hung from the ceiling and from each other. They used the wrong nuts. It's just that simple."

"Denjer wouldn't know a hex nut from a butter knife. Wouldn't that be on the engineers? Doesn't that mean that he just hired bad engineers?"

"Denjer wanted it finished. He wanted to open the hotel, so he cut corners. He didn't wait for the right materials. He didn't believe the engineers. I don't know what he was thinking.

You can't think how that man thinks. He had everyone fooled that he knew what he was doing and that it would all work, because he said it would. And now I can't walk and forty people are dead. Two more today. Two more who didn't survive their injuries."

"Shit," Jon mumbled.

"All because that man couldn't wait. You don't want to work with him."

"I can't believe it. How could someone be that ...? How could someone be like that? Do you think he knew? Maybe the engineers didn't tell him." But the Denjer's credibility was growing increasingly bad.

"If he didn't know, he should have," Gail said. "He's responsible. I'm still working on all the connections. As you can imagine, there is a pile of paperwork and assholes like this are going to be good at covering their tracks and putting the blame on someone else."

"I can imagine," he said.

"There are lawyers crawling all over this."

Jon thought of hundreds of black ants swarming over a pile of sand. That was construction, too.

"And Denjer has his own army fighting them off," Gail said.

"Of course he does," Jon said.

Another slug of silence.

"I remembered you had mentioned that you went to school with the guy and that you were thinking of working with him, so I thought I should warn you."

"Thanks. Yeah. I did go to school with him. He seems interested in my construction company. We could use some financial support. You should see his office. It's in the freakin' clouds in downtown Boston."

"Stay away from him, Jon," Gail said. "Stay away."

Confined Spaces

* * *

"I'm taking Stogie out," Jon shouted to Lisa after he had hung up the phone.

What now, Jon wondered. Every time you think things are coming together, some piece of it falls apart. It's like building a house out of cards. No. Worse than that, because cards have flat edges and straight lines. This is a like a gelatin house.

He clipped Stogie's leash to his collar while the dog enthusiastically pulled toward the door. His was a simple life with simple pleasures. Smell. Piss. Shit. Smell. Piss. Shit. Eat. Sleep. Head scratch. Head scratch. Excellent stuff.

The mid-March Cape Cod evening air was spectacular as Jon stepped out of the house - redolent of the warming earth, coming back to life. Touch of salt and seaweed. Buds on the branches. Grass greening, heading for the first mow.

Stogie bounced his way from new smell to new smell, marking the boundaries of his world.

He had started to think that things were coming together. The fact was that he didn't want to work with Denjer. There had to be an alternative.

And now? Jon kicked a branch off the street.

Well? He knew ... he had known that Denjer wasn't the nicest person. That didn't come as a surprise. The man was a businessman. He made no bones about the fact that altruism was not his goal in life. Profit. Making money. Prosperity. Those were his motivators. That's what made him tick. And wasn't that what Jon was looking for in a business relationship? So why should it come as a surprise that he wanted to optimize those things?

Jon looked up as a chevron of Canadian geese crossed the evening sky - shouting, calling to each other, adjusting their course, seeking a place for the night.

Was it really Denjer's fault that the engineers screwed up the design of those walkways? It was horrible that all those people had died. All those lives and all those families. Jon was lucky to have gotten out as well as he had. And Gail in a wheelchair. Shit. Her life must have changed a lot. Was she still working on toxics? Did she still have a job?

He should have asked her. Should've ... Should've... Should've ...

Stogie had found his spot and assumed the position, bending in the middle, smelling the surrounding ground seeking "reading material" while he pooped.

Jon looked around. Up at the sky. Down the street. And waited.

Should he keep working with Denjer? Was it a moral issue? Was it immoral to work with an immoral person? If that was the case ... a lot of business wouldn't get done. And maybe it shouldn't. Jon struggled to see a clear path ... A black and white direction.

* * *

BACK IN THE HOUSE, he unhooked Stogie's leash and banged the front door closed.

Sam was up in his chair at the table having a 'nack'. Jon kissed him on the top of his head and Sam reached up with a hand covered in peanut butter and grabbed his shirt. "What's that? It'll be like toast. Then you finger off the g'olive oil. Mommy 'ead so."

Jon pulled away and leaned back. "Is that right? Mommy said so? What did mommy say?"

"Garlic bread," Lisa replied. "He's talking about making garlic bread. We did that together, didn't we, Sammy?"

"Garlic bread? Yum," Jon said, smiling at Sam and grabbing

Lisa around the waist and pulling her to him. He leaned over the stove and lifted the top of the big pasta pot. "What else you got cookin'?"

Lisa pushed him away and told him to behave himself. He went back out to the front hall and leafed through the mail Lisa had left on the table. Bills and advertising fliers. No magic check from Publishers Clearing House.

Back in the kitchen, he dropped into a chair.

"Oh, I didn't tell you what Babs found on Nita's disk. It's pretty strange. Like weird names like 'Pinocchio's Plaza'. Babs thinks the numbers are bogus too. Like Denjer's making stuff up, seeing what works, trying to put together believable real estate scenarios. And it's strange that Nita got that disk from Denjer's wife."

"Desert!" Sam shouted.

"You have to wait, buddy. We haven't even eaten the spaghetti or the garlic bread yet."

"Desert!"

"Desert comes at the end of the meal."

"I'm done," Sam said and started climbing down out of his chair.

"So what's it have to do with you?" Lisa asked.

Jon wondered if he should have compelled Sam to stay in his seat until they'd all had supper. When he was growing up, the family all sat down together and ate together and asked to be excused from the table when the meal was finished. Parenting styles changed. Manners and mores changed. Parenting didn't come with an operations handbook, and Lisa's childhood had differed from his. Not better. Not worse. Just different. The key was to prevent Sam from growing up to be a drug dealing serial killer, and getting down from the table early seemed like a minor concession.

"Have you heard from Nita?" he asked as Sam thumped off

into the living room. Jon wondered when the Parlor had become the Living Room. And some houses now called them the Family Room or the Great Room. He could see why old-time builders like his partner were grumpy about constant change.

"I haven't," Lisa said as she poured the cooked spaghetti into a colander in the sink. She dumped a jar of sauce into the empty pot and put it back on the stove. "I would have thought she would have checked back about that disk."

"Do you know any of the people in her music group? They might be able to explain who that guy was that whisked her away. Maybe there's a simple explanation."

Lisa poured the spaghetti back into the pot with the sauce. "See if you can wrestle the Puddin' back up into his seat."

When they were at the table working on the spaghetti, Jon said, "And that's another thing. Don't you think it's surprising that Denjer didn't know about Pocatuck? You'd think he'd be monitoring ownership records and who dies. When real estate is tight - like apartments in Manhattan - people read the obituaries to find vacant apartments. And this is almost three thousand acres of land in Plymouth?"

"Maybe he doesn't look," Lisa said.

"'Have-your-people-call-my-people' to set something up' attitude? Must be nice."

"How are you going to handle it? Are you still going to ask him to invest in W and M?"

Jon stirred his spaghetti around on his plate. "It's going to be tough to do what he wants. I'm not going to ask Ace to retire and I don't know how I can get Minky Schmidt to sell him Pocatuck. At the core, W and M is just a construction firm. Ace is what makes it unique with his knowledge and craftsmanship. If you cut Ace out, what you have left is another construction company. Is the money worth that?"

The phone rang. They both looked at each other. Jon put down his fork.

"Ignore it," Lisa said.

"Can't do that. We can't hide in our own home."

He left the kitchen on the fifth ring, walked into the dim light of the hallway, and picked up the receiver.

Chapter Nineteen

Jon was relieved to hear Lash's voice. "Did you find anything more about those toxic sites?" Jon asked.

"Mr. Denjer has been up to some Machiavellian machinations," Lash said, once Jon recognized the voice on the phone.

"He's been up to what with what?"

"Weren't you an English major?" Lash asked. "Machiavelli was a wicked man, as I understand it. They say he was a counselor of evil."

"Outstanding!"

"And it turns out that 'Summer Meadows' is a Denjer Development project. Developers seem to like to be poetic, as though buyers will associate fancy names with fancy places. I would bet that there aren't any meadows around there."

Jon said, "And you would be right."

"And that's exactly right. That's what it was - a toxic waste dump. I told you that. They used to make thumb tacks around there."

"I remember you telling me that," Jon said. "How do you know Denjer developed it?"

Lash snorted. "Well, I did some digging into Denjer Development and 'Summer Meadows' was buried in the holding company's legal shit."

"Denjer?"

"Yah. Denjer. But wait there's more," Lash said.

"Great," Jon replied. He sat down on the floor in the hall with his back on the wall and the twisty cord to the phone bouncing from the handset to the base. Stogie came trotting in and stuck his nose in Jon's face.

"A bit of digging turned up that Denjer Development is buying toxic properties and building on them. The land is cheap and apparently lost in government bureaucracy."

"So, there are more toxic developments?"

"You bet," Lash said. "And get this, they're building one off the other."

"What's that mean?"

"That means that Denjer Development is paying for one project with the investors in another. It's a real estate Ponzi scheme."

"Oh, shit," Jon said. He pulled his knees up and twiddled the twisty phone cord around his fingers.

"Oh, shit, is right," Lash said. "The investors love the cash flow. They keep getting paid. They think Denjer is a real estate genius."

"Yeah, but the homeowners are getting screwed. I've got to get Brenda out of there. Her house is going to be worthless when this comes out."

"But wait. There's more," Lash said.

"More?"

"They're not all real."

"What? What do you mean 'they're not all real'?"

"Denjer makes up names and concocts fictional developments like 'Pine Valley' and 'Crest View'. Those places don't exist, but the investors are so convinced that Denjer knows what he's doing, they don't even ask for the prospectuses."

Jon jumped to his feet. "That would explain those weird names on the disk I got from Nita." He told Lash about the disk and how he had Babs read it because the disk wouldn't fit in his Mac.

"That connects," Lash said. "His investors just believe in him. They just give him money. Because he gives it back to them in spades. They don't ask if it's real. They don't ask to see the property. In fact, they're afraid to ask."

"What do you mean 'they're afraid to ask'?"

"If they ask about it, he gets mad and tells them that if they don't believe him, he'll send their money back, but that's the last investment they'll ever make with Denjer Development."

Jon said, "I remember my father telling me about shit like that going on in the twenties in Florida when they were selling swamp land."

"What are you going to do?" Lash asked.

Jon scratched Stogie's head. "I don't know."

"It's all fiction. It's all smoke and mirrors. It's all based on the wizard behind the curtain. Fairy tales are all about the suspension of disbelief. The Wizard of Oz. Peter Pan. The Norse gods. The Greek gods. People believed they existed. And they fought and died for them. People seem to think that Denjer is another one of those fictional gods."

Jon looked up at the stairs. "Do you think he took Nita? I'll call her. Let her know what we've found."

"I'll keep digging."

"This guy is pissing me off," Jon said, as he stared up at the water stain on the ceiling. "He really is starting to piss me off."

"Good luck with that," Lash laughed.

* * *

Nita didn't answer her phone when Jon called.

He had related his conversation with Lash to Lisa. She was stunned and told him again he had to stop dealing with Denjer.

"He's going to end up in jail," she said, "and I don't want you to go with him."

"Why would I go with him?"

"Because you're trying to get him to put that dirty money into your company. When the Feds find out about this - and they will, no doubt - they're going to tear apart every connection the man made."

"Shit," Jon said. "You're right."

Lisa smiled.

But Nita hadn't answered her phone. She didn't have an answering machine.

Jon asked, "Do you know where she lives?"

"Cambridge, I think."

"Can't you do one of those reverse look-up-police-search things?"

"Not from home," Lisa said.

Jon got up from the kitchen table and paced out into the living room. How far did Denjer's damage go? he wondered. He was a powerful man. An enormous web of mystique surrounded him, and that web was no doubt populated by powerful people with powerful interests.

Jon paced.

Who would he tell? He couldn't just call the FBI and tell them that Norman Denjer was a crook.

And then his father came into his thoughts. His father had suggested he seek Denjer's advice.

Jon called, and after the opening conversational preliminaries, he asked, "Did you ever invest in Norman Denjer's company?"

"Patera Healthcare has a diversified portfolio. I don't know all the individual holdings," Andy Megquire replied.

"No, but you were the one that suggested I should work with Denjer. Was that because you had investments with him?"

Jon heard family activities in the background.

"It's funny that you should ask," Andrew said. "I just got a call from his company today. They apparently have a new project coming up."

"Don't do it, dad," Jon said. "The man's a crook."

"What? What makes you say that?"

Jon explained what Lash had discovered.

"That can't be right," Andrew said. "The man is a renowned real estate genius. Everyone wants to invest with him."

"Think about it, dad. What have you always told me? If it's too good to be true, it probably isn't. Right?"

Jon could feel his father thinking on the other end of the phone line. He listened to his own house and heard Lisa trying to convince Sam to use the potty.

"Could be just a coincidence," his father said.

"What? That Denjer's properties are built on toxic sites? That his developments don't exist?"

"That's my point. If the properties don't exist, how did you find them?"

"Did you ever visit one of his properties?"

"No. I can't say that I have."

"Well, I have. Babs' sister, Brenda Downs, lives in Summer Meadows, here on the Cape. Her house is toxic."

"That's awful," his father said. "But maybe that's an anomaly. How do you know that the whole site is toxic? If the government thought it was toxic, they wouldn't have let anyone build on it."

Jon told his father what Lash had discovered about the thumb tack company. "And besides, Lisa is constantly finding kids from there with serious delinquency issues."

"Are they connected?"

"I've read the research. There's this outstanding book called *Crime and Human Nature*. You should read it. The author points out that exposure to environmental toxins - especially lead - early in life impact the anti-social behavior and can lead to elevated rates of crime in communities."

"I should read that."

"You should," Jon said. "It certainly impacts your business, right? Health care? I mean, come on."

"So, what are you saying?"

"You haven't visited any of the sites you're investing in. Have you ever read a property prospectus from Denjer? Does this sound like a Ponzi scheme to you?"

"If what you're saying is right, there's going to be a lot of very upset people - powerful upset people. People don't enjoy being told they've been fooled. You better be sure of your facts before you go public with this - or make accusations or report it to the ... I don't know... the SEC?"

Tomb silence on the other end of the phone line. Jon's father was a smart man. He had done well in his job. He was one of the most honest and decent people that Jon knew. It was almost impossible for Jon to believe that someone like his father could be suckered in by Denjer.

"I hope you're wrong," Andrew said.

Jon sucked in his breath. "I hope I am too. But I don't think so."

* * *

THE FACT WAS that they didn't have concrete evidence. The beauty of this crime, as Jon saw it, was that … it didn't exist. It was a crime of make-believe. Jon was not a real estate lawyer. He wasn't a lawyer at all. He knew nothing about any of this, which was why he had gone to Denjer for help. Denjer was the wizard-with-the-money who was supposed to boost Wentzell and Megquire into the big time.

That wasn't going to happen. It would be stupid to take it any further.

Once they had gotten Sam off to bed, Lisa joined Jon at the kitchen table, and Jon laid out everything that Lash had told him and his father's reaction.

"I can't believe that my father could be suckered in like that?" he said. "What is it about that guy? He has some sort of animal magnetism that makes people just want to believe him."

"You were," Lisa said.

"What?"

"You thought he was going to be our saving grace."

Jon looked up from his coffee cup.

"I did, but my father suggested it."

"Don't blame your father."

Jon changed the subject. "I hope Nita's okay. If Denjer found out that she knows what he's been doing … god knows what the man can do."

"He may be a creep," Lisa said, "but he's not a killer … is he?"

Jon snorted. "Hard to tell."

And then the phone rang again.

"Damn," Jon said. "Don't they ever leave us alone? It's like Grand Central Station around here. I hate telephones."

"We're not here," Jon said into the phone when he picked it up.

There was a moment's pause and then a man said, "That's too bad because I have something you might want to know."

That wasn't the usual opening for a bill collector, but it wasn't a voice that he recognized. "Who's this?" he asked.

"Reid Trask."

It didn't immediately register for Jon. There was no context. So many out of sequence events were flying around in his head. "Who?"

"Reid Trask. I worked for Norman Denjer. Went to Boundbrook. I saw you in his office."

"Reid! What the hell? I didn't recognize your voice. What's going on, man?"

"Denjer fired me."

Jon wondered if Reid was looking for a job. That wasn't going to happen.

"What's up, Reid?"

Trask said, "He did me a favor ... firing me. I was about to quit, anyway. The man's a bastard."

"I'm recognizing that," Jon said. "Why were you working for him?"

"Long story. Could we get together? Do you ever get up to Boston?"

"I build houses down here on the Cape."

"I know. You're married to State Trooper, Lisa Prence Megquire. You have a son: Samuel Reesor Megquire, and a dog named Stogie. You work with toxic land issues and your company built a house in Summer Meadows."

"Thanks for reminding me," Jon said with a snort. "How the hell do you know all that? Better question is, why do you know all that?"

"I worked for Denjer. My job was to get him all the information about everyone he worked with. Your social security number is 045-21 ..."

"Okay. Okay. I believe you."

"Why would he fire you?"

"Because he thought I missed that property that you brought to his attention."

"Shit. Sorry about that. Pocatuck. Belongs to the Schmidt family. Do you remember Dabney Schmidt from Boundbrook?"

Silence. Silence.

"Reid?" Jon said, wondering if he had lost the connection.

"I don't want to do this over the phone," Reid said finally. "Maybe we can meet half-way? At the bridge."

"The Sagamore or the Bourne?"

"Sagamore," Reid said. "Tomorrow? About noon?"

"Let me look at my calendar. Oh, wait, you probably already know my schedule's clear tomorrow, although I have no idea how you would know that."

Reid laughed.

* * *

In the shadow of the Sagamore Bridge over the Cape Cod Canal sat a chain family restaurant that presented a wholesome appearance with a replicable layout and color scheme. In this non-challenging environment, Jon settled into a booth to wait for Reid Trask. Jon had arrived first and was guided to the booth by the hostess, who appeared she had been waitressing all her life and called him "Honey" and informed him that Ramona would be there soon to take care of him. Jon thanked her and scanned the menu while he waited. Eventually "Ramona" came by, chewing gum, and asked him if wanted coffee. "Black," he said with a smile.

Jon remembered little about Reid, and he didn't know if he could trust him. They weren't close at Boundbrook. Reid had been in the class ahead of him and people change in ten plus years since they had left the school. Men grow beards, lose their hair, start wearing glasses, gain weight, and lose weight. Jon wondered what Trask couldn't talk about on the phone.

Trask arrived and stood momentarily at the reception desk, scanning the room. He was short and heavy and there were hints of gray in his wavy, chestnut brown hair. He wore aviator glasses and a black topcoat with the collar pulled up. He had one hand thrust into his pocket, which he extracted and pointed at Jon when the hostess approached him.

Jon raised his hand in a perfunctory wave, and Trask weaved his way between the other tables, pulling off the topcoat as he walked. They exchanged introductory smiles, greetings, and identifying remarks, and Trask settled onto the bench across from Jon.

They exchanged a brief rundown of what they had been doing in the intervening years since they had left Boundbrook with a few laughs and a handful of snorts and reminiscences of masters and other students. Jon asked if Trask had gone back for anything like reunions and if the school was still the way he remembered it when he was there.

"So, how did you connect with Norman Denjer?" Jon asked. "He was ahead of us, and in those days, seniors were gods. Ancient and worldly. Something to aspire to. Denjer, especially since he was president of the class. I don't think I ever talked to him when I was there."

Trask's expression grayed as though rain clouds had taken over his eyes. If his ears could have drooped, they would have.

"He fired me," Trask said. "For no reason at all."

"You told me," Jon said.

"Yah, well, the man's a lunatic. You do not know what goes on there."

Jon waited for further explanation.

Ramona came by with her pad and pencil at the ready, snapping her gum. "What'll it be?" she asked.

Jon ordered a burger while Trask quickly scanned through the menu and then said, "Same."

Ramona scribbled, smiled, took their menus, and walked away.

"So tell me," Jon said, leaning on the table.

Trask looked around at the other tables and then leaned in toward Jon and lowered his voice. "Part of it," Trask said, "is that Denjer develops on toxic sites. He buys cheap land and then develops them without telling the homeowners ... or anyone else ... that the land their homes are built on might kill them. The land is cheap so he can make a humongous profit. And he passes the profit back to his investors so they think he's a genius at real estate. I'm sure you've read the stories."

"I sort of figured that out. I did some research. I mean, the toxic stuff, that's what I do. A friend of mine lives in one of those sites here on the Cape. A place called Summer Meadows. My partner built one of the houses. Turns out to be one of Denjer's developments."

"How's that working out?" Trask asked.

"And my wife, Lisa ... she's a state trooper ... there is a lot of juvenile crime coming from there."

Although Trask hadn't added sugar or milk to his coffee, he stirred it thoughtfully.

"How long did you work for him?" Jon asked.

"Three years," Trask said. "He's a star. It was like getting a job with the Mars family - you know the Milky Way people - only Denjer wasn't into grand buildings and putting his name on them. He prefers a more subtle subterfuge and skull-duggery."

Jon wondered how a man could sleep at night putting families through hell. Just for the money.

"So, what are you going to do now?" Jon asked.

"Don't know, but that's not all."

Jon leaned back in his chair and waited.

"He's faking real estate."

"What do you mean?" He was confirming what Lash Ashton had discovered about Nita's papers, but where did Trask stand?

"He is so well known ... he's got so many connections and his projects appear to be so successful that people just hand him money."

"Really?"

"Yah," Trask said. "You ever been to Disney World?"

"No," Jon said. "Always wanted to go, but somehow we just never got around to it."

"Well, there are lines for all the rides."

Jon nodded.

"There are lines for all the rides, so when the park opens in the morning, people crowd around, waiting to get in and get to their first ride ... first."

Jon nodded again.

"So when I went there with my family, I swore to myself that I wouldn't run. Running to a ride seemed stupid, maybe even undignified. There's plenty of time to get in line and enjoy the day. But something comes over you. You want to be first. You don't want to be left out, and so, as undignified as it might be, you run. It's the same thing in emergencies—burning buildings, active shooters, that sort of thing. Something inside you makes you run. It's biological. It's a natural force."

Jon harrumphed to show that he heard what Trask was saying.

"People can't help it. That's the feeling around Denjer. He's generated this ... I don't know ... aura?"

"Okay," Jon said.

"Denjer takes their money, doesn't charge them anything, and regularly pays them dividends. It's like free money—money for nothing! The investors think that money is coming from the real estate investments. Denjer generates official looking paperwork for reports and statements. He mixes the make-believe properties up with the real ones—the toxic ones."

Jon said, "Hard to believe. My father invests with Denjer. These are sophisticated investors."

"It's not like buying a house," Trask said. "People don't go out and look at these places. They trust the seller. It's all trust. Investment managers like to diversify portfolios with an allocation in real estate offering growth while providing 'a hedge against market volatility and inflation. Unlike playing the stock market, investing in real estate lets you better mitigate risk without sacrificing potential returns.' That's what Denjer's sales material says."

Jon stared at Reid Trask. "Are you serious?"

Trask leaned back from the table as Ramona brought their burgers and set them on the table. "Enjoy," she said.

"Got any hot sauce?" Trask asked as he reached for the bottle of ketchup.

Ramona scuttled off and came back with the hot sauce. "Anything else?" she asked.

"I think we're good," Jon said with a smile.

They munched on their burgers in silence.

"Hard to believe," Jon said.

"Trust. You put in money and more money comes back. Better than any slot machine. What's not to like? Why wouldn't you want to keep doing it? And there's that overwhelming desire not to miss out and so you tell your friends and your family all about it. It's a religion. Everyone wants to go to heaven ... and if you don't, you'll go to hell. You just gotta believe!"

"Holy shit," Jon said. "How does he do it? The paperwork, I mean. Doesn't anyone check?"

Trask put down his burger. "The unreality is real," he said. "He has a separate department that only a few people go in. That's where the black magic happens. It's run by another Boundbrook graduate, Phil Bosun."

"The world is run by Boundbrook graduates."

"At least Norman Denjer's world. He likes to keep it tight around himself. What's he doing for you?"

Jon thought about it for a minute. He looked around the garish red color scheme of the restaurant, the laminated plastic table tops, the historical black and white corporate pictures on the walls, the scattering of diners spooning in their ice cream and forking in their French fries. What was he doing with Denjer? Severing all ties and getting as far away from the man as possible was the rational thing to do.

"Nothing," he said. "We just started talking a couple of months ago. I went to his house. Met his wife, Eleanor. Jon paused. A friend of my wife's, Nita Avant, works for them."

"Oh?"

"Yeah. It was strange. She invited us to a jazz session she was playing in Cambridge."

"Did you go? Was it any good?"

"I took Lisa, my wife. We made a night of it. She is good." Jon paused for a moment and then he decided to take a chance and trust Trask. "No, but the really strange thing was that she had a disk from Denjer's computer that Denjer's wife gave her."

"Why?" Trask asked.

Jon took a sip of his drink and shrugged. "Don't know, but I had my partner's wife read it on her computer and she came up with the same facts you were just telling me: that the real estate was fiction."

Jon sucked more of his drink up through his straw.

"But then," he said, "but then, at the end of her show, we went backstage to talk to her and some guy grabbed her and dragged her away."

"Really?"

"None of her bandmates knew who he was. They said she didn't stick around."

"Where is she now?"

"She's not answering her phone."

"Well, that could just mean that she doesn't want to answer her phone. Or maybe she isn't home. Who knows?"

"I mean, maybe Denjer found out about the disk and wanted her removed."

Trask studied Jon's face. Then he pushed his burger plate aside and leaned forward. "I wouldn't be surprised. Let me tell you something that I've never told anyone. Denjer is definitely capable of murder." He let that sink in.

"What do you mean?"

Pausing for effect, Trask said, "Back at Boundbrook, do you remember when that kid supposedly killed himself in the woods?"

"Dabney Schmidt. I've been talking to his mother. His father died last summer."

"Right. Dabney Schmidt. And Norman Denjer became president of the class. Because Dabney was dead."

Jon said, "I remember."

"Well, Dabney didn't kill himself. Norman killed him."

Jon leaned back in his chair. "What? No. How do you know?"

"I was there," Trask said. "I was there in the woods."

"Are you kidding me? What were you doing in the woods?"

Ramona came by the table with refills on their drinks and

picked up their plates. "Will there be anything else?" she asked. "Maybe some ice cream."

"No. Thanks. We're good." Jon smiled at her and then turned his attention back to Trask.

"What were you doing in the woods? I mean, that's pretty weird."

"I was on the Woods Squad just like Denjer. We were always out there on Sundays cleaning stuff up. I wasn't spying on them or anything, but I overheard them talking ... and you know, I got curious. They didn't see me. I know they didn't see me. They were upper classmen having a private conversation."

"So Denjer killed him?"

Trask sucked on his straw. "Well, not exactly. Denjer didn't take the gun and shoot him. They were playing Russian roulette. I heard them say something about that movie ... The Deer Hunter. But it was Denjer's gun, and I'm sure he set it up somehow so that when he pulled the trigger on his own turn, it wouldn't fire."

"Why didn't you report it?"

Trask looked around the room. "Don't know," he mumbled. "I mean, that would have been like squealing on an upper classman. He was a junior. I was just a sophomore. Maybe I should have ... In hindsight, you know? It was sort of the code. Denjer was the big man on campus. I probably should have."

Jon was stunned. "How could you work for the guy?"

Trask shrugged. "It was a job. And Bosun was there too. I mean, how bad could it be?

"You think he would kill Nita?"

"Don't know. All I do know is that he wouldn't stop at killing someone who got in his way."

Jon was getting uncomfortable. He needed to do something. Dead bodies and fake housing developments and toxic home sites were piling up.

"We can't just call the police," he said. "What would we accuse him of? My wife's a state trooper, you know."

"I know," Trask said. "Remember?"

"Yeah, but this is too crazy. I mean, she knows I'm nuts ... but in a nice way."

Trask looked around at the empty neighboring tables. "Did you have some guy warn you of the toxic investigation?"

"What?"

"I sent a guy to warn you off your toxic investigation down there on the Cape. The Summer Meadows place. There were rumblings in the office that Denjer was getting nervous about what you were doing."

"That was you? A guy stopped me on the street while I was walking my dog. I thought it was weird. This inspector shit is not supposed to be dangerous."

Jon shifted in his chair. "I'm going to use the head," he said and stood up, looked around, and spotted the Rest Room sign.

The men's room smelled of disinfectant and wet paper towels.

The key to this story was ... well; the key was Denjer, of course, but ... was there an authority who could put a stop to him? The FBI? The Secret Service? The Security and Exchange commission? The police? And then there was Pocatuck and the Schmidts and Nita. Was she really missing or just not answering her phone? And did Denjer make all this stuff up? There had to be someone who was managing all this for him. He didn't strike Jon as being all that smart and creative. There was a lot of baffling bullshit in this picture now. How much more was there that they couldn't see?

Jon stared at himself in the mirror as he washed his hands. No. If Nita was in trouble, that had to be his priority. Someone had to know where she was.

Back at the table, he asked Trask, "Who would know about Nita Avant? Who would Denjer tell to take care of her?"

"Phil Bosun," Trask said without hesitation. "Phil is his fixer."

"Maybe he knows where Nita is."

"So what's your plan, Megquire? Call Bosun and ask him if he kidnapped this woman and if he's killed her? Just as sort of 'by-the-way'?"

"We've got to start somewhere. What if she really is in trouble?"

"But what if he's already killed her?"

Jon looked at him. "Jesus, I can't believe we're even having this conversation. Does this stuff really happen?"

Trask shrugged.

"I'm going to head home and talk to my wife and see if there's anything the police can do."

Chapter Twenty

Jon's thoughts were dancing a polka by the time he got home. He found Lisa in the living room on the floor playing car crash with Sam, explaining to him how the police would survey a crash site and handle the crowds of spectators.

"Have you heard from Nita?" Jon blurted out.

Lisa said, "No."

"Call her. We need to find out if she's okay. Apparently Denjer killed Dabney Schmidt."

"What?" Lisa said.

"Yeah. Well, he didn't actually kill Dabney, but he got him to kill himself." Jon outlined his conversation with Reid.

"And this Reid Trask witnessed this?"

"That's what he says."

Lisa paused, and then she asked, "How much do you trust Mr. Trask?"

"I guess," Jon said. "Why would he make that up?"

"People do strange things. You said that Norman Denjer

fired him. Maybe he's looking for revenge. If it was murder, we could arrest him. There's no time limitation on murder."

"You think he could be lying? Didn't seem like it. He's the one that sent the guy to warn me on the street. Remember? I told you about that car that pulled up beside me while I was walking Stogie. But Reid sent the guy to warn me.

"But wait. There's more. Trask said that Phil Bosun might be the one that Denjer would send out to take care of Nita. Maybe Denjer found out about the computer disk from his wife."

"You've got to get this straightened out, Jon," Lisa said. "The man is a menace."

"You're right," Jon said. "But Denjer doesn't seem like the kind of person you can just walk away from."

* * *

WHEN JON AWOKE the next morning, Denjer dominated his thoughts. Rather than resolving his financial issues, Denjer threatened to make them more complicated. It had become the type of relationship that you wish you'd never started.

Throughout the day, he threw himself into the physical labor of building a house, moving piles of lumber, stuffing insulation into wall cavities, digging drainage trenches. The more physical the task, the better.

When he got home, he was still mulling over what Trask had told him and Denjer's implied threat. Denjer was a murderer and a con-artist. There had to be a way to put him in jail. He lied and cheated and ruined people's lives. People were jailed for life or executed for doing less. Where was justice?

Stogie welcomed him at the door with an enthusiastic tail wag. "Take you out in a minute," Jon promised him.

He was surprised to find the house empty and echoing. He

called Lisa at the state police barracks to let her know what he had been thinking about. "By the way, where's Sam?" he asked.

"Babs is watching him today."

"Oh, yeah. Hey, do you think that Denjer may have done something to Nita? I mean, if he's capable of murder ... Have you heard from her?"

"I tried calling her again. I haven't heard from her, but that's not strange. We haven't been that close."

"But that guy that grabbed her backstage ..."

"Maybe he was a friend."

"Don't know. Maybe," Jon said. "It just seems odd. I'm going to take Stogie out."

As Jon was clipping Stogie's leash on his collar, the phone rang. Jon hesitated. It appeared the Megquire financial pendulum had swung back down now that an investment from Denjer Development was out of the question. He would make it quick. Stogie was pulling on the leash.

"What?" he barked as he picked up the receiver.

People sound different on phones, but the oddly familiar man's voice replied, "Jon?"

"Who's this?" Jon replied.

"It's Norman," the voice said. "Norman Denjer."

Oh shit, Jon thought.

Denjer continued, "You have to understand how important Pocatuck is to me. I really need your help. I thought I'd see if I could catch you at home. Just to see how you're getting on. Seeing if you had any thoughts on what we talked about. Got to protect that lovely family of yours. Get your financial situation squared away. Families are so important, aren't they? We want to give them the best future we can. It's very nice to share with everybody. Yes, it's very nice. Good genes. Very good genes. Oh, they do a number, don't they? But when you look at what's going on, it's going to take them another one hundred and fifty years because libraries are a fun place. There's books there and everything."

The man was crazy. Stogie's tongue was hanging out.

Jon didn't reply to Denjer, who continued, "No, but I wanted to check on how you're doing with Pocatuck and Ms. Schmidt, convincing her that selling to me is the best option. It's really the best option. I need your help, Jon. You're my ticket to ride."

"I can't talk right now, Norman. I have to take my dog out. I'll get to it."

"I need to get this squared away as soon as possible. Can't wait. Can't stop. He who hesitates ... Ooh, you've gotten me so excited! So excited. We can get your business flying along the way we talked about. Give it a future. Give you a future. I can do that, you know. Better than anyone."

Everything in Jon wanted him to scream into the phone and tell the man to melt himself down to an ice cube puddle on an iron skillet and evaporate, never to be heard from again.

"I'm taking my dog out, Norman. We can talk about this later."

For a moment, Denjer didn't reply. Then he said, "Where are your wife and son, Jon? Wife's at the police station, isn't she? They don't call it a station for state police, do they? She at the *barracks*? She take Sammy with her? Of course, she wouldn't leave him alone, would she? Babysitter? Gone all day. Can't be too careful these days."

What was he getting at? Of course, Lisa was at work. Why would she take Sam with her? Sam was with Babs. Lisa said so.

Jon stretched the phone cord out until he could see into the kitchen. Jon dropped the handset and Stogie's leash, stepped into the kitchen. Nothing. No note.

Back in the front hall, he picked up the phone, hearing

Denjer's voice saying, "Jon? Jon? Are you there? Where did you go?"

Nita *disappeared*. Dabney *murdered*. Denjer had a gun. Denjer was behind it all. The assumption of Sam's location seemed obvious.

"What the hell are you talking about, Denjer? What's going on? What have you done with my son?" Jon demanded, struggling to keep his voice under control.

There was a silent pause that stretched on and on, as though Denjer was thinking.

Jon yelled into the phone, "Denjer! What have you done with my son? Where is he?"

Another breath snatching moment of silence.

Finally, Denjer replied, "I don't know, Jon. Is he missing?" Jon could swear there was a twist of glee in the man's voice.

"If you did something to my son .... I swear to god I'll kill you!"

"Jon. Jon. Jon. You mean he's not there? He's not where he's supposed to be? Oh, my. That's a shocker. That's a real shock, isn't it? To not know where your son is. Look away for just a moment, and 'Poof!', he's gone. Shame. Shame. Shame."

Jon dropped Stogie's leash. All the blood seemed to have rushed out of his body and he began shaking. He struggled to squeeze the words out, "What ...have ... you ... done? What ... the ...hell ...have ...you ...done?"

"Nothing, Jon. Nothing at all. Wow! We seem to have a situation here, don't we? But I'm going to help you. We're classmates. I'm going to help you. I swear. I swear. He's fine. He's all right. We'll find him together. Why don't you meet me at my office and we can talk to Minky Schmidt and straighten all this out together? Eh? She's coming in today to talk."

"I don't give a shit about Minky Schmidt! I don't give a shit about Pocatuck. I want you to tell me where my son is."

For a moment, Denjer didn't answer, then he quietly said, "You *need* to care about Pocatuck, Jon. You need to. If you want your son back. And you *do* want your son back, don't you?"

Jon wanted to twist the phone until it broke in half. Stogie sat down. "I'm not going anywhere until I find my son."

Denjer said, "I'm sure he's fine. I'm sure he's safe. I'm sure he's with his babysitter." Denjer actually chuckled!

"Oh, my god. What have you done to Babs?"

"She's pretty old, isn't she? That's something you have to take care of if you want my help. You can't be teamed up with that old man. But we can talk about all that later. Why don't you get up here, and we'll get this all straightened out and you can have your son back. See you soon. Make it an hour."

Jon could sense a giggle in the man's voice that made Jon's flesh crawl.

Stogie whined.

* * *

JON'S HANDS were shaking as he wedged the phone's handset between his cheek and his ear and held the base in his left hand as he dialed Babs' number with his right. When it connected, he dropped the base of the phone back onto the table in the front hall.

Ringing.

"Come on. Come on. Come on!"

Ringing.

"Where the hell are you?"

Ringing. It was the slowest, most drawn out ring he'd ever heard.

Ace would know where she was. But Ace was at a job site. Far from a phone.

Where would Babs take Sam? Why wouldn't she leave a note or call Lisa or something?

An hour wasn't a lot of time to get to Boston. He should leave now.

He cut the connection and called Lisa's barracks back.

She sounded impatient when she picked up the phone.

"Denjer's got Sam," Jon blurted into the phone.

"What?" Lisa nearly screamed. "What are you saying?"

"Denjer's got Sam. He's taken Sam, and he wants me to meet him in Boston. In an hour. I can't get ahold of Babs."

"What?" Lisa shouted. "No. No, Sam is with Babs."

"No way I can get to Boston in an hour!"

"What are you saying, Jon?"

"They're not here. Babs isn't here. Sam isn't here. They're not here. And I can't get her on the phone. She doesn't answer."

"Why would Denjer take Sammy?" Lisa asked.

"I told you. He wants me to convince Minky Schmidt to sell Pocatuck to him. The man is crazy. I mean, after he kidnapped Nita and killed Dabney Schmidt, he's capable of anything. I have to go."

"Are you sure Denjer kidnapped our son?"

"He said he did."

"He actually said that? He admitted that? The man's a liar. Where's Babs?"

"How the hell should I know?" Jon almost screamed into the phone. "Where's Sam? Where's Sammy? He's not here!"

"Do you know where Ace is?"

"He must be at a job site. He won't be close to a phone."

"Let me call Babs."

"She isn't answering," Jon yelled.

"All right," Lisa said, icy determination in her voice. "I'll see what I can find out, and we'll take this bastard out."

Chapter Twenty-One

How do you drive within the limits of the law when your child has been kidnapped?

How do you sit still in a driver's seat? How do you sit still when your mind is racing hundreds of miles ahead of you—to where you want to be?

Jon told himself to be calm. He tried to tell himself to be calm, to control his breathing. Take it step by step. He tried to be rational, to take it step by step. Get in the car. Put on the seat belt. Start the engine. Done this a hundred thousand times. He could do it again.

The tires screamed as he accelerated out of the driveway.

Slow down. He had to slow down. He had to get control.

He pushed his hair back from his face. He was sweating.

Was Sam dead? That took Jon's breath away. His mind filled with Sam's mischievous grin, his emerging baby teeth, his toddler's cheeks, his wide, blue eyes.

Was Denjer capable of murdering of a child?

Why would he kill Sammy? He wouldn't. It wasn't logical.

Denjer wasn't logical. He was crazy. Logic didn't apply.

Jon suddenly realized that what he had been doing wasn't logical either. It wasn't logical to run after Denjer to Martha's Vineyard. It wasn't logical to even consider asking Ace to leave the company. It wasn't logical to crawl into a coalition with Denjer. Denjer was just a shiny object he'd been chasing.

Jon squeezed the steering wheel as though he could squeeze the life out of it. The road that stretched in front of him blurred. He abruptly recognized the bulk of a truck immediately in front of him and swerved into the neighboring lane to the screaming displeasure of the car that he cut off.

Sam wasn't dead. Couldn't be dead. Oh, God, he couldn't be in pain. Why? Why would Denjer do this? What possibly could be the gain, the benefit, the ultimate success?

We're always trying to make the unexplainable explainable, he thought. One plus one always equals two. It has to. It has to —every time. But Denjer would make it equal six or three and a half because that's what he wanted it to be. That's what he believed. He would beat them with the loud whip of his voice until he would get everyone around him to believe that was the right answer too, because they were too afraid of him to tell him that he was wrong! They were too afraid of losing his ... love? Too afraid of losing his respect ... when he didn't respect them in the first place.

The air in the car was too dry. Jon powered down his window and wind roared through the car, picking up papers and spinning the dust. Jon pushed his foot down farther on the accelerator. He swerved between cars and lumbering semi's— flashing his lights and pounding on his horn.

And then—too late—Jon realized that he should have looked for Sammy and Babs in Tilley. He should have driven to the barracks and talked to Lisa.

He slowed down.

What if Denjer hadn't taken him? What if that was just another lie? Did he say he'd kidnapped Sammy? What about Babs? Maybe this was all just a sick, sick joke.

But what if it wasn't? If there was the slightest chance....

He accelerated.

And when he got there ... When he got there and had Denjer by the throat pinned against the wall and kneed him repeatedly in the groin until he screamed for mercy. What then? What then? He would tell everyone in the world what Denjer had done—what he was capable of.

Lisa had been right: Jon should have stepped away sooner.

Lisa was right. She was always right. Jon could smell her long auburn hair, dominant cheekbones, and that open brilliant warm and natural smile that always made everything right. Her face flowed into his thoughts in a wave of warmth.

Sam and Lisa were the essence and substance of Jon's life; not Denjer's money.

He should have seen it. Working with Denjer and his demands was playing with a lunatic. Lisa's police experience had shown her that people were capable of the most awful and surprising things - even the most proper among us. She had no illusions that Denjer, with his power and connections, would not be capable of removing people who got in his way. It was in the nature of power to demand control.

Stay in control.

How could you be confined behind the wheel of a car? How could you be trapped by the demands of a situation created by the mind of another person and yet be free to move, to think, to change the ending of the story? Jon swore to take control.

If you kidnapped someone, what would you do with him?

Where would you keep to him? How would you restrain him? How would you feed him? The thought of his son tied up somewhere in a closet or a box or a trash can made Jon push the car to its limit—to the limit of what you could do on the Southeast Expressway coming into Boston.

Chapter Twenty-Two

When Jon got to Denjer's office, he rushed past the receptionist and pushed past Denjer's staff, who turned toward the madman rushing through their midst. Jon didn't pause. He crashed through Denjer's door, and didn't stop moving until he reached Denjer.

Norman Denjer was behind his desk and Minky Schmidt was seated in one of the big chairs facing him, clutching her handbag on her lap. She wore a funky, old-fashioned hat that might have included a veil in times past.

Denjer was tilting back in his chair and holding a cup and saucer. He looked up when Jon burst in, but before he could say anything, Minky said, "Oh, Jon! Thank you so much for coming," leaving Denjer momentarily speechless.

Jon stepped around the desk, reached over, and grabbed Denjer's jacket by the lapels, and jerked him to his feet. The coffee cup and saucer flew out of his hands as he tried to push Jon away.

Rational thought flew out of Jon's mind as he felt the power of his arms and upper body. Denjer had no weight. "Where is my son?" Jon shouted. "What have you done with Sam? Where the hell is he?"

Minky leapt to her feet and held her hand over her mouth. "What's going on, Jon?"

Jon shook the smaller man like a rag doll. He felt the urge to smash him up against the wall, rip his arms and legs off, and leave him like the bag of puss that he was.

"Nothing!" Denjer screamed. "I haven't done anything. I don't have your son."

"Liar! Liar! Where is he? Where's Sam?" Jon shouted. "You're always lying!"

"No. No. You misunderstood. You misunderstood. I want to help you." Denjer tried to manage a weak grin as Jon shook him.

Jon pushed him back into his chair and stood over him.

"Where is Sam?" he yelled again.

Denjer cowered. "I don't know. I swear. I swear I don't know." He pushed his chair back away from his desk and toward the windows. "It's a misunderstanding. You said ...you said he wasn't home. I offered to help you find him. That's all. That's all."

"You said you knew where he was - where Sam was. So, where the hell is he?"

"What's this all about, Jon?" Mrs. Schmidt asked. "We were just discussing the future of Pocatuck and looking forward to hearing your thoughts. Mr. Denjer was explaining some of the legal issues for the transference of such a large piece of land. I'm not sure that I can understand what he is telling me. He said he would help me with the paperwork. Arthur had such admiration for Mr. Denjer - I guess everyone does."

Denjer glared at Jon.

Jon said, "He's a liar, and he's kidnapped my son. Don't believe anything he says. Don't trust him. He's done it before.

He kidnapped Nita Avant because she discovered he was cheating in his real estate business."

Denjer smiled at Minky Schmidt and shook his head. "You've got this all wrong, Jon. You've completely misunderstood the situation. Did I say that I kidnapped … that's the word you used, isn't? Kidnapped. I never kidnapped anyone. Never. I said I would *help* you *find* your son. I want to help you, Jon. I want to help you so you can help me. That's all I do. Help people." He leaned forward on his desk, angled his head coquettishly, and smiled.

Minky looked at Jon. "What do you mean he kidnapped Nita Avant? He did no such thing."

"I saw it," Jon said. "I saw her dragged out of her concert in Cambridge. She asked me and my wife to come backstage after the show. And she was gone. The other musicians didn't know where she had gone."

Minky laughed. "She wasn't being kidnapped, Jon. That was Phil Bosun."

There was a moment of silence. Jon wondered how Minky Schmidt would know Nita or Phil Bosun.

"I knew it! Right?" Jon said. "I knew it. Phil Bosun. Norman Denjer's enforcer. See? Denjer had Bosun drag her away."

"Oh, no," she said. "Phil's Nita's boyfriend."

"What?" Denjer said.

Jon's mouth dropped open. "Nita's boyfriend? Boyfriend? How do you know?"

"Oh, because Phil is a Wampanoag elder," Minky said with a gentle smile.

"What?" Denjer repeated. "Phil Bosun? My Phil Bosun?" He hesitated, looked around the room, as if seeking another answer, and then he said, "Oh, yes. He did say she was safe. I asked him about her when she didn't show up for work. He said she was safe. Well, that's good. That's very good. I'm glad we cleared that up. See, Jon?"

"Phil is a Wampanoag elder," Minky said again. "Nita is a very talented member of the tribe. I'm willing Pocatuck to them the way Arthur wanted. Phil and I have been talking about the tribe's plans."

Denjer jumped to his feet.

"No, no, no," Denjer said. He came around the desk and peered down at Minky who had resumed her seat. "You can't give Pocatuck to the tribe. You can't. Um, it wouldn't be good for you financially. Not at all. No, no. It would be horrible on your taxes. No, no. What we were talking about ...before Mr. Megquire interrupted us. Let me help you. It's what your Arthur wanted."

He turned back to Jon. "So, what's all this crap about your son? I don't have your son. I never did. I never will. I never said I did. I never ever said anything of the sort. But that's a problem ...Bosun. Bosun's a problem. Didn't expect that. Didn't expect it at all. So what are we going to do about it? How are we going to fix that? How are you going to convince Minky to do the right thing?" He winked at Minky Schmidt. "She's got herself all tangled up with these bleeding heart Indians. Can't let them win, can we? Can't do it."

This was ludicrous. It was a madhouse. Lies and innuendos and slurs were flying around the office like bats in a cave. Jon wasn't going to help Denjer. He didn't give a shit about Pocatuck ...or Denjer, for that matter. The man looked sick. Maybe that was a real observation, or maybe it was an observation of the person who Jon now knew that Norman Denjer was. He wasn't even close to the elevated, enigmatic, powerful figure that Jon had thought him to be. He was shorter. His hair seemed to have receded farther up his scalp. Jon had an urge to pick him up and dangle him by his ankles off the balcony of his fancy office.

"Why did you drag me up here? Why did you tell me you had Sam if you didn't? Do you? Do you have him? Where is he?"

Denjer said, "Of course not. Of course, I don't have him. Why would I have your son?" Pffst! He dropped back into his desk chair.

"Jesus!" Jon said, spun around and headed for the door. "I'm going to go find my son."

At that moment, he was shocked to see Lisa dressed in her State Police uniform push through the door, followed by a man he didn't recognize.

"Lisa!" Jon shouted. "Lisa, did you find him? Did you find Sam?"

Lisa said, "This is Special Agent Woody Adams from the FBI."

"Great," Jon replied. "But what about Sam?"

Lisa stopped. Jon held his breath.

"Oh, Jon. Sam's with Brenda at Pirate's Cove in South Yarmouth. He's probably in the cave."

"Oh, my God!" Jon said.

"The barracks notified me on the radio as I was racing up here. Thought we were going to take Mr. Denjer into custody for kidnapping, so Agent Adams agreed to come along."

"Why is Sam with Brenda? Where's Babs?"

"Babs had to rush Ace to the hospital. They thought he might be having another heart attack. He's having trouble breathing. So, she dropped Sam off with Brenda."

Jon wrapped his arms around Lisa and pulled her to him. "Oh my God," he said again. "Oh, my God. I thought Denjer had taken him ...hostage or something. I really thought he had kidnapped him. I mean, after Nita just disappeared and the gun on the Vineyard and everything. I was going to kill him. You can't imagine what was going through my head as I drove up here."

"I can imagine it," Lisa said. "I can, but it's okay. Sam's safe. Pirate's Cove just opened for the season. You know how Sam loves pirates."

"Is Ace going to be okay?"

"Too early to tell. Babs is with him."

Denjer grinned. "See? See? No harm. No foul. See, I told you. I told you. You didn't believe me." Norman stood and came around the desk.

"So now, Minky," he smiled ingratiatingly. "It's okay for me to call you Minky, isn't it? We're trusted friends, right?"

Minky smiled.

"We're going to get this tax thing straightened out for you. Your husband trusted me. You need to trust me, too."

"You can't believe anything he says, Ms. Schmidt," Jon said. "He killed your son."

The smile on Minky's face evaporated.

Minky leapt to her feet. "What are you saying, Jon?"

"Of course I didn't," Denjer smiled, putting out his hands to her. "Of course I didn't. I was there at the end to help him. He was so troubled. So very troubled. My only regret was that I couldn't stop him."

"What?" Minky asked. "What are you saying, Jon?"

She stood in front of Denjer's desk, clutching her handbag in front of her, beginning to tremble.

"Reid Trask witnessed it, Ms. Schmidt," Jon said. "There was a witness to what really happened. Reid was there in the woods. He witnessed you push the gun to Dabney. It was your fault."

Minky put her hand over her mouth and tears began rolling down her cheeks. "All these years. All these years," she mumbled. "I knew the story wasn't right. Dabney would never have just shot himself."

Even then ... Even then, in the middle of all this, Norman was still the center of attention, Jon thought as they watched the man's performance. Despite everything. Despite his lying, cheating, murdering deeds, he was still the center of attention. It was what he needed ...thrived on, what he thought, what he wanted, and he would continue to be that way surrounded by his lawyers and the press which he was bound to manipulate and to spin the stories his way. What was it about the man that compelled people to crave Denjer's attention? In terms of power and financial gain, he had been undeniably successful. But that success was built on fiction—just like the Man in the Moon or the Wizard of Oz.

Norman dropped back into his desk chair. "So, let's finish this thing, Minky. Let's finish this and move forward with our lives. Pocatuck is my destiny, Minky. You wouldn't deny me my destiny, would you?"

Ms. Schmidt, handbag in hand, stood in front of his desk. "You killed my son," she said.

Denjer smiled that greasy smile again and ran his hand back through his thinning hair. "No, Minky. No, he did it himself."

"You helped him do it. You helped him do it. He never would have done such a thing. And all these years I thought you helped him, thought you were a hero, thought you tried to stop him. Instead," her voice was rising, "instead you took him out into those woods and handed him a loaded gun, and he blew his brains out! Why? Why would you do such a thing?"

"That's just the point," Denjer said. "That's just the point. That's where this logic falls apart, doesn't it? All these years you've trusted me, believed in me, and now ..."

"I knew something was wrong. Something was wrong. Dabney never, ever would do such a thing on his own."

"And now," Denjer continued, "someone tells you something different and you believe him. Just like that, he tells you a different story. How do you know what he's saying is true? What might make you think that what he's saying is truer than what you've known for twenty years? And he," Norman slammed his hand down on his desk and the hula dancer danced and his human audience jumped, "he has kept this information to himself all this time. All this time! Why? I ask you, why? Why would he keep it to himself if it was so true and so damning?

"Your husband trusted me. He trusted me to invest. He begged me to take your money. Begged me! I was reluctant because Dabney was my friend, and I didn't want to spoil his memory. Shakespeare wrote Polonius advised his son Laertes to be neither a borrower nor a lender. 'To thine own self be true. And it must follow as the night the day. Thou can'st not then be false to any man.'

"Sign the papers and give me Pocatuck," he hissed.

Jon was tempted to pull out his wife's gun and shoot him.

Jon watched Minky Schmidt step back. "No," she said. "I'm giving Pocatuck to the Wampanoag. Just where it belongs. Just where Arthur wanted it to be."

Denjer scanned Ms. Schmidt from her handbag up to her eyes. Jon saw a depth of hatred in Denjer's eyes and face and body that transcended reality. It was as though he were inflating and would explode like a cartoon character.

"It's mine," Denjer hissed.

"No," she said. "No. It's not."

Denjer leapt to his feet. "It's mine!" he shouted.

Minky looked at Jon.

"Don't do it," Jon said. "He killed your son. Reid Trask witnessed it happening."

Denjer said quietly, "He's lying, Minky. He's a liar. Trask worked for me, and I had to fire him because he's a liar. Oh, Minky. Who are you going to believe? The man your husband trusted all these years or this sleazy, peeping-tom liar who claims he was lurking in the bushes who just wants to shatter your memories and make your life miserable just when it could have been so beautiful?"

Jon said, "He's not lying, Mrs. Schmidt. Norman Denjer is a cheat and a thief. He has been defrauding his clients for years. He's been running a real estate Ponzi scheme."

Mrs. Schmidt looked from one to the other of them. "Arthur trusted you," she said to Denjer. "He believed in you. He believed you helped our son at a terrible moment in his life. He wanted your help to transfer Pocatuck to the Wampanoag."

"He had no intention of doing that, Ms. Schmidt," Jon said. "He was going to keep it for himself. He has dreams of turning it into a massive resort. Has Norman told you what he intends to do with Pocatuck?" Jon asked.

"Pocatuck," Denjer said, rolling the word around on his tongue like caressing a pearl. It put a twinkle in the dullness of his eyes and curled the corners of his scrofulous mouth. "Pocatuck is going to be the most beautiful place in the world. There will not be any place like it. I'll take excellent care of Pocatuck, Ms. Schmidt, don't you worry. I'll take care of it. I'll take care of you. You'll be safe now. Safe. Pocatuck will be your mastaba ...of sorts."

"He intends to develop it," Jon said to Minky Schmidt. "Run bulldozers all over it. Rip out the trees. Rebuild the buildings in his own image. He took me out to Los Tres Pinos to show me what he intends to do."

"Lies!" Denjer screamed. "Lies and snakes. All I have done

in my life is to give. To give. To give. That's all. I've given people what they wanted. Been who they wanted me to be. And they just keep wanting more. Wanting more and more and more. And when I give it to them, they just want more and more and more."

"We have the Ponzi scheme evidence. Nita gave us a disk. Ask her. Ask Phil Bosun. It's true. There's more than enough evidence to bring this whole operation down. It's a scam. I'm sure there are people here who will testify to that."

Denjer stood with his back to the windows facing out over the blue sky and the city. Minky Schmidt glared at him.

Agent Adams said, "I think we should talk about this at the field office, Mr. Denjer."

Norman's face had turned ghastly pale. "My god," he said. "You can't trust anyone. This can't be happening. Do you know who I am? I have friends. Talk to the President. He knows who I am. Everyone knows who I am. They need me." He was backing up. He pulled his chair around, spun around, opened his private exit door, and slipped out, slamming it behind him.

Agent Adams said, "Where the hell does that go?"

"His private elevator," Jon said.

Jon, Lisa, and Agent Adams rushed to follow Denjer.

Lisa pulled her gun out of its holster.

"How do you open this?" Agent Adams asked.

They fumbled over the surface of the door until they finally found the latch. The door swung open, and they stepped into the narrow hallway and toward the elevator. The display showed it was descending.

"Is there someone in the lobby to stop him?" Jon asked.

Agent Adams said, "I'll get down there. Call it in, trooper."

Lisa made the connection on her radio and holstered her weapon as they returned to Denjer's office.

"Where is he?" Minky asked.

"Gone," Jon replied. "That's his private elevator."

"The Federal guys will be all over this place," Adams said. "They'll get him."

The office had become cloister quiet. Even the outer office seemed to be hushed as though the staff were tip toeing, holding their breath, not clear about what was going on.

"Oh, my," Minky said. "The man's a devil. Arthur had such faith …He killed Dabney. Oh, my."

"We'll get him," Jon said. "It would be best if you went home now."

Minky left the room, clutching her purse, her head bowed.

When Agent Adams returned from the lobby, he reported no one had seen Denjer leave the building. "Elevator's empty. He's a rock star. Don't know how they could have missed him. We locked the elevator just in case."

"He had me fooled," Jon said. "He had everyone fooled."

Adams said, "Well, he's done now. If he's been running a Ponzi scheme out of here, they'll rip this place apart. Hard to believe. He was so well known."

The day was fading, and the lights in the city were coming on. Jon walked over to the windows overlooking the Back Bay district, the Charles River, and over to Cambridge. "Hell of a view," he said.

Lisa stepped up beside him. "You gave me a scare."

"I did?"

"When you told me Sam was missing and Denjer had taken him. I was freaking out thinking about him and you hurtling up here. I know how you can drive when you get the bit in your teeth."

Jon reached out and pulled her to him. He felt the surge of relief now that Sam was safe and this insanity was over. Perhaps it wasn't proper to hug a state police officer in public. It was definitely prickly with all the equipment she had hanging from her body.

"Well, we should get out of here," Lisa said, pulling away.

They turned off the lights and, as they returned to the outer office scattered with desks and office spaces that were mostly empty, Cynthia stopped them.

"Excuse me," she said. "Did you find him? Did you find Mr. Denjer?"

"Not yet," Lisa said. "But they will. The FBI will arrest him within the hour."

"Oh," Cynthia said. "Oh. Okay. Did you look in his safe room?"

"His what?" Agent Adams asked.

"His safe room. He has a safe room in his private hallway. It's hard to see. He showed me. It's got everything. It's pretty small. I guess he is afraid of killers or something. He can lock himself in there."

"That's right!" Jon said. "I'd forgotten that. When we went out to lunch, he mentioned something about his castle and bishops' hidey-holes."

"Safe room," Agent Adams said. "I've heard about those things. They're like bomb shelters. Reinforced. If he's locked himself in there, I'll have to get the tech guys to cut him out. Is he armed?"

"Oh. I don't know," Cynthia said.

Agent Adams asked, "Do you know how to open it?"

"Oh ...no. I wouldn't. He's got the key."

"But you can show us where it is?"

"Yes," she said.

Jon laid his hand on Agent Adams' arm. "No wait. If it's a safe room, it would be locked from the inside. It would be designed so that no one could get in. So even if Cynthia shows us where it is, what are we going to do?

Knock on the door and say, 'Come out. Come out. It's time to go to jail.'"

"He has a camera in there," Cynthia said. "He knows if there are people in the office."

They waited.

"He needs to realize that he's failed," Jon said.

"To hell with it," Agent Adams said. "I'll get the tech guys to cut him out of there."

"We'd need a warrant," Lisa said.

They waited.

Agent Adams said, "Shit."

"Or," Jon said, "or we could just wait. Denjer is the kind of man who wants an audience. Being cooped up in solitary confinement is going to drive him crazy. I would bet that if we just shut the lights off and wait, he'll pop out of there."

Agent Adams crossed his arms across his chest. "Of course, we don't even know for sure that he's in there. I mean, the elevator was going down."

"He could have just pushed the button and ducked back into his safe room. No one saw him leave. You said so yourself. You have people at his house?"

"Of course," he said. "All right. Let's assume that he's in there. Turn out the lights."

"I'll give him twenty minutes - tops," Jon said.

"Fifteen," Agent Adams countered.

The four of them settled onto desks outside Denjer's inner office and waited.

Lisa said, "You know, when I was a kid, we played that game called sardines. We would hide, and when people found us, they would have to squeeze into the hiding place with us. I hated waiting to be found. I hated the suspense."

"It's like in the movies," Agent Adams said. "When the good guy is hiding behind the dumpster and camera follows the bad guy hunting him through the parking lot. The camera can see both, but the good guy can't see where the bad guy is."

"Can I get you anything?" Cynthia asked. "Coffee? Juice? Water?"

Lisa smiled and said, "No thank you, Cynthia. I think we're okay."

"I'm not sure I see the comparison here," Jon said. "The good guy is scared that the bad guy will find him? This is the opposite."

"Hide and go-seek was the same thing," Lisa added.

Jon got up and paced. "When do the cleaners come in?"

"I'm not sure," Cynthia said.

They waited.

"Those under-the-bed scenes in the movies freak me out," Jon said. "You know the kid hiding under the bed and there are these guys with automatic weapons stomping around the house, and you can see their shoes from under the bed."

Waiting. Jon hated waiting. Waiting to be found. Waiting for Christmas. Waiting for your son to be born. Waiting with anticipation shimmering on the horizon. Anticipating the best …or the worst. All of life was waiting.

"No, seriously," Agent Adams said. "What if he's not in there and we're just sitting around here twiddling our thumbs and taking up air? We're going to look pretty silly."

"We'll look sillier if we just let him walk out," Jon said. "He's not a patient man and right now, he doesn't have anyone to talk at. We have to be more patient than he is."

They waited.

"I can be patient," Agent Adams said, "if I know for sure what I am being patient for. Know what I mean? If I'm hiding behind the dumpster, I'm going to be reasonably certain that the bad guy is walking around in the parking lot, right? I'm not just going to be back there kicking the dirt."

They waited.

"So, what do you propose?"

At that moment, they heard the inner door in Denjer's office bang open, and they stepped back into the shadows of the outer office. Denjer pushed the door of his office open and stepped out, peering from side to side, holding his gun out in front of him with his hand shaking.

"Drop it," Agent Adams commanded. "Drop the gun, Denjer. Now!"

Denjer squinted, but he continued to wave the gun back and forth.

"Drop it," Agent Adams and Lisa yelled. "Drop the gun."

Looking stunned, Denjer let the gun drop out of his hand and crash to the floor. "It wasn't my fault," he said. "It wasn't my fault."

"Hands behind your back," Lisa commanded.

"It wasn't my fault. Everyone says so. We have the best numbers ever. It's disloyalty. Perfidious fickleness. Untrustworthy. All of them. It wasn't my fault. I did the best I could. I've spoken about it many times. Obviously, it was a terrible thing. I was great. Everyone said so. It wasn't my fault."

Agent Adams guided Denjer between the silent office desks.

Lisa turned, looked at Jon, and shrugged. She said, "Well, that's done. See you at home?"

Chapter Twenty-Three

About six months after Norman Denjer had been taken away by the FBI, the Megquire family met in the pavilion that Andrew Megquire had reserved in Plymouth Woods State Park for the Saturday after Labor Day for the family picnic. Jon and Lisa packed up Sam and Stogie and piled all the juvenile paraphernalia into the back of the mini-van and headed off up the Cape and over the bridge.

Plymouth felt different for Jon with the proximity to Pocatuck and all that had happened there.

The real estate world had trembled after Norman Denjer's Ponzi scheme was revealed. Jon had been sure that all the bulls had been let loose on Wall Street and were thundering up the alleys, streets, and avenues of New York, across Connecticut and up to Boston. The great codfish of uptight Boston royalty was flapping around on the docks. Nobody had expected the demise of Denjer's empire. People just weren't prepared to accept that they had been fooled by the king of a real estate scheme. And they had certainly had not expected him to get arrested by the FBI for so many crimes they would fill multiple courtrooms for decades. They would have to peel away all the guilty parties, including Phil Bosun and his staff from the 17th floor where they conjured up all the phony paperwork. Jon hoped that they wouldn't go too hard on him.

But Jon had been there, and it still haunted him. It haunted him that he could have believed ... no, wanted Denjer's money to solve all the problems.

"I was blinded by his aura," he said to Lisa. "I should have known better."

They were still talking about it as the highway hummed under the wheels.

"The man was crazy ... obviously. Money makes people crazy," she said. "I'm just glad he didn't take you along with him."

Jon had a sudden bizarre thought that there might be a children's song about falling objects. There were songs about everything else, from garbage to brushing your teeth.

When they reached the State Park, they exchanged greetings with the entrance guard who directed them to the pavilion, and they drove past all the cars and ball fields and people picnicking and found a place to park.

Although it had been an eventful year, the park seemed timeless and unchanged. As though they had just left it. Jon wondered if that would be the case with Pocatuck now that Denjer would not develop it, cutting down all the trees, putting in roads and septic systems and power lines. He hoped the Wampanoag would honor the land and not the dollars from some massive, garish casino and hotel complex. More and more Jon appreciated that land ownership is illusory. Ownership is relative to the society that gives permission to act upon it. Denjer's vision was also illusory. He saw the world the way he wanted it to be. Somehow, despite all his lies and double-speaking, he made his admirers feel safe and secure and see only what he saw. In some form or other, the land would continue to be there until the sun exploded.

Lisa lifted Sam out of his car seat and got Stogie on his leash while Jon opened the back of van and began lugging things down to the pavilion where they were greeted by the family. Hugs and kisses and laughter all around.

Uncle Langston lumbered up and with a grim expression said, "No more collisions this year. Right?" reminding Jon of their impact at first base in last year's softball game. "Getting too old for that. Too much time in the hospital this year." He went on to explain his bout with cancer. "But I'm still here!" He grinned and let go of Jon's hand.

"You've had quite the eventful year yourself," Langston said. "I heard he threatened to shoot you? What was his name?"

"You must be talking about Denjer. Norman Denjer," Jon's father, Andrew, interjected, putting his arm around his brother's shoulders. "Yeah. That was really something. My company had some money tied up with that guy. He fooled everyone."

Jon laughed. "He had a gun, but he didn't use it. He just waved it around. He was involved in a shooting at boarding school, though," Jon said.

"I don't know what I'd do if someone threatened me with a gun," Andrew's wife, Mirasol, said. "I'd probably scream."

Andrew smiled. "Let's hope that never happens."

"He did some bad things," Jon said. "And just last year, you were urging me to go to him to invest in our company."

"I didn't know," Andrew said. "The man was a genius at public relations. Seriously. People begged him to take their money."

Langston said, "I hear he was a big contributor to Dukakis's presidential campaign."

"That didn't go so well, did it," Lisa added as she spread out a tablecloth and began stacking plastic wrapped packages of paper plates.

"Dukakis looked like an idiot riding around in that tank," Langston said.

"Yah. And that story about setting murderers free didn't help either," Andrew added. "What do you think Bush is going to do to NASA, Cornelia?"

Jon's sister Cornelia, the genius aero-space engineer, had flown up from Texas for the picnic and Sam was hanging on to her hand and grinning. He had been eagerly expecting seeing 'Aunty Corny' again.

"I doubt he'll do anything," she said.

"In general?" Andrew asked with a smile.

"Things at NASA are long term. They don't happen suddenly. We're going to launch Galileo in October but it won't get to Neptune for six years. Most things that happen suddenly in space are not under human control."

"Let's get some meat on the grilles," Langston said, "before we dive deep into the space/time infundibulum."

Andrew slapped his brother on the back and laughed. "Where the hell did you get that word?"

"You probably never realized it, but I know lots of stuff," Langston said.

"Hey, Jon. How did that poop thing work out?" Andrew asked.

"It was just shrew poop in the wall, dad," Jon said. "The stink wasn't our fault. Just nature doing its thing. It took a while, but the lawyers finally went away."

"That's great!" Andrew said. "So, what are you going to do now? With your company, I mean."

"It's a long-term investment," Jon insisted. "It's like Cornelia and that Galileo spacecraft."

"My kids are thinking long-term, Langston. Can you believe it? Long-term!"

It was like they had just left. Memories were served up with the burgers and the steaks. Bart, Jon's step-brother, was lost in his Teenage Mutant Ninja Turtles game. Sam was happily listening to Cornelia's every word.

Andrew and his brothers - Langston and Michael - and their wives had moved further back into the past, reliving family war stories that only they could remember and envision.

It was great to see Ace there. Ace had become an honorary member of the family, but he and Babs didn't share the same memories and sat off to the side watching and smiling. Jon went over and sat with them.

"Well, I guess we won't be getting funding from Mr. Denjer," Ace said.

"I guess not," Jon replied. "But we dodged a bullet there. He took a lot of people down with him."

"Did you work things out with the bank?"

"Pretty amazing, isn't it? After all the fuss - all that nagging they made about our loan, the fact is that they're so happy with us they want us to borrow more money."

"What?"

"Yup. Said we'd been so good at making the payments that they want to do it again."

"No shit? Just like that," Ace said. "Should we do it?"

"Probably. You going to find more houses to build?"

Ace laughed. "You going to find any more toxic projects you can charge up the wazoo to fix?"

"Not like Summer Meadows. That was awful."

"I don't understand people like that," Babs said. "I just don't. How can anyone be that greedy?"

"When's Brenda going to move out of that house?" Jon asked.

Ace said, "Next month, thanks to that lawsuit of yours. Didn't know you could sue the federal government."

Jon laughed. "Gail really sunk her teeth into that. But it won't be quick."

"The government knew it," Ace said. "They knew. Don't tell me they didn't know that was a toxic dump. They never should have made that deal. It should never have happened."

"Brenda's lucky," Babs added.

"How so?" Jon asked.

"Well, she's older, you know. That house was just a place to live. But other people there have everything tied up in their houses. And their kids are ... well, who knows what will happen to them."

"The thing is," Ace said, "the thing is, how many more places like that are there? What about the other bogus developments that man built?"

"I know," Jon said.

"It's a good thing you're doing what you're doing," Ace said. "I mean your toxic ... stuff."

"Lots more to learn," Jon said. They sat back and watched the frenetic family activity while they sipped their drinks.

"Gail's going to be here," Jon said. "It will be good to see her again."

Babs lifted herself out of her chair. "Can't just sit here," she said.

Ace looked up at Babs. "I'm thinking that maybe it's time for me to stop. I've been doing this for almost forty years. Loses its magic when you see things like this."

"This?" Babs asked.

"Not this." Ace waved his hand at the group. "No, you know. People like Denjer."

"Seriously?" Jon asked. "What would you do? You sure as hell will not take up golf! Or retire to Florida."

"Don't know. Just thinking about it."

"Wentzell and Megquire doesn't have a lucrative retirement plan. I don't think we could even give you a brass watch."

Ace laughed.

"And besides," Jon said, "we haven't hit it rich yet. I can't afford to buy you out. I wouldn't want some other yahoo in there taking your place."

"Don't make me feel guilty," Ace replied. "As I said, just thinking about it."

A car pulled into the handicapped spot in front of the pavilion. Jon heard Langston say, "You know, some people really take advantage of those parking spots. They're not really handicapped. They just have one of those mirror tags, know what I mean?"

Andrew replied, "Not this time. That's a van built for a wheelchair."

While they watched, the side door of the van slid open and a ramp extended until it almost touched the neighboring car.

"Pretty fancy rig," Langston muttered.

They watched a woman dexterously roll her wheelchair down the ramp, turn, push a button, and the whole thing retracted back into the side of the van.

"We shouldn't be staring," Andrew said.

"All the same," Langston replied. "That's pretty slick. Looks just like any other minivan. Looks like yours, Jon."

"Might be handy for loading all the stuff," Andrew replied.

They turned away when Jon realized who was in the wheelchair.

"Gail!" Jon called out and hurried up to help her transit the rough ground from the car. "Oh, wow. Thanks for coming."

He hadn't seen Gail since she had been trapped under the rubble of the hotel. There was some gray in her curly blond hair, but she still had that gap between her front teeth that he could see when she smiled.

"I was so surprised when you agreed to come to this," Jon said.

And that's when she smiled, gripping the wheels on either side of her chair with her leather gloved hands. "Seemed like a hoot for a late summer day."

Andrew and Mirasol came up behind Jon and he introduced them. "Thank you for rescuing my son," Andrew said with a smile.

"Other way around," Gail replied. "Don't think I would have made it without him. It's funny what you think about when you're pinned under tons of concrete."

"Funny?" Mirasol asked.

"Well, maybe that's the wrong word. I wouldn't recommend it, but it can be a shape-shifting experience. Literally! Priorities change when your time is running out."

They all laughed appreciatively.

Jon asked, "Do you need help with that?" indicating the rolling of her chair.

"Nope," Gail replied, pushing out ahead of them.

When they reached the pavilion, Jon introduced Gail to Lisa and the rest of the family.

"So good to meet you," Gail said. "Jon talked about you a lot."

"You as well," Lisa said with a smile. "Don't know if I should be jealous of the two of you trapped together in a hotel."

Gail grinned. "Nothing salacious about it. You can see how it turned out for me," and she lifted her hands off her wheels and spread her arms out like wings.

Sam ran up and grabbed his mother's leg, and she introduced him to Gail.

"Cool chair," he said. "Can I get a ride?"

"Soon as I can get up," Gail said, and Sam ran off.

"So this is the famous Ace Wentzell," she said, rolling up to Ace, who heaved himself up to his feet. "Jon told me all about you. He thinks you're a genius."

"You the one who got him hooked on all the toxic stuff?" Ace asked.

"He did that on his own," Gail said with a laugh. "He turned over some nasty rocks. I've been having fun with the EPA. With the waste site development and all."

"Thanks for your help with that. Babs was just telling me that her sister Brenda is moving next month."

"Good," Gail said. "Don't know when we'll be going to court. These things take time.

"Hey, speaking of lawyers," she continued, "have you heard anything yet?"

Jon said, "Heard about what?"

"From the lawyers?"

"Lawyers?"

"You know. Because of the hotel. Money won't cure everything, but four point seven million dollars sure help me move around in this chair. They're paying out a lot of money."

Jon's mouth dropped open. "Wow!" he managed. "That's great ... I guess. From the hotel?"

"There were a couple of hundred lawsuits - individual and class action. They proved it was negligence. The developers and engineers cut corners. All the people that were injured or trapped and went through the medical triage should have been covered. You gave them your name, didn't you?"

"I guess. That was all such a blur."

"You should have heard from the lawyers by now. Did you ever call them? I thought I gave you their number."

"You did," Jon said. "You did. I just hate lawyers and insurance companies. Always have and probably always will."

Gail smiled. "All lawyers?"

"Present company excepted," Jon said with a grin.

"You should call them now," Babs urged. "Aren't lawyer's offices always open?"

"You think?" Jon said.

"Yeah. Do it," Lisa urged. "We'll save you some food."

"I have the number in my address book," Gail said, handing it to him.

As Jon set off to find a working phone booth, a variety of scenarios played out in his head, floating from elation to disappointment. Just because Gail had gotten all that money, didn't mean that he would have. He wasn't in a wheelchair. And why hadn't they called to tell him? But then maybe they had. They didn't always answer their phone. And they certainly weren't eager to talk with lawyers. He had heard that some sort of caller identification system was becoming available. That would be good. Something that would say, "Ignore this call. You don't want to speak to this person."

Jon felt a wave of urgency now. Maybe this was going to be like a lottery where, if you weren't present, they would give the money to someone else. He told himself that from now on, he would answer every call. No matter what. Ignoring it wouldn't make it go away.

When he found a phone booth, there was someone in it. He considered finding another one, but decided to wait, trying to find a place to stand that would let the caller finish in peace. It was like waiting for a table in a restaurant and not hanging over other diners, urging them to finish up and not linger in some dumb, meaningless conversation.

The person in the booth was illustrating her conversation with her hands - as though the listener could actually see the gestures.

He scuffed the dirt around, making a little pile of sand, and noticed ants running back and forth from a hole. The ants must have a field day in a place like this. Picnics everywhere. He wondered if the park rangers had problems with raccoons and bears. That would make a picnic memorable! A bear walking out of the woods. Jon wondered if there were bears in Plymouth, Massachusetts.

The woman finished her call and pulled back the folding door. "Asshole!" she exclaimed, glaring at Jon.

He was stunned.

"Oh, not you. The jerk on the phone. He's a pontificating asshole," she said, and stormed away.

Jon momentarily wondered what that was all about, smiled, but pulled open the phone booth door. He held the door open for several moments to let the chamber air out. The woman's perfume and sweat lingered. Traces of a person-once-removed.

He pulled Gail's little address book out of his pocket, picked up the receiver - the earpiece was still warm, recited his credit card number, dialed the number, and heard the thrumming indicating the ringing of the phone in the lawyer's office.

Well, it was a shot in the dark that they would be open on a Saturday, Jon thought, when the phone wasn't answered immediately. And it was probably too late, anyway. He listened to another couple of rings. He had his ten rings rule. It was up to six.

He imagined one of those huge lawyer farms like Denjer's office, with windows all around, and secretaries scurrying about. It had to be. If they gave out millions of dollars, the place had to be huge.

Suddenly he heard a woman's voice rattle off lawyer name, lawyer name, lawyer name, lawyer name, and lawyer name..

Jon asked to speak to the man whose name Gail had given him, Bill Nash.

The woman asked who was calling, and he identified himself and added, "I was in the Patriot Grand Hotel."

"Oh," she replied.

"Well, that was positive," Jon thought as the on-hold music came on. "Who plays these kazoo-concertos in C-Sharp minor?" he wondered. He tapped in time on the glass of the booth and looked around to see if anyone was waiting.

Moments later, the music stopped and a man's voice said, "This is Attorney Nash, and you are ...?"

Jon identified himself again and told him he had gotten his number from Gail Barker and that she had suggested that he call because he had heard nothing about the settlements that involved the disaster at the Patriot Grand Hotel the previous November.

"I'm well aware of it," Nash said.

Jon wasn't sure if he liked the guy, although, to give him the benefit of the doubt. It was probably a snap judgement based on a common dislike of attorneys. But the man was working on a Saturday, and he had answered his phone, so Jon had to give him a couple of points there.

"What can I do for you, Mr. Megquire?"

"I have heard nothing about some sort of insurance settlement? You know?"

"What makes you think that you should have heard something?"

"Well, I was there. I was trapped under the rubble with Gail Barker. We were trapped together."

"Ah," Nash said. "Yes."

Jon half expected more on-hold music to fill the pause.

"Should I have heard something?" he asked.

"Just a moment," Nash said, and the kazoo concerto resumed.

Jon thought again how lucky it was that he wasn't pouring

coins into this payphone, urged by an operator's voice. It was also lucky that no one was waiting. He wondered if the woman who had filled the confined space before him would return and pound on the door of the phone booth and demand the phone.

"Could you give me your social security number, please, Mr. Megquire?" Nash said, interrupting the intermezzo in the concerto.

Jon rattled off his social security number.

"Ah, yes. Thank you," Nash said. "We've tried to call you several times."

Jon laughed awkwardly. "Well, yes. Our phone doesn't always work. We have a three-year-old."

"Ah, yes. Well, according to the settlement list, you've been awarded one million one hundred thousand dollars for the pain and suffering caused by the hotel disaster. I hope that's acceptable?"

Jon nearly dropped the phone. "Excuse me?"

"I can repeat that if you like, Mr. Megquire. I'm sure that doesn't fully compensate you for what you suffered in that tragic event, but if you would come to our offices, we can provide you with a settlement check, and we can move on with putting all this behind us."

"Did you say, 'one million one hundred thousand dollars'?"

"That is the amount settled upon."

"Holy shit," Jon said. "Thank you. I'll stop by. For sure." And he hung up the phone and stood there looking at it as a smile filled his face—a day to remember, a holiday, a feriatum for sure.

Acknowledgments

One of the really cool things about writing fiction is that if you have a problem with someone, you can put them in a novel and kill them. It's very cathartic.

I began this book in early November 2021, building it around the concept of St. George and the dragon or that great movie, *The Sting*. Villains are hard to defeat satisfactorily. Many tales seem to make the villain less important and not the focus. And some have the demise of the villain implied but not clearly defined. I reviewed various villains in literature: Mrs. Danvers in *Rebecca,* whose demise is unknown, but she doesn't live happily ever after. Moriarity, who dies in a fight with Sherlock Holmes. Uria Heep, who eventually goes to prison in *David Copperfield*. Cathy Ames in *East of Eden* who is defeated by her son as a reflection of the evil in herself. Mr. Rochester in *Jane Eyre* who ends up marrying the girl despite his evil character. Mr. Potter in *It's a Wonderful Life* who doesn't get to crush the Savings and Loan after all. And the shark in *Jaws,* who dies spectacularly.

I don't know that Norman Denjer lives up to this hierarchy of villains, but numerous people helped me bring him down. I wanted a building collapse scene, so Joseph Lstiburek gave me input on how structural elements of buildings rot away. He told me "It could never occur in MA on the coast…not humid and hot enough for long enough…having said that…it is possible to corrode metal truss plates or wood trusses in vented roofs on the coast of MA." That reality made me turn to the collapse of the walkways in the Hyatt Regency in Kansas City in 1981.

Nancy Doherty, my official editor, wrote, "You are super-sizing this time around, with an uber-villain in Norman Denjer whose characteristics would seem to make him a bad guy for our times." Jeff May helped me elaborate on the shrew poop after I heard him discuss it at an indoor air quality conference in Maine. Knowing little about real estate law, I turned to Richard Scott at Scott Title, who was more than willing to talk with me about title pirates. And Marianne Gonsalves was my go to resource for the life and times of a Massachusetts State Police trooper.

And there are my fantastic early readers—Jason Wolfson, Bill Sims, Bill Boyer, Larry Ward, and Linda Hannon—who gave me encouragement when the entire project was going to hurtle off the rails and into the trash.

Above and beyond these terrific people is the Lightning McQueen of accurate and helpful editors: David Goehring. I cannot thank you enough. You make it look so easy!

On top of the pile of all these helpful souls is my dear wife Kate, who willingly subjected herself to reading multiple drafts and coaxing the best out of the pages. Thank you.

Paul H. Raymer
  Cape Cod, Massachusetts
  July, 2024

About the Author

Paul H. Raymer was born in New York City. He has worked as a teacher in a one-room school, an assembly-line worker in a television factory, a quality control manager for an under-water acoustics company, inventor of twenty-five different product lines, founder of ten companies, a building scientist for more than forty-five years, and the father of three excellent children.

He is the author of *Recalculating Truth* a tale that describes what happens when developing a product that uses computer integrated human tells to discern the truth—a far more benign and effective process than water-boarding. Even candidates for the Supreme Court can tell lies.

Death at the Edge of the Diamond introduces Jon Megquire to the world, bringing him to Cape Cod in 1979 to play baseball in the premier summer league. Unfortunately, it turns out to be less than a peaceful Cape Cod summer visit when a client uses the family mansion as a murder weapon.

In *Second Law*, Jon returns to the Cape in 1984 for a building science conference where a participant meets an unfortunate and ghastly end. Unnerved by the brutal act, Jon is shocked when he's plunged into the investigation surrounding the bizarre crime. But with all the confusion around supposedly cursed land and a lethal case of arson, he fears his fresh start is about to fall fatally flat.

Seeing a need for better understanding of the air quality in houses (indoor air quality or IAQ), he wrote *Residential Ventilation Handbook* which was published by McGraw-Hill in 2010, quickly becoming the go-to source for many building science training programs. He updated and self-published a second edition in 2017.

While he was trying to figure out what to do with his life, he moved temporarily into an old, seventeen room inn on Cape Cod in 1975... and never left. His wife, Kate, joined him seven years later, and she never left either. Their three children grew up there but they figured out ways to move on and create grandchildren to whom this book is dedicated.

Also by Paul H. Raymer

Second Law - A novel - 2022

Death at the Edge of the Diamond - A novel - 2020

Recalculating Truth - A Novel - 2014

Residential Ventilation Handbook - 2nd Edition - 2017

Salty Air Publishing Newsletter & Website

Salty Air Publishing, bi-weekly newsletter
Subscribe here

Salty Air Publishing Website
https://www.paulhraymer.com/

References

References

- OSHA Confined Spaces
- My House is Killing Me! - Jeff May
- Crime and Human Nature - James Q. Wilson
- Scott Title Services - Richard Scott

Music in Confined Spaces

- Wheels on the Bus Go Round and Round
- You're Special
- Skinamarinky-dinky-dink - Sharon, Lois, & Bram
- Harlem River Drive - Bobbi Humphrey
- Fast Car - Tracy Chapman
- Don't Worry Be Happy - Bobby McFerrin
- Perfidia - Mantovani
- Memphis Underground - Herbie Mann
- Danny Boy - James Galway